GALAXYS EDGE

THE RESERVIST

ORDER OF THE CENTURION

J.R. HANDLEY WITH ANSPACH + COLE

Galaxy's Edge: THE RESERVIST
by Galaxy's Edge, LLC

Edited by David Gatewood
Published by Galaxy's Edge Press

Cover Art: Fabian Saravia
Cover Design: Beaulistic Book Services
For more information:
Website: GalaxysEdge.info
Facebook: facebook.com/atgalaxysedge
Newsletter: InTheLegion.com

"The Order of the Centurion is the highest award that can be bestowed upon an individual serving in, or with, the Legion. When such an individual displays exceptional valor in action against an enemy force, and uncommon loyalty and devotion to the Legion and its legionnaires, refusing to abandon post, mission, or brothers, even unto death, the Legion dutifully recognizes such courage with this award."

98.4% of all citations are awarded posthumously.

RAGE CO., 9TH LEGION

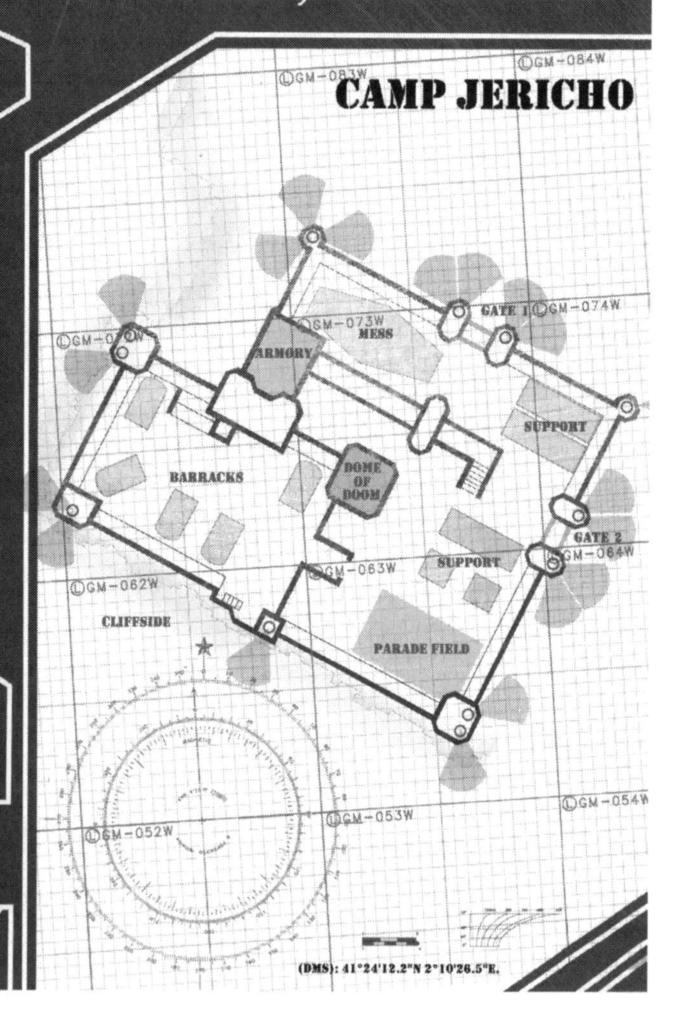

01

Nineteen months after the events of Legionnaire.

Gray skies over Utopion wept as I stood at attention in the pouring rain. I was receiving an award—the award—for living when so many of my brothers hadn't. A pompous affair, the Order of the Centurion ceremony was equal parts beautiful and grotesque—beautiful because of the bravery and heroism shown in combat, when life was as chaotic, dangerous, and real as it ever would be. Grotesque because of the self-satisfied officers who wore more medals than Oba aimed to hang their award around some fool's neck, and that fool was me.

The survivors of the 9th Legion were on Utopion for the festivities, and it was the usual Repub dog and pony show. We stood under an awning on Virtue Plaza, trying to pretend that it was a good day. If the torrential downpour was any indication, Mother Nature knew better. Thunder and lightning punctuated my gloomy thoughts and hid my tears. It was like the weather had confirmed that Oba was on the side of the Legion. If there was justice in the universe, it'd sure as hell never side with the political class.

Gritting my teeth, I tried to contain an anger that had been swelling in my chest since I put on my dress uniform that morning. I couldn't dishonor the ghosts of my friends. They were counting on me to bear their standard, to ensure their lives mattered. With the specter of my brother leejes peering over my shoulder, the ceremony felt like a cruel farce. Its very existence mocked the real heroes who'd bled out on the rocky Bevak Mountains. I'd stood under the shadow of truly valorous men, the sort that these mincing politicians couldn't hold a candle to.

I hated it, all the showmanship.

They didn't care about those who died. And they didn't care about me. This was for them. And their disgusting pageantry tarnished the memory of those who'd sacrificed their lives to protect the corruption on Utopion. Rather than give those heroes their due, we survivors were patted on the head by a bunch of pansy admirals who've never gotten their dress whites dirty. Never even left the core.

We were an island of Legionnaire dress blues among a sea of naval whites. That pompous gaggle of biddies with soft hands and calloused hearts sickened me. I remember, I could barely stomach them as they told us what great warriors for democracy we were.

Truth be told, though, I was barely listening. I didn't want to be there. I wanted to be dead... just a pile of bones. Like the others.

The betters.

We stood there, all of us survivors from the 9th, waiting for it to end. Because we had to. Because it was our duty.

Time dragged by. We disconnected from reality until we could salute and be dismissed. When it was finally over,

I excused myself from the cluster-hole of diplomats and big brass. I had a new mission: oblivion.

And I knew just how to accomplish that mission. I changed into civvies and then headed to the nearest leej bar I could find. The sign above the entrance said Sleeping Legion. It looked low class. That's saying something, when it's coming from a leej. It was the kind of run-down dump which spoke of hard times, hard booze, and harder patrons. The kind of place that promised trouble. I wasn't looking for any, but I didn't care if I found it.

I walked in to see a burly barkeep rubbing a dirty rag over the counter. He stood out; scars marred his face like he'd gotten too close to a plasma grenade's flash-burn. If this guy wasn't ex-military, I'd eat my bucket. Not that I bothered asking him. Instead, I ordered a Sible whiskey on the rocks, which he quietly poured.

Drink in hand, I walked over to a booth in the farthest, darkest corner of the bar. I slid onto the bench and did my best to look uninviting. I wanted solitude.

But it wasn't meant to be. I'd only just sat down when some wannabe thug slid into the booth with me. This guy was everything I wasn't. Brutish and crass. A brawler who was used to letting his muscles do his talking. I preferred to outthink my opponents, it made life easier.

Work smarter, not harder, my Ama always said.

Which isn't to say I couldn't throw down if that's what it came to. I'm still a legionnaire, after all.

"My table," the guy said. "Move, if you know what's good for you."

I knew where this was going. It's all the same in every dive bar from here to galaxy's edge. The guy was looking for trouble.

And while I wasn't, it had come. And I was in an obliging mood.

I slammed my whiskey and stood up, not saying a word.

For all this man's bravado, he lacked the killer instinct that I'd had beaten into me when I'd joined the Legion. With his bulging muscles, thick neck, and scowl, the dude looked physically tough. The muscles were pretty, like he'd spent a lot of time on them, but he was weak where it counted. Mentally, he was a cupcake.

I could see it in his eyes.

Now I'm not saying the guy was afraid. He was too stupid to be afraid. No, this chump's eyes were mean. Which told me that he was the type who got off hurting people and never went for the coup de grâce. My instructors at the academy would've laughed him off the dojo mat. With someone like this, they'll usually back down or leave when you show them that you ain't playing. That you don't mind getting a little hurt so long as you can hurt them back.

I should've walked off and been the bigger man, but I was in a mood to play. I tilted my head and let out a derisive snort.

The guy made a move right away, and if I'm being honest, it surprised me. He grabbed my shirt with both of his big, meaty hands. And then just... held on. I guess I was expecting too much.

Such a weak opening attack.

But he seemed pleased with himself as he held onto the front of my ragtag band tee. Like that would do something. Maybe bother me, my precious shirt getting all wrinkled and stretched. The shirt was cheap garbage I'd purchased from a street vendor after realizing everything else I had was Legion standard-issue. It was literally the first thing I could find.

The black shirt ripped with ease the moment the dude tried to use it for leverage.

And I started laughing. Belly shaking laughter.

He looked at me for a second, confused. "You think this is funn—"

I went in close and kneed him in the groin. A low blow, granted, but I fight to win. I laughed again as the guy bent over, hands on his package.

He didn't join me in laughing. Guess he didn't get the joke.

Still gasping for air, my visitor got a knee to his face. The satisfactory sound of his nose breaking made me smile. This would do for a little fun. A little steam that needed letting off. It could almost dull the pain of losing my fellow leej brothers.

Almost.

A well-aimed elbow strike later, and Mr. Brute was out cold.

Just like that.

I picked up my second shot of whiskey and drained it before realizing that this place was pretty cold without a shirt. I looked down at my unconscious friend to see if I might liberate his. To the victor go the spoils. But it looked a size too large and the blood stains weren't my style.

"You do okay for a tubby fella," the barkeep shouted at me. "If I hadn't seen the tatt on your arm, I wouldn't have believed it. Marine, maybe... but not a leej! House of Reason really lowered them standards, huh?"

I get this a lot. This time I didn't feel like answering.

"Another shot'll warm you up," said the barkeep, probably a way of telling me he meant no harm. Or maybe just because he wanted a few more credits. His voice was gravelly, and I struggled to understand him at first.

While my mind processed what he said, I pulled off the remains of the rag that was once my shirt. Balling up the fabric in my hand, I sauntered toward the bar.

"Whiskey, yeah?" he growled. "On the house."

Well, all right. I'd never met a leej who'd turn down a free drink. I wasn't gonna be the first. I walked over to the bar and slammed my palm down flat. "Sounds good."

I knocked back another tumbler full of the finest whiskey the Siblians could make. It burned going down, just like the good stuff was supposed to. I visited the distillery once. The Siblians looked freaky; that third eye, the horns, and scaly gray skin. It gave me the heebie-jeebies. But hot dog, those freaks made some smooth hooch.

The barkeep slid another round across the bar, interrupting my contemplation.

"This round's on your tab," he said. "Ain't runnin' a charity."

He poured one for the house and stared at me as he took a sip, then watched me down the shot I'd just bought.

I had the distinct feeling of being sized up, but his face gave nothing away.

Had I been found wanting?

I nodded at the man and took a swig of my whiskey. Drink fast on someone else's credit; drink slow on your own. I savored the balanced flavor, it had just a hint of warm, smoky goodness. Worth every credit. On a day like this, I wanted the top shelf stuff. It seemed right. Seemed a fitting way to honor my friends.

"Thanks, barkeep."

"Name's Kylie. Call me Wetmore."

I smiled. "Legionnaire Lieutenant Benjie Ocampo, but my friends call me Fetch. Thanks for the whiskey, and I'm sorry about the mess." I gestured toward the crumpled jerkwad still unconscious on the floor.

"Don't be," said the barkeep. "Had it coming. Up for another round?"

I was.

"To the Caledonian Corps!" Wetmore shouted.

We slammed back the shots and he immediately poured another. This was getting expensive. I waved him off.

"On me. So, was you with them?" asked the barkeep. "The 9th Legion?"

I didn't answer outright. Just grunted as I sipped the strong whiskey. The smooth liquid warmed its way down my gut and left the taste buds in my mouth tingling. The barkeep stared at me, patiently waiting for an answer. I didn't want to talk about it, but the man was paying for every other round.

"Yeah, I was with Rage Company, 9th Legion," I finally replied.

"So... was Rhyssis Wan as bad as the holos suggested?"

Shaking my head, I answered the barkeep. "Worse. They sanitized the reports while the politicos decided how to spin it. And our losses, we lost so many. They had to hand out medals, or the piles of dead leejes would look meaningless on the evening news."

The barkeep grunted. "I was with the 131st when I was young." He pointed at his ears. "These are prosthetics, but I can still listen. I'll even put our drinks on the Legion's tab."

I chuckle, the rim of my glass millimeters away from my lips. "Legion has a tab with you?"

"Someone from the Legion liaison office set it up. Just something to cover for the leejes that bail on their bill. It's easier than getting bad publicity. Especially here, on the capital planet."

That made sense enough.

The bartender planted his hands spread wide apart on the counter. Even at his age, I could see the muscle and definition of his forearms. His face went serious. Almost concerned, but not in a patronizing sort of way. Not like talking to someone who wants to help, but hasn't been there. Hasn't seen what you've seen. Done what you've done.

"Do you want to talk about it?"

I finished my glass, grimacing against the burn, then looked up at the man. My voice was soft. Speaking of the dead, of tragedy; it's a delicate matter. "One leej to another, I'll tell you how it really went down."

02

We were just starting to ramp up our training for the reality of a post-Kublar world when I was finally promoted. My superiors had pushed my advancement since I'd enlisted. I was a rarity, a legionnaire with an advanced degree. I'd graduated early and ended up with three degrees: hotel and restaurant management, baking and the pastry arts, and a general culinary degree.

People called me a prodigy. I called myself weak. And I needed to do something about it.

On my 17th birthday, I finished my master's degree and got offered jobs working for the most prestigious dining establishments on Pictavia. Instead, I enlisted in the New Caledonian Reserve Corps. It'd been a lark, the chance to play leej without the full-time commitment. A chance to prove that I had the strength of character to stick it through. I'd been controlled for so long, the boy genius adults coddled. Enlisting was my first act of independence, somewhere to finally stand on my own two feet.

I'd never thought I'd stick around. I'd be a once and done leej. Get in and leave after my first hitch was up.

Life didn't work out that way. When the Mid-Core Rebellion grew more active, I began paying attention to the news feeds. When the MCR atrocities occurred on Kublar, I reenlisted. And besides, New Caledonia had a reservist program held over from the end of the Savage Wars. The stuff on Galaxy's edge… it was all far away from me, or so it seemed.

I told my mom not to worry. A lot of us did.

My college degree at the Pictavia Culinary Institute qualified me for the officer's academy—I'd been too young for that at my first enlistment. And by the time that changed and I re-upped, I'd become jaded by one too many dismal point officers to want to try my hand at it. There are no points among the enlisted men.

Shortly after I reenlisted, my company commander promoted me to full sergeant and placed me in command of Berserker Squad. I was comfortable, and managing the ten leejes in a Rage Company squad was infinitely less stressful than the restaurants I ran during the rest of the month.

Life settled into a routine. They trained us nonstop when they had us, sometimes every weekend. As things on the edge got worse, it seemed the "one weekend a month" had gone away and our Reserve Company was on perpetual standby. The government of New Caledonia had gotten comfortable after the Savage Wars ended, but recent events convinced the elected officials that we weren't as safe as we thought. How could anyone be when a bunch of primitives and the MCR were able to bring down a Republic destroyer and wipe out almost an entire company of full-time legionnaires?

Funds for extra training were authorized, and I kept volunteering for all of it. I wanted a break from the stress of my day job and the chance to exercise in the fresh air. Time in the kitchen made me a little soft around the edges, as it tends to do, and even though I could outrun the entire platoon—genetically, I have an athlete's heart and lungs—I'd gotten sick of the jokes about my weight.

I heard 'em all, but my favorite was, "Holy hell, Sergeant, I think I can see the fat squeezing out of the seams of your armor."

I still don't know who said it. And, truth be told, I still have a hard time not cracking up about that one.

Something to know about New Caledonia is that we held our own during the Savage Wars. We worked hand-in-glove with the Legion and when it was our turn to face that nightmare from the stars that was the Savage marines, any Cally will tell you how we kicked their asses. We felt safe during the time of relative peace following the end of that conflict. We were close enough to the core that no one figured a threat capable of reaching us would ever be able to rise again.

And our military spending reflected that. The Parliament shuttered all of our legions, until only the 9th remained. They supplemented our Reserve Corps with militia, forces cheaper to outfit and maintain. Even still, we were holding on to an outdated notion that we were still Legion—still what we once were—even though our tech and training were anything but. Our fighting force was a relic from our pre-Republic history, a budgetary line item that the politicians wanted to get rid of in favor of vote-buying programs.

Legion reserve isn't really a thing anywhere else. But it is here. The beauty of Republic political negotiations. New Caledonia has a Legion Reserve Corps that the House of Reason treat as the real deal—and flood with points too afraid of getting hurt—and the rest of the Legion... well, they tolerate us, I suppose. We don't matter.

We weren't supposed to, anyway.

Once those MCR rebels stepped up the attacks, well, the politicians still tried to double down and continue with the spending cuts, but as the saying goes, "There'd been an army on Kublar too."

The public began to get fearful. It's only natural during times of uncertainty. Finally, the politicians responded. They increased the number of companies in the 9th until we were fully manned, and then added worthless militia to the Caledonian Legion Corps. Made us a paper tiger. But nobody on the inside—the men who'd have to fight and die for the Republic—was fooled. All that really happened was that they forced the recruiters to work overtime to fill the new slots. All around the system, reserve leej recruiters toiled around the clock to process the recruits.

When the talking heads began talking about several more Cally Legion companies, we tried to ignore it. I focused on my career and on becoming the best leej I could. Blustering was what politicians did. Any restaurateur knew to ignore it while milking the situation for better tips. I worked out and spent time enjoying the little moments with friends and family. Things were spooling up, but this would pass. And the little Legion Reserve on my home world would continue as a quaint formality.

Life drifted on and I'd just started settling into mine. I'd gotten a pay raise, married my school crush, and bought a house. My wife was pregnant, and the money from my promotion in the reserves definitely helped. College wasn't free and not everyone was lucky enough to get scholarships. About my wife: what she saw in me is beyond my comprehension. I married up, something her twin brother never lets me forget. He was right, of course, but then I think every guy who loves his wife thinks the same thing.

When we got the call to mobilize, I was floored.

There were no riots on the news feeds. The rebels had left our system alone. Some of the guys were excited. Not me. My mind had already divorced itself from everything else that happened in the galaxy. I can't say I was angry or scared, though. More... confused.

Like I said, nothing directly involving our planet had been reported on the holovids and our system was relatively peaceful. When the old man told us that we were leaving the New Caledonian system, I probably sat in a state of disbelief for a good five minutes. My mind just blank. This was something that we'd been told wasn't possible when we enlisted. Heck, I'd never thought my unit would leave the planet, even for training.

But I took the king's credits, so duty called.

After mobilizing, I reported in for the NCO briefing with the sergeant major, Sergeant Major Logan Scott. The senior Legion NCO in the New Caledonian Reserve Corps was one of the few full-timers gracing us reservists with his presence. He was full Legion, part of the deal with the Republic to make our planet feel special. He was standing in front of the assembly hall, in his full dress uniform with more ribbons than a point in a Unity Day parade.

Sergeant Major Scott was a perpetually angry little man full of scowls and vulgar language. This time he looked even angrier than usual, something I hadn't thought possible. He went into a rant about the state of the galaxy, punctuating his thoughts with his knife hand and off-world curse words I'd never heard. He referenced anatomical positions that I didn't believe were possible as he told us in no uncertain terms where the rebels could go and how they could get there.

I zoned out, waiting for him to get to the pertinent parts. I have a talent for tuning in on important information, a skill I'd first learned as a specialist and found useful in my civilian job as well.

"The Mid-Core Rebellion is stepping up their attacks on the Oba-fearing people of the Republic. There's a rebellion going on in the Rhyssis Wan system boys, and that means traitorous rebels are encouraging the cultists to challenge the legitimate rule of the Republic. If you don't read the news, I'll make it simple: They're seeking an independent state and think they can wrest control of the system from us. The House of Reason wants to show them, in no uncertain terms, that rebellion is not an option. And that means it's up to the Legion—and in this case that means you—to go kick a little ass."

The sergeant major had to pause, his deep commanding voice drowned out by the sound of his subordinates' cheers. I doubted that the other leejes cared that deeply. They were likely just carried away with the emotional tone of the NCO's diatribe. I wasn't sure that my fellow NCOs bought the company line. In private conversations, we'd all talked about how Utopion was a hotbed of corruption. Regardless, the battle of Kublar convinced me that the MCR rebels weren't the answer. My musing was interrupted by the sergeant major's booming voice.

"We'll be leaving the system with all of the New Caledonian Reserves. The recruits can finish their training en route. We're missing over one hundred leejes, totally unsat. Squad Leaders, police up your people. Involve the local law enforcement if you need to, I want those people here yesterday! Before I let you go, any questions?"

Please don't ask, please don't ask, I telepathically begged. But some idiot always asks a question, it never fails. That day was no different.

"Sergeant Major Scott," Sergeant Bello asked boldly, "our charter said we're only charged with defending New Caledonia. We can't leave the star system defenseless. The Repub has no right—"

The crowd of seated NCOs suddenly scooted away from the lanky young sergeant, not daring to incur the wrath of the advancing sergeant major. I regretted having taken the seat next to Bello, torn between the desire to flee from the advancing Curmudgeon of the 9th and staying to watch the impending train wreck. I didn't decide quickly enough.

"Let me stop you right there before you lose your stripes!" Sergeant Major Scott looked pissed. "Your little planet wanted to be considered part of the Legion? Well, that means you KTF when the Legion commander tells you. Now we're paid by the House of Reason. They tell Legion Command who to stomp a mudhole in and where to walk it dry and that's exactly what we do. Orders are issued and we're going to follow them. We've been ordered to put down the Bar Kokhba Revolt by any means necessary. Those cultists will not be allowed to join up with the MCR. Not on our watch! Now move out and round up your missing leejes. Dismissed!"

Astonishingly, Bello didn't seem willing to let it go, but stood his ground and continued to protest as NCOs piled out of the room. "All due respect, sir, but that violates the contract I signed."

The vein on Sergeant Major Scott's forehead began to tick as he struggled to contain his rage. "Listen here, Sergeant, that's not how things work in my Legion. The time to play dress up is over. You're in it to win it now, boy."

The belligerent young leej didn't learn. "You're voiding my contract," he continued, "so I demand to see the Inspector General to—"

Sergeant Major Scott's knife hand to the throat ended the complaint. "The IG works for me, son. Now, would someone get this prisoner to the brig, so we can KTF those rebel cranks?"

03

The pre-deployment training was brutal, and it was made worse when training cadre from the 71st Legion showed up to train us. These were more of the real deal. Legion proper. They were technically and tactically proficient killers who ran circles around the best Cally had to offer. Some serious KTF stuff, the kind of leej we thought we were and aspired to become.

The cadre smoked us nonstop with "conditioning runs" that served no other reason than to satiate their sadistic tendencies. They beat us near senseless in the name of learning proper hand-to-hand combat training. Our legs burned from the unending accumulation of conditioning miles. Our arms ached from the hours upon hours of D&C. Through it all, my cadre took special joy in singling me out. I was the odd one. An NCO college boy. The closest those maniacs could get to tearing into an officer, even if I didn't have the commission.

And, it definitely didn't help to have love handles.

"Come on, Fat Brain," Corporal Santos bellowed as he ran circles around me while we pushed our bodies to their breaking points. "I've seen quadriplegic sailors run faster than you!"

"Maybe he needs another donut?" asked the Curmudgeon of the 9th as he effortlessly jogged besides me.

"Holy hell!" shouted Santos. "Get me a donut and a stick right now. We'll get this lard ass breaking records."

Sergeant Major shouted into my ear as we ran. "Do you think the Bar Kokhba cultists in Rhyssis Wan care? Do you think they'll give you donuts, fatty?"

"No, Sergeant Major! I'm a chef, Sergeant Major! I'll make them myself, might even share!"

My bellowed response didn't seem to make a difference to the 9th's training cadre; they kept up their verbal tirade. But it did seem to tickle the old man's fancy. At least that's how I took his grunted reply to my snark. My reward was more of his undivided attention; we might've even been going steady. With the vastness of the years between us, it's sometimes hard to tell. It's like we were speaking different languages. Sure he abused me, but I think that's how some old timers show their love.

The extra attention from Sergeant Major Scott had the added boon of encouraging the junior corporals. The Curmudgeon joined in, adding to my discomfort as he ran beside me while the cadre kept up their insults. He laughed in that deep belly laugh of his, acting as if the torture we were being subjected to was a Sunday stroll. His presence emboldened the corporals, and the tiny martinets amped up their taunts.

Corporal Santos was the worst of the bunch. He was relentless.

"You're a real buffet slayer, ain't you? The cultists on Rhyssis Wan are gonna have to shoot you twice to get through that belly. Let's move it, Sergeant Fats! Stop jiggling, lard butt."

I really hated Corporal Santos.

And then when the fat obeyed physics instead of the training cadre... "Okay, I see how it is! We just gonna do squats, you and me 'til one of us drops."

A thousand squats later and my legs would seize up, almost useless. Then they'd run me back to the barracks for a unit of water and more berating.

It became a common refrain, and I became something of a connoisseur when it came to insults and fat jokes. If anything, my struggle wasn't so much with the abuse as trying not to laugh at the cadre's lack of vulgar inventiveness. I'd heard worse from my mother, and despite having a slight pouch, I knew I was in good shape. I'd never failed my physical fitness test; however, that wasn't good enough for our cadre. I was a sergeant who wasn't ideally suited for the Legion recruiting poster, thus I had a target on my back. I knew what they wanted. I was their primary target because if I broke, then those below me would as well.

"Come on, lardie, want a donut?"

Yeah. I knew exactly what they wanted, what Santos wanted. But I wasn't about to give it to them. I was too stubborn for that.

"Roger, Corporal," I gamely replied, "and the squad prefers chocolate glazed. Might as well grab us some kaff while you're out. And none of that Navy garbage, only the best for my boys!"

The laughter from my leejes was immediate, and soon the entire company joined in.

Eventually the cadre gave up. The training didn't slacken, but the laser focus on me as a worthless waste of a leej shifted so that I was just one of many worthless leejes. Reservists who didn't deserve to exist.

It had been made known since day one that the guys from the regular Legion didn't think of us as their leej brothers. The differences in our uniforms only made it more noticeable. Their armor was reflective and shiny, a new rollout from the Republic. And you could tell the guys hated everything about it except maybe how it looked on the parade grounds. Our LARKs by comparison were tan with black accents. They were boxy, ill fitting, old, and ugly.

But that didn't really matter. The regular legionnaires didn't give us too much guff about how we looked. Us looking unprofessional was almost expected. What made the situation tough was that the regular legionnaires knew our kit was better. The House of Reason did them dirty with the "shinies" as the guys called it. Looked great, worked like twarg dung. With about the same protection. It was armor designed for a fighting force that expected the galaxy to step aside when they showed up. And it debuted at the worst possible moment—just when the MCR showed that it was willing to go toe-to-toe. Even if it cost them everything.

Our armor allowed us to blend into the arid world we called home, at least that's what they taught us in leej training. It was designed after we'd expanded our colonies past the open deserts, but the color scheme was supposed to pay homage to our colonial founding fathers. I suspected it was a gimmick to hide the piss-poor quality of our kit. Remember, I only said our kit was better than the new standard issue. By no means was it good. Certainly, they weren't the Mark 1s. Still, I'd take them over the new shiny nonsense the House of Reason foisted on the regular Legion. Our armor was a self-contained system, one that cooled us, and our AI kept us operating at the optimal combat effectiveness. I wasn't sure the new gear was worth its scrap value.

Like all good things, the hazing reached its natural conclusion and we spent our final pre-mobilization days on the weapons range. We donned all of our combat gear, re-qualifying with our weapons in full battle rattle. Any seasoned soldier would tell you that firing a blaster in your armor was different from firing without it, and the skills weren't necessarily linked. So, we trained in our kit while the full-timers from the 71st rode us hard. We were the redheaded stepchildren, to borrow a phrase from antiquity, and even at that late stage, the cadre seemed disgusted by the very existence of the Caledonian reserves. But they didn't know what lay ahead. The bonds that would be forged.

None of us did.

If I had it to do over again, I'd go back and just enjoy the time with my mates. Back before Rhyssis Wan, after the boys of Rage Company had jelled into a cohesive unit, one capable of ferocious violence. Despite the martial trappings of our training, at our core we were kids playing dress up. Little boys waging war with action figures in the sand. We hadn't tasted the melted ozone from a field decimated by blaster fire. We hadn't smelled the tangy copper stench from the rivers of leej blood we'd wade through. If I could do it over again, I'd go back for one more precious moment with some of the finest men I'd ever known.

The cadre didn't know any of that, either; they were just doing their jobs. Admittedly they seemed to take a special joy in tormenting our junior officers and NCOs. We never saw our company-grade officers much. Those points were too busy scurrying around the Caledonian Parliament to worry about their legionnaires. Except Rage Company's CO, Captain Reyes. He was one of the few points worth a spit. Maybe it was because he was a local? Whatever it was, he was a man I was proud to call my friend.

Outside of drill, Reyes owned one of the companies that supplied my restaurant. If there was an ingredient that you absolutely had to have but couldn't find, Reyes was your guy. He was a man among men, an officer who motivated you from the front and a friend who'd have your back.

Too many of our other officers were interstellar nomads, points in search of a safe checkmark up the ladder of success. Hell, we'd even put down an invented riot just so some point major could get face time in front of the holocams.

I almost left the Legion that day. I'd put in enough time to cash out and go into inactive status. Being used as part of a made-up crisis just so some fool who wasn't even rifle qualified could look good for the House of Reason—it felt like a slap in the face to the Legion I loved. But my first sergeant, First Sergeant Phil Culpepper, called me into his office and talked me down.

"You've dealt with worse, Fetch," he'd said. "Pretend it's another day at your restaurant with loud drunks."

He stood there, Captain Reyes at his side, both men beseeching me to stay.

"Go ahead and get the point major blacklisted from all the nice eateries," Reyes added. "Have that soup sandwich of a leej barred from any of the hospitality businesses on Pictavia. Just don't quit, we need you. The Cally Legion needs you."

It worked, and I stuck around. I still hated most of the points, but I don't need to tell you that. You're a leej, too. You know about the infestation of points in the Legion. Let's just spit upon their graves and move on.

Like I was saying... many of the sergeants were close to breaking in those final days. But I wasn't mad. I planned on getting even. When we were fully mobilized, I'd be senior to these jerks. Many of the active duty leej training cadre were corporals, and my newly minted sergeant stripes would let me extract my pound of flesh off them. Besides, I knew something the cadre didn't. They'd been assigned to us, upon our final mobilization, to fill holes in our rosters.

It was about to suck real bad to be them.

Now I'd spent countless hours during my off time at the range and I'd become proficient in our NM-4s. They were cheap knockoffs of the N-4s used by the regular Legion. And while they still packed a punch—that was only when they worked. These babies had a tendency to overheat or have the charge pack get stuck in its well. Neither was a good thing in combat.

If I hadn't been a squad leader, I would still be one of Rage Company's designated marksmen, making impossible shots despite the low-quality weaponry. I found tranquility on the weapons line, and as we trained, I realized how much I missed it—the prestige, the extra time on the firing lanes, and the feeling of accomplishment.

Still, I heard the 71st leejes talking about us from the overhead catwalks. I'll grant that many of my peers were screwing up, but they were picking it up quickly. While I was waiting for my squad to get through the course again, my bucket on, I began hopping around L-comm frequencies and accidently found theirs. We weren't in combat yet, so none of the channels had been secured. I ended up catching the training corporals chatting.

"You know what's worse than a leej company commanded by a point? An Oba-damned RESERVE leej company! And dude, I never thought I'd say that. But… a bunch of fat civvies polluting my Legion? Hell nah."

I couldn't help myself. These guys weren't giving us a chance. This wasn't leadership, it was elitism. "That's on you, Santos. If these leejes can't fight, the blame stops with the instructors. So spend less time complaining and more time getting my men ready to KTF."

If Santos was surprised at my being on the comm, he didn't show it. "Lard butt, there ain't enough hours in three lifetimes to get your sorry asses ready to KTF."

"You've got a week."

Santos grunted a derisive laugh. "Ain't happening."

"That's not at all what I meant, Corporal. In one more week you'll report to me, Santos," I growled the words over the comm. "Might be a nice time to dust off your copy of the Legion's customs and courtesy manuals."

"Roger that, Sergeant," Santos replied. He sounded neither scared or repentant. But I know he got the message. "Don't get your panties in a wad."

The counseling that followed from Sergeant Major Scott, who'd also been listening in, was more of the wall-to-wall nature. I didn't see the scuffle, but Santos found the black eye hard to hide. He chose to keep his shiny bucket on for the next few days. Whatever our sergeant major said—or did—seemed to have the desired effect; the 71st left us alone until we rolled out.

Maybe it was the realization that they'd been transferred to fill our NCO shortages. Maybe my words had more impact than I knew. But Ama always told me not to look a gift-winnlie in the mouth.

04

We finished training, feeling more like heartbreakers and life takers than we ever had in our entire lives. We were Legion. We were born to KTF. We were ready.

And then the word came: Stand by.

We couldn't do anything but wait, not even leave the base. My guys didn't like this, but the justification was that we could leave at any moment. Behind the scenes, the Senate and House of Reason were in an argument with New Caledonia about whether the Repub would use our local Navy or send one of their many fleets to take us to wherever we were going.

The Caledonian monarchy demanded that the Repub Navy send its own ships to transport his "purloined" legionnaires into battle. If the news holovids were to be believed, the House of Reason replied with a "do what we say or else" ultimatum, forcing the Crown to submit to the will of the Republic.

Now, if anyone asked me—and why would they—the Crown should have known that this came with the territory when you formally join the Republic. At any rate, the inane bickering between the polities wasn't the best way to test the viability of mobilizing our reserves, but since I couldn't do anything about it... I sat back and watched the fireworks as they unfolded on the local news holos.

If nothing else, I'd have interesting stories to tell my kid when I got home.

Not surprisingly, the House of Reason got their way and our system's naval defense force was commandeered by the Republic for the duration of our active service. Denying us the ability to defend ourselves in the meanwhile. Of course, we were going out there—supposedly—to make sure that there would never be a need for a fleet back home.

The guys from the Legion made a point of telling us that our fleet wouldn't make a lick of difference against a formidable invading force, if such a thing were even possible.

And that stung. Even if it was true. Our fleet was pathetic—a few antiquated Ohio-class battleships, a dozen corvettes, and some freight haulers converted into troop transports. But it was ours.

And it looked impressive, at least. The Ohio-class boats were big, larger than a Republic destroyer. But they were made centuries ago and hadn't been well maintained or updated. Half their gun emplacements were missing, and the crews were woefully undermanned. Not to mention poorly trained. Their job was to make pirates think twice about buzzing around to pick off cargo freighters coming in and out of port. And ninety-nine percent of that job is just showing up.

After we mobilized our navy, the Repub "generously" augmented the manifests of our forces and sent us on our merry way. Two weeks of dickering around, and we finally ended up where everyone knew we would: the Rhyssis Wan system.

The trip was uneventful. At least at first. I don't know what I was expecting—it wasn't like the MCR was going to pull us out of hyperspace and attempt to board. It felt a lot like when we were confined to base back home. Not a lot to do and nowhere to go. So we hit the gym and used the open areas of the old boats to practice urban ops. It felt like we were back on Pictavia, spooling up for our deployment.

It was an almost magical time for Rage Company. We were a unit, a real deal leej company. During that first week, Captain Reyes managed to get us time in an auxiliary kitchen, letting me cook for the men. How he made that happen I never knew. I never asked; it would've broken the spell. But he had the ingredients for me to give the poor grunts of Rage Company the kind of meal they couldn't afford if they saved for their entire lives.

And they hated it.

So we gave that meal to the points, pretended we thought they were important. I grilled up some hot steaks and the CO came through with cold beer. None of that non-alcoholic stuff, real hops. The leejes stood a little straighter during that meal, puffed their chests out a little more. We were what we were meant to be, we were a family.

When we weren't training or eating culinary masterpieces, we spent downtime checking our gear, trying to pretend we weren't scared. I was on one of the battleships, the Cambria. We had plenty of room to train, and our officers took full advantage of it. Between all of those ad hoc training sessions, I wrote a letter to my wife on my datapad and prepped it to send automatically should my luck run out.

It was an emotionally draining procedure, writing that letter. I wouldn't have even written it, but Corporal Santos suggested the company write them. It seemed at the time like a fairly decent thing to do, given his attitude during training. He was a veteran of several Repub policing actions and said he never knew of one where at least one poor leej didn't die fighting. I prayed he was only being paranoid but encouraged Berserker Squad to heed his advice.

I'd just finished with the letter when I checked my clock and cussed. There was a company leadership staff meeting and I'd gotten so wrapped up in recording holo-messages to my family, I was in serious jeopardy of running late. I didn't want to have to deal with the leadership counseling sessions that Culpepper, our first sergeant, would administer for my transgression. I hated those damn meetings; they were mind-numbingly nauseating. But they were easy enough to avoid as long as you weren't a screw up.

Easier said than done.

First Sergeant Culpepper always insisted that we were thirty minutes early. Usually that just meant being more than on time for a meeting that perpetually started late. Which felt a little like adding insult to injury. There's something about officers and late meetings. I dunno. Hurry up and wait, same as it always was.

Hoping I could outrun the clock, I jumped into the shower to make sure I was presentable. Because being late is one thing, but being late and looking like I'd been sleeping in the field... I might as well have thrown myself into the airlock and hit the dump button. When Sergeant Culpepper went on the warpath, it was safer to play chicken with a rampaging donk. Or wrestle a wet wobanki.

I was rushing out of the shower back to my quarters when the alert sounded. I started instinctively scrambling out of my clothes, stripping as I made it through the hatch into my small room.

The AI announced over the internal com speakers, "General quarters. General quarters. All hands, man your battle stations."

The dreaded expression telling us that the fleet was in trouble. It could be just a drill, but you acted the same in either event. Better to be paranoid and alive than to die dismissing the warning. Fear was good; it kept you on your toes. Fear kept you alive.

The clanging siren was earsplittingly loud. There was something about it droning on like that—annoying and yet terrifying. Like this was all real and people were about to die. It was a shock. It felt surreal, my body moving on autopilot as my mind scrambled to process it all.

I tuned out all the noise, both mental and physical, and threw on my synthprene undersuit and then my LARK. My fingers were shaking—heck, I was shaking—as I fumbled with the various straps and buckles of my armor. As soon as I was kitted up, I made my bucket tune out the nonessential noises. The silence was gratifying, but the drawback meant too much time to think.

Unlike the sailors, leejes didn't have anywhere to be during battle stations. That was difficult. Because somewhere out there in the black outside the ship was a threat.

Some unknown thing existing in the great unknown of space. I hated that feeling of helplessness and I hated being uninformed, so I jumped into the command channels as I ran toward where my company commander and fellow squad leaders were already meeting.

"The Cambria's skipper says the fleet ran into a mine field," said one of the Legion commanders. "MCR proximity mines around all of the known exit points from the main shipping lanes, and we sailed right into 'em, like flies to honey."

"Unreal," commented a battalion commander. "Did no one think to send a probe bot ahead?"

"Skipper is a point, sir."

There was an audible sigh. "How bad is it?"

"Two transports down along with four corvettes," replied another voice over the comm. "No survivors."

The tactical discussion moved fast and furious, a sort of soundtrack that accompanied my sprinting toward the meeting room. I was having trouble keeping up with who was talking.

"Which transports? Do we have ID?"

"Reading Monarchs two and three."

"Oba, those were the main battle tanks."

"Most of the HK-PP Mechs too," replied the first officer.

By all that was holy, hearing that scared the piss out of me. I was halfway through the passageway toward the Rage Company command center in full battle rattle when the ship shuddered, knocking me to the ground. I must've hit my bucket on the deck, because suddenly my visor went black before quickly rebooting.

Then I heard the shrieking of oxygen venting out of the ship. The hull had been breached. On an Ohio-class, that meant a really big boom because those things could stand up to a super-destroyer's barrage for hours. Well, they could when they were lovingly maintained.

I fought back the panic that threatened to overwhelm me.

Please, Oba, don't let me get sucked out into the void.

As embarrassing as it is to admit, I screamed like a little girl. Thankfully my L-comm was muted, sparing me the embarrassment of living through something like that.

The pull of the venting oxygen wasn't so strong that I couldn't get back to my feet. The breach must've been somewhere farther back in the ship. I grabbed my NM-4 off the deck and continued toward the command center, using the emergency handrails to pull me along until the ship's blast doors had time to seal off the breached section of the corridor.

And then it stopped. An eerie stillness settled over the corridor.

Emergency lighting still flashed, but there was only silence. Which was odd, because those klaxons surely didn't get sucked out into space.

I needed information, so I checked my bucket for updates. The emergency blast doors had indeed sealed off the breach, making the hull breaches a nonfactor. They were temporary hull patches, much thinner than the hull that had just been shredded. But the Cambria was saved from losing an entire deck. None of the automated hatches were working. I had to go through each one manually, knowing that if there was a breach on the other side, I would be stuck. Finally reaching the hatch that led into the meeting room, I initiated the manual open, having to use my squad leader emergency access code to get inside.

Real VIP stuff.

When the door slid open, I stopped dead in my tracks. Instead of seeing an orderly military command center, I found only chaos. Chairs were knocked over, datapads strewn around, and scorches marked the bulkheads. Had the explosion done this? But if that were the case, I'd still expect to see Rage Company's command staff.

But the room was vacant, adding a haunting quality to the disorderly environment. Maybe the guys had evacuated the room and left to oversee the men when General Quarters sounded.

And then the reality of what happened hit me.

The conference room had three small portals made with transparent impervisteel. They were all covered by blast hatches—standard procedure across the ship whenever there's a hull breach. The center portal had a crimson smear staining its edges. I moved closer and almost tossed up my chow inside my bucket.

There must have been a blast here that ruptured the portal. The guys—my command team—had all been sucked out into the void. And one unlucky kelhorn was pulled so hard into the breach that it drew blood. A lot of it.

This wasn't supposed to happen. These safety doors should have activated immediately the moment a hull breach was detected. There shouldn't have been time for one guy to get sucked out a hole that small, let alone everyone in the room.

And those blaster marks on the bulkheads, why had there been weapons discharged at a staff meeting? Something wasn't right, but I didn't know what to do about it. There were only a few burn marks visible, practically covered by the debris from the mines that had gutted this section of the Cambria. I fought back the urge to retch, disgusted at the implication that one of my leej brothers could've done something treacherous.

My knees nearly gave out under me. I dropped to a squat and tried to catch my breath, cursing the Crown for failing to keep this ship adequately maintained. For putting the sons and daughters who'd set out to protect their home world at such unjustifiable and unnecessary risk.

Rudimentary scanning software would've prevented the blatant sabotage. Competent officers would've stopped them from sailing blissfully into a stellar mine field. Any officer who'd earned their seniority could've averted the wanton loss of life, but no. We had points, too many kranking points.

Gone. They were all gone. Looking around at the aftermath, I tried to remember what the damage control SOP was. As a sergeant, I should have known, and the fact that I couldn't recall meant that I'd failed Sergeant Major Scott and the rest of the command staff. And that was what was really eating away at me. None of my training had prepared me for something like this.

They were all gone—my entire company chain of command. All of the company officers, my fellow squad leaders, and the first sergeant were dead.

I'd like to say that I handled that stoically, a real frosty leej with nothing but ice and KTF in his veins. But instead, I screamed into my helmet, feeling an impotent rage boiling up from my gut. Tears poured from my eyes. I'm not too proud to admit it. I didn't even like all those guys, but they were mine. My leejes, and woe to the fool who'd taken them from me.

I'd been drilling together with these guys for years. I'd dined with them, I knew their families, and I'd been the godfather to some of their kids. I'd snuck Captain Reyes into the restaurant I worked at, back when I was just an executive chef. Hell, I'd catered the wedding of First Sergeant Culpepper's daughter. Now they were gone, and I was in shock. I don't remember how long I stood there staring at the datapads as they blinked on the deck. Then the Cambria shuddered again.

Another voice inside the same room snapped through my shock. "Fetch! We need ya, Sarge."

It was Corporal Santos. He'd snuck right up behind me, breaking through the mental haze.

Turning to face Santos, but still very much in shock, I saw the corporal's rigid form standing next to me. Our buckets concealed our faces, but the comforting hand on my shoulder spoke volumes.

"Sarge, we're it," he said. "The rest of the company officers and NCOs were here when the first mine struck."

I wanted to ask him how he could possibly know that. But as my thinking clarified, I could see it on the HUD of my bucket's visor. Each man from the command staff showed offline, presumed KIA by the Repub-Tek software. Their buckets and suits were telling the rest of us leejes that they either had all their armor blown off or, more likely, that their hearts had stopped beating. Out there. Outside in the relentless vacuum.

"We were the only ones running behind," Santos continued. "Secondary hull breach caught them all off guard. We're the only squad leaders left in the company."

I nodded because I heard him. But he sounded so... distant.

"I can't explain the blaster fire inside the room, but we will figure it out. Then we'll get pay back, you and me."

Still I didn't respond. My mind was a fog and I stared listlessly at the room. I didn't even know where to begin.

Santos seemed ready to help me along. It was a completely different approach to what I'd seen from him during training. He was trying to help me step up and lead. "Sarge, orders came down over the L-comms while you were assessing the situation in here. We're to report to the ALTOs now."

When I didn't say anything, Santos got in my face.

"Sergeant?"

"So many good men," I whispered. "How will I tell their families?"

"Sergeant, first we need to live long enough to bring home the rest of Rage Company's men." Corporal Santos's voice rang with firm resolve. He sounded like a legionnaire. The way you expected one—a real one—to sound.

I again nodded. Determined not to get squirrely. Not to behave like some point after my first encounter with the stress of combat. "You're right. Get the leejes to the assault landing transports and don't go orbital without me. I'll see if I can salvage any gear here before meeting you there. Dismissed."

As Santos left the command center, I looked around for any sign that things were going to be okay. The priests always preached that in trying times, Oba sent signs for the faithful to find.

I found nothing.

Only destruction. Only a bleak demonstration of my friend's final moments. On one corner of Captain Reyes's desk sat his bucket, strapped to the dummy head he'd kept to store his helmet. He never liked to be far from it. The tan dome sat there, its black trim and markings of rank taunting me.

That bucket was as lifeless as its owner now was. My longtime compatriot. Walking over to the desk, I gently laid my gauntleted hand on the helmet, almost petting it. Reyes was gone. Really gone, and this piece of equipment, just a serial number to the rest of the Legion, was the only physical connection I could see that he was ever even here. Ever alive like me.

But I was still breathing. And those breaths started to feel hot as they escaped my lungs. The shock was making way for anger. If I was the new CO of Rage Company, well that was fitting. Because I was going to KTF every single MCR kelhorn I saw.

05

Reaching the ALTOs took longer than I thought it would. I had to detour several times. Mines had damaged other parts of the ship along the only route I knew—they kept us reservists away from the inner corridors. Can't have us see how poorly they maintained the ship. Might make us question the value of the naval militia.

I was able to navigate a new route to the hangar bay despite the seemingly endless parade of blocked or sealed corridors and damaged ladder wells. The speedlifts were all dead, powered down during emergencies. Ship-wide SOP to stop electrical damage from spreading. Something about cascading overloads or some such garbage. Mostly, you don't wanna get stuck in a dead lift when you need to be free to move about and kill invaders or evacuate the broken tub. At least I remembered that little bit of damage control training and didn't waste time standing around waiting for a car that would never come.

I double-timed it, not wanting the shuttle to leave me behind on the ship. Launch windows were fickle things, and the navy gave the pilots very small margins for errors. They waited for no one, except for maybe Legion Commander Keller. He might be important enough, maybe.

I ran, cursing myself for not being in peak physical conditioning.

My heart pounded like it would explode, and my lungs weren't far behind. Maybe it was the shock, maybe it was the extra donut. Whatever it was, I vowed to hit the gym even harder if I made it out alive.

I was hopelessly out of breath when I finally got there, which may have been a good thing since it prevented me from yelping at the sight of the shuttles waiting for me in the hangar bay. These weren't what we had trained on. They were some other kind. These "Assault Landing Transports, Orbital" looked like flying coffins. Their large and boxy angled wings stuck off to the side and snubbed noses capped the front. Likely the design helped the shuttle cut through the atmosphere on reentry, but they looked like something drawn for a preschool art class.

How was this contraption aerodynamic?

I still can't figure out. And if I had to guess, these shuttles were yet another example of some House of Reason delegate awarding a contract to a company that had no business building military craft just because the delegate had an ownership stake. And yes, that does happen in our beloved Republic.

Regardless of their suitability, the ALTOs were all we had. There were countless rows of what I presumed were the newest version of the orbital entry shuttles, and leej companies scrambled to get in.

It was pure anarchy, with sergeants pushing and shoving leejes into the open ramps. Ironically, the more they tried to speed things up, the more they slowed the process.

Watching the spectacle showed me why the regular Legion boys from the 71st gave us such a hard time. If we couldn't load properly now, what would happen if we were loading under fire? It wouldn't have been pretty. We're talking total team kill kinda bad.

"We have to do better. We will do better."

Except there was nobody in my company's command L-comm channel to answer. They were gone, all gone.

"Fetch," Santos said and nudged my arm. "We're waiting for you by our bird. Your leejes need you to join us. We can't do this alone and this ride waits for no one."

I hated it when Santos got all compassionate. It was easier when he was trying to break me. But pride had to go, my leejes needed me. In the end, I activated the homing beacon to find the shuttles assigned to Rage Company and shoved my way through the crowd, following the prompts in my HUD until I was near our bird.

It was clear that the pilots were preparing for an emergency departure, because last I heard, we weren't supposed to be leaving for another few days. The master plan called for the navy to enter the Rhyssis Wan system, orbit Rhyssis Wan Prime, and preemptively bombard critical targets. Only after those threats were neutralized was the Legion supposed to be deployed.

But the intel guys never mentioned the system being mined. So already nothing was going as planned. I always heard jokes about military intelligence, and at least what the Navy brought to the table was making me a believer. Their errors cost lives, and if I ever met the scat-brained sons of a twarg hauler who let us waltz into that system the way we did, I'd knock his brains out.

But for that to happen, I would have to live long enough to secure the planet.

"Looks like we're going to be doing things the hard way."

I hadn't meant to say that out loud, but Santos answered me over the L-comm all the same. "If it was easy, they'd call us Basics. The galaxy saves the hard jobs for the leejes, Sergeant."

His words spurred me on, and I quickly caught up with my squad. Rage Company was loaded onto their shuttles, with Corporal Santos standing at the ramp of ours. I checked into the company L-comm channel, only to remember that it was just Santos and I, so I hopped over to the battalion net.

"Sergeant Ocampo reporting to the BC, sir. I'm the senior surviving member of Rage Company. What are our orders, sir?"

Major Leblanc, my battalion commander, answered, his voice grim. "We're aware of your situation, Sergeant. I'm sending the last unassigned captain from the 71st to command your company. One of the master sergeants on my staff will assume the first sergeant position. Sadly, dead leejes mean promotions are in order. You've got a degree, is that right?"

"Yes, sir."

I didn't like where this was going, but I knew better than to argue with an officer. Especially one with shiny major pins on his collar.

"I'm giving you a field promotion to LT. Move people around until you have a functioning Table of Operations and Equipment, then send me the list for approval. You'll assume command of 1st Section and I'll round up what spare lieutenants I can find for the other three. Now let's make them pay for this, Leej."

"Roger, sir," I stuttered out.

Evidently, Major Leblanc heard the uncertainty in my reply. He made an effort to put me at ease. "I saw your record, Ocampo. I know you haven't been a sergeant for very long, but your legionnaires need you to man up. Pray to Oba, scream into your bucket, do whatever you must to get your butt in gear, because Rage Company needs you. If it makes you feel any better, the brass will probably take away the promotion when this is all done. Can I count on you, Lieutenant?"

"Yes, sir!" I said.

Still reeling from the shock, I hopped over to the company command network and updated Santos. He had to know what was going on, so I was brutally honest. I latterly transferred him over to one of the vacant squad leader positions and let him know that one of the 71st's captains would be our new commander.

He didn't sound pleased.

"We're getting the point? Holy—"

"Enough, Santos," I said, cutting him off before he continued the thought. "Rage Company needs us. From here on out, let's try to remember to use our LR numbers over the comms. Might as well set a good example. LR-24, out."

"Yes, sir. But be careful around that guy, oh-two-four. He'll get the rest of Rage Company killed if you let him."

I wanted to argue, if only because I didn't want Santos to be right. But, deep down, I knew he probably was. "Roger," I said quietly.

Once the logistics were handled, I went looking for our new CO. I didn't have to try very hard. Our new captain was sauntering toward me, the first sergeant trailing behind. I prayed to Oba that Santos was wrong, that we hadn't gotten a useless point officer. It was the last thing we needed after our chain of command had been devastated.

I halted, snapped to attention, and offered a crisp salute.

First impressions didn't tell much about our new command staff, except that like Santos, their shiny uniforms made them stand out. Their kit was well maintained, at least that was in their favor.

I guess we'll have to wait and see, I thought.

"Sir, Sergeant… sir, Lieutenant Ocampo here." I dropped my salute. "I've copied you in when I sent the new TO&E to the battalion commander and entered your LS number into our system along with those who transferred with you. Our ALTO's over here. If you'll follow me, I'll make the introductions."

"Very well, LT," said Captain Archer. "I appreciate the update, but the BC already forwarded it to me. And everyone transferring from the 71st will have LR numbers to signify that we're part of your unit. We're Rage Company, 9th Legion Reserves now. Let's make the New Caledonian Reserves proud."

"Yes, sir," I said in surprise. For a second, I could almost forget he was a point officer. Maybe they weren't all bad. My experience with the Legion was pretty limited.

Archer looked over the shuttles. "We were lucky that the mines didn't destroy our ALTOs, or we'd be floating down to the surface."

I cracked a smile underneath my bucket. The captain was doing a nice job of welcoming me. "Yes, sir."

"I'm not gonna lie, Lieutenant Ocampo. We're making the drop as soon as we strap into the shuttle. Launching early means this will be a cluster. We were supposed to get orbital bombardments to soften the targets, but no time now. Looks like a small MCR fleet was reported on the sensors and the Navy needs us cleared out prior to engaging."

I nod again, taking in the reality of what was about to happen in. Holy strokes. This was going down. First my command team and now, surely, more of our boys in Rage would be facing death. And it was up to me to make sure that they followed their training and made it back home safely.

"Once we're dirtside," the captain continued, "the fight up here won't be our problem. We'll have enough of our own. Let's go meet the men."

06

The ride to the planet Rhyssis Wan was sheer terror. As the shuttle rocketed from side to side, incoming rounds from orbital defense guns boomed around us, and only our seat straps kept us from crashing on the deck at terminal velocity. This was the price we paid for failing to do a proper pre-invasion bombardment.

I doubt I'll ever think of that planet without breaking into a cold sweat.

At one point during the ride down, I blacked out. The pilot had juked around to make the ALTOs harder to hit and the G-forces of atmospheric flight were just too much for me to handle. I'm just glad I didn't puke in my bucket. Morris and Schultz had to carry their vomit around for hours before we could safely take off our helmets for some fresh air.

I thought we were going to die. The ALTOs flung us around like we were nothing. If it weren't for being strapped in, I can't imagine the number of busted faces and broken bones. And even though we were all wearing our buckets, keeping our faces hidden, I could still tell that the rest of Rage Company were as scared as I was.

My fellow leejes had death grips on their jump seats and blasters. There were no windows in the shuttle, so I couldn't see the planet, but I'm not sure I would have wanted to. All that would've been visible on the way down was the blinding light from the flames of our shuttle as we burned our way through the Rhyssis Wan's atmosphere followed by the explosive bursts and smoke clouds of the incoming anti-air fire. And, sad to say, the sight of more than a few shuttles going down in flames—all hands lost.

Instead of dwelling on the things I couldn't control, I focused my attention internally. I could control my breathing and mentally prepare for what was to come. I told my guys to do the same. I was most concerned about PFC Olvera. He was a skittish sort of fella—massive, a real bruiser, but high strung. The kind of leej you'd want on your side in a bar fight, so long as nothing serious was at stake. That worked in a peacetime reserve unit, not so well at war. I was worried; the entire command team had been. We'd spent too many hours worrying about who would cut it and who would break.

"Only difference between this ride and a repulsor-coaster is the cost of admission, leejes. Hang tight. You'll be fine."

Captain Archer's voice was a soothing balm piped in to our helmets over the company's L-comms. Maybe this was the difference between a leej serving full-time in the Legion and us. Whatever the case, it worked, and a heck of a lot of leejes loosened their grips on their blasters. He was turning out to be an okay officer, for a point.

I began to think about the mission. I stared at the combat overview displayed on my HUD during the rough descent toward the planet. Hundreds of shuttles swarmed Rhyssis Wan from our fleet, all trying to clear space prior to the impending battle. They appeared as small icons on the three-dimensional display on my visor, which I could control with my tongue on the toggle switch near my mouth. I could move my view around, giving me the full picture of the battle space.

Trying to take in all of the information was difficult. I began to have a new respect for our senior officers. They had a tough job, and even with AIs to handle the logistics, a human legionnaire still had to put his eyeballs on the data to verify it. As I scanned the information, I became increasingly alarmed.

The mine fields we stumbled into forced us to deploy directly over the planetary defense cannons. Those infernal guns were swatting us out of the air like we were slow, bumbling flies.

Our pilots saved us, even if it meant throwing us around like rag dolls. They flew like the devil's minions were on our six. I don't know what was out there, hiding in the inky void, I was too focused on the guns down below.

The pilot, Ensign Jonathan Clews, cut my prayers short.

"Can't hold this vector," he said over the comm.

"I don't care where you put us down," Captain Archer replied. "Just give us a chance to get off in one piece!"

"Roger... sir," Clews managed, his voice strained with a white-knuckled grip on the throttle.

The ALTO shuddered from another near miss and bucked wildly downward. Warning alerts from my HUD told me that a few leejes had been knocked unconscious from the jarring motion.

"Hang on, guys!" I shouted, encouraging myself as much as them. "Just… hang on!"

Because what else could we do?

"Rage Company, you are being diverted to an emergency landing zone, designation LZ Echo," said Captain Archer, sounding calm amid the chaos.

"Five minutes to LZ Echo," the ALTO's pilot announced over the comm. Ensign Clews sounded calmer this time. Maybe Captain Archer's cool rubbed off on him. Even with everything getting shot to hell, the man now sounded as smooth as any Dark Ops leej you'd ever meet.

The pilot came back on the comm. "Rough landing. Hang on!"

Clews wasn't exaggerating. I heard a horrible scraping, like layers of the shuttle's hull were being peeled back like strips of bark from a sapling. Turns out, that guess wasn't too far off. The landing zone was too small for the shuttles, and the pilots had to crash through a forest. We hurtled through the timber and bounced off a boulder before settling on LZ Echo.

The shuttle lurched to a stop.

"Up!" I shouted. "Get up and earn your pay, Legionnaires!"

I listened to the flight comm as my men scrambled to adjust themselves. It was clear that someone in the cockpit was hurt in the crash.

"What's the situation?" I asked.

"Tree freaking impaled Clews. He's alive, but we need some help STAT."

Holy strokes. Clews had saved us all, it didn't seem fair. I looked around at the swarming mass that was Rage Company as they assembled and waited for the doors to drop.

"Medic!"

Sergeant Virgil Dwyer, a paramedic in the civilian world, was nearby when I made the call. He was one of the few leejes who'd joined the Cally Reserves from the regular Legion. Another squad leader from my section, Chaos Squad, Virgil was someone I knew well.

"Fetch... LT, you hurt?"

It took me a second to realize that he was speaking to me. I wasn't used to being called sir, to being an officer. "I'm fine, but I need you to hustle up to the cockpit. Things are bad there, Virgil."

"Ooah, sir."

I checked the HUD. I was shocked that the BC had picked such an isolated location. At least we would be, if anyone else hit their original landing zones. Rage Company would be cut off from further support, on our own in the middle of this soup sandwich.

"Holy sket," I muttered.

"What?" Santos asked.

Sket, I'd said that out loud.

"Looking at my HUD," I answered. "Our units landed all over the place. By Oba, some of our militia even landed on the wrong kelhorned continent."

Santos only laughed. "Guess those lucky buggers get to sit out the fight."

"Right, while we die," Olvera grumbled, "and if we all live through this, those lucky buggers'd bash your twarging head in for saying that."

"Kill that noise, Olvera," I commanded, but we all knew it was true. The Cally Militia were touchy about perceived slights, though most lacked the training to do more than tilt at windmills.

Boom. The ramp dropped.

"Grab your gear and un-ass this bird," Captain Archer said, calm and collected. Seriously, I was developing a serious bro crush on this guy.

Looking out the open hatches, the full weight of our new location smacked me in the face. We'd landed in the mountains where the local Arthava had their stronghold. At least that tidbit of information was something the intel schleps got right.

"LT, you're gonna wanna see this," Virgil hollered, the urgency in his voice making my blood freeze. Since he had been a real deal leej, not like us reservists, if he was worried, this was bad.

I nodded to my men who were piling out of the shuttle and followed the sound of Virgil's voice. On elbows and knees, I crawled through the connecting passageway into the pilot's compartment.

Looking in, I was shocked at how little regard had been given to the pilot's survivability. The passenger compartments were protected, compared to the pilot's, whom the designers seemed to see as expendable. The ALTO's crew cabin was barely sufficient to handle the heat from planetary insertion, but a hot drop looked like a bridge too far.

There was blood everywhere. Not just the dramatically smeared handprint common to popular war holofilms, but full-on spatter. Drops of gore and intestine clung to every available surface. Clews, our pilot, sat upright in his chair, a large tree branch speared through his ribs. He gripped the wooden spike poking out of his belly, his face frozen in shock. Somehow in the battered landing, the pilot had lost his helmet, his final scream etched permanently on his pale lifeless face. Even in my isolated LARK, I could smell the coppery tinge of blood.

"He's dead," I said in shock, confused at why Virgil had called in me to see this.

"Open your eyes, Fetch."

I could hear the frustration in his voice, he was trying to show me something, but I wasn't seeing it.

"I get it, that could happen to any of us," I answered. "Bad luck, your time to go. No need to remind me of that, Sergeant."

"Look out the kelhorned window, Fetch."

Pulling my eyes from Clews's lifeless body, I looked out of the shattered cockpit window. I could see the slate gray tones of Bevak Mountain Range in front of me. The strangely purplish hue on the massive trees and something out there circling our location.

"Charkas." I saw what he was pointing at. "Like intel warned us about. Lots of them."

The sight of those ungainly monstrosities in the distance brought back memories of classroom training about our objective. The usual cultural sensitivity twarg that got good leejes killed, trash that most of us had slept through. Those long-forgotten lessons said these mutated dog-like creatures were large war mounts. Some ungodly mix between a wild boar and dog, amped up by a factor of ten. Not just in size, but in sheer ferocity.

"Ding, ding, ding, we have a winner."

The seasoned NCO was his usual brash self, but he had a way of cutting right to the heart of the matter with little regard for your feelings. These strange beasts looked like the war dogs from the stories of the Ancients. Creatures of myth and legend, but they were real. I don't know much about the beasts. What I can tell you is that after what happened next, I'd never look at my setter back home the same way again.

07

I might have stayed in that cockpit, mesmerized by the creatures, had Captain Archer's voice not jolted me into action.

"This is what we've been training for. Let's set a perimeter while I call in for guidance."

Shocked, I crawled back out of the pilot's compartment and rejoined the company. Virgil was several steps ahead of me.

The hooahs that followed were half-hearted. Mine wasn't any better than the rest of the company, barely above a low growl. We were scared, we were sore, and we didn't know what to expect.

Archer called me over, speaking to me over a direct comm channel. "The flight engineer says the shuttle's dead, but just because it won't fly again doesn't mean we can't use it. Get a tech working on setting it up as a comm relay with the fleet in orbit. I want constant contact. Once that's working, we assault the objective like the leejes we are."

"Yes, sir."

"And I want you to make sure your men are properly set up and ready to KTF."

"Yes, sir."

Captain Archer was right, it was time to be leejes for real. It was time to KTF.

"Let's go! Let's go!" I called, hoping to be even half as inspiring as the skipper was. I wasn't holding my breath. "Specialist Dominguez! Captain needs this shuttle set up as a comm relay with the fleet. Join him back on board. Now."

"On it, LT!"

Freezing cold gusts of wind shot up around me, venturing inside the shuttle, bringing in swirling dustings of snow. Snow—real, white, colder-than-an-aggrieved-point's-heart snow. Having grown up in the equatorial region of Pictavia, I'd only seen snow in holovids, but seeing it in person grabbed my attention. I wasn't on Caledonia anymore. Our mission's plan hadn't survived entry into the system, let alone contact with the enemy. This sket was real. I took a calming breath and ran out of the damaged bird as the last of my men rolled out.

"I'll set the perimeter, LT," Santos said. "Don't forget to coordinate with the old man."

The dude was looking out for me. Something was different between us, but I hadn't figured out what. By the time I did, it didn't matter anymore. But you know how it is—you compartmentalize things until you can deal with it later.

The cold was even more jarring outside the ALTO. The legionnaires without reserve kits must have had better climate controls because they were the only ones who weren't shaking. Our kit was designed for the extreme heat, and we had landed in the coldest icebox in the galaxy.

I never heard the guys curse so much as right then. Some of those words were new to me, and I'd dealt with organized crime families as a restaurateur. The men suggested anatomical acts that I wasn't even sure were possible. Didn't even bother looking it up, I was afraid of what I'd find. I focused on setting up a defensive perimeter instead.

I ordered Sergeant Dwyer, Corporal Moore, and Sergeant Michael Conn to set up a perimeter on the south side of the ship.

"On it, Fetch," Virgil said, speaking for the section.

They were good guys, any one of them more qualified than I was to be the section commander. But college degrees were king in the classist New Caledonian Reserve Corps. I had the paper, so I wore the shiny yoke of power. It was still so new that it felt strange watching leejes work. Pulling up my HUD overlay, I looked around the area and set the secondary defensive positions.

With the instructions forwarded to the section's NCOs, I bit the bullet and called the Old Man.

"Captain Archer, 1st Section is digging in. Well, attempting to. Check your HUD for our positions. We've interlocked them with 2nd and 4th Sections."

"Good job, Lieutenant. Don't worry about a secondary position, we've got nowhere to go. We hold the line and KTF or we die."

"Roger, sir."

I hope that he couldn't hear the fear in my voice. Anyone that says he wasn't afraid lied to you. Or he wasn't there.

After the landing zone was secured, our HUDs started lighting up. We didn't have a lot of time to dig in. Threat icons warned us of movement all around us.

"What are we seeing?" I asked my squad leaders.

"Relax, sir," said Corporal Moore. "If the AI in our suits can't recognize the source, it isn't a threat."

Dexter Moore had always been a cocky guy, a career corporal convinced that the Legion would fall apart without him as a team leader. He could've made sergeant, but he was prone to drunken run-ins with law enforcement. Even in the Reserves, that didn't fly.

Santos piped in his opinion. "Classify it as suspicious, LT. If we're wrong, oh well. If we're right, we've saved lives. I'll take over for our dead platoon sergeant and coordinate things for the section, sir."

He came through for me again. I was glad that the experienced NCO hadn't been in the company HQ when the ship had been hit. When I'd boarded the shuttle and laid eyes on him, it had been an emotional moment. This wasn't the last time I'd thanked Oba for that stroke of fortune either.

With Virgil's help, we desperately tried to create firing positions. It had worked in training, but the picks and shovels in our pioneer kits didn't even scratch the surface of Rhyssis Wan's frozen, rocky terrain. We couldn't dig in. Things just got a lot more complicated now that we were without defensive positions. The hard, black rocks of the valley where we'd landed just added another wrinkle to our battle plans.

"Check the shuttle for cutting torches," I ordered a private as he futilely bit into the permafreeze. The leej happily jumped up and run for the ship.

"If you wanted easy, you should've joined the Marines!" Top Walden grunted as his second shovel broke on a rock.

Things went from bad to worse. The valley was acting as a wind tunnel, adding strength to the wind which buffeted the area. We weren't able to turtle ourselves below the surface in proper fox holes, and the cold was biting.

"No torches on board, Lieutenant!" the private responded.

"Kneel or go prone!" Walden called.

First Sergeant Walden was one of the command team who'd transferred from the 71st. He was a hard man, and one whose shiny armor kept him warm. He might've been comfortable, but things got even more miserable for the rest of Rage Company. The cold rocky ground leeched any residual warmth from our bodies. We secured our perimeter as best we could, despite the conditions.

While the four squads in my section knelt, eyes fixed on the blinding snowbanks around us, I went around and checked on the leejes. It was weird, being responsible for so many legionnaires. I still hadn't processed this promotion, and I was actually hoping I wouldn't keep it when our reinforcements finally touched down. In an instant, I'd gone from being a sergeant managing a ten-man squad, to an LT serving as the Officer-in-Charge or OIC for four squads. Forty people depending on me not to screw the Drusic.

I knew that I couldn't dwell on the what-ifs, so I tried to force myself to think positively. Stop focusing on all the pressure. Of course we'll be fine! Keep your chin up. Never mind those flashing HUD warning lights.

Negativity wouldn't help—it might even hurt us since I was already prone to going to the dark places in my mind. I had to think clearly and positively. I needed to fake it until I began believing my own lies.

"Sir? Any word from the fleet?" Corporal Santos asked me. "I don't think your kits are gonna be of much use to you just sitting out in the cold, sir."

He was right. We needed to at least move enough to get some blood flowing. This was brutal.

"Captain Archer," I called into my comm. "Word on the fleet connection, sir? The men are struggling in this cold and staying still to turn into snowmen isn't helping."

"Negative," said Archer. "Still trying to get that set up. Having some difficulty with—"

The captain's voice was cut off by something that sounded like... wet fish slapping against the rocks above us. Even above the howl of the wind, there was an audible slapping sound. Like marching, maybe. A lot of boots.

"Sounds like company is coming," warned Santos.

I looked but couldn't see them. I strained my eyes to see anything, trying to understand what was happening. The sound had a chilling effect on the men of Rage Company, and the not knowing made it worse. I could almost feel the leejes collectively holding their breath, as they waited for the boogey man to appear.

I bellowed orders to my section. "Keep your eyes scanning the horizons but check your blasters before they appear. Don't let them catch you with your buckets off—your brothers are counting on you!"

Dark shadows appeared out of the snow. Waves of charkas loomed above us. They were an impressive sight, massive and majestic. Also deadly, very deadly.

I remember the picture the intel types had shoved in front of our eyeballs at Camp Lund, during our training on Pictavia. The charkas were sometimes used as mounts for the native Arthava population. These massive four-legged creatures had razor-sharp fangs in a maw as big as their heads. They looked like someone mated a wild boar with a war dog. Even the tiny ones were nearly five feet tall at the shoulder. I remember thinking that the wee beasties made the zhee look cuddly by comparison. Normally I'd respect the sheer splendor of such creatures, but a pack of these wild beasts were charging toward my leejes.

"Hold your fire!" I shouted.

"Wait for it!" My squad leaders seconded my order, relaying to their leejes.

The charging beasts weren't close enough that we could hit them with kill shots. Might as well save the energy, use it when it counts. I couldn't see their eyes yet, which was the mantra the Legion taught us at the designated marksman school. It sounds like they'd be kissin' close, but with our advanced optics, we could see our enemy out to smack dab in the middle of the effective range of our NM-4 blasters.

All I could see at that point were swirling blobs of fur, but I couldn't help but imagine those eyeballs containing a vicious predatory bloodlust. There were waves of the strange creatures flowing out of the hills around us. They charged down the wooded hillside, uprooting some of the smaller trees that were in their way. It was a stampede of snarling predators, and we were the prey.

Before I had a chance to prompt my section, our pre-deployment training kicked in. The monotonous drills helped us hide our fear. I won't lie, I was so startled at first that I yelped like a little girl. I guess that's something I do a lot of. Best just to own it.

We're talking tax day kind of fear. I had to do something, though. Inaction meant death and I had too much to live for. All around me, the leejes of Rage Company fired bolt after bolt from our blasters. It didn't seem to make a difference. If anything, those volleys seemed to make the charkas only angrier.

These things couldn't have been that strong, could they? Mission intel was clear that a standard blaster shot would have sufficient lethality. But that wasn't happening.

Every childhood nightmare and every horror movie I'd ever watched came back to me in that moment. My breath caught in my throat. My palms began to sweat. I wanted to run away. The sound was a terrible screeching, pure terror inducing, like an angry demon trying to break free from the pits of hell. The charka's bulky mass allowed them to pick up speed as they ran down the mountains, which they used to uproot still more sapling trees from the rocky soil. I began to worry that my section would be overrun.

It was Corporal Moore who identified the problem.

"LR-24, we're having weapons malfunctions. Only getting half charges from our blasters!"

That explained things. I kept my voice as calm as I could make it. "Roger, LR-11, stand your ground. Berserker Squad must hold the line. 3rd Section is sending their crew-served slug throwers over now. LR-24, out."

The rata-tat-tat told me that the weapons had arrived. Slug throwers are old tech, and if it weren't for the Cally militia being old and outdated, we wouldn't have had them in the field. But in this case, it ended up being a blessing. Those bullets had no problem punching through the charka's fur, muscle, and bone.

Soon afterward, the red lights on my HUD that signified hostiles began to dim. So far, so good, but I knew we'd be in trouble when they got within reach of us. It was time for us to go.

"Captain Archer," I called out. "Sir, we need to forget fleet and reach out to the rest of the battalion. The cold is messing with our blasters. We need to link up with other companies, or we'll be overrun."

There was no reply, just the dead hum of an unconnected channel. I doubted our comms were jammed—that wasn't supposed to be possible for L-comm. Maybe it was just the quality of our kits. Maybe the snow... This was craptastic.

Either way, the charkas were almost on top of us and all we were doing was giving them a slight burn and bruise with each trigger pull. I screamed the order I'd hoped to never have to use.

"Fix. Bayonets!"

Up and down the line there was the distinctive click of the bayonet clinking onto the barrel of their blasters. Our bayonets were largely ceremonial, a cultural thing. The Legion didn't have them. But with our blasters misfiring, we were desperate. The order came just in time. Seconds after we set the blades onto our weapons, the charkas flooded our perimeter. It was pure chaos.

The leejes who first made contact with the animals swung their blades like pros. Thrusting, jabbing, and slashing into the beasties' flanks like we'd been trained. I saw them from my peripheral vision as I monitored my sector. I trusted my suit's assisted aiming enough to check on my men. The blades weren't working. Some of them snapped in two, while other bayonets merely bounced off the animals' thickly muscled hides.

Soon the furry monstrosities knocked over leejes, crushing them under their massive weight as they bowled through our lines. Their charge cut through our position with such force that they end up slamming into the rushing onslaught that came at us from the other direction. It bought us the time we needed to regain our footing.

"Aim for their heads!" I shouted as I stood back up, blaster clutched tightly in my numb fingers. A half charge to the face at this range should still be enough to drop those things.

Trusting the leejes behind me, I began dragging my section back to our position on the line and focusing our fire. I had an unformed idea tickling my consciousness, but Virgil had none of my hesitation.

"Buddy teams! Fire in teams of two—you'll knock out the beasts. KTF!"

It worked. We began carving out a small section of land that was ours, an island of calm in the swirling seas of charka death. The unified volleys also began to warm up our frozen blasters. Soon our shots were having more of an effect, knocking out the charging animals. I focused on one of the beasts that had circled around our position, gently squeezing my trigger. A caress really, a lover's touch that unleashed my fury on the closest target.

Focus pressed against my chest like a cold weight. I forgot about the battle around me. I concentrated on the group of large furry beasts only feet away. I sighted, fired, and sighted again. Shifting my aim, I stared into the mouth of the nearest Cerberus. Froth drooled from the animal's gaping maw, flinging from side to side as it shook its head and roared. When the thing snarled, it was like Hell had unleashed its hounds after us.

I'm telling you, these beasts were the stuff of nightmares, and we had to stand toe-to-toe with them on their home turf. I see them still, every night in my sleep. Every morning I wake up in a cold sweat, some part of me afraid that the things are near. Kind of nuts. All the stuff that happened over there and this is what gives me bad dreams.

A charka charged at me and I was terrified, but the repetitive buurt sound of crew-served slug throwers strengthened my nerve. I stood up, aimed my blaster and fired several bolts in rapid succession. Just hoping that maybe the weapon would continue to overcome the cold and do some damage.

I couldn't tell if I landed any critical hits, but I kept pouring shots downrange anyway. It became reflexive—aim, sight, gently squeeze the trigger. It surprised me how quickly the charge pack on my blaster died, but I swapped it out and engaged the target.

I didn't get the chance to fire again, as the pouncing charka was practically on top of me now. This one was even larger than I'd thought, easily as tall as the average Caledonian horse. Up that close against something so big, my bayonet seemed laughably pathetic. Thank Oba our blasters are holding the line for us.

It swiped at me with its massive paw, intent on removing my head from my shoulders. I ducked and juked right, only to be slammed back by another beast. Stumbling, I fired a few shots at point-blank range.

I backpedaled until slamming into something solid, knocking my head before slumping to the ground. It was the ALTO; I'd hit the shuttle. I gasped from the pain. The bird had stopped me from careening farther from the protection of Rage Company's formation, but it hurt like hell. Not as bad as what Santos had managed with all those squats, but a close second.

I stood, struggling to shake off the floating pinpricks of light. I couldn't hear anything, just the ringing in my ears. A small voice inside of me said that I had to get back into the fight. Squatting, I grabbed the blaster lying near where I'd landed and fired at the furry charka. I got lucky, hitting one in the eye. I watched in satisfaction as the wounded animal panicked, plowing through the ranks of its horde mates. Soon several more charka were turning on each other, snarling and biting each other.

I couldn't dwell on the small victory, not when a battle raged on and my men needed me. I steadily advanced forward, encouraging my section while firing bolts. Soon I was among my section, directing their positions and interlocking their fields of fire. We'd managed to re-form a firing line and force the charging animals back. They still circled us, but they weren't in our ranks anymore. We fired recklessly, hurling our war cries into the mass of teeth, claws, and mangy fur assaulting our formation. We were entranced, lost in the fight.

While many of my section were swapping out batteries, the next wave of charka rushed straight at us. They were fast, and our frozen gloved fingers struggled to slot new packs into the battery well of the blaster carbines. But by now our rifles were charged and operating properly. Maybe those first packs were bad, but the beasts were getting mowed down much quicker, with only a few of the strongest getting close to our lines before dropping under the convergence of leej fire.

Of course, with my luck, a big one barreled right through and toward me as I struggled to swap out packs. I tried to back up and tripped over something.

A leej, it was a dead leej. I could feel the solid ceramic polymers of his LARK as I tumbled over his corpse—a corpse that had once been my friend and neighbor.

"Damn it!"

I roared my frustration into my bucket. Flat on my back, I stared up at the razor-sharp canines of the charka about to kill me. All I could do was pray that my end would be quick.

Then the creature's head exploded.

I'm not going to die, I thought I as I wiped the blood and brain matter from my visor. Those beasts smelled even more disgusting once their insides were on the outside, but I would happily have smelled that to avoid being eaten by one.

I'm not sure how long I lay under the beast, pinned to the ground by the massive weight laying across my legs, relieved to be alive. I could hear the blaster fire pitch and then slowly subside until the battlefield was quiet.

Someone shoved the charka corpse off me. Looking up, I saw a set of shiny armor leaning in toward me.

"Come on, sir, upsy-daisy."

It was Santos offering me his hand, grunting as he pulled me to my feet. I was sore, but very much alive.

"Switch to your sidearm, sir," he said once I'd regained my feet. "If your blaster is knocked from your fingers, or you can't change packs quickly enough, switch to your pistol. And drop your bayonets. Most of those krankers broke the first time we tried using 'em. Defective gear is dead weight, we can't afford to carry it around."

With that, Santos took off. Looking around, I saw way too many leejes milling around aimlessly. Inspecting the dead monsters up close or watching as medics tended to the wounded. I was seeing more men than there were in Rage Company. Where had they come from? I needed information, so I tried to the company L-comms again. Got nothing. Frustrated, I slapped the side of my bucket where the comms relay was housed. That worked, I could hear the comms again.

"LR-01, my comms were damaged. LR-24 requesting an update, how copy?"

No response.

"Any 9th Legion element, this is LR-24, Rage Company. Request immediate reinforcements."

This got someone's attention. "LR-01, Dragon Company. En route to your location."

"More charkas!" yelled a leej from the line.

I didn't respond right away, firing into a cluster of charkas trying to push through our lines. I was having serious doubts about how long we could do this if more waves of this pack kept coming. They didn't seem like quitters. Some creatures just live to fight.

"Oh, sket!" someone else called out. "This looks like all of 'em!"

"You better push the throttles or there won't be anyone left," I managed. "LR-24, out."

It was abrupt, but manners go out the windows when you're being tackled by the furry fiends of destruction. I tried to find my leejes. It wasn't possible. The entire company was intermixed, our lines broken with legionnaires fighting in desperate pockets, doing everything they could to keep the charkas back.

We had to re-form the lines, to push them back.

"Rage Company... gun run... I say again, pull back to your ALTO. Keep up your fire and make sure those things say out in the open."

The voice was abrupt. The message was interrupted by static, but the intent was clear. I began grabbing every leej near me, dragging them back toward the shuttle. I fired my blaster, not caring if I killed the charkas around us. I just needed to buy time, keep them back and get my men out of the line of fire.

"Santos, pull the men back!"

More and more legionnaires clustered around our damaged shuttle. If this didn't work, this would be our last day. When everyone I could see had pulled back, I radioed the pilot.

"We're clear! Rage Company is clear!"

Buurt. Buuurt.

The pilot didn't answer, but the chatter of his blaster cannon tearing into the clustered charka was the only response I needed. Men cheered, but none of them stopped firing.

The unknown pilot put his buzz ship's guns to good use, mowing down hundreds of the beasts and halting the momentum of the stampede. Our blasters took two shots to kill the monstrous charka—if we were lucky, at close range, and aiming on point—but a buzz ship's guns are significantly more powerful. The stampeding beasts were slaughtered, and our perimeter expanded. It was over pretty quickly after that.

With the situation stabilized, another ALTO set down near our landing zone.

"Sergeant Dwyer, organize our section. I'm gonna find Captain Archer."

I didn't have to wait for an answer, Virgil was already getting the situation in hand. Pulling up my HUD, I marked Captain Archer as the objective and started the methodical hunt. I found him inside our damaged shuttle, checking on the wounded. I called out to him over the L-comm, but the Old Man didn't respond.

That's when I realized his comms had been damaged as well. He was gesticulating but no sound came through. With some of the charka still showing signs of life, I couldn't let him finish taking off his bucket.

I slapped the side of Captain Archer's helmet, trying to jar it into working.

"Sorry, sir," I said. "That worked for me, though."

Archer nodded and I could hear his voice. "Thanks, Lieutenant."

I listened in as he repeated our sit-rep to the Dragon Company commander. We'd almost been overrun, but our sister company had reinforced us in the nick of time. During our initial landing, our battalion shuttles had tried to stay close enough that we could link up, but it hadn't worked. Only Dragon Company, 1st Batt, had succeeded in the unified battalion landing. Dragon Company's ALTO was still operational, and its crew uninjured. They'd risked anti-air guns and taken to the skies, saving us all.

"LR-01, will the shuttle begin ferrying us over the mountain to rejoin our boys?" I asked when the update was done.

"Negative, LR-24," Captain Archer replied. "Our orders are to secure the city of Kusiba. It's believed to be loyal to the Repub. We're to protect them at all costs."

"But there's only three hundred of us for a city of two million!" exclaimed Corporal Moore.

"Radio discipline, LR-11," I ground out over the comms channel.

I understood his frustration, though. I'd been thrilled when I'd heard that the rest of the 9th Legion was on the other side of the mountains. After a quick shuttle ride to join them, we could have been back with our brothers. It gave me a brief feeling of safety and well-being. But instead of enjoying the safety of numbers, we were being sent back out into the wilds. The Repub had done us dirty again. They were sending us to die. A much larger occupying force could have secured a city like Kusiba, but a mere company like ours? We'd be squashed like sin-ticks. I understood the logic behind it, but I was pissed. We all were. Leejes cursing as word spread. Someone needed to stop the toxic negativity from infecting the ranks.

"Stow that garbage, Rage Company!" I growled into the L-comms. "This is why they sent the 9th Legion. KTF! For Cally!"

08

"Medic!"

The screams echoed up and down the perimeter. Getting out of the valley was gonna take time. We had to treat our wounded and handle the remains of our dead leej brothers.

"Ocampo, send over anyone with medical training," Captain Archer said. "And process the field, the other sections will handle the defensive perimeter."

The captain was picking up the balls I kept dropping. We lucked out with him; made me wonder if he was a point after all. I came alongside Virgil.

"Dwyer, let Sergeant Moore manage 1st Section and come with me," I told him. "Doc Tran needs your help. Take anyone who's got the requisite skills."

While Moore started organizing our improvised fortifications, piling up the bodies of the dead charka that littered Landing Zone Echo, I followed Virgil over to the medical collection point.

Big mistake. Some things can't be unseen.

"Make it stop!" screamed PFC Allan Valdes.

He was a private from my section, though not from Berserker Squad. I didn't know much about him, but with his bucket off he looked so young. I couldn't even see a hint of facial hair. By Oba, now I was going to have to write his folks.

Doc Tran was working on him, but quickly. It was evident he was doing what he could to help the kid's pain go away until what came next arrived.

"It hurts!"

"Shhh, it's gonna be okay, Leej. It'll stop hurting soon," soothed Doc Tran.

Everyone could see what the Doc wasn't saying, that Valdes was not long for this world. His guts were hanging out, his legs had been chewed off, and one of his arms was bent at an unnatural angle. Without a hospital, one of those real top-of-the-line Repub versions, there was no way to save him. And he wasn't my only loss from that first engagement, not by a long shot.

Walking around the wounded, I saw one of the corporals from Berserker Squad. Cole Trueblood was one of those strong, silent types. Even after several years serving beside him, I still barely knew him. Now I never would. He lay there with a sucking chest wound, his chest crushed under those devilishly massive paws. Another leej whom the House sentenced to die.

Thinking my men would need the encouragement of seeing their lieutenant's face, I took my bucket off. Instant regrets. The coppery smell of human blood assaulted my nostrils, and I heaved. The pungently acidic nature of the smells wafting across the frozen field from the dead charka made me lose what little was left in my stomach. I don't know if it was the banging my brain pan took, or the stress of my first combat engagement, but it was too intense. I had to put my helmet back on. I'd wanted to show my face, my humanity, to my men when they needed that little gesture the most. But I couldn't. I failed those legionnaires.

It still kills me inside, even after everything that happened on Rhyssis Wan. But I couldn't take it anymore. I should've offered them aid and comfort as they prepared to meet Oba, but I just didn't have it in me. Not that day, after so many had already died. I was at the halfway point, straddling the line between human and warrior. Between Caledonian subject and leej. It was a difficult transition, feeling everything and nothing. I felt too much... and yet, I didn't feel enough. I couldn't be there for my men at the end.

I left Virgil to supervise my living leejes as we prepared to depart LZ Echo. When I returned, Moore had finished pushing the carcasses of those foul beasties into an impromptu barricade. With our defense handled, I began the grisly task of processing the recently departed. I wasn't quite sure what to do with them. Leaving them unburied was out of the question; they'd earned our respect and their final interment. I felt we had to make time to send them into Oba's welcoming arms, though burying them wasn't a viable option.

"What do you want us to do?" Sergeant Moore asked, as the last of Rage Company's dead were piled up.

"The ground's way too hard to dig graves," I replied, my hushed voice only audible because of my bucket. "We pile them together and cover them with rocks."

"What good will that do? Scavengers can still get the bodies."

I wanted to scream at the injustices of the situation, but Sergeant Moore didn't deserve that abuse. He was just doing his job and doing it well, despite everything. No, he deserved a real leej officer and instead he was stuck with me.

"We hope their LARKs, and the rocks, keep the scavengers at bay until the fighting's done and a cleanup team can do these men right. Yeah, it's a ceremonial gesture, but it's the best we can do for now."

It went unsaid that the Field of the Fallen, the veterans' cemetery on Pictavia, would have to add another plot after this battle. Once the Savage War had ended, it had become a mostly unused war memorial. Sure, we buried our native sons and daughters who went away to serve, but those were relatively few and far between. Because of that, those hallowed grounds became a place that politicians only seem to remember on Veterans Day or at election time.

I couldn't let that happen to these leejes.

Standing there over that first batch of bodies, I made a solemn promise to bring them home. Our fallen sons deserved all that and more. Until then, we protected their bodies as best we could and marked the spot on our maps. Kneeling next to the rocky mound, I placed an emergency transponder beacon into the pile and covered it with a rock so it wouldn't roll away. Moore had set the device to activate in forty-eight hours. We'd be victorious or dead by then, so giving away the site's location wouldn't comprise us.

A flight engineer stumbled over and placed his hand on my shoulder. "We won't totally abandon our fallen to the ravages of Rhyssis Wan's weather, legionnaire. We're leaving the damaged ALTO to guard them. The old girl still has some spunk left in her, sir."

"What's your name, spacer?"

"Petty Officer Taylor, I was the crew chief until yesterday, sir. Before... everything. I set the shuttle's auto-cannons to defense mode. It'll gun down anything getting too close to the graves."

I gave Taylor a suspicious look, though he couldn't tell from beneath my helmet. "Why didn't you use those in the fight?"

"I tried, sir. They were taken out in the crash. Just finished repairing the guns a minute ago. But since we can't save the shuttle, I figured at least we can protect our fallen."

"Ours?" I growled.

I shouldn't have snapped at him. He was a member of the naval militia, a part of the Caledonian Reserve Corps. He'd earned the right to be there, but I was protective of my leejes.

"Caledonia's, sir," Petty Officer Taylor replied, showing a resolve and respect that made me flush inwardly with shame. "We'll protect their remains until the ship runs out of power. Or is destroyed by the enemy. I've tweaked the shuttle's core programming, sir. It'll attack charkas on sight. I can send the specs to your HUD, sir."

I could only grunt in reply, I didn't have it in me for words. I was too busy trying not to cry. Looking over his changes, I saw that he'd added the charkas to the automatic threat status. If the shuttle ever managed to upload the new program into the navy's data network... it'd get pretty interesting for the planet's ecological makeup.

"Make it so," I finally managed. "Make sure the bird's ready by the time we're ready to leave."

"Sir, I've already done that. I need help stripping the ALTO of everything useful. We need to load it into Dragon Company's shuttle."

Nodding, I looked for Corporal Santos. He was beside me, right where he needed to be when I needed him. It was uncanny, but I wasn't going to complain.

"Santos, organize a detail to salvage anything we can from our shuttle."

"Already on it, sir."

With all our assigned tasks handled, I began checking on our situation. After I scanned the status reports on my HUD, I realized we weren't as poorly situated as I'd feared. If we could take out the local orbital defense guns, we'd have proper air support from those ALTOs capable of taking off, not to mention the slow but powerful buzz ships. The only wrinkle in our good fortune was how we would handle our walking wounded. In the mountainous terrain, we couldn't afford to use manpower to carry them.

Toggling the lever near my mouth, I switched through to the unit rosters for Rage Company. We'd lost thirty-four leejes from Rage and Dragon Companies. They'd survived the contested landing, only to be killed by a gargantuan pack of wild animals. Our first assault and we had at least twenty so badly wounded that they should've been sidelined. None of them were willing to stay with the shuttle.

Swiping through the map overlay on my HUD, I saw how complicated our situation truly was. Our trip into Kusiba went straight up steep and craggy inclines. We couldn't trust the roads; if the enemy were expecting us, they'd have ambushes and booby traps.

I saw Virgil returning from his duties with medical triage.

Pulling him aside, I asked, "Sergeant Dwyer, if you were the cultists, how would you defend this area?"

The grizzled sergeant didn't miss a beat. "Given the time to adequately prepare... and they had it... I'd leave so many anti-personnel mines on the local roads they'd shake the entire mountain when they went off. Really make the attacking forces feel the love."

"That's what I was afraid of," I said, trying to show more confidence than I felt.

We were in a time crunch, with very few viable routes to our objective. Every rolled ankle meant we went slower than before, and time was of the essence. It felt odd, assuming so much authority, but we needed every leej operating on all cylinders and the captain was too focused on the larger objective to remember the troops. He was trusting his subordinate leaders to handle that for him.

Me, he was trusting me to look out for the leejes of Caledonia.

"Rage Company, lighten the loads of the wounded. We need every leej on their game, so spread the gear around. Make it happen."

While Rage Company passed the kit around, my HUD started flashed with a private L-comm request from Captain Archer.

"What then, Lieutenant?" asked Dwyer.

"Once we're light enough on our feet, we're taking a climb. The hard way. The Legion way."

"Ooah," said Dwyer before moving to oversee my orders.

I keyed for Captain Archer. "LR-01, we've established the defensive perimeter and we're making preparation to climb. Our analysis suggests that we need to avoid the main roads."

"Well done, Ocampo," he said. "I needed my officers to step up, and you didn't let me down. I won't forget that."

Maybe he wasn't a point after all.

Feeling like my favorite teacher had just praised my work, I went to check on my leejes with more pep in my step than had been there since this whole fiasco began. They were checking charge packs and making sure their gear was on securely. Most of them were staging with their sergeants.

I stopped by each NCO and gave them the same message. "Nobody comes up unless you're sure they can make it the whole way. Legionnaire pride isn't going to slow us down and we don't have the manpower to carry anybody we don't have to. It's all KTF from here on out."

I saw that a few of the leejes were taking this opportunity to eat some rations. After a fight like that, I didn't blame them. I was feeling ravenous myself, but work needed to come first. The sight of those legionnaires blowing steam out of self-cooking ration packs made me think of what else a few of my reservists might be doing in their downtime. "Santos, check on Private Schultz. He tends to hide hooch on him, and I need him sober for the first time in his life."

Laughing, Santos responded affirmatively. It had to suck to be that kid; this was the worst day in the history of history to have to sober up. With that off my list of things to worry about, I checked on the other squads in my section. I hoped that the other LTs were doing the same.

"Listen up," Captain Archer said over the command L-comm channel, "we need to un-ass this LZ. I want your leejes ready to step off in ten, LR-01 out."

That time flew by. Officers and NCOs scrambled to ensure we'd forgotten nothing. Corporals checked the site for anything that could be salvaged.

And then Archer gave the final command to move out, ending our respite. Now we were about to more deeply appreciate the leej mantra. Kill them first.

The U-shaped valley we'd landed in was between two of the largest mountains in the entire Bevak Mountain Range. Whatever glacial hell that formed this geographic monstrosity had created some of the steepest terrain I'd ever seen. The glare of the snow taunted us with its cheery brightness.

Onward we marched, scrambling up the steep incline. We tried in vain to maintain tactical formations, but often the trails were only passable by single files of troops. Fortunately, a few of our leejes had brought along personal camera drones. We were able to send those ahead of us to scout the terrain. It wasn't perfect, but it was better than nothing.

"Sir, there's an enemy pillbox ahead," Private Olvera informed me. "Got it on drone feed."

That surprised me—not that there was an enemy pillbox, I'd expected that, but that Olvera had been the one to spot it. So far, that pretty boy had yet to impress me. He had been skittish in the fight, and loved primping in front of a camera.

"Show me."

That pillbox had to be dealt with. Looking at the footage, I saw the Arthava for the first time. They were dirty, stinking pack animals that looked like someone had taken a hyena from our plains and stood it on two legs. Only they were meaner and a whole lot bigger. Easily taller than the average human by more than a foot. Like maybe they were an evolved version of the charkas. I don't know. Rumor had it they could rip a man in half with their bare hands, but I wasn't sure I believed it. What really worried me about the Arthava reports was the tiny notation that the population liked to play with blasters for fun. That seemed like a bigger threat to our safety.

I forwarded the threat alert to Captain Archer.

"Lieutenant Ocampo, lead a small strike team to eliminate that target. LR-01, out."

Archer could've asked any officer in the two companies under his command. Captain Archer ordered me instead. Guess that's fair since it was my team who spotted it. I momentarily froze at the order, but my NCOs had my back again.

"I'll take care of it, sir," Dwyer offered.

I shook my head. "Negative, we need you leading this soup sandwich. I've got this, Sergeant."

"Follow me, sir," said Santos, already stalking toward the objective. "And try not to step on my toes."

Santos. For as rocky as things started off, he seemed like everything you'd want in a leej.

Some of what happed next ended up on the news vids taken from the drone footage. Maybe they were inadvertently leaked, maybe the recordings of the engagement were sent to the public on purpose. But what the public got was a messy affair. It always is when you KTF.

I advanced forward, stalking our new prey.

"Just provide overwatch, sir," Santos said. "I'll take Maas forward and silence those braying kelhorns."

The enhanced optics on my HUD gave me a front row seat, despite Santos moving on ahead. The pillbox was situated so as to look over the road we'd opted not to take—right at a bending switchback, meaning any column traveling up the road would be zeroed in right when they were doubled up and snaking around the curve. Wouldn't have been pretty.

Santos crept past scrubby trees and disappeared behind snow-capped stones as he moved toward the duracrete structure dug into rock, just a slight dome dusted with snow extending above the ground with a few slits where the heavy weapons inside could fire from.

I saw a hatch swing open, and then one of the Arthava climbed out of the pillbox and stretched, its breath sending up hot clouds of vapor into the chill air.

"Santos," I called, lining the sentry up in my rifle's reticules, "one of them is topside."

"I see it. Another one is following."

A moment later I saw the second. It moved in the opposite direction as us and found a tree to relieve itself against.

"Making my move," Santos said.

When it came to a knife work, Santos was an artist. The Arthava sentries never saw him coming. They never had a hint that they'd been flanked until his vibro-blade sliced their jugulars. Do hyenas even have those? I guess I could've asked them, but they'd lost their heads in the excitement of meeting a real-life leej.

He moved quickly from one Arthava to the next, sprinkling the white ground with each creature's blood. He then crept to the pillbox, fragger in hand, and gave a cursory look inside.

"Looks like it was just the two, Lieutenant."

"All right. Check them for any intel we can use."

"Already on it, sir."

Santos disappeared into the pillbox but returned a few seconds later. "Just a high-cycle blaster cannon and a charge battery."

By then I had reached the location and began to check the dead bodies. I found a couple of datapads but after a couple of tries couldn't unlock the pass codes so I stowed them in my tactical ruck for intel to take a look at later.

I called back a status report to Captain Archer. "Enemy pillbox neutralized, sir. No sign of further hostiles."

"Nice work, Lieutenant. Re-form and march. Kusiba is still a good march from here."

It took us several hours to get within visual range of Kusiba. The intel we'd received on the place didn't do the city justice. It was gorgeous—a modern enclave built over a rocky plateau. The designers clearly placed an emphasis on embracing the surrounding natural beauty. The buildings blended in with the slate gray rock of the local mountains, and didn't have reflective windows that are popular elsewhere in the Republic. The layer of snow powdering everything added a peaceful, serene look.

Designed to mimic the environment's rocky terrain, the rectangular buildings rose several hundred stories tall, allowing the densely populated city to have a smaller footprint. The city took up several square miles, but there were still only a couple hundred thousand buildings. And all of that was supposed to be secured by three hundred legionnaires.

"Are you seeing this, sir?" I asked the captain.

"Affirmative, LR-24."

I blinked in surprise. "Sir, how will three hundred leejes secure such a massive city?"

"One foot at a time, Ocampo. One foot at a time."

One foot at a time? What did that even mean? There was no way we could capture so much territory with so few personnel. Let alone occupy and secure it. I didn't know what to say, but I didn't want to look like a fool, so I shut my mouth. Instead, I focused on the footage from the drones.

There should've been more movement and activity in the city. Local citizens should have been going about their afternoon routines. Instead, there was stillness. Nobody was doing business, or walking the streets. And yeah, it was cold and mountainous—winter—but the Arthava were used to that. They were staying hidden for a reason. The only thing we did see were more of those stinking charkas running around. A few of them with saddles. They were sort of stalking the streets like a pack of feral dogs, looking for trouble. It dawned on me how tough the Arthava must be to deal with another high-level predator the way humans treat stray mutts.

I knew that the indigenous Arthava had domesticated the foul beasts; they'd taught us that in our cultural sensitivity training. Supposedly the housebroken charka were tame. Supposedly. I'd been around enough guard dogs in my life to know how they'd treat us. No matter how friendly the tame ones were, we'd still be strangers in their territory. It wouldn't make a difference how gentle the charka were when they bit the limbs off of my troops. Or when they crushed the boys under their massive girth.

"LR-11," I ordered Corporal Moore, "send your drone in closer, it's worth the risk."

"Copy. I'm having trouble getting these things to uplink with your HUD, so if there's anything you wanna see, you're gonna have to come on over and view it on my control screen."

I moved to do just that, but Captain Archer took my attention.

"Lieutenant Ocampo, I need a timetable on when you're set to move First Team into the city."

"Copy LR-01," I said, looking over to see Virgil set up his fireteam in a perimeter and feeling like I had too much to do at one time. "We're going to need some time to fully scout something this big."

"Affirmative." Captain Archer next ordered the two companies to halt. The men needed to rest, and Moore needed extra time to direct the drones deeper into Kusiba. As his section leader, it was my job to supervise him. No rest for the wicked, or so I've heard countless officers tell me.

I peered over Moore's shoulder since that was my only option. All up close and personal.

"You don't have to breathe down my neck, Fetch," Moore said, exasperated.

"That's lieutenant now, Corporal."

It was weird, correcting him. It hadn't been very long since we'd all been corporals together.

"Yes, sir."

"Lieutenant Ocampo," I heard Virgil say. "Sir, you should have authorization now to patch Moore's HUD feed into your own visor and see whatever he's looking at."

"Roger, thanks," I responded curtly.

I was authorized extra features, I belatedly remembered. I quickly toggled the officers' option screen from the command interface. I found the ones I needed, and my HUD blacked out before displaying Moore's bucket, my HUD's display miniaturized in a small box in the corner so I wasn't completely blind.

Moore looked around, his small fleet of drones skimming the streets inside the city. The roads were abandoned, devoid of life, except the occasional charka prowling the area. So that was something, even if it wasn't good.

Because it meant these weren't mere strays like I first supposed, but guarding charkas on patrol.

Seeing a minor metropolitan city abandoned in that way was like being on the set of one of those slasher horror holos I peeked at as a kid.

"Captain Archer," I called over comm. "I'm not seeing any obvious threats. Streets are empty except for some of those charkas. Sending a holo for your review."

"Copy. What's your assessment, Lieutenant?"

"Place looks abandoned, sir. Maybe the city has a fallout system or subterranean bunker left over from the Savage Wars. Locals do not appear aware of our presence, so I advise we move in fast and hard. Over."

I was confident that the commander would take my advice on this one. We were in range of any sensors that the Arthava might have. If we were going to stand any chance of living through this ordeal, speed would trump stealth. The longer we were stationary, staring at our HUD screens, the higher the risk of discovery. And with our drones flying around, we weren't likely to remain hidden for too long.

I stood beside Moore, still patched into his HUD as his drone swooped in for a closer view of the city streets. He had groups of drones flying at various heights so he could analyze the roads, roofs, and other points of interest. It was daunting, managing several camera angles at once, but we didn't have the luxury of searching the city any other way.

After clearing the roofs of activity, we searched the parks and temples.

Nothing.

Just stillness and silence. Moore then focused his drones on the ground level, searching the roads. The drones skimmed up against the buildings, exploring the city at dizzying speeds. I saw strange writing illuminated against the exterior of the buildings, some sort of projected advertising system. The same messages were on multiple holo posters and billboards, all positioned so they would only be seen from inside the city. Even the holo street signs near the roads had switched to the same message. Our HUDs translated the posters to Repub Standard. It was pro-Repub propaganda. All of it.

Communal Liberty Day is for everyBEING.

Kusiba is Republic Strong.

Or there'd be a picture of a Unity Day parade on Utopion where all the marchers were waving Kusiba's flag.

It confirmed the friendly status we'd been given, but it didn't explain the silence.

We'd just finished our reconnaissance when Captain Archer approached on foot. Moore and I were still occupied, reviewing the drone footage while the company rested. When the captain tapped me on the shoulder, I almost jumped out of my skin.

"LR-24, the drones have taken us as far as they can," Archer said. "We need more intel, and the only way to get it is with boots on the ground. Your section has point. Move out in five mikes."

"I smell a trap, sir," I said. "I feel we should go in force or take our time on this one—"

"Negative, LR-24. Move out at the best possible speed."

The captain's grim voice brooked no argument. I hadn't heard him use this tone before, but there was no doubt about it: his decision was final.

We were moving out.

09

"No time for stealth," I told my section. "Captain Archer wants us in and reporting back at fastest possible speed. We'll double-time it into Kusiba for a sneak and peek."

I observed the city in front of me as we started jogging in. Kusiba was the first alien metropolis I'd ever visited, and it certainly looked alien. It'd been built intentionally and lacked the urban sprawl I expected from major population centers. The city's footprint was neat; the lines demarcating the city from the wilderness were crisp.

"This city has no soul," said PFC Padagas over the L-comm.

"Stow it," growled Sergeant Dwyer, Chaos Squad's grizzled NCO. "Or you'll wish you'd have let that judge send you to jail."

Padagas had chosen service in the New Caledonian Reserve Corps over prison for slicing into the Royal Bank of Pictavia. He'd taken his share of abuse from the chain of command since joining Rage Company, getting picked for every crap detail and working party. Sergeant Dwyer took it as a personal offense that someone he viewed as inherently dishonorable had joined the Legion he loved—even if it was just a reserve.

But I had to agree with the code slicer. The city lacked a soul. Critically eying the empty streets, I couldn't help but notice that the downside of the city's layout was the inability to expand as the town grew. Maybe architectural engineers could find a solution, but it was beyond me. The buildings were large, slate-gray affairs, and taller than I could see from this close. The briefings said each building was over three hundred stories tall, but I suspected that was a propaganda-driven overestimation.

After a few minutes of running, we made it to the outer edge of the city. I kept expecting to see signs of life springing out to surprise us, but we found nothing. There was no civilian traffic, no movement save for the occasional listless charka. The beasts were behaving much differently from the wild ones we'd encountered near our landing site.

"Keep an eye on your blasters," I told my section. "I want a double-tap headshot on any charka that gets close."

My enthusiasm was met by laughter from Virgil. I chose to ignore it as my section moved through the roads leading into the city. I was watchful and wary. It was quiet, all too quiet, for a city of two million people. No vehicles moved. Every shop was shut up and dark. The city looked like it'd been abandoned during the night while everyone slept.

"Find me a terminal—I'll find out where the hyenas went," Padagas volunteered through a private L-comm message.

"Chain of command, use it," I growled back, projecting an anger I didn't feel at the moment. We were all on edge, still expecting a trap.

I halted our column when we hit the outskirts of the city. The silence weighed down on us, stoking our fears.

I rounded a corner and unexpectedly came face-to-face with a scrawny charka.

"Oba!" I shrieked and yanked up my blaster.

Before I could put it down, a hand dragged me back around the corner and Santos fired several shots into the throat of the equally startled beast. Its dying cries echoed down the street.

I was just glad that our buckets allowed us to scream without the world hearing us. We could scream our rage or fear, and do so in the privacy of our fully enclosed helmets. It helped create the illusion of the legionnaire as an unstoppable killing machine, emotionless and ruthless. It also allowed me to pretend I hadn't just screamed like a girl. Again.

"Thanks, Santos."

"Any time, LT," he replied, sounding almost cheerful that we were on our own in enemy territory.

I called a halt, letting my section rest while I studied the map on my HUD overlay. The empty city felt spooky. Almost haunted. We strained our ears as we rested but heard nothing. Eventually the stillness was broken by the growl of another roaming charka, cautiously venturing closer to my formation.

"If they get close, kill them," I reminded my team. "Unleash Oba's righteous fury upon them!" Those infernal beasts had killed enough leejes for one day.

But the growls stayed distant. We moved farther down the cavernous streets of Kusiba City. Had the city been abandoned en masse? It wasn't unheard of for such a thing to happen, everyone just picking up and moving. But often the reason was clear—religious wars, political coups, and terroristic attacks were hard to hide. All we had to go on was the sound of silence broken by the occasional growl of wildlife.

"Virgil, something isn't right." I gripped my blaster as the men fanned out in tactical formation down the street. "We haven't received any real-time intel since we walked into this city. Nothing from either of the two companies we left back at the rally point."

"Things always go to pot in a real engagement, sir. Nothing we can't handle."

His answer was everything I would expect from a seasoned veteran, but it didn't soothe my concerns. As a corporal I'd given similar pep talks to new point lieutenants while putting down the food riots. I knew the score, but in the end something wasn't right. I just didn't know what to do about it.

I guess it didn't really matter, because we had our orders.

I kept my suspicions to myself after that, but the whole situation had me concerned. We hadn't received any real-time intelligence for what was happening in Kusiba City. Even worse, this was an ad hoc mission. Impromptu assaults were the most dangerous, but such is the life of the legionnaire. Do the mission. And our intelligence officers had insisted that the loyalists would be here.

Silence was all we found. It was chilling—it felt wrong.

And all that pro-Repub propaganda? That seemed like it was laid out pretty thickly, even for the House of Reason. Again, why?

Sergeant Dwyer snapped me out of my thoughts. "What's it gonna be, sir?"

Evidently Virgil hadn't forgotten the mission, either, so I gave the order to resume the patrol.

"Time to get back to it, Leejes. Push into the government sector, keep up the sneak and peek."

"'Cept they know we're here," quipped Padagas.

We moved without much more talking and still didn't see anyone. Finally, all that silence got to me. I felt like we were making a mistake pressing on like this and wanted to evaluate what our sensors had picked up so far.

"Listen up, 1st Section." I pulled up the map overlay on the inside of my bucket, marking a waypoint in the alleyway ahead of us. "Rally point marked on your HUD. We're going firm while I review the data we've collected."

"You heard the LT," Sergeant Dwyer echoed. "Security halt at the designated spot." Then, turning to me, "Good call, sir. The alley's natural chokepoints mean we only gotta defend two directions if we're attacked. It'll cost the enemy greatly. KTF."

I wanted to ask "what enemy?" but I'd come to the same conclusion. It was nice to hear the gray beard affirm my decision.

When I got into the alley, I saw about what I'd expected: Heaps of trash piled up against the wall. But none of it was fresh. A light dusting of snow coated the refuse, adding to the ghost town vibe. And I could see it affecting my section. Their buckets hid their faces, but they clutched their blasters and nervously fidgeted as they stood watch.

Looking around the alley, I saw something out of place. A door had been left ajar. We now had access into one of the buildings without needing to break in; I knew we needed to investigate.

"We're going to have to search a few of these buildings," I sent to the squad leaders. "Might as well start with this one since they were so kind as to leave it open for us."

"How hard are we looking, sir?" asked Sergeant Conn.

I always liked Michael. The sergeant had a bit of a wee man syndrome, but he was always fun at the yearly company parties. He was a blunt man, one who could've advanced further than squad leader if he was ever sober long enough.

"Obviously, it's gonna be a cursory look," I replied. "There just aren't enough of us for more than that. We'd be here for days if we tried to clear the city properly. I'm updating the section L-comm, then you'll have your orders. We move out in ten mikes. Get your men to check their gear and hydrate."

That seemed to appease my squad leaders. It gave me a warm feeling, seeing my fellow NCOs approving of my plans. Those butter bars still felt surreal, like I was a pretender to the throne. To be fair, I wanted to hand off the responsibilities. Maybe those points could do better than I was. While the orders were sent up and down the chain of command, I tried to envision what we might encounter. I knew our close quarters battle training, or CQB, was top-notch. After countless hours training, we moved like a well-oiled machine.

A couple of minutes went by and it was clear that the men were ready.

"No use dragging this out," I said over the section's L-comm. "Move out."

Our maps showed that this section of the city was all government buildings. They were obviously wrong again. Or were we more lost than we knew? I took a quick glance through the cracked door and saw a narrow corridor full of doors, with the occasional welcome mat in front of it.

How are we gonna get this all done? I wondered.

We didn't have the manpower to secure even one floor of an apartment complex.

"LR-01, we're preparing to enter an apartment building in the government sector to investigate. Negative signs of life, I repeat, negative signs of life in Kusiba. Do we continue investigating or pull back?"

"Continue the original mission. LR-01, out," replied Captain Archer.

Orders were orders.

With no reason left to delay, we prepared to enter the structure. My leejes stacked, and on my command, began our assault of the building. The moment we walked inside, we stopped in surprise. My initial peek into the hallway hadn't shown me this.

How could I miss all the blood? It was everywhere. Not the red blood you expect from humans, but you could tell someone had been injured here. The blood had a vibrant orange hue, almost mesmerizing. As if the dead were calling out for vengeance—justice. Despite the insulating effect of my LARKs and the synthprene layer under it, I was struck with a chill, a cold that sank into my bones. Ghosts upon ghosts.

"Doesn't look good, sir," Santos told me over a private L-comm.

"I know, nothing has since we entered Rhyssis Wan."

"Affirmative, sir... I meant Kusiba. Something is off. Stay frosty, I've got a bad feeling."

Grunting a reply, I cut the comms channel and studied the blood spatter patterns. Something awful had happened, but how and why? We continued deeper in the hallway and found more tacky orange goo, a lot more, smeared all over the walls.

"Does anyone know what could've made these marks?"

"Looks like someone used their hand," Dwyer grunted. "Like finger-painting."

Santos nodded his head in agreement. "And you don't need your helmet to translate it, either."

That was true enough. The words were written in Standard.

"Death to the Republic."

"House of Reason—House of Lies."

MCR stuff.

"Looks like whoever wrote it has four fingers," I said, shuddering. "More Arthava, then. But who would do this to their own kind?"

"Dunno," said Dwyer, "but it looks like they were mainly writing their message out over these pro-Republic posters... and by the looks of what they've got to say, probably MCR."

I recorded snippets of the gruesome painting and marked it for the spooks to worry over later.

Looking around, past the macabre paintings on the walls, I tried to figure out what else was off. It tingled at the back of my head, but I couldn't quite place it.

Then it hit.

Rhyssis Wan's only value to the galaxy came from its raw materials, and their politicians had traded those goods for their own benefit. Predictably, the rank and file Arthava citizens suffered. Yet the dwellings in Kusiba were smart buildings. They were fully integrated homes, which meant we could slice into them and access all the security features.

"Sergeant Dwyer, let's get plugged into the building and see what we can find out through its systems."

"Rog, LT," Dwyer said with a nod. "Someone find Padagas a terminal, might as well make him earn his pay."

The building's interfaces were interconnected holo-networks managed by a non-sentient AI. Those models were expensive, too expensive for such a poor planet. The stuff I was seeing in this building would cost a leej two months' pay, so the occupants must've been important. Which, being in the government sector, made some sense.

"He can start with the doors," Olvera volunteered.

His attempt at humor only earned him the ire of his team leader. "You can start with shutting the hell up, Olvera."

I hoped that Padagas could open the doors, but I wasn't sure. A slicer kit was a special order unless you were Dark Ops and the intel guys had sworn that we'd be able to use the standard gear to gain digital entry. So everything was riding on Padagas's ability to figure out how to use the terminals in front of each apartment door.

With a slicer, we'd be breezing through, though. It felt like more proof of how the House's micromanaging directly interfered with what they claimed they wanted accomplished.

While Padagas worked his digital magic, I ordered the section to perform overwatch and waited. The quiet was still unnerving. Just the gentle tap of PFC Padagas's fingers on a nearby data screen.

I was almost afraid to break it.

I checked on my squads in whispers, though I could see that everyone was okay. The entire section knew we weren't in the most defensible position, and it had us all uneasy. I couldn't shake the feeling that we were missing something important. Maybe I'd become paranoid since the botched landing, expecting boogey men around every corner. Unsure what else to do, I decided to err on the side of pushing the issue up the chain of command. I was preparing an update for Captain Archer when I heard cursing coming from the terminal.

"Sir, I mean LR-24, sir. The residents. They're all dead, sir," Padagas said, the panic thick in his voice.

"Say again, LR-133. All residents are dead?" I asked.

"Roger. All of them." Padagas sounded as if he might throw up. "The closed loop air filtration system was injected with lethal aerosol toxins. I don't recognize it. Neither does the diagnostic system. It's a designer cocktail; the building's air scrubbers couldn't decipher it. Snuck past their safety measures, the AI couldn't clean it quick enough. We might wanna keep our buckets on, sir. When I patched the information through my HUD, it detected trace amounts of the stuff in the air."

Cursing, I switched to the company L-comm. "LR-01, I'm sending your HUD a data packet. In a nutshell, the entire city was executed."

"Say again, Ocampo. Did you say all dead?"

"Yes, sir. Someone gassed the whole city overnight. I can't fathom the logistics of this. There must be survivors. If we're going to cordon and search, we'll need both companies to go house to house. How should we proceed?"

"We're coming in. Clear the building you're in but stay put."

After the captain cut the signal, I ordered 1st Section to begin clearing the first floor. We went room by room, searching every apartment for signs of life. It was futile but informative. We found many of the furry, dark-skinned hyena-like Arthava in various states of rigor mortis. Hands grasped at throats, an obvious indication of their desperate struggle to breathe. Some Arthava stopped forever in the middle of a task, others collapsed with their kin in a final embrace.

When we finished searching the first floor, I ordered Berserker Squad to remain behind. They were my original squad, and I trusted them. The rest of the section continued the investigation, moving up to the second floor. It was a repeat of the first floor. More dead. The search progressed, representing much of what we would find across the city in every skyscraper. Kusiba was a ghost town full of the hollow bodies of Repub loyalists.

When we got to the twelfth floor, the squad leader from Berserker Squad announced that our company had rejoined us. I quickly switched back over to the command channel.

"LR-24, the Skipper sends his regards," Walden said, the disdain thick in his voice. "He's updating Fleet, they'll relay the message to the BC across the mountains. LR-05, out."

I joined Chaos Squad in clearing the top floor. There things took an even darker turn.

"LR-24, you're gonna wanna see this," Corporal Singh called over the L-comm.

"En route," I replied. "Dwyer, on me."

Pulling up the HUD, I scrolled through the floorplan Padagas had sent us until I saw where Corporal Singh was waiting. The top floor housed the access to the air scrubbers. I stopped dead in my tracks as I walked in. Blood was everywhere. Someone had created a gruesome inkblot test, something the House would approve of. The vibrantly hued orange blood painting every surface twinkled under the low light HUD setting.

"Gets worse in here, sir," Singh called out.

Rounding the corner from the main room of the apartment, I followed the voice from the Dagger Squad team leader. The room was filled with strange egg-shaped pods centered around a crystal.

Oba.

All those bodies.

So many in one place.

The bodies of several family units clustered around the apartment's communal bedding. The families had been killed the old-fashioned way. No, killed is too soft a word. What happened to them was barbaric.

"Damned mass-execution. In all my years… worst I've seen."

I looked at Virgil in surprise. He'd been around the Legion for decades. Close to retiring even. He'd seen some stuff in his time on active duty. If Virgil thought this was the worst, it carried some weight.

"Gather whatever intel you can, Legion Command is gonna want it. Let's search the rest of this floor as well."

"Roger, Sergeant," I said, forgetting which one of us was supposed to running the show.

Everyone else in the room hopped to as well. Luckily for us, if you can call it that, one of those apartments belonged to the building manager, and his dwelling had cameras installed.

"Padagas, get up here," I ordered over the L-comm. "I need you to gain access to this feed."

"On the way, sir!" Padagas replied.

"Dwyer, prioritize what intel the points are going to want."

What I was looking at, all the dead, it was butchery. Not just a blaster bolt to the head. These Arthava had been ripped apart. Picture an artillery strike with no explosions, no burn. Just the twisted flesh and gore.

"Check your HUD," Padagas said, cutting off any reply Virgil might've had. "Transmitting feed from the apartment's cams."

The recording was cued up to show the Arthava cowering together, like this was a last stand—more like a final hiding place. And then a pack of hyena soldiers rushed into the room. They tore into the huddled natives with claws and teeth. I still have nightmares from watching that security video.

However the MCR had gotten into the building, either by collusion or stealth, they'd tied up the families around the poisoned air scrubbers. Then one of those walking mongrels, I couldn't even guess its gender, cut a baby apart while the hyena's compatriots ripped into the mewling Arthava cubs. The holo footage was vivid; I could almost smell the fear. And if the corpses at my feet could draw a breath, I'd guess they could smell the fear in me.

"They're torturing those cubs," Padagas breathed.

"By Oba," Corporal Singh whispered.

I could hear several of the leejes who had chosen to watch the holovid puke inside their buckets, spraying their disgust in the worst way imaginable.

After they'd tortured the young cubs while the parents watched, the soldiers had their way with female captives. I had to look away; I wanted to scream and rage at this perversion. The Arthava rapists wore a mix of MCR uniforms and cultist robes as they repeatedly ravaged their loyalist prey. It was brutal, but quick. When it was over, they murdered the women and then the men.

I wish I could say that this was an isolated incident, but the continued search through Kusiba proved otherwise. In their fanatical pursuit of power, the MCR had slaughtered two million loyal citizens of the Republic.

"We won't forget this," Virgil grimly said. "We won't forget nothin'."

10

It took us the rest of the day, and two more, to clear the city. We took big risks and ended up sending one leej per floor in most buildings. Some of the floors were cleared entirely by the drones. Our searching only confirmed what we'd already learned. The MCR had massacred two million sentient beings—men, women, and children. The rebel scum hadn't discriminated.

During the search, we sought refuge from the cold in an abandoned residential building. It was another of those massive numbers, but we were able to open the windows to fumigate it. Once it was safe, we turned it into a fort Legion Commander Keller himself would've approved of.

"Santos, look after the leejes," I told him. "Dwyer, Chaos Squad, on me. We're going on a resupply run."

"Anywhere in particular, sir?" Virgil replied.

"Affirmative, I marked them on your HUD. There's a sporting goods store and a local police garrison."

"Roger, let's make a point of not just grabbing charge packs. Grab food, weapons, and anything else which could augment our basic kit. Not everyone's rucks survived the landing."

Sket, why didn't I think of that? Blasters wouldn't fire indefinitely, I knew that. But it hadn't occurred to me to consider food. The Legion always resupplied us on our training operations. But now we were on our own. We'd have to forage what we could, even if that meant riffling through alien garbage.

"All right, let's make it happen," I said, and moments later we were scanning the deserted gray streets.

In the end we got lucky. Thanks to the Arthava's cultural fascination with shooting things, we found an overabundance of civilian knockoff legionnaire blasters. Rearmed by the locals, we were ready to avenge their ghastly murders, all two million of them.

"We're gonna need a larger work detail, Top," I called in to the first sergeant. "We hit pay dirt on charge packs. Could you send more leejes to my location? LR-24, out."

There was some grumbling, but Top Walden did send leejes to be my mules. We carried the supplies once Virgil said we'd cleared everything useful from the stores.

I sent a HUD update to the company commander.

"LS-001 this is Lieutenant Ocampo. Resupply complete and preparing to rejoin the 9th, over."

"Negative, Ocampo."

"Sir?"

"Just got off comms with Fleet and the navy has its hands full with an ad hoc MCR force."

That sounded crazy. I mean, the Republic Navy has no equal in the galaxy. But then it dawned on me that this wasn't the Republic Navy that was constantly appearing in so many holos meant to show the breadth, scope, and might of the Republic. This was our Navy. The thrown together Caledonian fleet made up of Ohio-class battleships that were inferior to modern capital cruisers in just about every way but size. And all the advantage that gave them was that it took 'em a while before they blew up.

So if Cally could put some Ohios in the field, why couldn't the MCR? And if they did... yeah, that would be a fair fight.

"Fleet's not dealing with pirates," Captain Archer continued. "This is a fight to the death up there and they've got no word when a destroyer might show up and help them clean house. We are to continue on foot toward the planet's orbital defense cannons. The Republic has numbers but those guns are what's tipping the fight to the MCR."

"Yes, sir." I quickly muted my comm and called on externals, "Everybody up. Sergeants, get your men up now."

Captain Archer relayed our objective in my HUD. Intel said that those guns would be well defended. With insurgents dug in with the hopes of surviving the inevitable orbital bombardment and bombing runs—the ones that never came because of the fight that began the moment we reached the system. So now it was up to us. And we had to do all of that... alone. Two leej companies against the unknown.

"Again, I'm counting on you and your men to get this done," said Archer. "Get. It. Done. LS-001 out."

By now my men were gathering around me, standing behind their squad leaders.

"Listen up, Rage Company. I want blasters cleaned and serviced. I want an updated count of your charge packs. Verify whatever your bucket tells you with visual inspection."

"I'll take care of redistributing charge packs," Sergeant Dwyer volunteered.

"Good call, LR-57," I replied. "Everyone else, eat your rations and tend to your wounds. We'll be pushing hard to the next objective the moment we're able."

Taking charge and seizing the initiative was starting to get easier. Giving orders to a leej with decades more experience in the Legion than I had alive still felt weird. It left a bad taste in my mouth, but it had to be done. We wouldn't have a lot of time once the commander acted on the orders from above. I'm glad that I did, otherwise our boys wouldn't have eaten.

Captain Archer was a driven man, as ambitious as he was competent. And anyway, those guns were a real problem. There were men dying above us and they were powerless to do anything about it but stay and keep fighting (and dying) or cut and run, leaving us stranded on-planet. Archer knew that as well as I did and wasn't willing to let it happen. We'd lucked out getting him. I know I'm not a seasoned legionnaire by any stretch, but I'd never heard of a point working out. Ours was.

My HUD pinged and I was taken into a secure L-comm channel with the captain and my fellow officers. I felt out of place.

"Gentlemen, our next objective's a beast," said Archer solemnly. "We're to take out those orbital defense guns, and I suspect it'll be heavily defended. The MCR think they can push us off this rock, and they went all in here."

"How'd they muster up enough troops to pull this off?" asked Captain Hatton, Dragon Company's commanding officer.

Archer spoke with the surety of a prophet. "The MCR stoked up these lunatic cultists to do their bidding. Once we capture these guns, we will karball 'em to the next planetary system before reporting in for our next objective. We will move as fast as the slowest wounded leej can travel, but we don't have time to dawdle. You are to move out in five mikes. Make it happen, Leejes."

A moment later, orders were sent to each unit. Once again, my team was taking the lead. I keyed in a comm line with my NCOs. "Listen up, 1st Section. We've got point. I expect you sergeants and corporals to do your thing. And with so many sergeants lost on the Cambria, each leej has to carry his own weight. LR-24, out."

In a story as old as the Legion itself, the real work was done by those still wearing the stripes. The House of Reason gave me the medal, but those boys did all the heavy lifting.

"Where are the guns, sir?" Padagas asked.

I took the opportunity to uplink a battle map to each leej under my command. "The orbital defense guns are due south, about twenty klicks."

His groaning was silenced, probably by an elbow to the gut. Likely some Legion sergeant stepped in to administer discipline. But inside, I was groaning too. The march to the guns was going to be a stretch. Our leejes were exhausted, pushed to the breaking point, but we didn't have a choice. The sooner we got to those guns, the more likely our ride back home would be safe. Those navy boys were counting on us, and when crap hit the fan, the Legion delivered.

With the comm still live for my entire team, I broke down what to expect. "I'm gonna be straight with you, Rage Company." I looked what legionnaires I could see in the eyes. "This march will be tough, but it won't be worse than Corporal Santos and his friends in the 71st running us back in Cally!"

"Least it's not uphill," Santos quipped, laughing with us.

I wait for the laughter to die down, replaced by that awful, nervous purgatory before the start of a mission. When warfighters remember that they're also sons, brothers, husbands, and fathers... and they worry about those who see them as such. "We're going to be okay, and these traitors are going to experience firsthand what happens when you square up with the Legion."

After checking the strip map overlay the commander had sent, I saw that Santos wasn't just making a joke about the route. We spent most of the exhausting jaunt skirting one of the largest ridgelines of the Bevak Mountain Range. There no longer was an uphill climb—we would be able to take surface roads to get near the guns.

But that didn't mean the journey would be easy.

We double-timed along one of the winding roads, not expecting trouble for several klicks. It was brutal; running in full kit with wounded leejes was never easy. We knew we didn't have a lot of time. Every second we delayed meant more rounds fired at our ships.

The cultists would've had to seize those guns from under the noses of the citizens of Kusiba. Likely around the same time they'd committed their genocide of Republic loyalists. That gave me some hope. The massacre was fresh; the murderers likely wouldn't have had time to fully make use of the gun emplacements or defenses. Those systems take time to learn, and saying security on a planetary defense system is tough to crack is an understatement. But again, that didn't mean it would be easy. I had to assume that the MCR and the Arthava cultists were at least as tactically proficient as I was. During my years breaking up fights among drunk restaurant patrons, I'd learned that you underestimated your opponent at your peril, and I didn't plan on letting my hubris cost the lives of any of my leejes.

Our usual forced march pace was definitely slowed by the wounded. Rage Company normally marched six klicks an hour; we only managed half of that.

"Keep it moving, Leejes," Captain Archer told the company. "A few more klicks and we'll rest. Never been prouder of a leej company!"

Our wounded did their best during the march, but they were only human. Their bodies had limits and we were all operating on very little food and sleep. Under ideal conditions, we'd have sent our wounded to field hospitals, but this battle wasn't ideal. If anything, it was a textbook case of what not to do from start to finish. I was learning the hard way what every real leej knew: no battles went down as planned. Like I'd been taught at the NCO Academy, war was a democracy and the enemy got a vote.

While my squad leaders managed their small units, I tried to maintain my situational awareness. I monitored the world around me, observing my surroundings. If we were attacked, I'd need to quickly formulate a response. I constantly checked on the location and vitals of my leejes, paranoid that I'd left one of the wounded behind.

"Sergeant Conn," I called over the L-comm, "check on Sterns. He's lagging."

I could see that the leej's vitals were close to WorryVille.

"Already on it, sir. Organizing litter detail now."

I had good leej NCOs, best in the business.

After I'd cared for my leejes, I took it all in. I couldn't help but notice how stunning the Bevaks were. I wished I could come back when the dust settled, show my wife and unborn son.

If I ever do go back, I'll definitely bundle up better. My LARK struggled in the cold. Some leejes reported cracks in their seals and electrical issues. The longer we were exposed to the snow, the thicker the layer of ice on our armor got. This caused us to use more energy to simply move forward. But after seeing the beauty of the trees and snow-covered mountains, I knew why the Arthava thought they were worth fighting for.

"Keep going," Archer called out. "Hot kaff to the leej with the first kill!"

"Rum, if the traitor is an officer!" added Top.

I don't know if we had any booze with us, but we didn't care. Top had lightened the mood enough to bolster our flagging spirits. Onward we pushed, our walking wounded desperately trying to complete the mission.

"Think of home," I added over the company L-comm. "It's warm back in Cally!"

"How's that one weekend a month treating you right now, LT?" Top joked.

I blinked in surprise but rolled with it. "Think that recruiter deserves a punch in the gut, Top!"

Top was right—this wasn't what any of us had expected when we'd enlisted. Most of us joined up on a lark. Life as a reservist would be a grand adventure without any of the risks of actual service. We'd been promised one weekend a month and three weeks in the summer. For most of the 9th, it was easy money and a chance to get away from the monotony of daily life.

The joke was on us.

Like soldiers since the dawn of time, we got screwed by the small print of our enlistment contracts. Ama always said the devil was in the details. Boy, was she right about that. The Repub included a clause that let them activate us without warning... for the good of the Republic, of course.

And maybe, when I really think about it, that was the difference between what I was—what I am—and the real Legion. There's no trickery with them. No one is there because they want to get out of a prison sentence or because it was the only way to get some benefits package. They were legionnaires because they wanted to be. Because they believed in it.

"Halfway there, Leejes," Archer said. "Head on a swivel now, boys!"

I reinforced the message with my boys. "1st Section, slow and steady from here. This is where things start to get serious. We're within range of the guns' defenses."

I hoped I sounded tough, the real deal leej. That guy who could KTF in his sleep.

Even though we'd already fought the charka, this would be our first battle with an armed enemy. Surely there'd be cultists or MCR troops waiting to kill us.

I swear, tree slugs moved faster than we did at that point. We spread out, wary and watchful. The enemy could show up anywhere. If it were me in charge of those MCR orbital guns, I'd have had scouts out, with several fallback positions already located. Defense in depth. Make the invading enemy pay for every inch.

But that's not how whoever was running this rebellion was doing it. At least not that I could see. If there were scouts about, we'd need eyes in the sky to spot them.

"Olvera, we need overwatch. Keep the drones high enough that their roving patrols won't look for it," I ordered.

"And beneath the window for any high altitude sensors watching out for the big guns," Dwyer added. "We don't want them to know we're here."

"MCR is definitely here," Santos said. "My team's spotted footprints in the snow. Fresh."

I was right to be cautious. I raised my right hand, halting my section. Kneeling in the snow, I looked around. I quickly tuned the noise actuators on my bucket to max and gestured for my leejes to do the same. I was hoping to detect the enemy before they identified us.

And then we heard it, the crunch of heavy boots tramping through the frozen underbrush. An enemy patrol was nearby. The entire section began scanning the area around us, looking for the threat. Our HUDs were acting wonky;

the LARKs couldn't seem to process the extreme temperatures of the Rhyssis Wan. And a nagging worry wondered if that same cold would sap the strength of our blasters again after such a long period of inaction. If so, we'd have to hope killing the Arthava cultists or MCR or whoever was out there would warm them up.

I always figured the cheap imitations of legionnaire kit we were using would bite us if we ever needed them for something more than crowd control. I remember telling my marksmanship instructor that. He laughed at me.

"Calm down, Fetch, they'll only deploy the Reserves if things get so out of hand that they have no choice. By then, we'll be so screwed that we'll welcome death."

I wanted to hunt down that old sergeant just to wave the "I told you so" flag in his face. At a minimum, I'd demand a beer for being proven right. But I didn't have time for daydreams. The enemy had stopped moving.

We've been made, I signaled to my men.

I scanned the area through the scope of my NM-4, my HUD not picking up any life signs beyond my fellow legionnaires. I was on the third pass before I saw it: the glint of light reflecting off an enemy rifle scope. It was an Arthava soldier, wearing a white and gray camouflaged uniform. Probably a layer of biorhythmic suppressors beneath that to stay hidden from Legion tech. The outfit almost worked, I almost missed him.

The scope was perfectly still. But blasters don't fire themselves, I knew someone was there behind the scope.

Taking a deep breath, I touched the trigger.

And then the bark flew off the tree next to me, scorching the wood underneath. The Arthavan had fired a hair before I did. The shock of the near miss startled me, and I went wide of my mark. I quickly found the target again and lined up the perfect sight picture. This wasn't the high tech sniper rifle I'd trained with—I'd lost that beauty when I made squad leader. Still, at this range I couldn't miss.

Legionnaires all around shouted out warnings and dropped into the snow.

With the traitorous rebel perfectly situated in my scope, just off-center of the crosshairs, adjusted for the inconsistencies I'd found in my blaster, I caressed the trigger. My blaster bucked as it fired one short pulse into the enemy soldier. Zooming in with my visor, I searched for my prey. The Arthavan's rifle was lying to the side of its hide amid the snow and I could clearly see the shooter's face. There was a neat hole between his eyes. My shot rang true.

"Got ya," I whispered.

Scanning around the fallen soldier, I began to detect other silhouettes.

"More hostiles!" I called, tagging the location in my HUD.

And then they either ditched whatever was keeping their bio-signatures hidden or my bucket was able to determine their presence. Either way, red lights lit the screen on my bucket, momentarily distracting me. I quickly isolated the signatures: one, two, three... I fired shot after shot at the enemy.

The rest of the legionnaires joined in within seconds of it all. Soon my team was unleashing a hellish fire and the enemy in my HUD kept dropping.

Nine cooling bodies.

Another one popped up.

I sent him down for good.

"That's for Captain Reyes."

I called for a cease fire and held my breath. The rest of my team likewise remained motionless. We scanned for other threats. As we waited, I called in a sit-rep to Captain Archer, who'd heard the echoes of blaster fire from the rear. Ten minutes passed before I waved my right arm in a circle, signaling the section to move out again.

"Watch your footing," Dwyer cautioned 1st Section. "Could be mines, or traps."

His voice had a strangely gentle quality to it. Soothing. It hit me then, we'd just killed ten men. Aliens. Whatever. But sentient humanoids. We'd ended ten lives.

"Right, move out and watch for traps," I parroted over the section's L-comm.

"At least the cold didn't freeze our blasters again," commented Top as we pushed toward the enemy patrol. "That would have sucked."

We reached the dead we'd just sent to meet Oba. They were set up in a natural embankment. The shooter who started the failed ambush lay over the lip of it, with the rest of them scattered around it. They were scorched and peppered with blaster holes; all of them showed dead in my HUD by the time we reached them.

"Check for intel," I ordered, motioning at the corpses below. "But carefully. And then take any gear you can salvage."

I didn't expect to find any usable intelligence, but you only had to get lucky once... so we searched.

Sergeant Dwyer climbed out of the embankment to reach me. "Not much here except some blaster packs—we took those—and some old fraggers that I wouldn't trust not to blow my liver out if we made the mistake of clipping them to our belts, sir."

I nodded. The MCR, despite being the biggest threat to show itself to the Republic in recent memory, was known for being ill equipped. "Thank you, Sergeant. Let's leave those suckers behind. Only rearrange them so they can be a nasty little surprise for any of their buddies who might come back to check on 'em."

Dwyer hopped back over the embankment with what seemed like glee. "KTF in absentia! You're all right, Fetch—a little twisted with a mind like that? But that's a big roger, sir."

There was a dark enthusiasm layering his gravelly voice.

After setting the traps, we gave a warning to any legionnaires following us and continued the push toward the orbital guns. We made good time, spread out in a thin skirmish line. Our job was to screen the rest of Rage Company as well as the units from Dragon Company who were spread out behind us. We'd been trained to maneuver like this since we joined the Legion, but this was the first time I'd done it with a real-life objective in mind.

And never with so many leejes.

"1st, spread out! I want a long front—we're not getting flanked on my watch!"

"Good call, sir," Dwyer replied, keeping up that habit of encouragement. I was grateful for it. "If those kelhorns see us, they'll have to engage us head on. Nobody can stand toe-to-toe with leejes like that, KTF!"

Our success so far seemed to have really lifted his spirits. And I could sense it in the rest of the men as well. We had encountered the enemy we'd been sent to fight and we weren't found wanting. I was feeling a sort of euphoria myself. We were death dealers, bringing justice on behalf of a Republic mourning the slaughter of its citizens.

It felt good. To be the monster who came to slay the beast. It felt... right.

For the next few hours, we wove in and out of the trees that dotted the mountainside. I tried to maintain spatial and situational awareness since I felt I still couldn't trust my knockoff HUD in the cold. They helped keep us connected, but they routinely crapped out in the frigid conditions.

My skirmish line was spread out along a three-quarters of a kilometer front, the mountainous terrain giving us a wave effect. At that length, our extreme flanks were at different elevations. As the section leader, I was in the center of the line where the snowy terrain was relatively flat. I felt guilty for it; my fellow leejes were having such a hard time maneuvering on slopes.

The trees prevented the height differential from making any difference in visibility, and the snow and incoming fog made it even worse. My leejes kept their composure, and there were minimal complaints. When we were eight klicks from the objective, we ran into another enemy patrol. They were again camouflaged in a white and gray patterned uniform, but our HUDs caught their heat signatures.

"Contact!"

A brief firefight erupted, but it was clear that we were the only ones who knew where to shoot. The Arthava were running from cover to cover, firing wildly in one direction only to be gunned down from my legionnaires above or to the side. Though there were at least twenty of them, a decent-sized patrol, they were quickly neutralized.

"Almost don't seem fair," Olvera said, recalling one of his drones. With the fog and snow coming in the way it was, all he was likely to do was ruin the thing. It wasn't helping. "We see them but they sure don't seem to know when we're here."

We moved past the dead, using knives to make sure there was no one left alive behind us to hit us in the back or ambush the rest of the force following us. Their bodies were left lying in the snow where they fell.

They had helmets, but no optics to speak of. No night vision. No motion sensors or bio-scanners. I kicked a helmet out of my path and then stepped over an Arthava whose throat had been shot out. "Be glad that their gear is so low tech; it gave us a stealth advantage."

"Roger, Lieutenant," piped up Santos. "Trust me when I say this to the rest of you reservists: you run into a force with those goodies just one time, and you won't complain about things not seeming fair again."

I bring the focus back to our mission.

"Let's pick up the pace and get this over with. LR-24, out."

We were soon moving out at a slow jog. I was proud of them—they sucked it up and endured it with the typical leej stoicism. And Rage Company had earned our right to be called leej. I'd break the face of any puke that said otherwise.

We were moving closer, closing in on where my HUD said the orbital guns were. It became clear that the last patrol of Arthava we encountered wasn't out here in isolation. More of the cultists were dropping back, running with reckless abandon toward the gun emplacements. Whether they had broken and run when we'd encountered the earlier patrol or were following orders to fall back to some predetermined rally point, I didn't know.

But we had them in the open with backs turned, and that wasn't an opportunity I was going to waste.

Sergeant Dwyer yelled into the 1st Section L-comm channel even as he began blasting. "Weapons free, I repeat, weapons free. Blast those twargin' freaks back to whatever pit of hell they escaped from!"

I aimed at an Arthavan as he climbed up a rounded boulder, scoring a direct hit between his shoulder blades as he prepared to jump down to the other side of the rock.

One less traitor in the galaxy.

A few pockets tried to rally as we charged, but they were quickly overrun and dispatched. We had caught up with a retreating enemy, and the route was on.

"Get some!"

"For Reyes!"

We rushed forward, screaming and firing as we went. Bolts flew, grenades exploded, and the enemy knew they'd messed with the wrong people. The Legion was there to make them pay in blood, buckets of it. Some of my leejes aimed, but our goal was suppressive fire. The noise had already told them we were here, if they hadn't figured it out already. Stealth wasn't an option; violence of action was our only choice.

"Contact... advance elements... cultists," I panted, sending Captain Archer an update in the event he couldn't figure it out from HUD reports and the sound of battle carrying over the rocks and snow.

The rest of the Dragon and Rage Companies soon joined the fray. The enemy kept falling back into the snow-laden trees, until we reached the first series of bunkers. They were squat primitive structures, surrounded by an earthen barricade encircled by razor wire. The outpost surrounding the orbital gun was highly defensible. We'd bleed good men to take it conventionally. But there was another way. It was a gamble, but I was going to take it.

"Bear Claw 2, this is LR-24. Execute singed boot contingency, authorization Delta-Echo-Tac-2-4-9-3-4-5. And watch out for their guns. LR-24, out," I said into the joint Fleet-Legion comms channel.

Once the buzz ship pilot acknowledged his orders, I pulled my section back. We ducked behind whatever cover we could find, before beginning a slow and steady harassing fire. I didn't really expect us to hit anything; the point was to keep the enemy's head down. While we distracted the militia, our pilot came in for his strafing run.

The sound of the high-cycle auto-cannons sending bolts into the enemy was exhilarating. Hearing our bird rain holy hellfire down on those kranks made my skin tingle. I felt more alive than I ever had before.

Maybe it was being so close to those powerful guns. Maybe it was the potential for that proximity to go horribly wrong. I don't know, but the risk of being on the wrong side of the gun moved me. The rush of adrenaline, the fear, all of it... I felt alive. In the end, the reason didn't matter. I didn't completely understand my euphoria and didn't care. The enemy was in front of us, and we needed them dead. They probably felt the same way about us, since they sent bolt after bolt into our ranks.

After the buzz ship passed, I popped up and fired my rifle, adding more suppression before calling for my men to do the same. "1st Squad! Don't let up! They're gonna take this opportunity to get bolts on us while the buzz ship makes the turn!"

Corporal Singh, who had been hunkering down next to me during the strafing run, didn't hesitate. He popped up and sent disciplined bursts into the Arthavan line. And then his firing abruptly stopped.

I looked over and saw the corporal as he fell back, a smoking hole right in the center of his helmet.

He was right next to me one moment, screaming his battle cries with the rest of us, and then he was gone. His HUD already showed him dead.

"Medic!" I bellowed. It was too late, but I had to try.

As Dwyer ran over to look at Singh, I kept shooting. I could focus on the mission or I could worry about things I couldn't control—like what happened to the corporal. I knew more would die if we failed to establish a strong position and push past the Arthavans, and I couldn't let that happen. Failure was not an option.

We fired even faster, burning through our charge packs. We managed to get the rebels to keep their heads down even without the buzz ship, but the price in munitions was steep. And then the low buzz of the aptly named buzz ship sounded again and the craft made another slow, almost hovering pass. It chewed up the ground and bunkers where the cultists hid, sending clouds of dust and pieces of MCR into the air wherever its blaster cannons focused on a target.

Errant smoke trails from shoulder-fired rockets streaked around the buzz ship, and then it moved on, leaving us to again press the attack as it turned for a third pass.

This time the Arthava broke and ran from the trenches where the pilot put down more brutal punishment. Honestly, I don't know that I would have been able to hang in there and take it the way the MCR did. I'd like to think so, but it was brutal. That didn't stop me from joining my squad in celebration as the rebels gave up the field.

I stood and cheered, shaking my blaster at the sky while the ship strafed the enemy position. Its cannons chewed into the walls of the bunker behind the trenches and flushed out the trenches themselves. Together, our coordinated assault tore into the defenders and the outpost bunkers.

"Looks like you've got an opening," the pilot calmly reported in before moving out of sight.

Once the pilot pulled off, we charged forward, surging into the enemy's defensive bastion. They were more than dead—they had been blasted and chewed up to the point that they were mixed with the mountainous soil. Pre-buried. Our pilot had earned his pay. He'd pulled off several dangerously close strafing runs and hadn't hit a single friendly fighter.

"LR-24, hold your position while I send an update to Fleet and the 9th," the captain ordered. "Raid these rebel scum of anything useful, but watch for trickery."

"Roger, sir. We'll make it happen," I replied.

11

With the trenches and bunkers that constituted the first line of defense against the guns secured, Captain Archer ordered us to move out.

As secrecy was no longer a concern, both companies spread out along the front, not caring how much noise they made. We weren't bunched up, though—I don't care what the talking heads on the news channels said. The 9th were professionals, despite being reservists. We knew that if we bunched up, one lucky shot would take us out.

No, we assaulted spread out. Our extended front allowed us to envelop the orbital guns lying like spires before us, booming with such ferocity that I could feel the vibrations in the soles of my boots. Those guns were nasty beasts, with barrels as big as hover tanks, mounted on what looked to be small buildings.

We moved fast through the bunker and trench complex, finding no resistance until we reached the end of the defensive bunkers, spilling out to the open ground where the guns were operating.

"Brace yourselves, this is gonna get ugly," Sergeant Dwyer said over the section L-comms.

Before us were even more trenches, and if the bunkers we'd worked our way through earlier were full of Arthava, these were brimming. The large dozers they'd used to tear up the ground and dig the trenches looked like they'd been repurposed to serve as combat vehicles with large guns mounted on them. Not quite tanks, but close enough for those of us on foot. We needed that buzz ship to resupply and get back here as soon as possible, because I was seeing more blasters arrayed against us than I'd ever imagined I'd encounter.

"Remember your training and you'll be fine," I added.

We pushed forward, moving behind the natural cover and closing in to engage the waiting enemy.

"Oba," I whispered, "there are so many of them."

Crap.

I'd forgotten what L-comm channel I'd said that on. Was it my direct line with Virgil? The whole section?

"I know, sir," Dwyer said cheerily—from the 1st general comm. "Competition to bag the first officer is gonna be fierce. Don't hog them all, will ya?"

Virgil again, always saving me from myself.

"Yeah, I've seen you shoot," Santos added. "Wouldn't be fair to the rest of the company. Maybe miss once or twice, just to even the odds?"

The channel buzzed with laughter from the whole section. Maybe the whole company?

"What's the plan, LT?" asked Top.

We were as close as we would get before the shooting started. There was no shortage of targets to engage.

Already the jumpiest among the Arthava were sending ineffective fire over our heads.

"Plan is to all push at once. Dragon and the rest of Rage are flanking and we keep the MCR's attention while they finish encircling."

"So we push up and engage?" asked Santos.

"Not yet."

I waited a beat and then heard whistles followed by distant crumps! Among the Arthavan line, an explosion and dust cloud blossomed heavenward. With our full companies present, the boys working the mortar bots had gotten set up. And they were softening up the entrenched enemy.

"Push up!" I shouted.

"Go, you sket-eating sons of tyrannasquids!" bellowed Dwyer.

My team moved forward, laying down suppressive fire on an enemy already scrambling due to the incoming mortar fire. If we had air support too, we'd be golden. But still no sign of the buzz ship.

We hustled forward, flinging ourselves behind rocks the size of speeder sleds—as close as we could get without crossing a no-man's land and waltzing into the MCR foxholes directly.

"Make 'em know the Legion is here!" Top shouted. I could hear the discharge of blaster fire whining in competition with his comm transmission.

We were all shooting. Changing packs. Shooting again. Those of us blessed with the kinds of arms capable of throwing a seamball at the semi-pro level tossed fraggers, which detonated almost on impact in the foremost Arthavan positions.

The makeshift tanks, caked with dirt clods from mortar bots doing their best to hit a track or repulsor array and ground them, swiveled their heavy guns, sending a stream of what felt like N-50 fire crashing into the rocks we ducked behind.

But where one group of legionnaires was pinned down, another picked up the fighting, shooting with such ferocity that I thought if we had the ability to step back and watch ourselves, we would wonder who the men doing the fighting were. It didn't seem like us. It felt like someone else, as though some warrior spirit had possessed our bodies.

It was pure chaos.

But it wasn't going to break the MCR lines. We needed the rest of Dragon and Rage to finish their flanking and add more pressure. As it now stood, the cultists were reinforcing the line where we were attacking and we started to feel the heat.

I called into Captain Archer while Sergeant Dwyer and two of his men fired nearby. "LR-01, are we going to be able to utilize the buzz ship again? Sure would be nice to soften those lines."

"Negative, Ocampo, the ship ruptured a coolant hose. Flight engineers should have it up soon, but 'til then, 'fraid we're on our own."

"KTF, sir... how soon on that air support? We're getting close to being pinned down."

I left unsaid that the other option was for the captain to get the rest of the company up in position.

"Engineers haven't nailed down a time for us, Lieutenant. Just keep fighting. We're moving slower than you but we're getting in position. Official word from buzz ship is 'a while.'"

"Copy. LR-24, out."

I hissed a curse to myself. This didn't bode well.

"Ocampo." It was Captain Archer again. "I need a sit-rep. How long until you can get your men in position to begin taking down those guns?"

What in the world? I didn't understand why Captain Archer was asking me this. The plan was for us to draw forward fire and for him to flank and break the lines. Then we'd get the guns down.

"Sir, we're not in a position to touch the guns. The MCR is throwing everything at us."

"I need those guns offline now."

"Yes, sir."

But those were just words. There was no way I could do that. Not unless he spotted me a destroyer to some precision orbital bombardments.

Switching channels, intentionally checking the frequency, I pinged my right-hand man. "Sergeant Dwyer: our gear only takes us so far. How do we stop the enemy from using their numerical superiority? Because I have a feeling a countercharge is what comes next."

"No special trick, Fetch. We just kill them first, sir!"

"But you think they'll come for us?"

"I'd be surprised if they didn't. I would. Think we'll be able to get that buzz ship into the fight, sir? It'd even the odds a fair bit."

"Doesn't look like it. So how 'bout it?"

"How about what, sir?"

"Killing 'em all." I didn't know how else to achieve what Captain Archer was asking of me.

Dwyer seemed to reflect for a while. "Probably all die trying, Fetch. We need those flanks pressured or the buzz ships."

Thwack.

Stone from the rock beside me erupted into shards as a bolt slammed into the boulder's face. I peeked to get a better idea of where the shooting was coming from. It didn't seem to belong to one of the tanks—it was just a single blast.

Thud.

The MCR blaster bolt hit me square in the shoulder and knocked me flat on my butt.

"Fetch!" called Sergeant Dwyer. "You okay?"

He could see that I was already getting back up. The enemy round hit the armor, but at that range the LARKs held. I wasn't thrilled at the idea of being hit in the same spot but... "I'm fine, Sergeant! KTF!"

We were killing the enemy, the combat interface on my HUD kept a running tally. More popped up in their place. Like a sort of military hydra—dust one MCR, two more take his place. I growled under my breath, Arthava produced large litters and this was their planet. They could afford to bleed troops without sacrificing their endgame. Meanwhile, we couldn't replace our dead. We would feel the loss of every leej.

"Ocampo!" Captain Archer again. Something was up his butt. I hadn't ever heard him like this before. "Status."

Everything in me screamed to run, find somewhere safe and hide. I tried to ignore that fear, but it bubbled up from my guts as we continued our firefight. It's suicidal, I thought. Only an idiot sticks around and waits for their death! We're going to get overrun.

"Sir, we're in a bad way here. They have us pinned down and we're concerned they're going to counterattack and overrun our line. We need some help here, sir."

"We're almost in position," said Captain Archer. "I want your unit to charge. One final push, Ocampo!"

"Is he serious?" yelled Top.

Looks like I wasn't the only one who had occasional trouble remembering to use the proper comm channel.

"Sir," I began to protest, "the MCR are shifting their focus directly on us. Even with the mortars I'm not sure that—"

"Kill that gutless talk, Lieutenant!" Captain Archer shouted over the comms network. "Maintain unit cohesion, Ocampo," he warned me privately.

Unit cohesion be darned, I wasn't ready to meet Oba that day.

"You're the most feared damn fighting force in the galaxy, Leejes," Captain Archer told everyone over the comms network. "Let our courage show them our might. Fear will overwhelm them, and they'll break! Just like they taught in training, boys! LR-01, out."

That was that. It was decided. He was a point after all.

"Captain Archer, sir," I said over the command L-comm channel, "I know you want to intimidate 'em, but—"

"Stow it, Leej. Go in fast and roaring and they'll run in fear from our might."

I tried to fight the rage that boiled up inside of me. The captain's orders were insane. I couldn't think of anything more idiotic. He'd seemed competent so far; I'd almost forgotten that he was a point. I had faith in his skills, and then he punched all of us in the gut. Here I'd come to believe that he saw us as men, as comrades in arms, warriors worthy of respect, but now he was ordering us to waste our lives on this foolhardy objective. Just like every other point blindly following textbook strategies, strategies that would get good men killed. He reminded us that his most saleable skills were his political connections with the overlords in the House of Reason.

"Sir, I beg you... reconsider?"

"Get moving, Ocampo, or I'll send in someone who isn't afraid to do the job!"

His voice sounded shrill, but I understood where Captain Archer was coming from. He operated from the doctrine the political classes mandated. It was clear that he was feeling some kind of pressure to get this done. And my team was the closest in position to do it. Except... this was going to get us all killed. And yet, I knew he was serious about replacing me. If I didn't call the charge, he'd relieve me of my command and put in place someone who would. And the thing about the reserves was that there would be a guy who would do whatever a point asked him to do.

Our training had been intense, but I'd be fooling myself if I thought it made every man in the Caledonian reserves an actual legionnaire. A lot of them still resented the Legion for how hard its cadre pushed us. And a point taking charge was exactly the type of thing they might ally with.

In the end, I couldn't leave my men. I keyed the comm to my NCOs.

"Captain Archer needs us to charge."

There was a stony silence in reply.

And then Dwyer said, "All right."

Archer's voice boomed over the comm. "Get that line moving, Ocampo!"

And then the hard voices of my squad leaders motivated their legionnaires to get up and get moving. We rushed the objective, firing from the hip as the MCR—who seemed to be gathering for their own charge—looked up in surprise.

That run was surreal. I could hear my heavy breathing drowning out the blaster fire. Could feel my rifle drain its charge pack. I was dimly aware of my team shouting instructions and rallying calls over the L-comm. But it seemed distant. Like I wasn't really there—until I got eyes on a single Arthavan and then things sped up as I took my shot and dropped the insurgent.

The mortars kept falling, taking a toll on the MCR behind their entrenchments. One scored a direct hit in the cab of one of the modified dozers, leaving a shattered corpse behind the wheel.

A scream sounded to my right. Looking over, I saw Corporal Moore writhing on the ground, clutching his throat.

"Medic!" I screamed as I knelt beside him, searching for his individual medical kit as my heart pounded in the back of my skull. My helmet flashed a warning about my heart rate and oxygen levels. I was too winded, too spent to even give the cancel code for the notification. It just sat before me flashing as I searched.

In my haste I couldn't find it. I tried to staunch the flow of blood as I waited for Doc Tran—assuming he was even up and with us. Moore's comm was still on, and he didn't have the mindset to mute his shrieks of pain. That wasn't a blaster burn; he'd been hit by a sliver of rock from a ricochet. In this cold, the LARKs might shatter when hit at high velocity.

"Someone help Moore!" a legionnaire shouted over the comm.

The corporal's screams were unsettling, and knowing the impact it might have on the men, I found my focus and muted his comm remotely from my helmet. I kept searching, and the HUD warning went away as I calmed myself.

Ah, found it. I pulled his sealed med-pouch from the webbing on his armor. Moore was left-handed; he'd oriented his gear backward.

His shrieks silenced for everyone but me and our direct link, and his jerking movements stilled. I ripped open the pack and the contents scattered in the snow. I grabbed the lone skinpack and slapped it on his torn throat, but by then it was too late. Moore was gone.

"Moore? Moore!" I shook him.

No response.

Damn it, I thought. How many men are gonna die for this point's orders?

I could hear an electric snap and hiss from one of those improvised tanks starting up in the background. It wasn't shooting blaster bolts—they were shooting us with industrial nail guns, building equipment designed to nail spikes into the bedrock.

Standing, I quickly looked around at my men. They'd slowed down, still moving but lingering behind whatever scrubby tree or rock they could find. I knew we couldn't take much more of this. At the same time, we were a lot closer to the lines. I could see the MCR clearly, making out the lines in the Arthavans' muzzles.

"Ocampo," Captain Archer's voice was back in my ear. "You're almost there. Don't throw it away, son... get moving! Now!"

I nodded, not bothering to reply and not caring that Archer would have no way of knowing I'd even heard him. Then I called in to my team to warn them about the spike drivers. "Be advised: MCR utilizing improvised slug throwers capable of breeching our LARKs. Assault at best possible—," but I didn't even finish my order to charge the rest of the way to the lines.

The leejes of Rage Company didn't need to hear me finish what I was saying. They knew as well as I did that what was done was done, and we either showed them our faces and delivered some KTF, or we broke and painted targets with our backs.

Legionnaires from 1st Section rushed the line, exchanging blaster fire and ducking beneath the fixed nail guns on the dozers at close range. I saw Dwyer reach a wide foxhole and unload his blaster rifle into the pit at full auto in a sweeping motion. He then jumped inside, motioning for his squad to follow.

Corporal Santos sprinted and leapt over a trench, dropping a fragger into the midst of the MCR attempting to follow his movements and then shooting the driver of a dozer once he landed on the other side. The fragger exploded, sending a spray of blood and dirt into the air as Santos used the neutralized dozer for cover.

"Keep moving!" he shouted to the rest of us.

By now I was running, sprinting to join the rest of my element.

"That's the spirit!" I screamed, frothing a little.

The leejes of Dragon and Rage Company didn't want to get left behind. I could finally see them on the battlefield, picking up speed until both companies charged the enemy's flanks. They were a good way back compared to us, firing bolts at the Arthava as they ran, but I doubt they hit anything.

I loosed primal screams of rage as more of my men punctured the MCR line—and more of them fell on the way.

"Umpf."

A blaster bolt hit me in the chest, hurling me to the ground.

I must've been unconscious for a second, because when I came to, Rage Company was pulling back from its attack on the flank. The Arthava, seeing the larger force coming, had shifted away from us and were engaging with everything they had, reorienting all their dozers and snarling as they spent every charge pack they must have had to send a punishing barrage into the flanking legionnaires who were getting caught in swirling strands of concertina wire.

Behind all these defenses were the guns themselves. So close that I could see the small crews working and guarding the weapons. And in my chest, I could feel each boom sent up toward the fleet in orbit.

My boys were mixed in with what was left of the MCR defenders in front of them, fighting up close. But there weren't enough of us to push forward.

Meanwhile, I was caught in no-man's land. I'd missed the charge that got my men close and in the lines.

I scrambled to my feet, dragging along a wounded leej who was near me. I tossed the leej's last grenade toward a pocket of MCR and grabbed him by the carry strap on the back of his kit. He shook off my arm and regained his feet to stumble back with me away from a fusillade of raw blaster bolts.

It kills me, but I still don't know who was running beside me. Whoever it was stumbled along next to me, and we pulled back to the first natural dip in the topography that offered shelter, and hunched in the bushes, with some other legionnaires who'd been separated or driven back and were sending sporadic fire toward the enemy guns. The leej I'd pulled along with me took a glancing blow on his head from a nail as we scrambled into the ditch. It dented his bucket, but he'd live.

"Oba," I breathed in shock.

The round didn't kill him, surprising everyone around him. It surprised him too, but he crawled into the ditch with me and took his place on the line. He felt along the back of his bucket but wasn't satisfied.

"Hey—" I said as he started to take off his bucket.

Thud.

The Arthava's sniper was good. Without his bucket, the man's brain exploded from the back of his head. Gore went everywhere, splattering my helmet's visor. My hands went up as though the gruesome projectile could physically harm me.

Get a grip, Fetch, I told myself. If you panic, more leejes die. I couldn't let that happen. We had to make it home. I had to bring them back to Cally; I'd promised their families.

"Head in the game," I muttered and grabbed a handful of snow to wipe that leej's blood off my visor.

"LR-01, our charge has stalled," I said, knowing that his had as well along with Dragon's on the other flank. "Check on the kranking buzz ship, sir."

The captain didn't respond. Maybe he was in shock that the craptastic tactics he'd demanded weren't working.

I quickly checked my HUD to get an idea of how my men were doing.

"Oh, no," I whispered to myself.

Top Walden was now dead, and many others had died around him.

The buzz ship chose that moment to come back online.

"LR-01, this is Bear Claw 2. We are inbound and ready to go. Auto-cannons are looking to join the fight. Send me targeting data via interface. I'll be airborne the moment it arrives. Bravo-Charlie-2, out."

Finally. I quickly moved my tongue along the nozzle in my bucket, toggling the various features on my HUD. I forwarded the info to the buzz ship pilots the moment it popped up. Oba was once again on our side, because the foolish rebels hadn't thought to defend the orbital guns with anything capable of shooting low enough to defend itself from a planetary aerial assault. Or maybe they didn't have anti-aircraft batteries at all. It was the MCR, after all.

Once the message was sent, I toggled the screen back to standby mode and returned fire at the enemy. I desperately tried to ignore the screams coming from the wounded as I sent bolt after bolt.

The MCR shifted their attention from us to the buzz ship, sending up every manner of small arms fire they could muster at the lumbering bird. But those bad boys had thick skin and the bolts either dissipated against its limited shielding or bounced off its armored hide.

"All units!" I shouted into the L-comm. "Push!"

I left the screaming of those laying wounded in the field and charged back to the lines, taking advantage of an enemy divided by threats from all sides—the buzz ship being the most pressing. As I got nearer, most everything was drowned out by the roar of the buzz ship's auto-cannons firing bursts into the enemy.

The pilot kept the shuttle in a hover over the enemy defenses, destroying anything within sight around the orbital cannons. I guess he had to allow the gun system's targeting algorithms time to lock onto the enemy, trusting the sturdiness of the ship's build to keep him from being shot down. Meanwhile every round he fired was one less fur-brained MCR firing at us.

The shuttle hovered over the enemy and cycled through bolt after bolt, its barrels glowing in the frigid Rhyssis Wan evening. Our buckets compensated for the lack of light, but the buzz ship's cannons shone like a beacon, making it an easy target. Which meant the cultists were no longer focused on shooting our heads off.

It made me wonder what the point of it all was. This thing was doing Oba's work for us. Why hadn't we waited? Why push to our deaths if this was all that we needed to have happen. Our sacrifice certainly didn't seize the guns any faster.

But then, neither would the work of those brave pilots if we didn't follow up. I was with my team, fighting through the defensive trenches, past wire, over and around smoking dozers. But the rest of Rage and Dragon had to do the same.

"LR-01, sir... seize the initiative. Push forward, sir!"

To my surprise, the captain immediately agreed. I'd expected resistance.

"All units: Charge!" he screamed over the joint company L-comms channel.

Reflexively gripping my blaster tighter, I screamed, following Archer's wild call for a charge deeper into the enemy fortifications.

We blazed past the dugout holes and fighting pits, shooting the MCR still left alive by the buzz ship, which was tightening its fire as we moved closer and focusing on the last defensive line protecting the guns.

It was an outwardly sloped, waist-high wall around the big weapons. An aboveground trench for the rebels, covering their attack. Given how rocky the terrain was, it made sense. Whatever they'd built the wall with seemed indestructible, deflecting or absorbing everything we had to throw at it. Instead, I concentrated on firing above the wall. My grenadiers seemed to understand the situation as well; they'd already lobbed their rounds over the wall. But for every rebel fleabag we killed, another one took his place.

One of their snipers aimed a clunky barrel at the buzz ship. Pausing in my wild charge, I targeted his hairy maw.

The Arthavan dropped.

"Got ya!" I yelled as I resumed my charge.

When we got close to the wall, the rebels paid closer notice to us again. They weren't having any luck on the buzz ship, and the buzz ship wouldn't actually be able to destroy those guns. Vehicles and infantry, yes. But something that big would take more than the bird had in her.

But the increase of MCR fire was coming too late. By the time they'd swung their fire concentrations to meet us, Rage and Dragon Companies bounded over the barrier, converging from all sides and looking for vengeance.

I clambered inside, shooting an Arthavan in the chest who rose to stop me before sliding down the other side, in the midst of a chaotic storm of close fighting. But that served us well. While the indigs had a certain biological ferocity and low light vision, our helmets were better, and our armor could stand up to their teeth and claws. Unless more charkas showed up. But those were nowhere to be seen.

"Get some!" I shouted as I punched one of the MCR in the snout, pulling up my blaster in time to smoke a hole through another snarling attacker, then dusting three more.

It was like that everywhere else, too. Legionnaires unleashing holy hell, dancing right on the edge of animal madness while never losing their ability to outthink and outfight. But we were getting savage. The whole thing was.

Blaster packs were spent and rifles were dropped, replaced by pistols, knives, or even tomahawks from some of the Legion regulars. Blood was everywhere, staining the snow orange and crimson.

The shuttle pilot seemed to have been expecting our maneuver, shifting the rest of fire to the area on the opposite side of the fortified defenses. His bolts chewed up the buildings surrounding the guns.

I was getting physically tired of killing. Like I'd been lifting weights too long and my arms and body pled that they could do no more.

Oba, there were so many of them.

But I had to keep pulling the trigger. I shouldered into MCR and shot them while they lay on their backs. I kicked others in the gut and crushed their skulls with the butt of my rifle as they yelped and doubled over. It was brutal, bloody work.

It became a battle of strength and determination, as we all grappled in desperate hand-to-hand combat. I fired when I had the room to bring my blaster to bear, using my NM-4 as a club when I couldn't. My bucket's visor was splattered with blood from head butting so many of the creatures, fracturing their snouts from the blow. I'd done that to the furry Arthavan in front of me when I went down as its buddy tackled me from the side.

I rolled, struggling to get out from under him as it attempted to send a knife blade plunging down beneath my bucket and into my neck.

I wanted to live, to breathe, to punch this rabid hyena who had his arm around my throat. Abandoning my weapon, I reached between the creature's legs and hoped some facets of biology were universal. I squeezed as hard as I could. Still don't know Arthava anatomy, but the one on top of me loosened his hold.

I wrestled the blade from his hand and stabbed him with it.

I aimed for his throat, assuming it'd be a fatal wound. I was right. More hot orange blood sprayed across my visor. I slipped my new blade into the cargo pouch on my armor, thinking that another backup weapon would be needed before all was completed. Retrieving my blaster with my other hand, I stood and searched for another target.

It wasn't hard, there were so many. But we were making a difference. We were winning. They were breaking under the relentless onslaught of men trained to be the very best the galaxy had to offer.

We were kelhorned killing machines.

Bringing my weapon up, I fired as fast as my finger could depress the trigger while advancing toward the nearest cluster of MCR. Soon our concentrated fire pushed the enemy backward.

"Don't let up, Leejes! KTF!" I shouted.

The enemy broke and ran, abandoned their own massive guns. We cheered like loons as the Arthava ran howling in retreat, disappearing into the forest outcropping beyond the last of the guns.

When the air grew quiet, I checked on my troops. There were too many black and tan LARKs lying motionless on the icy ground. The numbers were staggering.

In the end, I lost a quarter of my section. I had to consolidate my forces down to three squads instead of four. All those leejes, men whose family I had let down. I wanted to cry. I wanted to scream. I wanted to hunt down those rebel kranks, and bathe in their blood.

But justice would have to wait. Our mission wasn't over yet. We needed to secure the orbital guns before the MCR returned. No one had any illusions about what we accomplished. We'd gone up against Arthavan cultists working with the MCR. There had been no charkas, but the mission was accomplished. Still, there were plenty more out there.

We had to prepare and defend this position for however long it took. We weren't done by a long shot.

12

This time I knew better.

This time I stayed away from the aid station.

While my surviving leejes received medical care, I organized the defense of the big guns and got the men clearing space for landings inside the small fort. And with the guns out of the fight, word was the fleet was going to send down some transport shuttles to be our mobile ambulance, but first we had to make room.

"How do you do it, Virgil?" I heaved another Arthavan corpse over to the edge of a hastily dug pit, made courtesy of the dozer-tanks. "How do you shrug off our losses and carry on?"

Virgil hefted an Arthava to the lip of the mass grave, then gave it a shove. "I care, sir. I care too much," he grunted. "But we can cry over our whiskey later. Right now my concern is for the living."

That gave me an idea. I found myself a quiet corner, then hailed our computer criminal—I mean, "tech"—on a private channel.

"Hey, Padagas, I need your expertise on something."

"Fire away, LT."

"These guns... do you think you could find a way to override the locks in place and give control of them to the Legion?"

Padagas was quiet for a while. "I think it's a real possibility. Depends on what kind of security software they have and how long until we're expected to move out again. But if all goes well, I could do it, I think. Yeah."

The brass wanted us to destroy them—that'd been the order Captain Archer had given me—but that seemed foolish. If we could harness those guns, we could turn them on the enemy fleet in orbit and assure our ships a victory.

"Padagas, keep this quiet," I said. "Do whatever you have to, but I want control of those guns. If we lose our taxis off this snowball, we're as good as dead."

"Sure don't wanna be stuck here... On it, LT."

While Padagas went to work, a hovering shuttle finally touched down, the back blast kicking up a small blizzard of snow around the fort. Just the fact that one of our cruisers was able to send it down suggested that the battle above us was no longer as desperate now that the guns were out of the fight. But with nothing going as planned, who could say whether the tide would turn again. How many ships did the MCR have? What if they managed to steal a destroyer?

I moved toward the ship to oversee it being loaded with the wounded when I heard, to my surprise, Padagas.

"LT, the guns are ready," the legionnaire whispered over a private channel.

That quick?

"Say again, Padagas... they're ready?"

"Copy that, sir."

I changed course and jogged over to the weapons control center. There he was, his gloves and bucket off, grinning like he'd just farted in a cathedral.

"Put your bucket on, LR-133, and police your kit, for crying out loud," I said. "Now, where are we with targeting the rogue fleet?"

Padagas shook his head, an exaggerated frown on his face. "Hello to you too, LT! You wound me, and here I thought we were buddies. Whatever will I tell my friends back in Ogham?" He didn't even try to keep the snark out of his voice.

"You think I give a crap what your so-called 'friends' think? Just tell me where you're at with overriding the targeting protocols," I replied in irritation.

"Roger sir. But first: I slice a lot better without gloves and helmets on. And second, you only said to take control of the guns. Not—"

"Padagas," I interrupted. "We need to use them against the MCR. Why else would I give a rip if we had control of them?"

Padagas gave a wobanki grin. "Roger, sir. Didn't say it couldn't happen. Just that I didn't do it. Hit the green button on the display here, and you've retargeted the guns."

I nodded and moved the panel to get a closer look.

Padagas's tone changed, becoming uncharacteristically serious. "Now, I'll be leaving, sir. I don't want to be between you and the brass."

I leaned over the console and hit the button. At first it seemed like nothing happened, but eventually I could hear the energy cannons cycling back up. And then the computer terminal shut down. I was about to call Padagas back, but the system started rebooting.

I don't exactly know what he did, and I didn't get the chance to ask him before the system started back up and got right to business. Once everything stopped flashing and beeping, an option to initiate the updated targeting sequence appeared. Trusting my leej, I accepted the prompt and waited. I could hear the crackle of the energy flowing around the cannons. It was working! The ground rumbled and the air hummed with gathering power.

"What's happening with those guns, Ocampo?"

I jumped at the captain's sharp voice in my ears. Evidently he could see my locator flashing on his HUD from the gun's command center.

"Working on it, sir!"

"Get those damn things back offline!" Archer bellowed. "The fleet can't handle much more of them and remain combat effective!"

The threat targeting screen appeared, indicating every spaceship in its field of fire. I scanned the list of ship classifications—none of the targets were Republic ships.

"Captain, we've adjusted the systems to fire on the enemy fleet now!"

The gun fired off two rapid salvos, loud thunderous cracks.

Everywhere legionnaires began to scramble, donning their helmets and picking up their rifles. The light from the blast of energy was blinding, and anyone not wearing their bucket had to look away. Captain Archer rushed into the orbital field gun's control room. The game was up. Before the point could say anything, I launched into my defense of what I'd done.

"Sir, if we let them destroy our fleet, we'd be hosed," I said, imploringly.

"Shut the hell up, Ocampo." Archer verified with the fleet that the guns were indeed firing on the MCR and not on our own craft.

I could see legionnaires scrambling, and the L-comm was flooding with reports and requests for information as they all struggled to find out what was happening. I got a sinking feeling in my stomach... this was good work, but I handled it in a bad way.

Archer went over the L-comm to inform all legionnaires to "Cycle down and await orders. The guns are not an immediate threat."

I was worried at that point that he was going to shut the weapons off again. "Sir, nothing else matters if we're stranded here in a system captured by the rebels. If this goes wrong, you can blame me."

"You're damn right, I can blame you. You went off half-cocked and made a monumental decision without conferring with the chain of command!"

"Yes, sir. But that was only to give you an out. With the guns doing their thing, we can achieve a much stronger hold on the planet. And we can still demolish them if we're ordered to move out and can't leave behind a force sufficient enough to guard them.."

Captain Archer stared at me, bucket in hand, his paper-white face looking exhausted. I could see him weighing the options, but ultimately, he saw the wisdom of protecting our ride home. We'd lost too many leejes taking these guns. From thirty-two squads, we were down to twenty.

Our leejes wanted blood, and they were cheering with every renewed salvo now that they knew what the guns were shooting at.

"We'll let the guns work for now," Archer finally said. "With Dragon Company hit so hard, we're folding both companies into one unit. They lost all their officers and too many of their NCOs. You'll have five squads under you now. Send Sergeant Dwyer to straighten that out. We're resting here tonight. Tomorrow we're heading out to a Repub Army base that went silent when this shindig kicked off. We'll spike the guns in the morning."

"Yes, sir."

"Make sure they're ready to blow these weapons in the morning."

"Yes, sir. I'll make it happen," I said, relief obvious in my voice.

Archer turned to leave, and then stopped at the door. "One more thing, Ocampo."

"Sir?"

"Two times today you've taken to the habit of thinking that you know best. I had to argue with you to obey orders before the charge, and turning these guns back on could have been a disaster in more ways than one. If either of those things happen again, I'm relieving you of command. Is that clear?"

"Crystal, sir."

13

We spent a long night defending the orbital guns from a counterattack that never came. The guns never stopped, we never slept, and time passed slowly. When the brilliant sun broke through the predawn fog, Rage Company was ready to abandon the massive cannons. We'd taken out enough of the MCR fleet that our navy had consolidated and re-formed. I didn't know how long it would take for our spacers to get full control of the fight, but it was the best we could do.

Maybe this was me being ground and not having the technical knowledge of a spacer, but I thought those guns made a much larger impact than they actually did. I figured they were blowing up ships left and right. But with there even being an MCR fleet left after a full night of firing suggested that either the guns weren't the edge I thought they were or that the battle had shifted outside of their range. If nothing else, we bought the Republic Navy time and gave them room to breathe.

"Rage Company, we're leaving as soon as we destroy these kranking guns," bellowed our commander over his suit's speakers. Most of the men were gathered in a school circle around Archer as he addressed the company.

The pause drew out, well past where things got awkward. We just didn't have it in us to respond in some motto manner he seemed to want.

"There's a Repub Army base, Camp Jericho, that's gone silent. It's due north of us, quite a ways past Kusiba. We need to beat feet, because it's a long hike. The biggest challenge will be avoiding local air power, because our path will take us across several valleys."

The legionnaires audibly groaned. Air power was something we weren't supposed to have to deal with. First, because planets rarely had anything even closely resembling a working starfighter force—that's what the Republic was for. And second, because it hadn't been a factor at all to this point.

"I know," said Archer. "But you're going to have to suck it up because those crossings will be dangerous, the lack of foliage means we'll be exposed. The longer we take, the more time for the rebels to prepare. Then it'll get even worse for us. Dangerous levels of suckage. I know you're tired, but let's show the rest of the Legion what the Caledonian Reserve can do!"

The boys gave a tired cheer, then we broke up to each get our jobs done before pulling out. As I hurried over to the gun control center, I called Dwyer on a private channel.

"LR-57, help Lieutenant Challen install the det cord on those guns."

My neck was on the line, I wanted to know it was done right.

Next, we needed to destroy the computer interface. I knew just the coder for the job.

"Padagas, can you give that computer a cold?"

"You mean a virus, sir?"

"Yes, something that makes it unsalvageable. Virus, cold, whatever."

"Sir, they're gonna blow the thing. It's not coming back from that much det cord."

"Not what I asked, Padagas. Can you do it?"

"Roger, LT. On the way."

Satisfied that I'd covered my bases with the operating system, I went to supervise the other officer. Challen had transferred into Dragon Company from the 71st Legion. He was a demolitions expert who'd come up through the ranks, but in the end I needed eyeballs watching these guns blow. My eyeballs.

Captain Archer had been clear about how thin the ice I was skating on truly was. We had to make sure these guns couldn't be rebuilt, not until we'd reconquered the planet.

"Here's some kaff, Challen." I handed him a cup while I stepped back to watch him work.

"Thanks," he said after taking off his bucket and setting it on the table. "Just what the doctor ordered."

It took us an hour, but we managed to completely corrupt the guns' computer cores. Then I watched Challen add more detonation cord, just for good measure. When the fireworks were prepared, Captain Archer ordered the company to move out.

"Burning daylight, people! Let's roll!"

This time 1st Section wasn't walking point; we got to pull up the rear. This meant I got to click the button and blow the guns. I can't lie, I was more than a little thrilled.

Challen was pissed to not do it himself, but he'd get over it. Like all good leejes, he could be bought off with a bottle of top-shelf hooch.

It was hard, but I managed to keep my itchy finger off the clicker until the time was right.

"Fire in the hole," Archer called over the L-comm.

I happily hit the button, might've even chuckled a little.

"Almost wanna grab some marshmallows, really enjoy the campfire!"

"Can it, Padagas," Sergeant Dwyer growled.

At first there was only a slight popping sound.

"That'll be the computers," Santos said.

I had my bucket's speakers maxed out to listen for the explosion. So did the rest of my section. We were like kids in a candy store, wanting to enjoy every moment. While we weren't close enough to see it all, we damn sure wanted to hear it.

Boy, was that ever a poor life decision.

When the follow-on blast came, it took us by surprise. Our cut-rate buckets short-circuited. It didn't last long before they reset themselves, but most of us had ringing ears for the next couple of days.

We pushed hard for Camp Jericho, and I spent part of my day rounding up stragglers. We were pushing well past the breaking point for most men. But we weren't men, we were leejes, and enduring hardship is what we do. So we put one foot in front of the next while keeping an eye out for any cultist hyena warriors looking to slaughter us in the name of the Mid-Core Rebellion.

Rage Company retraced our steps back toward Kusiba, trying to move quicker than we had before. Our dead and wounded rode in the shuttle, giving us the ability to push harder. But it didn't last long. We'd only been on the march for an hour when Corporal Santos pulled me aside.

"Sir, take a look over there. It's to your right, just past that ridge. See that?" he asked.

Movement. The mountains rose up all around us, the monotonous color palate tending to bewilder the eye. But that worked to our favor, because the white snow made dark shapes difficult to conceal. Only one beast would be that large from that far off. Charka.

"We're being followed," I said.

"Obviously, but look at their uniforms. That's the important part, sir," replied Santos.

I zeroed in my visuals, magnifying the optics on my bucket. The targets weren't wearing the usual white and gray of the cultist fighters. I didn't know if these warriors were loyalists, rebels, or some unknown third faction. They were armed and though they weren't clearly identifiable as MCR, that didn't make them friendlies.

"I see them," I replied, before switching to the channel with section's NCOs. "Dwyer, are you seeing this?"

"If by 'this' you mean the force shadowing our movement, then yes. For now, I suggest you flag it on your HUD and stay frosty."

These warriors shadowing us forced us to alter our behavior; we had to sacrifice speed for an increased tactical awareness. Every step we took, we knew the crosshairs were on our backs. I called it in.

"LR-01, unknown force east of our location surveilling our movements. Permission to neutralize the threat."

"Negative, LR-24. Remember the rules of engagement," Archer said over the L-comm. "Don't fire unless cleared by higher authority—"

"But, sir, if they shoot first—"

"Report any hostile enemy action up your chain of command."

"But—"

"Are you listening to me, Lieutenant, or are those comms malfunctioning, because you sure as hell aren't questioning an order."

"No, sir," I agreed, studying the dark shapes in the distance.

"It's clear they're Arthavans riding charka. And that's all that's clear. Now a lot of those were slaughtered for supporting the Republic, and I'm not going to allow some impulsive legionnaires to add to that tragedy by ignoring the Republic's rules of engagement for this operation."

Boy, did my trigger finger itch. But I had my orders. So I kept my finger off the trigger and bit my tongue. The rules of engagement were clear, but to hell with them. I didn't care. Not if it meant that more of my guys might get dusted.

"1st," I called over our section comm. "I'm updating the ROE. When in doubt, bolts out."

It was a risk, making such a policy known. But you can't court-martial a dead man. I was confident nobody would bring us up on charges for trying to survive, not even the House was that bad. Were they?

It was exhausting, but we pushed through it and maintained our vigilant posture. I knew that if our attention to our surroundings faltered, even just a little, we'd be easy prey. We were in enemy territory, unsupported. One reinforced company performing the role of an entire legion.

When we got within a few klicks of Kusiba, I noticed our shadow acting strangely. One of them was riding his charka hard up and down their line, yelling something that my bucket couldn't make out. He shook his blaster at the sky, and the icy wind brought back their screaming cheers.

"Get ready, they're about to attack," I told my section.

We all crouched as we advanced forward, weapons ready, all five of my squads on alert. We'd been looping our way down a winding mountain road, and we were vulnerable. Our sole focus was on our left flank where the mounted Arthava were following us. I expected contact at any moment, my mind ignoring everything else around me as it tunneled in on the threat. It was right there, I could feel it in my bones.

Something was going to happen. The wind howled, snow swirled around our feet.

"Turn the external sound down," I ordered. "At least until the snow settles."

"Negative, sir. We need full situational awareness," Virgil sent over our private channel.

Sket. There he was, correcting me again. Hot lava anger rose in my gullet, but in the cold and snow with Arthava near, I couldn't let my pride get in the way. So I swallowed it.

"Belay my last, we can't afford to sacrifice our situational awareness."

Then I heard it. The crunching sound of thousands of feet moving down through the frozen underbrush. It appeared to be coming from the opposite side of the trail, but sound was funny in the mountains. It could be a trick of the natural acoustics.

"Steady, boys," I urged.

A blaster bolt streaked toward us.

Our HUDs' red lights lit up like Cally police busting a H8 drug nest. Someone had fired at one of our leejes, but the only Arthava we saw were the charkas shadowing us.

More blaster fire began to sizzle in.

An energy bolt streaked by my bucket and I swore. They'd been stalking us from the opposite side of the pass. I'd been so distracted by the obvious threat, I missed the one sneaking up in front of us.

"Where'd that come from?" shouted a leej in the confusion.

"Who saw the gunman?" demanded Captain Archer.

"Wasn't from the group!"

More shouts of alarm echoed across the L-comms for each section.

"Can it and find the kelhorn," growled Dwyer.

We grabbed whatever cover we could, though there wasn't much to hide behind. I scanned the area but couldn't find a target. I kept looking, desperate to find the threat so I could neutralize. The landscape was snowy, with tall, pole-like trees interspersed between large stretches of rock. Then I saw the cultists, their white and gray camouflage telling me that they were rebel trash. I began firing, knowing I probably wasn't hitting anything but it'd keep their heads down. Any of my boys with a clear shot would take it.

Though the fight hadn't reached a fever pitch, we were effectively caught in the middle of two Arthava elements as we moved along the mountain road. The MCR cultists were farther down the slope—these are the ones who had sent the initial shots at us. Their heads were down as I suppressed them with the rest of my company, but we also had to keep an eye on the mounted strangers moving above us at the top of the ridge.

"Any brilliant ideas, Virgil?"

"KTF, LT," he said.

Right. Got it.

"Gladiators, move out—cover our rear," I yelled frantically into the section L-comm, all the while searching for specific targets. The squad hustled to obey.

"Permission to adjust Gladiator's positioning, LT?" asked Santos, as he slid into the snow-covered bush next to me.

"Do it."

Santos was up in an instant and sprinted to join Gladiator squad.

After adjusting the positioning of my section, I ran to take a knee behind a fallen tree. Bringing my NM-4 up, I started tracking targets. You have to give 'em just enough of a lead to hit them as they run. It's tricky to hit moving targets, but the spike of adrenaline helped me narrow my focus to what I could see from the scope of my blaster. The rush from the hunt allowed me to forget that I was shooting sentient beings.

They weren't living souls anymore, just targets to eliminate.

Aim... fire... and repeat.

I pulled the trigger as fast as my fingers could move. The Arthavans above us had thrown in with the cultists beneath, and we were taking fire from two fronts. The MCR were hanging in there, sending return bursts of fire as we tore into them, but the sparsity in training was evident to me. Here, we weren't charging an entrenched position. We were essentially on equal footing, and our shots were dropping Arthava with a consistency that had to be alarming to the rebels. In the background I could hear our crew-served blasters sending controlled bursts at the enemy. Just piling on.

Captain Archer called in to the buzz ship over the command channel as I fired. "Bear Claw 2, this is LR-01. Concentrate fire on the larger group of rebels."

"Affirmative," the pilot replied.

As the firefight continued, I noticed my sector wasn't caught up in the middle of the assault. It freed me up to begin looking for ways to roll the rebel flanks. I toggled the HUD interface, studying the map details.

"1st Section!" I was about to give the order to start flanking the rebel assault when they charged directly at us. I changed instructions on the fly. "Here they come, right for us. Steady now... hold your ground!"

"Don't give up an inch," Dwyer added.

"Not an inch!" echoed Santos.

The howling MCR that had been shadowing us rushed our position in an alien wave, with no apparent concern for battlefield tactics. The rebels seemed to be relying on sheer numbers, and they had us there by at least five to one. I continued firing bolts from my blaster, the barrel glowing red from the heat. I shot as they charged down the mountains, throwing enough energy toward them that I depleted two charge packs.

Rebel after furry rebel dropped to the ground. I don't know how many I killed. I don't know how many Rage Company killed, but it felt like for every rebel traitor we shot, ten more seemed to pop up.

"Don't let up!" I yelled into the comms as I shifted my aim.

The front ranks of the MCR troops were closing the distance and soon got within arm's reach. Our rate of fire plummeted, as each leej focused solely on the furry kranks in front of them. I got a bead on a sprinting Arthavan and squeezed the trigger.

Crap. My NM-4 was dry.

I stood up from the fallen log I'd been crouching behind and pulled my pistol. I fired one aimed bolt after another, until I spent its charge pack as well.

"Reloading!"

My primary weapon was dry, and there wasn't time to holster the secondary. Dropping it, I tried to bring my blaster back up. My hands fumbled through the motion. The rebels were too close and I couldn't get the pack changed and rifle up in time. Leejes waged small wars all around as each warrior sought to survive the melee, but my attention focused on the grinning Arthavan in front of me.

"For Cally!" I screamed as I charged the MCR warrior.

This thing was huge, not so large as a charka, but a lot bigger than me. And it had worked itself into a frenzy; steam wafted off its kaff-colored fur. The beast swung its blaster like a club, and I dodged to the right but tripped over my own two feet. I wish I could tell you that I tucked myself into a graceful combat roll, but it was ugly. I face-planted, losing my blaster rifle.

I flipped over just in time to see the traitor swing his weapon down at my head, but Oba be praised I rolled out of the way, the rifle's butt smashing against the snowy rock where my head had just been. I tried scrambling back, using my feet to kick myself away from him, but he jumped on top of me. But not before I managed to pull out my vibro-blade and wildly stab upward. Oba was with me again in that moment, because I sliced clean through his throat.

"For Cally!" I bellowed again as my blade cut through heavily muscled flesh.

The Arthava's vibrant orange blood spilled onto my hands. I had to clench my fingers even tighter on the handle of the vibro-blade to keep my grip from slipping.

Thrust, withdraw, and repeat.

I stabbed the creature, ignoring the arterial spray. I stabbed until my arm grew tired and I realized that the alien lying on top of me was no longer alive. I don't know how long I lay there, with that hairy corpse smothering me like a massive wet parka. With one last heave, I chucked the dead rebel off me.

Oba!

Rolling onto my knees, I sheathed my knife and crawled toward my blaster rifle, my hand prints staining the snow orange with blood. Before I could grab my weapon, a booted foot smashed me in the solar plexus. I gasped in pain but couldn't suck in breath; pinpricks of light danced around my vision. Hauling myself across the ground, I'd just grabbed the blaster when the attacker stomped my gauntleted hand. Grunting, I used my other hand to again yank out the vibro-blade and stabbed the krank's calf.

"Rowowow!" he yelped like a drowning pigasaur. I took grim satisfaction from his discomfort. But I didn't want him to be uncomfortable; I wanted him dead.

I was expecting to die myself at any moment, so I had to be quick about taking this one with me. "For Cally!"

Roaring in rage, I stabbed him again. And again. He still stood on my right hand, despite my attempts to free my limb. He slammed his rifle into my back, but my armor didn't fail. Frustrated, the hyena started beating me with his blaster. I felt every blow, one after the other.

While he beat me, I slashed his calf again. And again.

"Fall down already!" I screamed and swung my blade while he bashed me with his blaster-club. It continued until I'd inadvertently severed the booted foot. Suddenly the beating stopped, and he toppled over. Groaning in pain, I managed to get out of the way.

This attack was telling me two things: the MCR were low on charge packs and they were hopped up on something that allowed them to withstand a ghastly amount of physical pain. No humanoid I know of could have taken the kind of punishment my blade was dishing out to that thing's leg without falling back. It's not natural.

Feeling like I'd just escaped the seven circles of hell, I regained my feet and brought my blaster up to bear, slammed in a charge pack and killed my foe. It was more of the same throughout my section. I searched for pockets of MCR and then sent bolts at every rebel cultist I could see, firing until this pack went empty as well.

"Changing packs!" I called out, not sure who would hear me or what it mattered with things so up close and sticky. I quickly changed out the energy pack, while I looked for a new target. I found one, fired until the rebel dropped, and looked for the next. We killed so many of them, but they kept coming. They seemed to wash over their own dead, a relentless tide of killers desperate to reach us. Our forces were in trouble.

Cries of "Medic!" echoed up and down our line. There were too many cries for those with the necessary training and still alive to reach.

On my HUD, red leej names blinked and faded out. Coyle. Malloy. Ortiz. On and on. I had to toggle off the updates. Virgil was right... worrying about the dead would have to wait. I needed to focus on the fight in front of me. Blind to the overall battle, I focused on the leejes closest to me. Acquire target, eliminate—next target. I fired and fought. Move, kill, advance. My vision tunneled until all I could see was the next slavering hyena.

"Where's that buzz ship?" I heard Captain Archer shouting over the comm.

We needed it. Badly.

The blare of a fog horn brought my head snapping around to the mountain ridge to see what caused the noise.

"Oba!"

The trampling of hundreds of feet followed the horn as the mounted warriors from the opposite ridgeline rushed down the slope toward us

"There's more of them!" shouted a leej.

"Too many!" yelled another.

Crap—not what we needed!

I started tracking the nearest mounted Arthava, when one of the cultist MCR pukes fighting amid our ranks hit me in the bucket. I stumbled but managed to keep my feet, barely.

The fuzzy tried to brain me again, but I dodged and stepped into his attack, elbowing him in the gut then kicking him in the groin. He lost his balance, and I took advantage of the space to bring up my blaster and fire in his face. Whirling back around, I looked for another immediate threat.

I couldn't believe what I saw.

Wielding blasters, spears, and everything in between, the mounted Arthava assailed their MCR counterparts.

"Don't shoot the riders!" I yelled into the open L-comm.

With the help of our new allies, Rage Company turned the tide of the battle. Soon the MCR was retreating up the hill with the mounted Arthava in hot pursuit. The mounted warriors wore handsewn furs and were bundled up from paw to ear. Many of these forces slung their blasters in favor of throwing primitive spears. They were deadly accurate, and speared rebels dropped to the ground, unmoving.

"Aww, yeah!" Padagas hollered into the open comms.

The strangers let their charkas join the fray. One angry mount reared back and swiped its massive paw across the bellies of several rebels at once. The creature wasn't satisfied with that but started to eat the screaming Arthava. Blood flew everywhere as the battle swirled around the hungry charka.

"LR-24, halt your forces!" Captain Archer roared order over the L-comm, cutting through the battle fog.

That command brought me back from the brink.

My men were pursuing the fleeing MCR, shooting them in the back as they fled. They were almost as wild as our newfound Arthavan cavalry, and I was right in the middle of them. I desperately wanted to track those krankers down and slaughter them all. They'd killed so many of my friends.

"Sir," I panted out. "Yes, sir."

I keyed in my section comm. "1st Section! Halt and reform lines!"

My NCOs echoed the call and I watched during a few tense moments to see if my legionnaires would obey, or follow that darker instinct of mankind and continue in the shedding of blood. Slowly, they turned back, leaving the rout for the Arthavan cavalry.

14

"Consolidate on me!" bellowed Archer over the L-comms.

Up and down the line, section leaders echoed the orders.

With the aid of our unlikely new allies, the battle had turned. The enemy had broke and run, and now our mounted allies were hot on their heels.

"Look at 'em go!"

"Hot damn!"

The cheers grew, following the fleeing forces until they reverberated off the mountains. Once the screaming died down, I assessed the situation. We'd lost nine leejes from my section, and another eleven were wounded. Other squads were hit harder. The attack had been a cluster, from start to finish. The ambush was perfectly planned and their use of wave tactics paid off in steep leej losses. We fought like demons, and the rebels bled heavily for each leej they took off the chessboard.

But this was their planet. And there were more of them than there were of us.

"Rebels don't fight like this," said Santos, sounding confused as he shook his head.

"Affirmative," said Dwyer. "Haven't fought like this since we encountered the donks at Zastos."

Santos laughed. "Oba… you're old, sergeant! That was thirty years ago!"

Growling, Dwyer picked up a nearby rock and threw it at Santos as he went about tending to our wounded. The corporal ducked the projectile and laughed again.

"Careful, old man, you'll pull a muscle!"

The show of morale was something. Because on paper, things weren't looking good. We'd become an over-strength company after we'd absorbed Dragon Company. Now we were smaller, much smaller. Even after consolidating squads, we were down to an anemic four squads in my section.

"Virgil," I asked, joining the sergeant's side, "are we as hosed as it looks?"

"Worse."

His simple reply chilled me to the bone.

"We're down to fifteen squads, sir. Most of those have holes in the roster you could drive a dozer through. Cut off, in enemy country, and forced to scrounge from enemy dead."

He paused to pour rockwell powder on the plasma burn on Stern's leg. With hardly any skinpacks left, we were resorting to last ditch—and painful—alternatives to helping our wounded. Stern shrieked until he passed out from the pain.

Dwyer put his hands on his hips while Stern was carried to the casualty collection point set up by Doc Tran. "But that's why we get to call ourselves leej, Fetch.

Situations like this are where we shine. You're doin' fine, kid. We'll get through this, then we'll make 'em pay, sir."

I thought about his words while the computer in my bucket began shifting troops around to optimize our chain of command. Quickly presenting options for my approval and then logging those decisions for the battle net.

I used my command access to check on Archer because he was showing as wounded in my HUD. His shiny leej armor experienced a catastrophic failure after one hit. It didn't kill him, but he'd need knee surgery to walk normally again. All Doc Tran could do was give him a shot of pain meds and slap a precious skinpack on the wound.

"Captain Archer," I said, "what are our orders on those new friendlies? Are we waiting for them to return and see what's what?"

"No," Archer growled into the L-comm, his voice heavy with pain. "We need to get out of this kill zone, yesterday. The fuzzies have retreated, but we're twarg-stomped if they come back. Time to move on, but make sure we're prepared to get back into the fight. LR-01, out."

I saw Corporal Pool running by me at that moment and waved him over.

"Corporal Pool, I want you and Gladiator Squad to collect all of the gear you can from our dead. They don't need it anymore. Put everything in a pile near the CCP and get it done fast. Sergeant Dwyer will be over to sort things out and you don't want to make him wait."

"Yes, sir! Gladiators..."

Corporal Pool sounded harried as he began issuing orders to his squad. While he set his men to their task, I checked on the status of my own gear.

"Give me OES," I said into my bucket.

The HUD responded:

> Operational Effectiveness Status:
>
> LARK, operational, 97% ...
> NM-4, operational, 76% ...

The list went on, but I ignored everything after that.

"End report."

Sometimes the AIs running our buckets glitched, so I'd eyeball the situation myself. But those first two, my armor and my rifle... I wanted more than one opinion on their status.

Once my gear was squared away, which hadn't taken very long, I followed my HUD to Captain Archer. He was near the medivac station, loopy from pain drugs.

"Sir, we need to get the shuttle back down here. The sooner we pass off our wounded, the sooner we can continue the mission," I said.

"Negative, Ghost Rider," he slurred. "Quarters are too tight, pilot can't land. We'll eat the Arthava and bury the dead. Go mark the location for Fleet to retrieve the bodies, they might be hungry too."

What the hell? I thought. Those meds must be strong.

"Sir—" I put in, using my most diplomatic tone.

He smacked away my hand. "Challen didn't make it, but we won't eat him. Still, I'll need you to assume command of his section. The Republic needs you! Let's get our wounded to Camp Jericho, you hear me?"

I saw Doc Tran looking at me, but whatever expression he wore under his helmet was a mystery to me. I'm thinking he was as concerned as I was about the captain giving orders in this state.

I didn't want to hear this; our leejes needed medical care and our combat medics could only do so much. It wasn't the captain's fault, but it was a crappy situation all around.

"You could relieve him," Virgil said, popping into a private L-comm.

"We're not there yet, Sergeant."

My answer sounded stiff, even to my own ears. I wanted to complain about the situation, but Archer was high and I was a leej. Legionnaires don't whine; we left that to the marines. Leejes got the job done.

"We'll monitor the situation, reassess as needed."

I hoped that was good enough for Virgil, because it was all I had in me.

Oba, please just make me a private again, I prayed.

The Man—or Woman—up there didn't answer, but I wasn't really expecting him to. That was the moment that I developed a whole new respect for the officers who led us. Not the points—those were a crapshoot—but those who'd managed to claw their way up from the ranks.

"Move with a purpose!" some sergeant shouted as we processed the field and buried our dead under a cairn of rocks.

"Do you wanna join 'em?" Corporal Pool shouted when one of his leejes sat down to rest.

It took hours for us to cover our dead in the loose rocks. It was an ugly job, but we hoped it'd keep the scavengers at bay. We passed from morning into the midday before we were ready to continue the mission. Prior to starting the march again, the mounted warriors returned.

So much for getting out of that kill zone now.

Sket.

One of the Arthava stopped in front of me. He was tall, taller than most of the others. Over his fur were handsewn robes and garments made of leather and furs of animals I couldn't recognize. While they were all pretty much dressed like this, the one before me seemed to be more elaborate. I assumed he was their chieftain. But that was a complete guess. The locals we expected to encounter were like those murdered in the city. Civilized. This group had a wild, barbarian feel to them.

The chieftain spoke in a strange dialect. I didn't know if it was a translation issue with my bucket, but I wasn't sure what he was saying exactly. His growls were sent back in a very formal-sounding standard.

"I see your head covering has markings different from the rest," he growled. "You must be the Great Chief for these warriors in tan and black. We have much to discuss."

"Good afternoon, sir," I said. "I'm an officer in the 9th Legion, but the burden of overall command rests with another. Let me take you to Captain Archer."

I don't know why I tried to mimic his speech patterns. Maybe for the same reasons people speak loudly and slowly to people who are blind? I felt like a fool the moment the words had left my lips and was thankful my bucket hid my blush.

The chieftain followed me in total silence, even his mount didn't make a sound. It was unnerving how quietly his charka moved.

Captain Archer was still resting when we found him, nearly asleep.

"Hearty greetings to the enemy of mine enemy!" the chieftain's voice boomed. "We would offer you our lives and spears in this war against the mutilators of the sacred womanhood. Let us escort you to your destination. For this battle, we shall interlock our shields and bring justice to the Great Mother Rhyssis Wan."

Captain Archer seemed taken aback, but he was a consummate politician if not soldier and recovered quickly. I could see how the man had earned his appointment into the 71st Legion.

"I do not have the authority to place civilians in harm's way." Captain Archer slurred his words, though he seemed otherwise coherent. "But the House of Reason thanks you for your assistance. The Legion will handle it from here."

I watched dumbfounded as the captain politely but firmly turned away the help that could be the difference between living and dying. We were bleeding forces—people I knew. They weren't just fellow soldiers, they were my family, friends, and neighbors. We played in the same recreational leagues. We'd known each other for years. A leej often spent his entire twenty-plus-year career in the same company. Sometimes even the same squad. I felt each loss like a blow to the heart, but I knew I didn't have time to dwell about that. I needed to get those of us who were still holding blasters to Camp Jericho, so we could live.

Hopefully we'd get reinforcements at the Army base, maybe even get pulled off the line to somewhere safe. I was confident that we'd win. If the Repub couldn't handle capturing one rebellious planet, it meant that the MCR were right.

They couldn't be right.

Not after what they'd done on Kublar.

No, we needed to win. The MCR were evil. Their actions had shown me that beyond any shadow of a doubt. It was only a question of how many of us would live to see the victory parades.

The Repub needed her leejes to stand fast, hold the line. My fellow citizens needed us, they needed us on the wall. They just didn't want to know how the sausage was made. So, I bit my tongue, saluted, and left Archer and the stunned Arthavan to return to where my section was gathered.

"Listen up, 1st Section," I said. "We'll be merging with 3rd. Lieutenant Challen didn't make it. I'm gonna need everyone to step up here. We move out in five mikes. Check your gear and grab something to eat. Dismissed."

While the men prepared to move, I took a seat on the ground and grabbed a bite of one our disgusting nutrition bars. They looked like what came out of the back end of a donk and tasted worse. But it was packed full of nutrients. In theory, one bar would keep you going all day long. Ignoring all the internal protests from my inner chef, I managed to get the gastronomic disaster into my gullet before I rejoined the troops.

My section ended up pulling rear duty again, but this time the pace was slower. We were limited by our wounded, who had to be carried on stretchers. We had to detail several able-bodied legionnaires to carry these injured leejes, creating a chain reaction of sucktastic fun.

We split up the gear from the stretcher bearers, so no one walked away unscathed. It was brutal, especially on the steeper parts of the mountains. What else could we do? We couldn't leave the wounded; it wasn't an option. Getting to a place where the shuttles could land was difficult, worse than even our cadre in Cally had prepared us for. Other than backtracking to where we'd staged before assaulting the guns, the only places available were the LZ or Kusiba.

"One step at a time, keep it up," I panted, partly to encourage the other leejes, but mostly to keep my own feet moving. At this point I had two goals: getting the wounded to our shuttle and continuing our mission. The mission came first, so we continued heading toward the city of the dead.

The sun was setting when we finally reached Kusiba. While we were en route the shuttle pilot had circled our marching line, ensuring we made it there safely. Not that it made any difference; the tree cover made them unable to provide much by way of support anyway.

"Don't fall back now, we're almost there!"

Once we got to the outer edges of Kusiba, we found an open area and the shuttle landed. The second the ramp dropped, several of the walking wounded from our first engagement staggered off the shuttle. They walked up to the closest officer they could find, me.

Their spokesman saluted. "Sir, Gimp Detail reporting in for duty."

It was a poignant moment; those men were heroes I proudly call family.

Returning the salute, I managed to respond without tearing up. "Welcome back. We need every trigger puller we can get."

Once everyone who could exited the shuttle, we began the process of loading up the critically wounded. There were too many of them, and yet not enough. So many were dead.

Every once in a while, a wounded leej would get hurried onto the waiting bird a bit too quickly for my tastes. They would shout out in pain—the results of too few narcotics and too long a march.

"Gentle now," I shouted as the last of them were loaded up to return to whatever ground support base had been established. I knew they couldn't be flying circles for fun, and with our guys limping off the ship, it was also evident that these shuttles weren't returning to the ships in orbit.

So where were they headed? I didn't know. And when the men asked, I didn't have an answer except, "So long as the pilots know, that's all we need."

That's one of the more frustrating things about fighting a war. There is just so much that you don't know. So much trust is required. It gets hard, especially when things turn bad.

Every wounded brother tore at my heart, but the injured had a chance the dead would never get. Nobody had time to process those emotions, not with an enemy still out there somewhere. The raised altitude of Kusiba gave us a clear comms signal. We'd finally gotten in touch with General Ponce, the 9th's commander, who gave Archer an update. I shamelessly listened in on that conversation.

"Well done, Captain. Your update was received. Adjusting your orders and using those guns saved the Cally Fleet."

"Thank you, General. We bled for that objective, we're down to an understrength company. Any chance to divert from the previous objective?"

"Negative. Legion wants answers from Camp Jericho. Continue the mission, I'll try to get you reinforcements. But the rest of the 9th was hit hard too, so it might be awhile."

"How bad was it?" Archer asked.

"Wave charges the likes of which we haven't seen since the Savage Wars. With orbital control established, we're all sending our wounded to the med bays on the Cambria."

"Any chance some of those fit to fight will make it back down, General?"

"That's up to Old Saw Bones, above my paygrade. Just continue the mission, KTF-style. 9th, out."

I wanted to ask, with orbital control ours again, if that meant we could finally get some kelhorned starfighter support. But I knew that chiming in would be a critical mistake.

The surviving officers and NCOs were thrilled to hear that our actions at the rebel guns mattered, to hear about what we'd accomplished for the spacers in orbit. But we'd paid a steep price for it. And we couldn't expect any help from the rest of the 9th Legion. Our leej brothers had their hands full. Rage Company was on our own.

I quickly moved to spread the good news, hoping that our boys would benefit from knowing how our actions had helped our brothers. We'd done something useful when we'd captured those orbital guns and turned them on the traitorous bastards.

"We broke the back of the ships that had lured us into that mine field," I said. "Even took some prisoners."

"I volunteer for their firing squad, sir," Dwyer threw in, his grim laughter showing little sign of mirth.

"We'll draw straws for the privilege," I replied.

I knew that we needed to boost the flagging morale. Being cut off and on our own was difficult for our leejes. I hoped that knowing what they'd accomplished would give meaning to it all, especially after having lost so many of our brothers.

It seemed to work.

Once we got the wounded onto the shuttle, Captain Archer ordered the pilot to take the shuttle back to Navy. They'd link up with our fleet in orbit while we bunked down in Kusiba, none of us eager to spend another night with the ghosts of the dead. The wounded turned out to be the lucky ones; they spent the rest of our campaign in the medical bay with cute navy nurses. The rest of us, we mucked around in the freezing mountains of Rhyssis Wan.

"Corporal Pool, scout for a secure location," I told ordered, "one we can easily rally at and defend."

"Roger, sir. But I'm thinking we can bunk down where we did last time, our defenses should still be built."

"Alrigh—"

"Negative," Sergeant Dwyer cut in. "If the enemy came in behind us, that location could be compromised. Find a new hidey hole."

We could've used our local allies here; they'd have been able to help us find somewhere to hunker down.

"Stupid point," I muttered to myself. But... I don't know if I was really angry at Archer or at myself for going with a flawed plan so quickly and having to be corrected again by Sergeant Dwyer. I had the thought, and not for the first time, that Dwyer was the one who should have been promoted. Not me.

My leejes searched for a camp site while I searched out Captain Archer.

"Lieutenant Ocampo," Archer said, some of the clarity back in his voice. "We've found some civilians huddled in one of the smaller buildings on the outskirts of town."

"Were they here the last time we rolled in?"

"Not sure. It's possible we just missed them, but I want you along to speak with them."

"They might have wandered back after the cultists culled the city."

"That's a possibility, too."

I nodded and walked in stride with the captain before he added, "Let me do the talking, Ocampo. I don't want another mix-up where we have to explain Republic wartime procedures to the natives."

"Aye, sir!"

It was frustrating, Archer couldn't seem to think outside of the constraints that the House shackled him with. Either way, I had to follow orders. We were honor bound to offer the civilians what little aid and comfort we had at our disposal. It wasn't much, just the advice to hightail it out of town and hide until the planet was secured.

When we got closer to the building where the civilians were clustered, a single Arthava approached us. She was clad in the same fur outfit that the mounted ones had worn.

"Greetings, Legionnaire. My father tells me you are fighting the ones who enacted the great purge on Kusiba?"

"Yes, ma'am, we fight the traitorous rebels of the MCR and their cultist allies," replied Captain Archer.

"Then we are shield family," she said. "Join with us to push them from Rhyssis Wan forever."

"Negative," replied Captain Archer, a genuine sorrow in his voice. "You need to take your band of civilians and leave the region. Once the planet is secure, the House of Reason will send representatives to facilitate the rebuilding of a stronger Rhyssis Wan system, and more specifically the city of Kusiba."

"Your House of Reason is full of mewling cubs," she said, "and holds not to the ways of honorable warriors. I am here to speak to you, a new ally."

I nodded along, knowing she was right. But Captain Archer didn't consult my opinion.

"I can only offer assurances that the Legion will secure your home for you. When we've destroyed the Rhyssis Wan cultists and their Mid-Core Rebellion allies, you can then negotiate with the politicians who will follow. I'm not authorized to offer you anything else. I'm sorry."

15

We left Kusiba the next morning, before the sun had crested the frost covered horizon. Unsurprisingly, we found our civilian allies had departed the city during the night. They left no trace that they'd ever been there, virtual ghosts.

"Creepy," I muttered as I surveyed the abandoned city in the predawn light.

The rest of the legionnaires of Rage Company were still shaking off their grogginess when we marched into the fog. I'd been up for over an hour. Rank has its privileges... right?

"Pick up the pace," Dwyer growled at everyone and no one.

We didn't have far to go, but the terrain was treacherous, and we still had wounded leejes. Nothing so bad as before, but with our numbers so strained, anyone who could march on their own power and pull a trigger was coming along.

Headquarters provided us an assault shuttle to give covering fire, before returning us to the 9th once we'd successfully captured Camp Jericho.

"If we capture it," I muttered.

"There's a clearing three clicks ahead," Captain Archer called into my comm. "Shuttle should be waiting for us there. Adjust course to the following."

I saw a new vector pop up on my HUD. A slight change of direction. Uphill, of course. We trekked on, one boot in front of the other until we reached the shuttle.

The only real assistance the shuttle had been able to bring to the table was a resupply of blaster packs, nutrient bars, and whatever gooey nonsense that kept the medics doing their jobs. At least Doc Tran seemed thrilled with what was sent. Good enough for me. If Doc was happy, then my grunts were doubly pleased.

"Ocampo, get that gear redistributed. LR-01, out."

Archer again, sounding more officious than he ever had. Pain was getting to him. I could handle the asshat mode, dealt with worse in the restaurant. Still, it was a letdown when I needed perking up the most.

We hadn't even handed out the last blaster charge pack when the captain gave the order to move out. More curt sentences, clipped with a funny accent I hadn't noticed before.

"Ocampo, 1st has rear guard again. Check your HUD, the TO&E updated as well. LR-01, out."

In the final reshuffle to accommodate our wounded, I'd disbanded Gladiator Squad. Those leejes had been transferred to Lieutenant Larsen's section and split up, filling out his own depleted teams. Larsen had a formidable fighting force at his disposal. And I… was given all the walking wounded. We labeled this collection of wounded warriors the Gimp Squad. The joke made by those exiting the shuttle was too good not to use again.

One of my new leejes stumbled over what would otherwise be an easy branch to step over. He grabbed my kit to steady himself, nearly taking me down in the process. "Sorry, sir."

"All good, Private," I said, once I righted myself and was sure that we weren't both going down to take a snow bath.

I watched as Sergeant Dwyer halted long enough to let the trailing reservists hobble past, and then reclose ranks. He never complained or grumbled about the men. They were true legionnaires, despite their reserve status. I stood a little taller when I had to stand bucket to bucket with men like that.

The trek out of Kusiba was exhausting. It was a constant starting and stopping as our line of advance struggled to maintain tactical spacing. I can't explain why the constant starting and stopping was more exhausting than just pushing on, but it was.

As if that wasn't miserable enough, we again had hostiles trying to kill us. I don't know how they were managing it, because we never saw them on our HUDs. Probably more of those bio-sig suppressing liners in their clothing.

We should've gotten some warning, but our screens remained blank. Our front line walked right into an ambush. It was textbook—I didn't think that the rebels had it in them. The Repub propagandists certainly never let on that the Arthava were this competent.

"Contact!" yelled a leej from the front.

"Where's it coming from?" I called back, watching my HUD for the battle net to update.

I couldn't sit back doing nothing.

Doctrine said I should hold tight, secure the rear of our perimeter while the men in the thick of it took the brunt of the attack. That was something I couldn't do.

"Movement to contact," I said into 1st's L-comm. Don't know how I managed to sound so calm.

Panting from his mad sprint toward the front of our stretching line, Dwyer said, "Stay back, sir. I'll lead the assault."

"Follow me!" I yelled as I ran, picking up my speed in the steep decline.

I could hear Dwyer curse over the L-comm and that immediately made me second-guess my decision. I wasn't just ignoring his directive, I was ignoring Legion doctrine meant to protect all of the company from disaster.

Luckily for me, I made the right decision; otherwise, the political pukes would've hung me out to dry. No. I'm giving myself an out that I don't deserve. The Legion would have hung me out to dry and they'd have been right to do so. You do what you think is best at the time.

My HUD came to life with targeting updates.

> Combat protocols initiated. Enemy movement detected.

"Now you work," I muttered.

The rebels were hitting the front of the line hard. According to the stream of data now flooding my HUD, casualties were low, but we weren't in a position to meet our objective if the wounded piled up, unable to move on their own power. I turned my section over to Corporal Santos, and then rushed up with Chaos and Lance Squads.

"Try not to do anything dumb, sir," Santos hollered at our backs.

"Good advice, LT," Dwyer added. "Maybe listen to it this time!"

Our tactical assault down the path was horrid—definitely not textbook. No instructor in the galaxy would call it anything other than a lesson on what not to do. We moved quickly down the narrow, winding path toward where our fellow leejes were being hit. I knew from my training that we shouldn't have used the roads to travel, but the terrain didn't give us much choice.

"Almost there," I told the two squads with me.

"Watch your footing," Dwyer encouraged us, as we kept moving toward the objective.

I reviewed the footage from our leejes in contact with the enemy, while trying to simultaneously move up the road. We had to relieve our troops at the front. We needed to give the rebels another target, so the rest of Rage Company could kill them. KTF and continue the mission.

I needed more information to formulate a plan, so I had my bucket's AI run a tactical analysis of the data. The enemy had mined the road ahead, forcing Captain Archer and our front element to halt. The lead element had tried assessing the situation. Textbooks would've told Archer to determine if the mines could be cleared, or if they'd have to go around them. Archer was a point; he'd do it by the book unless doing otherwise was a good career move. Sadly, the bad guys had read the same books.

"Virgil, can we blow the mines and charge through the kill zone?"

"No, it could trigger a landslide. Buried alive under tons of rock, having the life slowly crushed out of you, would be unpleasant, sir."

Damn it.

Skimming the footage, I saw what happened. As Archer stood around discussing how best to handle the obstacle, the rebel Arthava opened fire. The MCR pukes had picked and bracketed the spot flawlessly. It was the perfect spot, situated on a bend in the road, one with a steep drop on the other side. The enemy had placed crew-served blasters on the flanks to pin us in a kill zone, with plenty of trigger pullers in between to pick the rest of us off.

Moving the toggle, I checked every angle on the map interface. Some of Archer's lead element had managed to charge toward the fuzzies, finding cover in the drainage ditch that ran parallel to the enemy's guns. It wasn't much, but it kept them back and bought us time.

"Bear Claw 3, this is LR-24," I called in to the pilot. "Request fire suppression on the following—"

The new pilot cut me off before I could finish my request for air support.

"Negative, LR-24, unless you want a rockslide on your laps. You'll have to shake them off that rise yourself."

I cursed up a storm from the privacy of my bucket, and then began reanalyzing the data. My HUD lit up a vivid blue while I was processing the information. The computer had found an alternate path running parallel to the road, one the naked eye had missed. It was likely how the enemy had gotten to their position. The slope of the path led upward—this had to be how the rebels had reached their location, it had to be. I gestured for my squad NCOs to fall in on me. While they took a knee and assumed the standard defensive position, I reviewed the plan over their squad L-comm.

"Lance Squad, listen up. You're gonna follow me up this path, I've marked it on your HUD. Chaos, bring up the rear. Hold your fire until we're close. Fire only on my command. If they see us, we'll return fire and withdraw. We need to take out that crew-served blaster before they know we're there, or we all die. Let's do this—KTF!"

I headed up the slope, picking my steps carefully. Any little noise could alert the hyenas to our sneak attack. Maybe it was overkill, what with the cacophony of the ambush drowning us out, but I just couldn't risk it. Not with so much riding on our actions. We moved slowly and methodically up the path, the ground slick with the thawing ice as the midday sun melted the ground frost.

The closer we got, the slower we moved, and the louder the battle raged. I could hear the Arthava cultists hurling insults at our leejes down below. Our buckets dutifully translated each one.

I saw red. All pretense of tactical movements disappeared. In a moment of fury, I charged the last few meters up the slope. I might have screamed my own vulgarities in response, I can't remember. I probably said things I wouldn't want my wife to hear come from my mouth, but I really cannot remember the specifics.

What I do remember was tossing one of my last grenades—an incendiary—among the rebels firing the crew-served blaster. The Arthava loader noticed it, but it was too late. It exploded with a massive fireball, sending super-heated plasma in every direction. I'd thrown it dangerously close, but my LARKs protected me from my own exuberance. The unarmored cultists weren't so fortunate.

"Better luck next time, kranker!"

I ran forward, firing my blaster at the rebels in their neat little lines, the rest of my squads following suit. I gunned down a few of them before they reacted. By the time they'd recognized the threat, they had no ability to turn the other crew-served weapon on us. They barely had time to cover themselves from our charge. Running ahead, we were soon among them, standing with them as we fired.

"Get your credit's worth!" I roared at them.

We'd had that motto beaten into our heads during close quarters combat training. In aggregate, the Caledonian monarchy paid two-tenths of a credit per blaster bolt. Charge packs weren't cheap. The Legion had taught us to fire two pairs of bolts into their chest. Center mass, always center mass. Those four shots were to be followed up with a blast to the head of the foe, before we took the fight to the next target of opportunity. Added up, each dead enemy cost the Republic a little over a credit in pure energy.

I kept firing until I was too close to a snarling Arthava to continue using my blaster. I wasn't concerned about being unable to shoot the kranking traitor. A leej is a versatile warrior and we had other weapons at our disposal. I flipped my bulky NM-4 blaster and swung it at the rebel's snout.

"Die!" I bellowed in rage, swinging my impromptu war club at the fuzzy in front of me.

Lance and Chaos Squads flowed around me as they joined the melee. I hit the Arthava in his furry face, screaming my anger at those we'd lost. I cried and swung and cried some more. When I looked down and saw pulp where his head had been, I moved on to the next rebel. He was crouched behind a big boulder, firing at my leejes. He was so focused on those legionnaires closest to the crew-served weapons that he forgot about me. His mistake.

"For Cally!"

I charged ahead, pressing the trigger. I wanted to deliver lethal bolts of energy into the very teeth of these traitorous clints. Except nothing happened. I'd broken my blaster when I'd pulverized the skull of the last dirty twarg. I stopped and checked the battery pack. It was oozing its coolant gel.

Cursing, I chucked it at the enemy and knelt down to snag a one of the blasters off a dead Arthava—that seemed better than going to my sidearm; I wanted the extra power another rifle would bring me. Rearmed, I fired until the target dropped. I advanced the entire time, until I was within arm's reach of another downed rebel. Staring into the eyes of the wounded cultist traitor, I watched him suffer. The battle around me ceased to exist; it was just me and the murderer. I brought the blaster up to my shoulder and fired one final bolt. It landed squarely between his eyes, causing his head to explode.

Ignoring the orange blood everywhere, I scanned for my next target. Except there were none. My leejes had hit 'em like a wrecking ball. Every rebel krank was down. Some were still twitching, but they were down. Rage Company knew what to do, and soon blasters fired their final bolts.

We began to clean up. A single shot and another enemy stopped twitching, and we moved on to the next traitor.

We continued systematically until every single rebel was dead. We couldn't take prisoners and we weren't feeling charitable. Those traitorous twarg haulers owed us a steep debt, and they paid it with a blaster bolt to the cranium. When the last rebel was out of the fight, I moved on to policing up the battlefield.

"Sergeant Navin, have Lance Squad search for anything. I mean anything—let the Brass figure out what intel matters."

"Roger!"

In the end, the only surprising piece of information we found was on the leader of the dead rebels. Well, we assumed he was the leader because his black and white cammies had some shiny emblem on the breast pocket. He had the codes needed to listen to our fleet communications.

"LR-01, we've got a situation here," I said over the L-comm. "Sir, I've scanned the documents with my bucket and forwarded all of the data to you. The important takeaway is that Fleet comms aren't secure."

"Thanks, but we already knew they were listening in," replied Captain Archer.

I was shocked, though I supposed I shouldn't have been. Not like that info was critical to tell a lowly lieutenant like me.

"Sir, Lance and Chaos Squads are good to go," I said, unsure of what else to add now that the additional triumph I'd secured beyond stopping the ambush turned out a bust. "The rest of my two sections are still in the rear and only saw minor action. My boys will be ready to go in five mikes. LR-24, out."

There was a distinctive double-clicking sound, so I knew Captain Archer had switched to a private comms channel. I toggled the switch inside my bucket with my tongue, and sure enough he was waiting for me on a secure channel.

"Fetch," Archer said quietly, "mind if I call you that? Of course you don't. We lost Larsen and Peck. We're the only two officers left alive in Rage Company. I'll handle the front, you keep monitoring our rear. I've given you access to regimental and Legion comms channels, but unless I'm dead, ignore it. We've only got fourteen squads left, and half of our leejes are nursing some sort of injury. It's looking grim, but just keep KTF-ing. Good leejes never die alone!"

"Right, we're always with our brothers," I replied.

"Negative, we're always surrounded by spent charge packs and the bodies of our enemies."

16

"Doc, is he gonna make it?"

Tran didn't bother looking up as he continued applying pressure to the wound on Aidan Maas's throat. It was a desperate losing battle; throat wounds never seem to seal up properly. I didn't expect much, but Doc Tran had worked miracles before.

"Fetch, sir... he's not gonna pull through," Virgil said from behind me. "Seen it a hundred times before. Your men, the living ones, they need you."

I knew he was right, and the doc's body language only reinforced what Sergeant Dwyer was telling me. But I had to ask, hoping I was wrong. I wanted to be wrong. Aidan had enlisted when I did, a chance for a better life. Service in the Cally Reserves gave him access to better housing, better food, better everything. Like many of the leejes in the 9th, he'd enlisted for his family. Sure, the House and all the patriotic prose made for good recruiting holos... but leejes mostly joined for a better life. Or to avoid prison—like I've said over and over, the Cally Reserve Legion is a totally different animal from the Legion proper.

It ended up taking us longer than five minutes to get our wounded situated. We used the last of our skinpacks treating them. We were going through them quickly, dangerously so. We still hadn't reached our objective, and already we had suffered heavy injuries.

Doc Tran stood up, his eyes still fixed on Aidan's throat to see whether the skinpack would do the job. "Sir, that last resupply is pretty much spent after this ambush. If we don't get more med supplies soon, there is nothing I can do for Aidan or for anyone else who gets wounded here on out."

"Not sure what I can do, Doc, " I replied, as worried as he was. "I'll prioritize the supply list in the command HUD interface. Best I can do."

We couldn't keep this up. Our LARKs dispersed the effect of blaster bolts, but that didn't mean we walked away unscathed. Get hit in the right place and you'll end up with a gnarly burn that requires a skinpack. Get hit in the wrong place and we're talking massive tissue trauma and burn damage. Those injuries add up, and over time our medic worked his way through the meager med supplies we'd received.

Tran was unwavering in expressing his need. "Do the best you can, then do better. I need supplies, sir."

He was right. Tran was one of the best combat medics in the 9th and was a nurse when we weren't playing weekend warriors. He had just been accepted into medical school when the call came. Now he played lick and stick for the dead and dying.

"Doc, I updated the command HUD interface. In the meantime, we'll organize another burial party."

His grunt was the only answer I received.

When the last of our wounded were treated, we redistributed their gear for what felt like the millionth time. We had to lighten the load of our wounded in an effort to allow them to keep up. It felt like every time we turned around, we had more leejes getting hurt.

"The entire mission is cursed," I muttered.

"Stop it," I replied.

Great. I was talking to myself. Answering myself. I'd lost it. But I had to push that thought from my head; defeatism was a surefire way to get my boys killed. They counted on me, and I'd personally promised the wives of my original command, Berserker Squad, that I'd bring them home. I'd already failed in that mission; we'd lost Morris, Schultz, Olvera, Moore, and Trueblood. I needed to knuckle down, or more would die.

"LR-01, sir, check your map overlay. There's a valley ahead that a shuttle could land in. We need to get these wounded to the Cambria, or they'll die. Want me to call Fleet?"

He took my blatant hint.

"I'll handle it, Fetch."

Our shuttles couldn't land on these steep hills, but that valley ahead could be their salvation. We could send off the wounded there, before the final push to Camp Jericho. We just had to hump twenty klicks across the worst mountains on this side of the galaxy.

Piece of cake.

Cake.

Great, that made my mouth water. Those nutrient bars weren't cutting it.

I got my head back in the game. I had to focus on the mission. An arduous twenty klicks. On the flats at home, twenty klicks would be an easy day. Not so much in these steep mountains. The cold continued to multiply our misery. But it was worse for the injured; their armor was compromised, their synthprene undersuits torn or burned away, and their bodies were damaged. I can't imagine the biting cold they had to endure on top of everything else they had to deal with. It was bad enough with a fully functional kit.

Worn and bedraggled, Rage Company pressed on to our next objective. The klicks dragged on, one step blending into the next. We kept our tactical posture, but I'm not sure how attentive we were. I often wonder if they'd hit us then, could we have fended off the attack? I don't know, but our shuttle stayed overhead like a comfort blanket. But then again, it was there last time we got into it and couldn't fire for fear of burying us all in a landslide...

"Is it worse than Zastos yet, Sarge?" Santos asked quietly, breaking the monotony of the hike.

"The Op is young, Corporal. The Op is young."

Virgil's answer brought cold comfort that not even the frozen terrain could compete against. Every step brought us up a slope and then down the other side. Going downhill was the worst, especially where the rocks were slick. We slowed down even further to keep from slip-sliding down the slope. Still we pressed on.

"Santos, you ever try the LT's cooking?" Sergeant Michael Conn asked.

"No, I missed that day. How bad was it?"

"Well... I did volunteer for seconds of the mess hall sludge, just to avoid it. Sorry, sir."

"Not my fault you're an uncultured swine, Michael," I replied. "If I'd known, I could've fed you the dog chow we keep for our patron's pets."

We'd been going for four hours, the terrain and our wounded slowing us down to a mere three klicks an hour. The beat-up leejes were barely able to make that pace and were sucking wind from the exertion. Even the able-bodied leejes were slowed by the extra kit they'd shouldered to relieve their wounded brothers, not to mention the stretchers carrying those hurt too bad to march.

We were falling behind, but I made no effort to speed up our line of march. I wasn't sure Rage Company could stand the added pressure. We were tough, but couldn't have gone any faster. We'd need every leej to be in top shape to survive what might be coming.

I remember Captain Archer trying to convince us that there'd be Repub Army guys waiting for us at Camp Jericho, but my gut said they were dead. If we were lucky, all we'd find were their ghosts. If not... the cultists would have a highly defensible position to use against us.

The shuttle pilot, who had popped in and out of covering us from the air to refuel, called us as the sun began its descent behind the mountains. "LR-01, getting dark. We'll start scouting for a suitable bivouac. Bear Claw 3, out."

"Affirmative." The one word answer was all the wounded captain could manage.

I couldn't help but feel that this would have all been a lot easier if Archer had accepted the help of the loyalist Arthava. Would we have avoided the earlier ambush? Could our injured legionnaires have been in a better place if they'd had the tamed charka to ride? I'll never know, but I was again reminded that we'd twice turned away the help of local warriors.

"Damn points," I muttered. "We could've been riding in like conquering heroes."

Instead of enjoying allied campfires, we were in for a cold night. We couldn't risk any visible heat sources, but at least we would be off our feet. We'd been forced to abandon some of our field gear so we could help the wounded, but there were enough mats and mobile tents to allow us sleep in shifts. The thin, insulated fabric would keep us off the cold, rocky soil.

"LR-01, this is Bear Claw 3," said the pilot over our secured comms line. "There's a cavern about a klick northeast of your current location. I've verified that it's clear of enemy activity and sent the data to your HUDs. Our shuttle's running on empty and the cold is messing with the lateral repulsors. We have to get back to the squadron for a retrofit."

"Roger, Bear Claw 3. See you in the morning, we'll move out just after dawn. LR-01, out," replied Archer.

Captain Archer sounded tired and resigned. We were on our own for the night. Not that there was much the shuttle could do against the enemy hiding among the trees, not without risking my leejes. We still hadn't seen any atmospheric fighters. Intel said the fuzzy cultists had them, but they'd been wrong about so much on this Op already.

And then with the Navy having control of orbit, those fighters may have already been splashed somewhere else. I had to remind myself that this was all bigger than me and what I saw. You feel like your battle is the war… but it's not.

We plodded along toward the cavern where we'd be spending another night on Rhyssis Wan, too exhausted to put up a fight if the rebels attacked. I don't think I'll ever look at mountains or cold winter nights the same way again. That planet was brutal, sucking the life out of us. And to make it worse, we'd run out of kaff tabs the day before.

"Bear Claw 3," I called as the shuttle roared overhead, departing from us. "Don't forget the warm kaff with the morning turndown service. Maybe throw in a few donuts you spacers are famous for."

The pilot guffawed like I'd said something funny. "Drink your own kaff, ours is too good for you leej types."

"The end is nigh, and we're out of the heavenly stuff. Lend us a helping hand, spacer," I pleaded.

The thought of that warm brew kept many of us going, except the odd crazies who preferred tea. We tried to be charitable to our less intelligent leej brothers. It was hard, though. Stupidity will only get you so far, even in the reserves.

The thought of the dark ambrosia carried me the last klick toward the cave where we'd bunk down for the night. Every shadow held a cup, every rock a donut to pair with it. I knew I was hallucinating; the cold was playing tricks on my mind. The sleep sack I carried in my pack would be my salvation.

The lower leejes began to grumble as we drew closer. "Are we there yet, Dwyer?"

The sergeant growled his reply loud enough to stave off any other questions of the kind. "Do you like living, Padagas?"

"Yes, Sarge! I get to spend my days frolicking in the mountains with you! And my nights... oh my nights!"

Any response was cut off when Captain Archer enthusiastically told the company over the L-comm that the lead element had secured the cavern. I yelled as loudly as the rest, though our buckets and strict radio discipline kept our cheers from giving away our positions. We'd made it, and within the hour had erected a temporary shelter, secured a perimeter, and were waiting out the night.

I could barely stand upright as my men moved into the mouth of the cave. "Sergeant Dwyer, organize a watch rotation. Leave the wounded leejes off, let them rest."

"Roger, LT."

The rest of us would pay for it in the morning, but our wounded leejes needed to recover so they'd be fit to fight the next day. The narrow avenue of approach to the cave meant if the fuzzies hit us, we'd be toast. Best as our scouts could determine, it was one way in and one way out. Your classic death trap. Our salvation could be our doom if the MCR attacked, but we rolled the dice and prayed for the best.

If there was a bright side, it was that the lack of escape routes did mean that we could limit the guard mount, letting more of us sleep. I munched on a nutrition bar as I set up my tent, before taking the first watch. I paced for several hours, through the first three shifts. I wanted my boys to rest; we'd need to be sharp tomorrow.

When my eyes started drooping, I knew my body couldn't do any more. I woke the relief and crawled into my tent. It was already warm, thanks to the other leejes who'd crammed themselves in. I basked in the joy of that feeling. It was designed to house two leejes, but we'd be cramming four into each of the tents, letting us share body heat. We'd stripped off most of our kit, letting the glorious dome of wonder, otherwise known as our tent, work its magic.

Morning came too soon, followed by cold water and more bland nutrition bars. We were up before the sun. Leaving our warm tents to don our LARKs was pure torture. The cold was biting, sapping your will to live. Taking a morning piss was horrific. We endured it, along with all of the accompanying discomfort, with our usual aplomb.

Once everyone in both of my sections was back in their armor, I clipped my bucket to my kit and went looking for Captain Archer. It wasn't hard. He was one of the few remaining leejes from the 71st in our unit and his shiny armor stood out like a sore thumb.

"Sir, 1st and 3rd Sections are ready to go," I said. "Gomez didn't make it through the night."

Archer nodded grimly.

"Any updates from the 9th?" I asked, desperate for some good news.

Archer ignored my question. "We lost three from 4th Section—Osorio, Bello, and Etrone. They were loners. Wouldn't join a cluster of leejes huddling together for warmth. Individualism is good, but not when taken to the extremes. They didn't have to die. They froze to death from sheer stubbornness."

"I'm sorry, sir. I'll organize the boys to strip their kit. We can send the bodies back to Fleet when the shuttle returns," I replied.

"Negative, Fetch. If the shuttle could have ferried bodies, it would have taken the wounded up with them last night. Bury them, mark the cords, and the Mortuary Affairs pukes can retrieve them later. Make it happen. I'll see about getting the shuttle pilots on the horn."

"Yes, sir," I replied.

Saluting, I headed over to where my boys were eating. I nodded to Corporal Santos, tasking him with getting the bodies buried. We stripped the kit from our dead, cannibalizing their armor to repair the gear of their living brothers. It's what all of us would've wanted, knowing our deaths saved other leejes. It didn't take long since there were enough loose rocks on the floor to cover the bodies. We made it easy for whoever arrived to bring the bodies home and used the cave as an ad hoc mausoleum. We did the best we could, given the situation, and said a few words over the fallen.

After sending their souls to Oba, we got back to the task of securing Camp Jericho. Locked and loaded, we departed our temporary home. Our blasters were fully energized, but I knew that didn't mean much. They'd been periodically shooting half-charges since we'd landed on this frozen wasteland, depending on how cold things got. Good leejes had died for want of a capable weapon. They started working again after being warmed up, but those wasted bolts drained the charge packs.

Resupply was marked a few klicks northwest of us, so I double-checked every leej's blaster. You could never be too careful, but I hoped we wouldn't be hit on this leg of the trip. We made horrible time, but the sun was still up when we finally reached the so-called valley, which was basically a pass between the mountains, where we could offload our wounded.

"Think they'll get the resupply right?" I asked Dwyer over a private L-comms channel.

"Nah, expect the civvies in uniform to mess it up. If you're wrong, great, but we're too low on the criticals. We need food, water, kaff, and ammo."

"At least that pass is all that stands between us and a long trek up the mountain to Camp Jericho." I pointed to a narrow path that snaked up the mountainside.

"Check your map overlay again, sir. We're moving uphill again and the incline is gonna wipe all of us out before we reach the top."

"Happy thoughts, Virgil. Knowing that the end is in sight will lift our spirits."

17

All of us were exhausted when we reached the valley.

I patched into the L-comm and sent a message to Captain Archer.

"LR-01, we should hold back from the valley. Stay under the cover of these trees," I said. "Send the drones out, verify things for ourselves."

"Agreed, send out the drones. I'll patch into the feed and decide accordingly. LR-01, out."

I toggled my tongue and got Padagas on the comms.

"LR-133, drones out. We need to see what's out there," I said.

While Padagas sent the drones airborne, I began checking on Gimp Squad. It had grown to twice the size of a standard squad, as the injuries added up. Doc was tending to them with his usual brisk bedside manner, and most were doing well.

"Not much longer until you men are heading up for a nice hospital ship," I told the group.

The knowledge that they'd soon be getting treated buoyed the mood of the wounded until they were almost jovial. Most of them figured they'd be treated on some naval ship, get a hot meal before being covered in skinpacks and sent back to the field. We didn't blame Gimp Squad for wanting to leave; they were a liability. I knew that they'd feel worse about departing than we would.

"Fetch—" started Padagas.

"Radio discipline, you were trained better, LR-133! It's LR-24—sir, even," I snapped.

"Roger, LR-24," said a chastened Padagas. "I've scanned the area, nobody's out there. Fleet would've alerted us to an air presence, so I focused on looking for fuzzy ground troops. We're good to go, sir."

I didn't bother responding, but sent his update to Captain Archer while surveying the valley. We were a quarter klick up the slope, shielded by the winter fir trees. The valley was wide, maybe half a klick.

"Just because we can't see them, doesn't mean the fuzzies aren't out there somewhere. Stay frosty," Dwyer ordered.

With the death of Top, Virgil had taken over as senior NCO for Rage Company. Nobody had officially appointed him to the role, and he wasn't the only sergeant left in the company. But Dwyer was a naturally charismatic NCO. Given his years of experience, his advice carried extra weight.

"You heard the sergeant—eyes on the prize," the captain growled over the comm.

The expanse of open land was rocky, and my HUD began noting several places where ankles might be twisted. A narrow road wound through the valley, and a few trees littered the area, but otherwise it was a wide-open plain.

Such a weird concept, after several days marching under trees and in the mountains.

"LR-24, move out with the wounded legionnaires," Captain Archer ordered. "Secure an LZ but stay close to us so you can pull back to the tree line if needed. The shuttle will land when you give the all clear."

"Roger, sir," I replied.

"There's some good news, too: the pilots scrounged up reinforcements for us. Load the shuttle, then pull back to us once the ship's airborne."

Archer sounded cautiously optimistic. Good—we needed that after the tough road we'd traveled. Grunting, I double-clicked the toggle to acknowledge his order.

"Dwyer... don't let the boys shoot themselves in the foot while I'm gone. Santos, on me."

"On the way," Santos replied, all business.

"Organize the reinforcements once they disembark, any supplies they bring too. Oba only knows what Fleet sent them with."

"Look alert," Santos called into the L-comm, turning around to look at the gathered wounded. "And smile for those pretty nurses."

"Let's roll," I said, cutting off any excess chatter.

We moved out tactically, scanning the area around us. We kept our communication to hand-and-arm signals. The valley was devoid of activity, and within a few minutes we'd secured a landing zone. I kept it tight, just large enough for an ALTO to touch down. That was good. It meant we'd get reinforced by something larger than the single squad a shuttle could deliver.

When we were set, I used my tongue to toggle the pre-arranged signal to Captain Archer and waited for the shuttle. We felt the air pressure change as the bird screamed down. About time. It was a classic hot drop maneuver, one we'd seen hundreds of times in training.

"Head on a swivel. If the fuzzies are gonna hit us, it'll happen now," Santos cautioned the detail.

Before the dust settled, the ramp dropped from the back of the shuttle and a company of Repub marines poured out.

The leejes groaned.

"Bloody hell, marines?"

"Stow it, Stern," Santos growled before I could. "Don't make me regret not sending you out with the gimps."

Standing up from my crouch, I strode over to the marine commander. Checking my HUD, I saw that he was Captain Stanton. Curious, I moved my tongue, and pulled up his file. He was the commander of Red Company, 3/4th SOAR.

I whistled to myself, thinking, The navy must think we're in trouble if they sent a company of Special Orbital Assault Regiment marines. I hadn't even realized that we'd had any on board, but my experience was limited.

"Fleet sends their compliments," Captain Stanton said as his marines fanned out to reinforce our perimeter. "Said you ladies need the Men's Department to come straighten out this mess you've made."

"That'd be the day the Legion needs bailing out from a bunch of Marines," I replied.

"You ain't Legion. You're reserves."

I bit my tongue before changing the subject. "Did they send you with my resupply?"

Stanton didn't reply, he merely pointed behind him where boxes of our equipment were stacked. I smiled to myself, glad that my bucket kept my facial expressions hidden.

"Captain Archer's compliments," I said, nodding. "You're to carry those boxes to the co-ords I marked on your HUD. Let's establish a secure comm channel between your team and ours. I'll follow you when I get the wounded handed over to the onboard medic."

Turning my back to him, I walked over to were Santos squatted. He wasn't even trying to hide his body-shaking laughter as he observed the situation.

"Damn, LT. That was ballsy," Santos said, shaking his head. "Not saying the hullbuster didn't have it coming, but they're carrying the boxes to the rest of the company? Sleep with one eye open, LT. Those SOAR bubbas are no joke. Almost leejes."

"Maybe our inbred cousins?" I ventured.

Santos laughed again. And that he was a real legionnaire treating me as a peer soothed some of the sting of what the marine had said. He stood up and clapped me on the shoulder, the mirth in his voice leaving completely. "Seriously, I'd still watch out."

I nodded to Santos before addressing my remaining detachment on the section L-comm. "Gimp Squad is loaded for transfer back to the Cambria. We're pulling back to Captain Archer. Let's not draw unnecessary attention. Move out, I'll be right behind you."

I sprinted after my leejes, who were pulling back to the tree line. I knew the plan. The shuttle would return to drop off our wounded.

Captain Archer pinged my L-comm. "Got the word that we're two hours solo until the assault shuttle can return. Something about a delay in retrofitting. Let's not waste time. Once we sort out these supplies, we're going to beat feet across the valley."

"Roger, sir," I said, still moving for the tree line.

Padagas was scanning the perimeter, eyes up on the ridges as we pulled security for the marines hauling the resupply back to the tree line. "Think those Army bubbas are alive, Sergeant Dwyer?"

"Negative, Padagas. They're gone. We're just investigating so the politicos can close out a line item. We'll fill some body bags and wait for exfil. Now close your lips and move your feet."

My team returned to Rage Company, the marines with us. I turned and watched—the ALTO was spooling up, kicking up clouds of snow like a localized blizzard and sending pebbles clinking into the trees and mountainsides. There was still no sign of enemy activity, not that I expected any. The shuttle lifted off, while the captain figured out how he would fit Red Company into our command. We couldn't be commanded by marine officers; the leejes wouldn't stand for it. Heck, even as a sergeant I would not have been happy under the command of a non-legionnaire.

The marine company was full. They hadn't lost people from combat attrition. And a SOAR regiment had twenty squads, four more than a fully staffed leej company normally staffed. I was also pretty sure they didn't want to follow a leej officer. They probably felt the same about following our orders. We weren't SOAR qualified, probably a cardinal sin for them. I was just glad I wasn't the one who had to hash that out.

Letting my mind wander, I almost missed Captain Archer's request for a private chat. I'd been watching the slow lifting of the shuttle.

"You were supposed to maintain the LZ until the ALTO was airborne," Archer snapped.

"Yes, sir, but I didn't have enough men to form an LZ once Gimp Squad left. So, I got my boys to safety and trusted the pilots would beat feet out of town," I replied, frowning to myself inside my bucket.

"Dammit, Ocampo! I keep giving you the benefit of—"

Before Archer could finish, a single rocket streaked out from across the valley. There were shouts of alarm from the marines and legionnaires.

I watched in horror as the rocket slammed into the port repulsor, sending it up in a ball of flames. Immediately the shuttle dipped as though it were going to roll on its side. The nose angled down and swung wide toward the canyon wall as its remaining repulsors screamed at maximum power trying to right the big ship.

And then the canopy slammed into the wall, sending a sickening crunch as the metal crushed and twisted against the unyielding stone. The pilots were pulverized in an instant.

That was the point of losing all hope of the ALTO surviving.

The ship dropped, its remaining repulsors still functioning, sending it bouncing back and forth between the hard ground and surrounding canyon walls.

I looked away, but my mind could imagine those legionnaires on board being thrown about violently. Slamming into each other, literally shaken and battered to death until the ship drove itself firmly and finally into the ground looking like a crushed egg.

Secondary explosions boomed as the ALTO's limited ordnance on board cooked off, catching the aft section of the craft on fire and spewing black clouds of smoke into the air.

They were all dead. All of them.

"Sweet Lord," Dwyer muttered.

And I knew in that instant, that this was as bad as it ever was. As bad as the sergeant had ever seen it.

It was the marines and the men from the 71st like Santos who reacted first. They began calling out targets from across the valley sure of mounting MCR cultists who had done the deed. But visuals were still clear. No combatants showing in the HUDs.

Yet that rocket wasn't imaginary and neither was the damage it wreaked.

I just stood there. In shock at what happened. A million thoughts running through my mind—excuses, vows of revenge... and why. That one came back to me a lot.

Why?

I was dimly aware that my private comm with Captain Archer was still open. I tried to speak. "I... I..."

But Captain Archer was already issuing orders to Rage Company. "We've got to get across that valley! Check your kit and get ready to kill those fuzzy scum. KTF."

The marines were organizing behind Captain Stanton, moving in fire teams up the valley.

My mind focused on the here and now. I sent Captain Archer a request for a private messages. I didn't have to wait long for his reply.

"Send it, Fetch, but be quick," said an emotionally drained Captain Archer.

"Yes, sir," I said, "You need to—"

"'I need,'" growled Archer, cutting me off and mocking my words. "What I need to do is own up to the fact that promoting you to lieutenant was possibly the worst mistake I've ever made. You see that out there? That's on you, Ocampo. You pulled back against orders and gave the MCR the opportunity to enter the valley and get that shot off. LR-01, out."

I didn't have a comeback ready. Truth be told, I was just hit in the face with the cold water of truth and it took my breath away. I had been going back and forth between praising Archer and hating on him for being a point, all the while ignoring my own tendencies to make the wrong decisions.

That had to change. Fast.

I monitored the feed coming from Padagas.

"Hold it steady, Padagas," Archer ordered when the drone hovered over a strange outcropping.

"Yes, sir."

Scanning the feeds, I watched the drones skim the valley toward the missile's point of origin. Glancing to the interface, I saw that officers from Red Company were watching too.

I pinged the drone operator on a private comm channel. "Padagas, go back... check that copse of trees again. Just past it, to the small clearing."

"You got it, LT."

I felt sick, Archer's words weighing down my heart to the point that I might puke. I felt keenly aware that this time Dwyer or anybody else didn't have anything nice to say. No words of encouragement.

Sket... I really fouled this up.

I studied the trees, unsure what else to do and expecting to see a small group of cloaked rebels. Instead, I saw a Fiend-class fighter. It had a forward bulbous nose where the pilot was housed and V-shaped wings that protruded backward. Each wing had an array of weapons and were fed by the barrel-like center that connected them together. This design feature gave it a butterfly-like appearance and allowed the cockpit to detach from the fighter in the event of combat related damages or catastrophic failures.

"You seeing this, LT?"

"Roger, Padagas. Zoom in as close as you can without tipping them off."

Those fighters were so old that they'd been obsolete during the Savage Wars. I'd seen one in a museum once.

"LR-01, are you seeing this?" Captain Stanton asked over comm. "Did you authorize a landing with that thing lying in wait down there?"

"Of course, not, Captain," Archer responded, sounding agitated, but without the spirit to get into it. "We would never risked something like that."

Stanton seemed suspicious. "Seems odd the ALTO didn't detect the fighter, is all I'm saying."

"It's not exactly cutting edge, Marine," Archer said, his voice weary but growing stronger. "They don't have a sophisticated sensor array. Get in, unload, get out. All as quick and cheap as possible. Be thankful that thing wasn't able to tag you on the way down the way it did my boys on the way back up."

I didn't know what to say, so I wisely kept my mouth shut. This meant it wasn't an MCR cultist wielding a heavy launcher who did the dirty work—it wasn't because I had pulled back. It was a ship that, for some reason, was there waiting for us at our pre-secured landing zone.

But at the same time... just because that's how it worked out doesn't mean it couldn't have been that way. I needed to do better.

"Looks like a job done," the marine captain said over comm. "So why isn't this bird taking off. The pilot has to know we're out here."

His fire teams had halted when it became apparent that their rush into the valley wasn't being met by the enemy. Other than what we were seeing on the drone feed, there was no sign of the MCR.

"Could be the ship's grounded," Archer suggested. "Weapons system's all that they got functioning."

We were all under cover now along the valley, waiting as the drones continued their reconnaissance.

"Padagas, pan around a little wider," Archer quietly ordered.

I spotted several more fighters covered with tarps like giant butterflies tethered to the ground. Oba! That would explain why neither the ALTO nor our own sensors had picked up their signals. I was about to tell Padagas we'd seen enough when the enemy spotted the drone, and a blaster bolt knocked it out of the sky.

"I added the data to the HUD map overlay, sirs," Padagas said once his drone was out of operation.

I started analyzing the information. Working on a way to redeem myself, maybe. At the very least thinking of how to use 1st Section to the best of its ability in conjunction with the marines and the rest of Rage. Captain Archer was pissed, I knew, but he hadn't relieved me of command.

Not yet, anyway.

"Virgil, I need some tactical solutions. Any suggestions?"

"Already on it, sir. I ordered our missile mules to prepare."

"Thanks," I replied.

Virgil grunted a half-laugh, making me feel like this new intel—this fighter—had absolved me from what happened. It felt good. Only because it had felt so terribly awful to have been the leej responsible for what happened. Even for those few brief minutes.

"They've humped their Aero-Precisions Missile Systems this far—the leejes are happy to get to use them. They'll probably thank us. LR-57, out."

"Santos, you used to carry an A-P launcher, right?"

"Roger, LT. Don't miss the weight either."

"Then supervise our guys. I want eyeballs I trust on this. We won't get a second chance at those Fiends."

I watched as Santos jogged over to the legionnaires wielding the weapon systems. The launchers each had view screens that popped up, where the user could sight them and use a laser designator to track the target.

"Captain Archer, I have a solution ready," I said.

I don't know why I said it. Legionnaires live long enough to be called old leejes by being smart. Piping up to your CO when you know you're in the doghouse isn't smart. But neither was what I was about to say next.

"I'll volunteer to take a squad out to draw any MCR fire."

Volunteering is the dumbest thing a leej can do, but our situation called for it. I was willing to roll the dice and take that gamble. Unfortunately, being an officer meant that I'd voluntold my brethren too.

"Sir," I repeated, now growing a bit apprehensive to after Archer gave no response. "The missile mules will hunker down with the A-Ps ready. Once those fighters sense a big enough attack is coming for them, they'll either come out and counter-assault or attempt to go airborne. So we gotta go in hard enough to make 'em jump."

Archer sighed. "With the fighters covered by the trees, those launchers will be effectively baffled, and we won't be able to destroy them. And we need to take them down."

I paused, waiting to hear what the captain would say next. That he wasn't screaming at me I took as a good sign.

"All right. Try and flush them out so we can get a clear shot of them once they're in the air. Only volunteers—it's likely a suicide run. And you'll need two squads to sell what I have in mind. Prepare to depart as soon as our guys figure out how to make you too sexy for your own good."

I don't remember my reply. I didn't expect to make it out of this run alive. So, I walked off to the side and waited to see who would volunteer to join me.

Santos stepped forward first. "We're with ya, sir."

"We'll make 'em pay, sir!" added Dwyer.

In the end, everyone tried to join my little forlorn plan. Even knowing it was likely a one-way trip was not enough to keep them from sticking together. Some of the Repub marines from Red Company offered to join.

My eyes started to shine with moisture—just some dust inside my helmet. These men were willing to die for me, and I knew I'd do no less than that for them.

18

I stood alone while a couple of field engineers threw together a bit of machinery that Padagas lovingly called the tricky bomb.

I stared up at the clear blue sky, wondering how long I'd be around to see it.

"Oba, protect my family. Make their lives long and fruitful. Protect my men. Bring them home to the arms of their loved ones. Make my feet swift, my aim deadly, and welcome me into the embrace of my ancestors."

I made my peace with the almighty while the engineers worked. It took almost ten minutes for our guys to create a passible contraption, one which would motivate the enemy to go airborne. It was shaped like some massive explosive mounted to a bunch of welded-together repulsor carts. On the one hand, it looked ridiculous. On the other, it looked like it could blow up an entire mountainside if it went off.

"Looks good." I gave the metal monstrosity a kick. "But will they pick up what we're laying down?"

"It better, 'cause our lives depend on it. We'll find out soon, LT," Padagas replied, the normal boyish exuberance gone.

"Simple plan, men," I said to my ad hoc team as we gathered around the 'super bomb.' "We're going to push our way into the forest, moving this little monster with us."

"And then?" asked a marine.

"Then we hope that the sight of this thing in proximity to those ships is enough to make the pilots crap their flight suits and get off the ground for the missile team to wipe them out."

"They'll first try to stop us from deploying the bomb," Sergeant Dwyer added. "And they have to know we're here and have likely been preparing for an eventual assault. This won't be easy."

I nodded. Waiting at a time like this was a morale killer, so I took a deep calming breath and sent Captain Archer a message over the officers' L-comm channel.

"LR-01, the device is ready. Time for us volunteers to make their peace with Oba, because it'll get frosty real quick. LR-24, over," I said with more conviction than I felt.

"Copy. You're clear to begin."

Toggling my helmet, I set my bucket to record one last letter home. "Ashley..."

And the rest... that's personal, y'know?

After preserving the recording into the memory banks of my LARK, I waited for the other doomed leejes to gather up. The group was made up of grunts from both companies, some of the best men the galaxy had ever spawned. The Brass should've given every one of them the medal, but dead men can't do photo ops. It's a wrong I'll spend my entire life trying to right, but I digress.

We formed up around the floating contraption and moved out. I spread the troops out into a diamond wedge around the device. Had to make it look believable. We moved out at an angle, aiming toward the source of the rounds. They had to know there were Repub forces nearby; they'd seen our drone and ALTO. But they weren't shooting at us yet.

As a precaution, Captain Archer moved our company as far from where we'd made our hasty launch positions as possible. I heard him talking as I flipped over to the command channel send him a HUD update.

"Listen up, Rage Company," Archer said, "we need to angle away from those grounded fighters. We need to move with all possible speed—I want us ready to cross the valley the moment their fighters are off the chessboard."

His calm demeanor under pressure buoyed my spirits. No matter what happened, he was prepared to capitalize on the risks my new detachment was about to take. While they changed positions away from the rebels, our missile mules angled closer as we'd planned. They needed the best shot at the Fiends taking off. Since I was risking my life to give them that shot, I didn't want them to miss.

"Don't act squirrely, Stern," I said. "We need to sell it."

"You heard the man," Santos jumped in, "slow and steady. Move like you've done this before."

My detachment got halfway across the valley, angled northeast toward the enemy. The lead element of volunteers fanned out tactically while four men oversaw the movement of the tricky bomb.

Still no firing. And we were right on the edge of the tree line where the drone had been shot down.

"This is where we get it done, Leejes," I said and looked for the confirmation that we were ready to move.

"One sec," Padagas said. He flipped a switch that caused our dummy bomb to seemingly hum to life.

Just like the real thing, I thought with a chill.

"Ready for that blaze of glory, you heartbreakers and life takers?" Santos asked, poised to run on the order.

"Thanks," I quietly told Santos.

"For what, sir?"

"These leejes weren't your neighbors; you haven't spent years with them. They're just a bunch of reservists. You didn't have to come—"

"Let me stop you right there, sir. The time for questioning who's a real leej has passed. You bleed for the right to don that mantel. Now let's focus on the mission, all right?"

I nodded and shouted, "Move!"

We pushed from our position toward where the fighters were hid among the trees and tarps. I was leading the men into an ambush, and we all knew it.

The incoming fire came in static bursts. Small arms only. Just blaster rifles kicking up the snow and rock around us or careening harmlessly into the "bomb" that pulsed and glided behind us as fast as we could make it.

"Give 'em hell!" shouted one of the Repub marines.

We opened up at the winking flashes of blaster fire near the staged fighters. There were MCR Arthavans there, the regular soldiers, but they weren't dug in. I began to wonder if this was really a trap or just the result of an opportunity too good for the MCR to pass up. That made some sense. If this was the only place in the area an ALTO could land, it stood to reason that it was also the only place where they could get a squad of fighters down and hidden.

I watched a trio of cultists drop under the sustained burst fire of my team, and cursed as a marine dropped, shot straight through his heart. Those marine flak jackets were all right for some things, but I think the shiny armor the Legion proper now wore might've done a better job.

"Don't let up!" Dwyer yelled, pushing up to a tree and using it for cover. He popped around the trunk and fired into the flanks of another MCR defensive position.

This was no ambush... this was the MCR the Republic always talked about. Ill-prepared, tactically unsound. If this kept up, the thought occurred to me that we might actually take the ships directly.

"Fighters are spooling up their engines," yelled a marine. "They see what we're bringing!"

"They're taking the bait," I shouted to my troopers. "Once they're in the air, fall back."

The fighters began to lift off, just skimming above the trees. They pivoted, facing our direction. My heart sank. This had all the looks of a gun run. And we were definitely the targets.

"They're hovering around on us!" I shouted to my team. "Keep 'em occupied until our mules get their shots off. Hold here as long as you can. If you must run, run toward Camp Jericho. Do not lead fire to our rear elements. KTF."

"Hold the line!" a marine sergeant bellowed in response.

"'Til death!" the six other marines in the detachment shouted in response.

And then the gray, metallic fighters screamed toward us.

"Remember to lead the target," I reminded my men.

While Fiend Fighters were older craft, they were gorgeous. Long, sleek wedges of destruction. But our gunners only needed to get off one shot, and the fighters were dust.

"Don't run!" I reminded my leejes. "Keep 'em bunched here so our gunners can get locks!"

The fighters roared toward us, moving so slow that it seemed surreal. Clearly they were taking the time to get us sighted for maximum damage. They weren't aware of the trap, but that didn't mean that our time wasn't at an end. We fired our blasters; bolt after bolt lit the sky. It was a gruesome festival of death and desperation, but it didn't slow down the fighters.

The Fiends began spraying blaster cannons at my team, chewing up the mountainside in fantastic explosions as the strafing run made its way toward us. We kept firing back. Raging against the inevitable.

"Where the hell are those missile locks!" I shouted into the L-comm.

The blaster cannon fire from a craft this old was rail technology. They didn't make the whine of a blaster so much as an electric popping followed by a crack as the slug broke the sound barrier and zipped toward us. And by the time we heard that noise, it was already tearing my volunteers apart.

Men were blown in two, literally cut in half as the spray of fire shot between their legs and continued past them. I saw legionnaires go KIA on my HUD status report. I saw one massive shot rip through two marines unfortunate enough to be standing in a line.

"Hold!" I yelled, never letting up from firing my weapon.

The survivors stood firm, sending their own blaster bolts into the rolling clouds of death. They shouted curses, fired, and died.

The marine sergeant took a round to his neck. Blood and bile flew everywhere, leaving a crumpled body ruined. And I didn't even know his name.

The ships passed overhead. Still nothing from our A-P launchers and I knew damn well those things didn't take that long to target.

"Where the hell is that missile lock!" I screamed into the L-comm. "We're getting murdered here!"

The Fiends circled around for more.

"Keep firing!" Dwyer ordered.

The fighters were moving faster now, which meant their time over target was short. It was our salvation.

They chewed through more of my team. It felt as though I'd been standing there forever, shooting. But it wasn't until that second pass had ended that I actually had to change my charge pack. I had a fresh one in when they turned back for the next pass.

We fired wildly at them.

None of it mattered. Our actions were futile, we didn't even ding the enemy.

We did, however, manage to distract them long enough to allow the missile mules to fire off their A-Ps. The fighters sped past us, eating up more souls when, finally, all ten of our gunners got their missiles into the air. In the blink of the eye, our missiles locked on the targets and destroyed them. I watched as our boys blew the enemy fighters into uncountable pieces and then ducked as flaming pieces of debris began raining down around the site of our grisly last stand.

With the air threat neutralized, I pinged Captain Archer. I didn't first take an account of who else made it through. I think I was stunned to still be alive myself. And… and maybe I just didn't want to face the reality of what happened to so many of those other volunteers.

"LR-01, get the boys across the valley. I'll handle our wounded here. Their sacrifice has to count for something."

I knew I was again ordering my commander around, but I knew we both wanted the same thing, to bring as many of Rage Company home as possible. A mission I'd already failed.

And that's likely why I was so quick to fall back to old habits. The red tinged snow from our Legion dead reminded me that more had died because of orders I'd given.

In hindsight, the grace Captain Archer showed me is beyond remarkable.

But there in that valley, I knelt as the tears started to flow. Only my bucket kept my shame private. "Oba, I'm sorry for whatever I've done to anger you. Please don't take any more of my boys."

All around me their broken and battered bodies stood as gory testimony against me. It was hard, and that realization still haunts my sleep. I barely managed to snap out of it and get to work moving the fallen into a pile near the toppled grav-sleds.

The captain hadn't needed my advice. He'd already had the boys moving out. While they leapfrogged across the valley, I knelt and checked on my wounded along with a pair of marines. It didn't take long, too many of my volunteers were dying.

"You two," I barked at the Marines. "Get that contraption off our grav-sleds. We'll load up our wounded and beat feet. When we regroup, Doc can work his magic." I don't know how I did it, but I managed not to cry as I gave the order.

"Our company has a few corpsman, leej," one of the marines said back. "I'll call in and see if Captain Stanton will let 'em stay a while."

Leaving the two marines to deconstruct the fake bomb, I finally set my bucket to record all of the data from our dead and wounded.

It was something I'd held off on doing. Because I didn't want to know. I wanted to keep the hope alive that the guys I last saw alive were still breathing. But the time had come. We'd have no MIAs on my watch. We would bury our dead, find our missing, and KTF.

It was the Legion way.

I was still trying to ignore the HUD reports listing the names of legionnaires who were reporting as KIA. And then I saw the sight I'd dreaded.

Corporal Enrique Santos.

He lay at an unnatural angle, his shiny armor streaked with fresh blood and his chest unmoving. The pilot had hit Santos center mass and walked the rounds up as its ship passed. The round to Santos's head had shattered his bucket. His face was an unrecognizable pulp.

Kneeling beside him, I grabbed his hand and sobbed. I barely knew him. And when we'd met during our pre-deployment training, I hated him. But now, he was mine.

My legionnaire. My battle buddy.

My brother.

"We'll make them pay," I whispered to him. "We'll make them all pay."

I stripped Santos's body of his personal effects, before standing, sliding the few tokens of his individualism into my cargo pouch. Turning, I saw that the SOAR marines finished clearing the grav-sleds and were loading the dead onto it. I went to pitch in. It was rough work, but we got all of our dead onto the cart.

"Damn shame," Virgil said. He, at least, I'd known survived the attack. He was blazing away the whole time. Right next to me. The Fiends never touched him, not even close.

"Yeah."

"Had to be done though, LT."

"Yeah."

Virgil was still urging me on. Trying to build me up.

Once all twelve leejes were piled up, we loaded the remaining five wounded to the top of the pile.

"Keep up," I told the marines.

Bending over, I activated the grav-sled and began pushing it the second it lifted into the air. I angled us toward where my HUD said Rage Company was gathered. They were on the opposite side of the valley and getting farther from us. Grunting from the strain, I began picking up speed. It didn't take long once we were jogging. We reached the opposite end of the open valley and kept running until we reached the medic.

"Lay 'em down gently," Doc Tran briskly ordered us. He was being helped now by some of the corpsmen the marines had with them.

We unloaded the wounded and continued to where the company was squatting. They were in a small dent in the landscape, taking what cover they could from the howling winds that never seemed to stop. After a while you could almost forget the wind. Until you stopped moving and the cold seeped into your bones.

"Help me strip the bodies," I told my section the moment I rejoined them. "Divvy up anything useful. We'll use this dip to bury our brothers."

I didn't have to tell them twice. We all knew our solemn duty to our comrades. After we laid the dead in the ditch, we piled rocky soil over them and marked the site on our maps. It was sobering. We were losing our brothers every time we turned around.

"These brave men died in the valley, sacrificing their lives for ours," I said. "Let us never forget these heroes. And let's take every opportunity to avenge them. KTF."

Those of us so inclined said a brief prayer over the dead and then we got back onto the trail toward our final objective. We'd make it to Camp Jericho, even if it killed us.

It probably would.

19

Finally, Camp Jericho was in sight.

"Look alert, boys," Sergeant Dwyer ordered.

I scanned for signs of life, searching for anything that indicated recent activity. The rocky area around the fortified position was littered with thick trees, the ground blanketed with snow.

"Don't forget to scan the trees—there could be snipers hiding out," Dwyer cautioned us.

Zooming in closer, I saw that attacking forces would have to cover several hundred meters of open ground before approaching the walls of the camp. The Repub Army had created excellent fields of fire for themselves, and some of the area had been cleared recently. I attempted to increase my bucket's magnification again, but the resulting feed blurred.

Still, I noticed that no guards patrolled the walls, and there were no comm signals. There should've been something coming from the Repub soldiers stationed there, but there was only silence.

"Does anyone have anything?" Archer asked.

"Negative, sir," I replied after it was clear that nobody else was going to speak. "Guard towers aren't manned, but we're going to have to get in closer."

Dithering around wouldn't get us anywhere. With our drones shot up during our last reconnaissance, we couldn't investigate further. Not from a safe distance anyway. That meant we had to enter the facility to get eyeballs on the target.

"All right, halt here," Captain Archer ordered.

We stopped several meters back from the cleared area as he and Stanton, the SOAR officer, decided to send a leej in to investigate.

"Paige, you're up!" Archer yelled.

I didn't envy the man. But without a word of complaint, PFC Paige headed into what we all feared might be another trap. Still, that calm confidence gave me a good feeling about the man. He was one of the legionnaires folded into Rage Company from Dragon. He slowly jogged past me toward the open kill zone between our cover and the camp.

"Screw stealth, get in and get out," I told the private. "Good luck."

Nodding, Paige took off sprinting towards the fortified camp. We all watched, holding our breath as he moved up to the wire.

"Careful, kid," I whispered as he climbed up the solid duracrete wall surrounding the base for a look inside.

It was clear that he was communicating directly with Captain Archer. I watched him climb back down just as the captain's voice came over the encrypted comm we shared with the marines.

"Camp looks empty or abandoned. It's vacant, either way. I smell a trap."

"Signs of a battle?" Stanton asked.

"No sign of a fight," Archer responded. "Our scout saw a few Arthava rummaging through the empty buildings, but they took off when they noticed us looking."

"What does that mean?" Padagas asked.

"It means we can expect the unexpected if those represented anything except local looters," Archer replied.

"So nothing useful, as usual," Padagas mumbled into the 1st Squad channel. Captain Archer wouldn't have heard that, but I did.

"Cut the chatter," I ordered.

"Let's move out toward Jericho," Archer ordered. "We need to occupy and control that camp before dusk."

"Sir, let me take a squad to investigate. I'll meet PFC Paige at the walls, make sure we're not walking into a trap," I offered.

"Negative, Fetch. Our back's against the wall and we don't have enough forces. I won't split our numbers any further. We'll go together and push through any resistance we find," Archer said, the resolve making his voice unusually harsh.

We moved out as fast as our wounded leejes could move. But it wasn't just the wounded. All of us were exhausted, physically and mentally. While Paige had made a straight run for the camp to inspect it from one of its walled sides, there was no way our band of walking wounded would be able to do the same. We had to make for the main gate, which meant one more winding march as the daylight burned itself away.

"Look lively," Dwyer said into the L-comm, but even he couldn't muster the enthusiasm to sell it.

Warily, we approached the winding path up to the camp. It was like walking into a medieval castle, something I'd only seen on holovids in school—knights on horses, armed with swords. I could picture the pre-tech Arthava fighting here with shields and blades—actually, I guess the modern Arthava might do the same given the element we encountered earlier riding charkas with spears.

I know modernity scoffs at such things, but I felt the presence of something there. It was peaceful, which struck me as odd for a fortified military encampment. Oba, it had to be Oba. Nothing else made sense. I couldn't imagine the ghosts of aliens past would side with the Repub, when modern man rarely did.

"Spread out, I want to verify that this place is empty," Captain Stanton ordered over the joint comms.

My leejes didn't need to be micromanaged; we silently moved out through the seemingly empty base. I couldn't see anything that screamed recent occupation, a fine layer of snow covered everything... except for the Arthava footprints. Looking around, it was clear that humans hadn't occupied this fort for some time. There was no activity, just the stillness of nature, occasionally accompanied by the howling of the wind through the buildings. It sounds creepy, but there was something surreal about the place. It felt like home, warm and loving. Odd for the snowy Bevak Mountains.

"Split up by squads," I ordered Dwyer after we'd verified that there was nobody roaming around Camp Jericho. "I want every building swept, then report back to me."

"Will do, LT!" Dwyer replied, suddenly full of pep after dragging throughout the approach to the fort.

I tagged along with Gladiator Squad, feeling like a fifth wheel. We moved to investigate our assigned building, one of the barracks. I admired the stone construction and castle parapets on the rooves as we approached. They were gorgeous, but they hid dark secrets. We entered the building and found row upon rows of bunkbeds in the massive open room. Much like every open bay barracks since the dawn of armies... except this was different.

My HUD told me that the room wasn't heated, that the ambient temperature matched the frozen wastes outside. I quickly forgot all of those details. The room was horrific. It was littered with bodies... hundreds of them. Every bunk had Repub soldiers sprawled out on them—men and women who'd died in their racks. They were frozen in repose, marble edifices to the once robust warriors they had been.

"Oba," Kowalski whispered into comms.

"Check for a pulse," I whispered, afraid to break the stillness.

"They're gone, sir," Corporal Pool replied.

"Check anyway, we have to be sure," I insisted.

"You heard the man, make haste. LT wants a head count," Pool ordered his squad.

Time crawled, but we checked every corpse. Every icy body. We found seven hundred of them, sleeping peacefully. Eternally. They never had a chance, never woke up to fight off whoever had killed them.

"We've seen this before. Test for the poison we found in Kusiba," I ordered Corporal Pool.

"I thought so too, sir. Test strip should be—"

"It's ready now, LT," Kowalski cut in. "Same stuff. I swabbed the ventilation and heating ducts. They were gassed in their sleep."

I was stunned. I didn't know what to say, I just stood their staring blankly through my visor.

"Sir… you need to call it in," Pool said quietly, clapping my shoulder.

"Right… thanks," I replied, nodding my appreciation.

"Sergeant Dwyer… Virgil, we've found one of the RA battalions. Gassed, just like in Kusiba," I told my senior NCO and newfound mentor.

"It's the same throughout the base, LT," he replied quietly.

"What do we do, Sergeant? Tell me what we do?" I pleaded. These weren't my men, but they were soldiers. They were our brothers, despite the different branch they served.

"Only thing we can do, keep fighting. We go way back, Fetch. I know you. You can do this. We make their deaths matter, that's what we do. We make the enemy pay. You readin' me, sir?" he asked, more drill sergeant than subordinate.

"Roger, we make them pay. KTF," I said, ending the transmission.

Switching to a private channel, I called the CO. "LR-01, we've found the basics stationed here. They were gassed in their sleep. We verified that throughout the four battalion barracks and the fifth building housing the officers. Everyone not on duty was gassed."

"Check the support buildings, report back to me as quickly as possible," Archer replied.

He didn't seem shocked by our discovery. He just sounded tired. Not the "I couldn't sleep" kinda tired either. He had the kind men get when they've lived too long and seen too much. It was chilling. His tone was devoid of emotion, detached from mundane things like survival.

"Roger, sir. LR-24, out," I replied.

"Dwyer," I said after switching channels, "we need to check the support buildings."

"Ooah, LT," he said grimly.

We moved out toward the first building, jogging to ward off the chill. I suspected we'd find more bodies, but we breached the buildings like it was just another kill house drill back on Pictavia. Our performance was textbook, even Santos would've been proud.

Oba... Santos.

I couldn't even wipe away the tears, taking my bucket off could expose me to the bastards' nasty gas if it was still present. And even if it wasn't... it was so cold in these rooms that the tears would have frozen to my cheeks.

When we entered the office building a few moments later, we found a gruesome crime scene. Another enduring moment, frozen in time. Literally frozen. The bodies had been killed, savaged by the Arthava. Claw and bite marks showed on the soldiers' bodies. And the fuzzies had shed, leaving evidence of their treachery. Intel would want to do tests, get evidence that a court would approve of, but we knew. It was the MCR and their Arthava allies. Oba help them if we found them before the government did. We'd make them pay.

The Repub soldiers, our soldiers—they'd been left to rot. No, to freeze. They lay pooled in their own icy blood, their horrified expressions etched into my memories. Only the thin layer of snowdrift gave an indication of the passage of time. I don't remember calling it in, but I must have. Or maybe Dwyer called it in? It was a blur, obscured by rage and hate. We moved on, checking the other buildings. We had to know, had to verify that there weren't any survivors.

We'd only searched three of the numerous buildings when our search was called off.

"Rage Company, I want you checking out these defenses," Archer added. "The marines will clear the rest of Jericho. Check out those walls, we want to be ready to fend off another assault if it comes."

The captain pinged our private comm channel. "Ocampo, personally oversee setting up defenses. I'm gonna try to reach Fleet and tell them the bad news. No help from the army today."

"Roger, sir. Same as every other day."

My voice sounded cold, even to my own ears. I wanted to scream, to cry, to shake my fists at the heavens. Anything to make the world make sense again. Instead, I lost myself in my duty. I got to work making sure we didn't have to send any more of our boys home in body bags.

Looking around, I took stock of the empty camp with an eye for defense. It was a squat facility, made of four high walls that were several meters thick. They appeared to have been built from local rocks and blended in with the surrounding mountains. It had a dark gray color that was both impressive and intimidating. The military base appeared to have once been a fortress that was reclaimed from Rhyssis Wan's pre-spaceflight history.

"Virgil, lead a team and search for any arty," I said. "That'll be our best force multiplier if we have to defend this place."

The base had a large armory, five barracks, and various support facilities, all enclosed by those monstrously thick walls. What made the place so defensible was that two of its walls sat on the edge of sheer natural cliffs. It would be extremely difficult to scale those walls unnoticed, leaving only two sides that were approachable for ground attacks.

"Padagas, go see if their anti-missile systems are operational."

In the center of the base was the standard dome of doom, a man-portable anti-missile defense system. It was a strange contraption, not one used by the Legion, and for the life of me I never knew how it worked. One of those times grunts hit the "I believe" button and rocked on. Long as we didn't have to service the blasted thing. Overall, the place should've been able to withstand anything shy of a massive orbital bombardment or an aerial strike. So how had Jericho fallen in the first place? How had they gotten in unopposed to plant their airborne poison?

"Lieutenant Ocampo, continue evaluating the defenses while I take stock of the available supplies," Captain Archer ordered.

"Already on it, sir."

I began scanning the available assets again; we couldn't afford to miss anything.

Walls, check.

Multiple anti-air emplacements, check.

Rapid-fire crew-served heavy blaster cannons, check.

Troops to man these assets? Not so much.

I knew we were in trouble if a fight came to us, though it wasn't readily apparent just how badly. As I ran an inventory from Rage Company and the marines, it made the issue glaringly clear. We'd lost a lot of good leejes. Camp Jericho had been designed to house a regiment and be staffed by a full battalion. We had a company and a half.

"Can we hold it?" I quietly asked Virgil.

"Not on your life, sir. We can make 'em bleed for the privilege, though. Assuming there's an army nearby looking to take this from us."

"Assuming that, how bad is our situation?"

"Sir... Fetch... if we worked around the clock, we still couldn't man all of these guns. We might fully man a quarter of the defenses, if nobody had to eat, sleep, or visit the crapper."

"We really could use those local Arthava Captain Archer turned away right now," I said grimly.

"Yes, sir. But in his defense, a lot of leejes have been stabbed in the back by indigenous allies. And don't forget—those charka riders were using spears. No guarantee they'd be able to do anything but add some numbers and charge the MCR if it came down to it. I understand you want to make sure we can defend this place, but sir, let's just do as ordered for now and take inventory, come up with a plan, and then hope it's all for naught and that there's a shuttle coming down to pick us up and get us gone."

"Roger, Virgil," I said, shaking my head. "Just... got a feeling that's not how it's gonna be. Read the operational history of this planet en route. This base was the first one the Repub manned in this system. The MCR love their symbols. If they get wind that the Repub is back in possession of it, they'll have to force us out. I'd bet my last credit the brass will want us to hold and defend until it can be reinforced."

"Yes, sir. Probably."

It was time to get creative if we were going to come up with a serviceable plan to defend this place. We could utilize the sensors on the cliff facing sides, leaving us manning only half of the walls. The A-A guns would have to be fully manned, though; fighters didn't need to worry about the sheer rock walls that made up Jericho Ridge and there was no word on whether we could count on the Fleet to send down their own fighters should the need arise. There had been scant few so far. And since we weren't anticipating ground attacks from that direction, the anti-personnel guns could be moved to focus on where foot soldiers could attack.

"Virgil, I agree that we can't man all four walls. Why don't we concentrate on the two walls that are accessible by foot?"

"Good thinking. If we set up lean-to shelters against the walls, we could man the fort more efficiently. It's a temporary solution, sir, but it'll buy us time."

"Then let's do it," I replied, thrilled at having found a solution.

Virgil hesitated. "The plan's still overly optimistic. It doesn't factor in the two squads' worth of wounded leejes. Or the five wounded in the valley. They likely won't make it through the night. No matter how we slice it, the math isn't on our side, LT."

"Then help me make 'em pay for every inch."

"Ooah, sir! And an ALTO can easily land inside the camp."

"Virgil, what good does that do us? We need a bird in the air if we want to use its firepower."

"It'll save our butts when it's time to bug out. I'm still holding out hope that we get rotated back or receive more reinforcements here—even if it means another company of marines."

"And you called me optimistic," I said with a laugh.

We needed relief and reinforcements, but there was no telling how long it would be until that was a viable option. Once I had my plan formulated, I dictated it to my HUD computer and sent it over to Captain Archer. It was time for him and the SOAR captain to earn their captain's bars.

While I waited for their reply, I called up my two sections.

"LR-59, get the squads to assemble on—"

Before I could finish, Corporal Pool interrupted, "Sir, he's gone. Santos is gone. I'll assemble the troops, LR-24."

"Roger, thanks."

I bit my lip as a wave of nausea washed over me. Calling on Santos had become something of a habit. He and Virgil had easily become my two top men. In all this, despite seeing his dead body… I was still thinking of the legionnaire as though he were alive. "Okay, Pool," I said, "we ought to give you Dragon Company leejes LR numbers for Rage Co. Only change the ones who have numbers matching living leejes. Solid communication will save lives. Make it happen."

"Yes, sir," replied Pool.

While Corporal Pool gathered up my combined sections, I began assigning sectors and performing other such tasks. I was helping one of the squads manhandle one of the crew-served weapons when Archer pinged my HUD.

"Fetch, I'll be straight with you. It doesn't look good. Fleet can't get us help any time soon and a large mass of locals is headed our way. We've got to hold the line until General Ponce and the rest of the 9th can reinforce us."

"Why can't we maneuver around the fuzzies, link back up with the main body, and take Jericho later?" I asked.

"When Fleet gives you orders, you follow. I didn't ask questions," Archer replied briskly.

Sket.

The MCR force was out there somewhere. I knew the main body of the 9th had them on the run, but that just might push them toward us. If we got hit, it'd be a bloody affair. I wasn't sure we could hold against a determined foe. The best we could hope for was to kill them first and go down swinging.

"Fetch, I've checked your defensive plans," Captain Archer continued. "I've signed off on them and detailed our forces accordingly. Made a few tweaks, nothing too major. Let Corporal Pool get your section onto the walls. Report to me. LR-01, out."

I wasn't sure what he wanted, but when your commander ordered you to stand to, you did it with a bounce in your step. Even when all hope was lost and you had your back against the wall. Especially then. Despite my exhaustion, I jogged over to Captain Archer. He was standing in the command hooch, a Quonset hut design, though infinitely sturdier than what my ancestors had played with. I rapped on the door, sharp and proud.

"Come in," replied Archer.

Quickly checking my kit before entering, I realized there was no way I'd pass an inspection. Giving up, I checked the air quality and took off my bucket. Once it was clipped it to my belt, I stepped inside.

I was in shock. Don't know why, after everything else we'd found. But I still expected to find neat, orderly rows of work stations. Monitors, data entry pads, and other office paraphernalia. It was there, but not how I expected. What a slow learner I was in the ways of war.

The room was covered in freeze dried blood, slashed from a dozen bodies of Repub soldier in fatigues and soft tactical armor. They'd been thrown about and broken like dolls. Whoever had killed them had taken their time. This was worse than what we'd found in the other buildings.

Limbs were ripped off, fingers and toes littered the floor, and several heads were stacked in the corner. Taking a closer look, I saw some of the familiar four fingered blood smears on a few of the desks. Those MCR fuzzies had been here too. It was every bit as grisly as what I witnessed in those apartments on Kusiba, only much worse. These were our men, ours.

My stomach immediately emptied itself of its nutrition bars and water. "What the..." I said, rubbing the slime from my lips and chin. "Sorry, sir. It's just..."

Captain Archer had a kind, understanding look on his face. "I know, Fetch, I know. No shame in puking. You've seen too much in the last hour."

"Sorry, sir." I looked around for a maintenance closet. "I'll get that cleaned up."

"Don't bother," Captain Stanton replied. "Does this room look like we're about to set up HQ any time soon?"

"No, sir." I tried not to stare too closely at the carnage. "I'm not sure we have the men to spare for another body detail..."

"We don't," Archer said. "These boys and girls will have to stay this way until, well, until whenever General Ponce relieves us."

"This looks like more MCR work. More personal than gassing someone in their sleep."

Archer nodded his head. "Probably."

I didn't envy the intelligence officers who would have to investigate this. The whole camp was like something out of a horror entertainment.

But the captain hadn't called me to see the brutality of the cultist demons; we'd already seen that in Kusiba. There had to be more here.

"Sir, they tortured the army boys, but what could they hope to gain? This was just a security garrison. Why these men? The krankers gassed everyone who was off duty. They killed those in the HQ, it was bloody, but efficient. Why torture these men? Unless there were covert ops here, these troops didn't know anything special. What am I missing, sir?"

We'd managed to enter the base, just like Fleet had ordered. As expected, everyone was dead, but what significance did that hold? Sure, we'd encountered a few local Arthava. They were scavengers, looters picking at the carcass of a once proud warrior station. It didn't give me any indication of what Archer was hinting at. I grew frustrated.

"What you are missing is what was taken," Archer said. "Those heads stacked up over there belong to the regimental officers of the 124th Mountaineering Regiment. They were experts at mountain warfare. No way they lost this fort without an inside man. And those heads, notice anything?"

"They're not attached, sir?" I asked.

"The eyes, Fetch, the eyes," said Archer with more enthusiasm than the situation warranted. "They took the eyes. Why would they do that?"

"Retinal security checkpoints," I exclaimed. "They'll get senior officer clearance with those peepers. Wait, won't that be changed now that we've verified their demise?"

"Now you're catching on," Archer replied, his demeanor changing. He'd become increasingly grim as he coaxed me along to the correct answer.

"Yes, sir," I replied.

"Captain Stanton and I have sent our reports up our respective chain of commands already. You needed to be brought into the loop, in case we bleed more officers when the Arthava hit us. There'll be a lot of counterintelligence work that comes after this and the three of us are the eyewitnesses who might help it go a lot faster. No telling what the MCR will do with whatever it is they're after."

"The MCR is inbound?"

"We're operating under that assumption. Fleet verified that troops are coming our way, but couldn't tell us more than that. But the force engaging the 9th broke off contact and we're sitting in a possible path of retreat. If the 9th is giving them hell the way they ought to, it might be that falling back to this camp is the MCR's best hope of surviving. We will deny them that opportunity unless the Fleet provides other orders."

"Yes, sir," I replied, chilled by the prospect of the worst possible scenario edging closer to reality. "We'll make 'em pay, sir."

"For every bloody inch. Once you've set guard mount, start looking for anything we can use. Don't forget the kit from the army personnel. It's likely still in wall lockers or in the armory. We'll need it soon."

I saluted, clearly dismissed. When I got to Captain Archer's section, I pulled aside the NCO in charge of Viper Squad. After a quick explanation of where I wanted him to position the troops for his section, I jogged over to where Corporal Pool was at work. He was supervising the repair of the LARKs and weapons from my leejes, tasks I should've remembered to assign my squads.

"Pool, we've already cleared the camp, but we've been ordered to search the facility for anything useful. We need beans and bullets, and we need 'em fast. The leejes have to finish their repairs as quickly as possible, we're expecting company soon. I've uploaded a task list to your HUD. I'll shadow Berserker Squad, you take Gladiator Squad. I want leejes moving to their assigned defenses in five mikes."

An entire army regiment destroyed. A base too big for us to defend. An MCR operative working from the inside to let this all happen… and no sign that this problem was going to fall to anyone else. This was all just great. Each hour on Rhyssis Wan seemed worse than the one before.

20

As rapidly as humanly possible, we all headed off to our assigned tasks. I followed Private Padagas, who'd been transferred to lead Berserker Squad. We'd lost so many NCOs that privates were leading a few of our squads. It was brutal, but legionnaire NCOs led from the front and often suffered the highest casualties when the fighting started. Many of the non-point officers operated the same way. That had certainly been the case with Rage Company.

"Padagas... Remo... you're doing great," I said. "Just sound like you know what you're doing. Fake it 'til ya make it."

"That explains a lot, LT."

He laughed as he answered me. Maybe there was still some of the defiant boy left inside. Padagas had matured since we'd arrived on Rhyssis Wan. Combat having forced him to grow into the legionnaire I'd always suspected he could be. His childish antics disappeared, replaced by a grim determination and a thirst for vengeance.

Archer had assigned me to personally clear the armory, so I followed Berserker Squad and headed for that building. We found what we'd expected when we got there. Racks of blasters, stacks of power packs, and extra sets of the soft black armored vests worn by Repub Army soldiers. It was telling that the MCR didn't take any of this. It added validity to the idea that what they were after in bringing down Jericho were retinal clearances from the officers, because they left behind a lot of useful equipment. Useful, but unfortunately not of the type we could use to repair our LARKs. But at least we wouldn't run out of blasters or charge packs.

Scanning the room, I saw a few crew-served blasters. There was no sign that the MCR had even come in here until I saw it... the decapitated body of the armorer.

Why?

His peepers wouldn't grant clearance into anything useful, right? The death looked gratuitous.

"Damn, Lieutenant," Padagas said as his eyes rested on the gory scene. "They took the time to do that but didn't take no weapons? Seems fishy."

"LR-133, secure the blaster packs first," I ordered. "We need to get that to the walls pronto. Then snag those crew-served weapons. I want an inventory of functioning blasters, and how many fully charged universal battery packs we have. Our half-charged bolts are burning through our energy reserves."

"The more we warm up the NM-4s, the less of a problem it is, LT."

"I know," I said, "but we could use extra on our walls, so that's our second priority. Swap out these Miif-7s with our Caledonian blasters. That'll help some, though it's only a drop in the bucket compared to what we need. When we're done, we'll handle processing the remains of the armory. I'll look through the records for anything I can send up the chain."

After I'd given Padagas his orders, I went searching for the armorer's terminal. I was right to trust him to get the squad moving. I tried observing him, while trying to look inconspicuous. I saw that Padagas was leading most of the squad out to the walls with all the large blaster packs for the crew-served weapons piled onto a grav-pallet.

"Hold it steady," Padagas hollered. "They're useless if you break 'em!"

Thankfully the pallets had been left in the armory, and Padagas had wisely chosen to repurpose them. He'd also managed to get half of the crew-served weapons balanced precariously on top of the pile. Nodding to me, he led the gear toward the walls, with two leejes remaining to start counting the blasters.

"Captain Reyes would be proud of you," I told him. "He always said you had potential."

I was proud of him too. He'd adapted to the situation like a seasoned professional. I was confident that he could handle things, leaving me to focus on my own duties.

I found the data terminal right where it was supposed to be, and started to see about getting my way in. I wasn't sure if my leej security codes would work, and I was desperately trying to remember what we'd learned in training for such an event. It turned out to be for naught, as the terminal was left open and unsecured.

And empty.

Someone, likely the MCR who had raided the base and done the dirty work to the officer corps, had been here and left the system in near ruins. The memory had been erased, but I knew that didn't always mean it was gone. Scanning through the administrator's menu, I found the folder full of recently deleted files, and restored all of them. They knew what they were doing... but they weren't tech experts by any stretch.

A quick glance through the records showed what they were trying to hide. The regimental XO had been funneling heavy weapons, A-P launchers, and missiles along with other controlled armament. He'd tried to clear the cache of data when he'd defected.

I had to pause and take it all in. One of our own, a senior officer in the Repub Army—named Major Sabo, if you'd believe it—sold the Repub out. He'd sure as shootin' murdered his entire command. And the damning docs in front of me told me exactly how many credits he'd done it for.

"Was it worth it?" I asked the empty terminal.

Oba, but I hoped I'd get to be the one who hunted him down. I knew that would be a Dark Ops mission, but seeing the ripped bodies of the other officers pissed me off. Those dead soldiers were his people, men he'd worked with, lived with. He'd set them up to be tortured to death without a second thought.

How could anyone in command do that to his boys?

"Was it worth it?" I asked, growling louder this time.

I took a calming breath and heard several of the leejes from Berserker Squad returning to the armory for the rest of the crew-served weapons. When I was sufficiently calm, I toggled my tongue to get onto the officers' L-comm and reported in.

"LR-01, I know how the base fell. The regimental XO defected to the rebels after selling them our heavy kit. I've sent the full data pack to Fleet and the 9th. I've sent you and Captain Stanton the details as—"

BOOM.

I was thrown to the ground, my body landing among the mutilated remains of the former armorer. An explosion had detonated inside the armory, leaving behind a tangled mess of blood, gore, bodies, LARK armor, and twisted metal. Where two leejes had stood counting blasters, there was now nothing.

Groaning in pain, I stood on shaky legs and struggled to regain my equilibrium. I was covered in the remains of whoever had been on duty when Sabo betrayed Jericho. Fortunately, I'd put my bucket on to talk to the commander. That bit of dumb luck prevented me from getting my clock cleaned by the explosion. I tried to talk, but I couldn't hear myself over the ringing in my ears. I looked around, trying to focus on the world past the pinpricks of light.

"Sir, are you okay?"

I recognized that voice, but I couldn't place it. I didn't remember the name, but I knew I'd heard it before.

Padagas.

He was still talking, but the ringing was lapping at my ears in waves. I couldn't hear every word and understood even less of what was said. I felt him shaking my armor, I just couldn't figure out what he wanted. That's when my bucket kicked in with air, washing my head in a cool breeze. It worked... I began to slowly refocus.

"—and your LARK is reporting a mild concussion, LT. CO wants you to report in person; he's at the TOC. I'll handle things here, sir."

"Wha—what happened?" I said, not sure how loud I was saying it.

"Some kind of booby trap," Padagas said, and I could tell in his voice that he was blaming himself for what had just happened.

I nodded and patted Padagas on his armored shoulder. This kind of situation, and the guilt associated with it, came with the territory. Didn't make it any easier, but it's the truth.

Still a little loopy, I didn't think to reach Archer over L-comm and report in. I just stumbled toward the TOC. Not so bad that the legionnaires running toward the blast stopped to help me on my way, but enough to turn a few heads.

"You okay, LT?" one called out.

"Fine," I managed. "Don't go in there until Padagas gives you the all clear. Traps."

My gait was unsteady, and it took me a while to make it to the command center. It felt like I had the world's worst hangover. At least those involved the pleasurable taste of whiskey, or other delicious alcoholic beverages. Instead, I'd been blown up by a booby trap left behind by the traitorous Major Sabo. Now leej blood added to the fratricide that stained his dirty hands.

I'd worked myself up to a righteous fury, and I wanted blood. Thankfully that distracted from the pain. I made it to the TOC and found the two company commanders talking to the 9th Legion's commander. I'd never met General Ponce, and I would've been perfectly happy to have kept it that way. But I walked in to find Archer and Stanton chatting with him over a live holofeed. When I realized what was going on, I quickly halted and snapped to attention.

"At ease, Lieutenant Ocampo," commanded General Ponce. "We've been waiting for you to arrive. Tell me what you found. We ought to at least converse face-to-face if we're going to accuse a fellow officer of treason."

Nodding inside my bucket, I started to speak.

"Bucket off," Ponce commanded. "I want to look into your soul when you report a finding of this magnitude."

I quickly took my helmet off, clipped it to my belt, while trying to remain at attention. I was still dizzy, and I wasn't as rigid as I would have preferred in retrospect, but it was the best I could do.

"Sir, Lieutenant Benjie Ocampo reporting in to the general, as ordered, sir."

"Enough of that crap, son. There's a war going on. Just tell me what you found in the armory."

"Yes, sir," I replied promptly. "When I reached the armory, I found several racks of Repub Army blasters, crew-served weapons, and stacks of ammunition. None of the larger armaments were there, and the armorer was decapitated. The armory terminal had been wiped—"

"Then how did you determine a senior officer was a traitor?"

"Whoever did it forgot to or didn't know how to fully delete it from the cache, General. I retrieved the data and sent that information up my chain of command—to my commander, to you, and to Fleet. The records indicate that Major Sabo and the armorer sold the weapons to local cultist cells. The rest of what was in my report was my speculation, based on what we found throughout Camp Jericho; the barracks, the support buildings, the TOC and the armory."

"Do you certify that, on your honor as a legionnaire?" demanded General Ponce.

"Yes, sir," I replied.

My answer came out stiffer than I'd intended, and General Ponce's frown indicated his displeasure. I'd clearly been dismissed, so I remained at attention and waited. Both captains and General Ponce continued for several more minutes, before the conference ended.

When Ponce cut the feed, Captain Archer gave me a weary smile. "You did all right, Fetch. We need to get everyone ready to man the walls and set up a rotation so we can let our leejes eat and sleep. I sent a brief to everyone in Rage Company to watch for more traps. Let's not have any more surprises if they can be prevented. That issue should be resolved soon, and we'll have the base secured in the next several hours."

"And the bodies, sir?" I asked. "We need to bury our army brethren. Our leejes too, if there's anything left of them."

Captain Stanton stepped in. "Negative, Lieutenant. My marines are piling the dead into the kitchen's freezer. Once that's full, we'll have to stack 'em outside and let the mountain freeze 'em. That'll hold them over until Fleet can retrieve their bodies. Focus on getting the defenses manned, or we're all screwed."

I saluted and turned to leave the TOC.

"And Lieutenant," Captain Stanton said, stopping me at the door.

"Sir?"

"The 9th confirmed that they've pushed that MCR force toward us. We can expect to get hit in the next few days. Make sure your leej boys are ready. But if you krank it up, SOAR will swoop in and save your bacon."

I chuckled on my way out the door. I had a lot of work left to do if we were going to be ready to hold the line. I felt overwhelmed by it all—utterly unqualified to prepare the defenses for Camp Jericho. My leejes were counting on me. I couldn't let them down.

But I knew what to do. My drill sergeants had made it simple enough. Shoot first, shoot often, and don't stop until they're dead. Not just dead, but good and dead. And never show mercy. Save that for Oba.

21

In the end, preparing the defenses for Camp Jericho wasn't as difficult as I'd feared. The few remaining senior NCOs handled their squads, showing those new to the position like Padagas what to do. Every leej worked harder than they'd ever done before.

I was beyond proud of them. We were all so tired, but those men didn't let it show. Didn't complain—well, hardly complained.

We had our backs against the wall and knew that we would fight or die in this place. As far as last stands went, Camp Jericho seemed suited to the task. Its defenses were formidable, even at less than full strength. Of course, I'd prefer not to make the stand at all; I'd rather burn the rebels in the righteous fire of an orbital bombardment.

Sadly, that wasn't in the cards. The ships in orbit weren't destroyers and weren't capable of sending down the kind of pinpoint accurate fire the Navy proper could have done. I found myself wishing the monarch had won his little tiff with the Republic and kept our relatively useless fleet protecting New Cally. Just one destroyer would have completely changed the face of this assault.

But it was no use dwelling on what was beyond our control. We had our orders and would fulfill them or die in the attempt. We were legionnaires—it was our way.

"Got the boys prepped, LT," said Corporal Pool. "Watch rotation is set, and now we wait. You look beat, sir. You covered most of the night watch in the cave. Go get some sleep. You're no good to us if you fall asleep when it hits the fan."

I took his advice and climbed into my tent—everyone was racking out close to the line, despite there being otherwise serviceable and warm barracks in the base. One of my leejes had set the tent up, and there were several other leejes already in there snoring. It was loud, but their body heat made it nice and warm. I fell asleep the moment I crawled into my sleeping bag and was out for several hours.

Sadly, that rack time seemed like only seconds. Corporal Pool woke me up for breakfast. I felt a lot better, my equilibrium had improved, and now I had hot food in my belly. The boys had raided Jericho's fridge and made us synth eggs and bacon. And kaff, real honest-to-goodness hot kaff. Not synthetic, real. For that brief moment, my world was heavenly. I was among my leej family, and we were savoring the feeling of truly being alive. Combat does that to you, but even in retrospect I'd hold that meal up against any of the finest gourmet dishes I made back home.

"Morning, LT," Padagas said.

I didn't reply, my mouth was full. I merely grunted. When he didn't continue, I waved my left hand, splashing kaff, indicating that he should continue.

"I sent a SitRep to your HUD," he said, the pain evident in his voice. "I've also updated our losses. We lost most of the squad, sir."

My eyes opened wide, registering the shock of what I'd just heard. At the time, I only saw two legionnaires get hit by the blast and I hadn't checked records before meeting with the general and then catching some sleep. Almost an entire squad. Oba...

"I'm sorry, sir." Padagas was close to crying, close to completely breaking down. "I... should've been there with them. I'd stayed behind to plan where to drop the supplies... and caught up right after the bomb detonated. If I hadn't done that, I would've been by their side in the end. I—I should've died with them. I'm sorry I failed you, failed them."

I knew exactly how he felt. But we couldn't afford that, not when the final showdown was coming. Besides, his guilt was nonsense. I had to buck his spirits.

"Padagas, you didn't do anything wrong. You didn't fail them. The traitorous scum who sold out his own regiment did. The XO in charge of this facility, a Repub Army major, sold weapons to the MCR. He then let those terrorists in to murder his brothers and booby-trapped the place. He set out to kill anyone who investigated his crimes. Take heart. Hold on to that rage. When this is done, we will hunt down this traitor."

"Yes, sir," he said, sniffing.

"Good. I'll retire Berserker Squad, since there aren't enough of us left. You'll fall under Corporal Pool in

Gladiator Squad. Salvador will join you. And don't worry. We'll make them pay. KTF."

"KTF, sir," Padagas replied despondently.

We spent hours fine-tuning our defenses and overlapping our fields of fire. The morning dragged on. Sergeant Dwyer rotated leejes through the chow line and ensured that everyone was rested. It was the best we could arrange. As afternoon morphed into early evening, Rage Company flagged. If we didn't get reinforcements soon, our leejes would start slipping. If that happened, we'd begin to become more of a danger to ourselves than to the rebels. I couldn't let that happen.

"Anyone not on watch, take ten," I ordered. "Send runners to the mess tent for hot kaff."

As fate would have it, nobody received their breaks. The passive sensors began chiming incessantly. We'd strung them along the pathways into the camp on the way up, the best early warning system we could manage. Rebels were out there. We just couldn't see them yet.

Headquarters was on top of it instantly, ordering all units to their stations. "This looks like it may be the lead elements of the kelhorns the 9th drove off. Everyone in position."

"Hold your fire until you have a target, Leejes," I grimly ordered the Rage Company L-comm. "But when you have a positive ID, KTF!"

I wish I could've been more creative. Rage Company deserved a better motivational pep talk than that, but it was all my fog addled brain could come up with. I focused on the rocky wooded areas in front of Jericho's walls, and flicked through the various filters—infrared, heat sensors, chemical signatures, motion detectors, and magnification functions. Nothing, yet.

I was so distracted looking for the cause of the alert that I missed the aerial signals indicating an incoming attack.

"Fighters coming in," a marine yelled into the comm.

Several fighters, Preyhunters, screamed toward us. The anti-air defenses were already at work targeting them, and soon the base rocked as they sent their AI-assisted bolts into the snub fighters. MCR ships exploded in flames, littering the trees and mountainside with their smoldering wreckage. But a few got through and raced overhead, their cannons spewing bolts, strafing the leejes and marines manning the walls of Camp Jericho. The bolts slammed through the defenders of the Repub fortress. I watched the vital signs of several of my leejes go flat, and the wounded screamed.

"Medic!"

"Doc, down here," some called from the base of the walls.

"Virgil, help Doc Tran!" I shouted into the chaotic L-comm.

The A-A chased them as they passed overhead, splashing them before they had the chance to make another pass. I was thankful for how the defenses took the airpower out, but we really weren't in a position to lose more men. That initial rebel punch was brutal, but we were armed and angry. They bloodied our nose again, but we finished the fight for those pilots. We cheered as we watched the fireballs crash to the ground.

"Get the wounded over to the aid station," Archer ordered. "Everyone else, get ready... they're not done with us yet."

We didn't get to rest for long. The MCR charged the walls before the last ash from their flaming fighters had fluttered to the ground. Astride their howling charkas, they fired blasters wildly, as if hoping to blow their way through with a single blaster bolt. It would've been comical, if it weren't for the earnest nature of the deadly threat.

"Look at 'em go," Stern hollered, whooping in joy.

"Keep firing!" Dwyer bellowed.

We poured an unending stream of fire with weapons that hadn't been half-incapacitated by the cold. This was a much different fight. The killing zone was piling up with Arthavans and charkas.

But they continued to press, seemingly unfazed by the damage they endured. Their tactics reminded me of something out of the historic holovids, but their blasters were decidedly modern. Bolts sizzled by my bucket. Only the height advantage that the walls of Camp Jericho afforded us prevented the fuzzies from scoring a solid hit. We weren't so restrained: our forces rained holy hellfire on them.

"Got one!"

"I'm ahead of you!" Salvador gleefully shouted.

"Aim, damn you!" Padagas yelled.

The fuzzies dropped like smoked mummy-bees, but more always seemed to pop up to replace them. We spewed our rage, hungry for vengeance, sending our anger at them one blaster bolt at a time. It was nice to finally have a defensive advantage. We'd been ambushed so many times, to dish it out this way was cathartic. I enjoyed the target practice—it was like being at the local county fair, shooting targets for cheap prizes. I lost focus on the situation, we all did.

"Too easy!"

Padagas was right. This was a slaughter-fest.

We never questioned why they'd behave so insanely. We should have, because they caught us with our pants down again. They'd expected the fighters to do more damage, but the subsequent assault had been intended as a distraction from what came next. It was devious, just what you'd expect from the traitorous scum.

The Arthava rebels attacked in cyclical waves. They'd rush, we'd beat them back, the rebels would break and run for cover. And the process would repeat, again and again.

"Watch your charge packs," Dwyer cautioned us. "They'll be back."

The fields around the walls of Camp Jericho were strewn with the bodies of dead and dying rebels. We'd only lost one leej, who'd been taken down with a lucky shot. It'd hit him in the neck joint on his armor, right where the extreme cold had compromised it. His death barely registered—my sole focus was on throwing as many bolts as I could at the Arthava. I was so focused on the enemy on the other side of the walls that I missed Captain Archer. He'd had to use his commander's override to isolate my bucket.

"LR-24, maintain your situational awareness. Rebels are inside the kranking camp! Grab a squad, find out where they're getting in. Shut it down, now. LR-01, out."

Shaking off the war fog, I got Corporal Pool on the L-comms.

"LR-59, bring Gladiator Squad to me. Rebels are inside the lines, and we're going hunting."

While he got his squad ready, I sent an update to the two company commanders. I didn't want any friendly fire incidents.

"Sirs... request permission to re-task the crew-served teams. I need to get them to turn their focus inward."

"Make it happen, but be quick about it," Archer replied.

Toggling channels, I called Dwyer. "Virgil, the leejes are yours until I get back. Don't let 'em waste rounds."

"Wouldn't dream of it, LT. Don't get cocky—the attack on the outside of the camp was likely a diversion. This could be a sizeable force."

"Agreed, I have the crew-served turning their focus to protecting our compromised internal flank. If we stop the assault from within, we can still win the day."

"We can and we will, sir. KTF!"

I knew the stakes. Everything we did was contingent on Rage Company holding until reinforcements arrived.

I turned to Pool and ordered him to follow me. By using the company-wide HUD network, we found out where the enemy had been sighted, and headed in that direction.

"Speed is key, Pool. Fuzzies know we're here already—stealth isn't something to worry about."

"Ooah, sir!"

We rushed from one covered location to the next until we neared the row of barracks on the other end of the camp. I could see groupings of dead MCR—presumably killed by the marines inside the camp.

"Double-time, leejes," I said, feeling lucky to not all be dead right now with hostiles having made it that far under our noses. I didn't look back; I knew my leejes were following. Most of the enemy signatures seemed to originate from the barracks closest to the armory. A sudden intensity of the red dots indicating hostile biosignatures on our HUD convinced me that the breach had to be from there.

"Has to be a tunnel," Pool said, "but how did they manage to dig through solid rock into the camp without getting caught, LT?"

"Doesn't matter—they'll die either way."

Still, I reported what we suspected back to command. Just in case.

We got to the rear of the barracks and got visuals on no less than fifty confirmed fuzzy warriors. I know the Legion always talks about being as good as five fighters for every one leej, which should have made my single ten-man squad even. But these were exhausted warriors going up against fresh MCR. And with every second we dallied, there were more coming in through the breach. I didn't have a lot of time, and we weren't in the line of sight for support from our crew-served weapons. I needed more men. But if I took them from Rage Company, we wouldn't be able to maintain our portion of the defenses.

"Red Company Actual, requesting reinforcements to my location," I asked over the marine channel. "Counting fifty confirmed rebels near the source of the breach. We are moving in position to engage. Need as many marines as you can spare. LR-24, out."

I knew Captain Archer would be pissed that I'd jumped my chain of command, but we didn't have time to play politics. I needed trigger pullers, and I needed them now. I assumed that the bodies would be sent, so I didn't wait for the official confirmation. Instead, I ordered teams of two leejes to the roofs of the three surrounding barracks. I couldn't cover the entire space, but at least I could have Gladiator Squad sniping them from the only heights available to us.

With six of my ten leejes climbing to the roofs, I took the remaining four.

"Pool, join Kowalski on the rooftop. If I buy the farm, you're in charge."

"Moving, LT!"

"Padagas, you're with me. If we run into any captured tech, I'll need you to decrypt it."

Selfishly, I also wanted a leej I trusted watching my back.

I needed to keep the enemy bottled up. Other fuzzies were already roaming the base, but for now I had to focus on stopping them at the source of the incursion. We could seek out and destroy the rest of those kranking murderers later.

"Make your shots count," I told Gladiator Squad.

Scanning the area, I looked for anything which could be of use. And then I saw it—a blessed dumpster.

"LR-133, move the dumpster," I ordered. "We'll block the area between the two barracks. It'll give us a chance, a small defensive position."

"I'm tracking, LT, we'll make it work. KTF," said Padagas.

"No heroics, Padagas. We need you alive and killing these kranking traitors. You got me, son?"

He didn't verbally answer, just a solitary clicking of his tongue on his toggle switch. I helped him shove the dumpster. It groaned as its rusty wheels struggled to regain mobility. I wonder how old that thing was to not even have had repulsors. It took hard work, but we managed it. Meanwhile, the other three leejes with us watched our backs.

Once the dumpster was in place, I assigned our fields of fire and waited for them to come out.

"They're massing by the barrack's doors, LT!" Pool told me.

If I was in charge of the rebels, I'd be preparing to break out and hit us from behind. They were probably waiting on what I now assumed were scouts to return. But those Arthavans were good and dead. And the rest of these mukkas were about to join them.

22

We kept low behind the dumpster, waiting. Looking around at the area, I took stock. The large barracks stood like miniature castles ready to repel the flea-ridden masses. The buildings had low parapets running along their roofs. I could almost imagine the ancient Arthavans standing up there with their spears, defending hearth and home, fighting to the bitter end.

The parapets gave the perfect cover for my leej teams on the roofs, allowing them to safely search for and acquire targets of opportunity. Without something larger than a blaster, those bubbas were safe. If the fuzzies did have something bigger—rockets, missiles, mortars—my leejes would be in trouble. That's why I'd stayed dirtside, to ensure that didn't happen.

"What are they waiting for?" Pool asked quietly over the L-comm.

"Any moment now," I replied. "Wait for it."

I was ready for it. In these close quarters, our training and doctrine proved its worth. Finally. We knew how to use our surroundings to their most devastating effect. We'd all been trained to use the enemy's perceived strength against them. Combat was a fluid thing, and we'd been trained to swim in those waters.

Larger forces often felt invulnerable, but a smart leej could negate that in a close quarters battle. We mostly called it CQB, because military officers loved acronyms and we loved confusing the civvies. But whatever you called it, we knew how to be deadly in tight situations. The scenario unfolding around me was like every boring training evolution I'd done since I'd enlisted all those years ago. It was so on the nose that I feared a trap.

"Wait for it..."

I couldn't let fear of messing up stop me from acting when the time came. Doing nothing was deadlier than making the wrong decision. Satisfied that we'd taken advantage of the heights, I focused on the ground level. We had the advantage here too, but it took some adjustments to our HUDS.

"Max your audio feeds," I told the four leejes who'd remained with me. "We wanna be sure we hear them coming in case the HUDs update bio-sigs slower than real-time. Trust your brothers and ignore the rest."

I felt safer knowing that the slate rock in front of us would give us an additional early warning. I was about to assign everyone's sector of fire when Padagas sent me a request for a private chat.

"Be quick, Padagas, they'll be here soon," I said.

"Roger, LT," Padagas replied. "This dumpster has a lift feature. I used to play on these in the slums where I grew up. If I tweak it just right, we can have one of us go prone underneath it. Snipe them from cover. They'll probably not think to aim that low. Even if they try, it'll be a small target."

Looking around, I took a second to reassess the battlefield around me. I nodded, he was right. If the lift function he mentioned still worked, then it was a solid tactical move.

"Make it happen," I ordered.

With the final touches made to our assigned sectors of fire, we waited. The assault had to be coming any second now. I decided to check in with Captain Stanton, who was now leading two squads of marines to our location.

"Red Company Actual, adjust movement to the angles marked on your HUD." I sent the data to his optic overlay, a two-centimeter thick square piece of smart impact-glass that could extend from his helmet in front of one eye. Not a full-surround helmet like the Legion, but enough for him to see what he needed seeing. "You'll flank them and push them into my meat grinder. LR-24, out."

Surprisingly, the two company commanders were trusting my judgement. I didn't know if that would happen again after the incident with the ALTO. Desperate times.

All our forces in reserve were being channeled my way.

I gave a final command, just to fill the silence. "Check your blasters, make sure you've got fresh charge packs."

My order was unnecessary, but it made me feel like I was doing something productive. Knowing that the entire camp could stand or fall in part because of my decisions was scary. I'd rather switch places with Virgil and face another charging horde of wild charka than be the officer in charge of these decisions. But Oba never asked for my opinion; he ordained what he wanted, and I was stuck with it. It was our lot in life to accept the divine wisdom and bend our will to his.

"I've got movement!" Pool called down to me.

My theological musings were cut short as enemy soldiers finally streamed out of the barracks in front of us. We couldn't see them yet, but they seemed to be massing for a large push. They weren't even trying to be quiet. I said a quick prayer that I could turn their hubris against them. They hadn't made it easy; the fuzzies were exiting through the door closest to the cliff. That was the worst angle of fire for my team.

"Can you maneuver and put eyes on for me, Pool?"

"Negative, sir."

Cursing that we didn't have many troops up there, I thought about re-tasking the anti-air gunners, but they were needed in case the MCR had more fighters at their disposal. Gladiator Squad would have to stand alone until the marines showed up. And they were taking their sweet time. Clearly, they needed more PT when we got home. If we made it home.

Stop it.

I couldn't let my defeatist attitude get me down—my men were counting on me. I had my duty as a leej officer.

Keep going, Fetch, one step at a time.

"Make ready!" I had my blaster trained for the barracks wall, ready for the first kranker to pop his hairy head around the corner.

The rebels charged without war cries or shouts. They seemed to think of themselves as undetected. They ran into a wall of legion bolts for their trouble, but it didn't seem to matter. I'd kill one, but it seemed like ten more were right behind. They just kept coming.

"No head shots! Aim center mass!" I bellowed at the four leejes with me.

I lost track of the number of souls I sent to the afterlife... maybe that was for the best. Either way, we were about to be overrun.

"Prepare to pull back," I shouted, trying to be heard over the adrenaline rushing through our blood.

"Hold what you've got," Captain Stanton ordered. "I'm almost on them!"

"You were supposed to flank them, sir!"

"Gunny took that route, we split our forces."

I made a snap decision.

"Sir, go around us," I told him. "We'll stall 'em for a few more moments, throw our last grenades. We'll pull back in retreat if we have to. We'll keep the fuzzies focused on us. Your marines hit their other flank."

"Affirmative."

I got onto the Gladiator Squad L-comm. "Use whatever grenades you have left. Pool, I authorize you to throw them danger close."

"These army blasters are overheating, LT!"

"Keep firing anyway," I ordered. "We'll swap it out when we get back to the walls."

We kept firing as the fraggers boomed amid the massed MCR. That, combined with our relentless blaster fire, broke the rebel charge. We forced the fuzzies to pull back behind the barracks. They began to open fire on us and it became apparent that they'd acquired Legion weapons from their fighting with the 9th.

Clank, clank, clank went the metallic wall of the dumpster as the hyenas took their shots.

"They know I'm down here, sir!" shouted a near-panicked Padagas.

"Prioritize anyone with grenades!" I shouted to him and to everyone else. "Just keep shooting! For the love of Oba, take out that SAB. I'll be damned if we're killed by our own weapons."

CLANK, CLACK, CLANK.

I could feel the heat of the blaster bolts warming the dumpster as we pressed against it for cover. At this rate, the thing was liable to turn to slag.

"They're overcharging their shots," I called out. "Hit the shooter when he tries to change packs. It'll deplete pretty damn quick."

"Die already!" Padagas yelled, dropping a trio of MCR who attempted to break away from the pack to move to new cover.

"Ignore the horde—shoot the damn gunners."

CLANK, CLACK, CLANK.

"Red Company Actual, where is your Gunny?" I asked Captain Stanton. "We're getting our asses chewed up over here."

"He's pinned down by another group of fuzzies, same as us. He's hard pressed; we're on our own."

Looking around at my men, I knew what I had to do. I was going to bring them home. I was going to keep the promise I'd failed to keep with the men of Berserker

Squad. Ducking, I grabbed Padagas's ankle, alerting him beneath the dumpster.

"I'm going to flank them," I said.

"You're gonna what, sir?"

"Gonna circle around behind those barracks. I need you to keep their heads down, use every grenade you've got."

"I'm out, sir!"

I checked my webbing and pulled off two fraggers, handing them to Padagas as he extracted himself from beneath the dumpster. "Take my grenades and give me your pistol."

He started to object, until I tightened my grip on his arm and shook him. "Now, Padagas!"

He got the message. Nodding, he drew his pistol and checked its charge. "Be careful, LT."

"Thanks." Saying a quick prayer, I started to take off but stopped short.

"If this goes belly-up, Padagas, tell Ashley I'm sorry. Tell her I loved her, that I did it for her."

I had to stop, I was getting choked up and couldn't start crying now. Instead, I thumped his chest with my gauntlet and started running with every ounce of strength I had left. I was winded. I could feel the cold burning in my lungs as I pushed my body. I cursed myself for not having spent more time in the gym, but I pushed onward. I ran past the barracks we'd stationed ourselves between, toward the wall that butted up against the sheer dropping cliffs. Turning right, I headed along the wall toward the other cliff facing wall.

Man, these buildings are huge, I thought.

I kept running, fighting the urge to head away from the fight. I stopped as soon as I got to the last barrack and peered around the corner. I could see the fuzzies massing for another assault. If I didn't do something, they'd likely break our small barricade. I had to stop them. Had to buy the marines time to flank them from the other side.

My life for my brothers. I was at peace with my decision. I checked my weapons one last time, slung my blaster around my back and pulled my own pistol. I'd never wielded two guns before, but I'd gotten in so close that I couldn't miss. I had a straight shot down the street into the clustered cultist group.

Taking a deep breath, I said one last prayer.

"Oba, protect my family. Make their lives long and fruitful. Protect my men. Bring them home to the arms of their loved ones. Make my feet swift, my aim deadly, and welcome me into the embrace of my ancestors."

It took another few moments to bring myself to move from the shelter of the building. I knew waiting would lower my odds of making it out alive. Tightening my grip on my blasters, I turned the corner and sprinted toward the enemy.

I resisted the urge to immediately fire at them, wanting to get close enough where I could have a more devastating effect. I found myself wishing that I'd held on to those grenades. That would have done the job! I just hoped I could get those shots off before they gunned me down. This only worked if they ignored their flanks, if their battle lust overwhelmed their discipline. If they were alert and aware, I was dead. I had to try anyway, or my leej brothers died with me.

Kill them first, indeed, I thought as I ran.

Still nothing! The fuzzies were ignoring me.

I reached that spot where I could unleash bolts into their ranks sooner than expected, adrenaline pushing me past what I thought I was capable of. The rebels were howling. Stamping their feet. Beating their chests and shaking their weapons in a sort of blood lust. As though they were pushing themselves in a berserker rage for a final charge that would not be turned back. It was terrifying, but I was well past the point of no return. The realization that I was already dead freed me to do my duty.

Miraculously the rebels still hadn't noticed me. They were too busy howling like loons. It almost sounded like laughter. Many of them were jumping up and down, like some primitive ritual. They hadn't noticed me, but they would soon. If I was going to die, then I'd KTF like a leej. Kill them first—it was all that I had left.

"For Santos!"

I pulled both triggers, firing as quickly as I could. I wasn't trying to be fancy, there wasn't the time for that. I was aiming center mass, just like I'd been taught. I let my HUD aim-assist help me put my bolts on target. But there were so many hairy hyenas clustered together that I couldn't miss.

I watched those closest to me drop, thudding to the ground. I kept running, until my borrowed pistol beeped. Empty. Cursing, I threw it into the massed enemy as they turned and opened fire on me. I skidded to a halt and crouched into a shooter's stance as I fired my own pistol. I was more accurate and precise that way, and my body count increased. But it wasn't enough, as there were too many of them.

Standing still, I kept firing, reloading, and firing some more. I didn't duck or make any effort to evade their fire. I just fired my weapon—calm, cool, and collected. Another day on the range.

Blaster bolts danced around me, none of them finding their way to my armor. The MCR was starting to panic, and their aim was showing it. My luck wouldn't hold out forever, and I was starting to feel the singe of the bolts flying around me. It'd be over soon.

Beep. Pack empty.

"For Santos!" I screamed my rage and hurled my pistol at them. The shock had worn off, and with me temporarily disarmed, they started charging toward me. I was so hyped up that it took me a moment to realize I wasn't done firing, and I scrambled for my blaster. The Miif-7 was on a combat sling, and I quickly had it in my hands again. I threw more bolts at them.

"Stay dead! Take that!"

Too few hyenas dropped and stayed down.

I remember what happened in those next few moments vividly. It was like watching a holovid in slow motion. One of the fuzzies got desperate and dove at me with an active grenade in his hands. He fell well short, but the blast knocked me off my feet. In his haste, the Arthava had inadvertently landed on the grenade, absorbing the worst of the blast.

It still hurt me. The fall to the rocky pavement did what the grenade hadn't, rendering me unconscious. Not a kill, but the rebel had traded its own life to take the threat out of the fight.

***

A blast of cold air from my bucket woke me. Shaking my head, I fought off the blurriness and heaved myself up for one final stand in the intersection between the barracks. I wasn't aware at the time, but I was unintentionally giving Gladiator Squad a show.

I got to see that stand through Padagas's bucket cam later. Gladiator saw the enemy grenade explode near me. They'd watched as I'd flown into the air, gravity doing what the rebel hadn't. I wish I could say my landing was graceful, like in our repulsor landing training. It wasn't that nice. In fact, it was an ugly fall.

Still, my actions did stall the fuzzies long enough for the marines to hit them from behind.

"How do you like my hullbusters?" I shouted at the Arthavans who were in the process of being routed by the SOAR bubbas who had broken their lines and were now cutting them down with their vibro-blades. Theirs were actually intended for combat. Not bayonets like ours, which had only been intended for parade grounds. No, the marines had real-life combat knives that they used to make a bloody mess of the cultist fuzzies. The sheer brutality was beautiful, in its own grisly way. Rebel blood stained the cobblestones as they went to join their ancestors.

It was about the most beautiful thing I could've woken up to see after being knocked for a loop.

By the time the fog cleared and I could think clearly, the marines had turned the tide of that battle. They'd sent over a hundred of the furry hyenas to the afterlife. I wondered at the reception the Arthava rebels would get from Oba but decided I didn't have the charity in my heart to care. Their reception wasn't my concern. My job was to arrange the meeting.

"Toughen up," I muttered to myself. Breathing deeply, I waited until it felt like the world stop spinning. I had to make sure this entryway into the camp was off the table for the MCR.

"... LT, we need... wall... how copy?"

I could tell that Corporal Pool was trying to reach me, but couldn't figure out what he was saying. Tapping my bucket, I walked over to the clustered marines. They'd encircled the body of one of their own, and I lamented the loss. I didn't know who he was, but I mourned with them.

"Comm errors, Pool," I said. "Wait one."

But the corporal came through nice and clear a second later. "They need us back on the wall—we need to wrap this up, sir."

When I got closer to the marines, I saw that the dead body was Captain Stanton. Red Company had lost their commander, a harsh blow to their esprit de corps. They'd fought this battle to support us. That made them my leejes too. Kneeling, I laid my hand on the shoulder of the dead captain.

"Rest easy, sir. We'll make 'em pay."

"Enemy blaster got him, sir." The marine sergeant struggled through his tears. "But Cap kept fighting, right until Oba claimed him."

"He did SOAR proud today," I said, "and I gladly call him brother. But we can't mourn now, there's work to be done. Krankers to kill."

"Never enough, sir," the sergeant said, conviction returning to his voice.

"Of what?" I asked.

"Never enough charge packs for the bodies we're gonna stack, sir."

"That's the sentiment that I'd expect from SOAR marines. Revenge now, mourn later. First, we need to quickly search the dead. Look for any useful intelligence. Get two marines to lay Captain Stanton off to the side, we'll bury him as soon as we can. Once we search the dead, we'll blow the tunnel they entered from. This can't have been for nothing."

"Ooah, sir."

I joined the rest of Red Company as they searched for anything useful. The dead often provided more useable intelligence than the living. A quick L-comms message had Padagas joining us with his small fire team that had fought from behind the dumpster, adding eyes to the search for useable intel and consumables. The expanded search for intel found nothing, though I hadn't really expected it to. These MCR knew they were going into the belly of the beast for a fight. Usually not the best place to bring your secrets.

Convinced we weren't finding anything of immediate value we could exploit against the enemy, I adjusted our search for equipment that could help us out. "Marines, look for any gear we can salvage."

While they looked, I retrieved my pistol, and reloaded it from a universal charge pack I'd found on a rebel officer. The dead kranker wouldn't be needing it. His pistol was clipped to my armor, a war trophy. Should his family protest the loss of their inherited property, I figured I could return it, one plasma bolt at a time. Fully rearmed, I hunted down Padagas's pistol, and reloaded it as well.

He seemed pleased when I handed him back his sidearm, replying with more pep than I'd heard from him since the night in the cave.

"Thanks, sir. This pistol meant a lot to me." He gave it a fond look before slipping it in his webbing. "The judge who sentenced me to the reserves gave it to me. It was a gift for finishing boot camp, for making the cut. She saved me from the work camps, told me I reminded her of her late father. I like to think he's watching over me. When I get home, I want to return it to her."

I didn't know what to say. I put a hand on his shoulder, and stood there with him for a moment. He broke the spell, clearing his throat, and the moment passed.

"Let's go blow the hole, sir," he said. "If we're quick, we might make it back to the walls in time for some target practice."

Slapping the back of his bucket, I turned to the barracks where the enemy had managed to find an access tunnel. The marines of Red Company had secured the opening and had it wired to blow. They were just waiting on orders now. I stayed back and sent a quick update to Captain Archer.

"Well done, Fetch. I've talked with their lieutenants and assumed command of all forces here. Blow that hole and get back on the wall. There's work to be done, and we need all hands on this one. LR-01, out."

23

I can still feel the bulk of him, of Captain Stanton. He was a solidly built man, and his armored flak vest only added to his weight. I set him aside, pulling him out of the morass of dead MCR and marines from that last skirmish. There really wasn't time for anything else, but I wanted to be able to easily find Stanton and make sure he was given all possible honors if we survived this attack.

"Red Company Marines!" I shouted, taking an initiative I hadn't seen their surviving officers show. "Follow Corporal Pool back to the line!"

"They fight like us," Padagas said as the hullbusters hustled with us back to the walls to keep the MCR waves at bay. "Now they're fighting with us. Has the world turned topsy-turvy, LT?"

"Maybe, Padagas, maybe. But as far as I'm concerned, those SOAR marines are leejes. Honorarily so, at a bare minimum."

It was a sentiment I heard from the other leejes, as well. If we made it home, when we made it home, I'd petition to have their names added to the Caledonian Hall of Honor and Remembrance. They deserved nothing less.

"Does this mean we can't tell marine jokes now, sir?"

"Hell no," I said, cracking the first smile of the day.

When I rejoined my leejes on the walls, I was surprised to find that the enemy had gone silent. Captain Archer had sounded as though the battle was still raging on, and I didn't put the lack of blaster fire being exchanged together in my mind until I saw the stillness on the walls myself.

"Were did the rebels go?" I asked Dwyer.

"They stopped once you broke their assault inside Camp Jericho, LT."

"Do we have eyes on their location now?"

"They faded back into the mountain mists, sir. Left their dead, though."

"Is that significant?"

"Would we leave our dead?" Virgil kept scanning the rocks and hills, any little movement catching his attention.

"Not if we could help it. But that's a whole helluvalot of dead MCR down there. Not sure they could take them away even if they wanted to."

"Huh," grunted Dwyer.

I knew the sergeant was trying to get me to see something. Maybe another teachable moment. "Listen: Sergeant. We don't have time for this... Tell me what I'm not seeing."

"They'll be back, sir. They aren't done with us yet. Not by a long shot."

Hundreds of bodies littered the open field in front of us. Charka and Arthava lay where they'd fallen. Piles of bodies showed where his most effective marksmen had been stationed.

"Virgil, find out whose sectors those piles of fuzzies belong to. I want their names. We'll move those men wherever the enemy mass."

"Already have the list. Check your HUD, LT."

I magnified my HUD's view, still wanting to review the battlefield. The list could wait. I scanned through the piles of enemy rebels, pondering. What could motivate their strange fanaticism? Sure, the Repub had its issues, but slaughtering a city of two million innocents and then throwing themselves in successive suicide charges didn't seem to fit the problems the MCR were constantly highlighting in their endless propaganda holos.

"What could be worth all of this?"

I asked my question in the sanctity of my bucket, but I doubt any answer would've satisfied my curiosity. Chaos and anarchy, that's what the rebels seemed to be after. Anything less would merely swap the names but leave the failings of our Republic. It wasn't malice that caused our woes, just the unfeeling nature of rank bureaucracy. But smaller governments couldn't protect us from the malevolent forces that lurked within the shadow. Smaller government couldn't protect us from the crime families hiding on the edges of the galaxy. Heck, they couldn't even protect us from the evil inside the core of the Republic.

"Does it bother you that the fuzzies have gone silent, Virgil?"

"It does," he said grimly.

It worried me that Virgil also thought the delay seemed ominous. What was coming next?

"LR-01, it's silent out there," I called in to the captain. "Any news from the 9th, or from Fleet? If something doesn't happen soon, the men will break, sir."

There was only silence at first, but I knew the other LTs from the marines were listening on the comm, wanting answers too. Everyone in Camp Jericho wanted answers.

"Fleet is on the other side of the planet right now," Archer's voice finally crackled through my helmet, "and won't be back in range for several more hours. The 9th is engaged with another force out there. We've just got to hold what we've got for now. Things are quiet now, so pull half of the men from the line and let them rest. Fetch, you've got what's left of Rage Company. I need to oversee the larger element now. I'll be in touch when we know more. LR-01, out."

It wasn't the most helpful news, but I knew that no news was worse than bad news. I took a moment to process the information, before the implications of Archer's last comment hit. I was in charge of Rage Company. Could we rightly call it a company? Only eight squads remained of the sixteen we started with. Half of our men were dead. Friends and neighbors. Gone, just like that.

"Will this all matter in the end?" I asked Virgil. "Were my friends' deaths worth it?"

"It matters, LT. We'll make it matter. As long as we remember, our leejes will live forever."

Hardening my resolve, I connected with my corporals.

"Pool and Faulkner, pull half of your leejes from the line. Consolidate Rage Company into two sections, you'll each lead one. Reassess your firing lanes and update them at your discretion."

"Sergeant Dwyer outranks us all," Pool replied. "Shouldn't we be reporting to him?"

"Sergeant Dwyer will coordinate with both of you, but I need him free to help Doc Tran as needed. Pool, you've got command of 1st Section. Faulkner, 2nd is yours."

"How do you want to handle the rest cycle, LT?" Faulkner asked.

"Figure it out. You don't need me to tell you how to lead. Dismissed."

I hoped I was making the right call. Pulling one section off the line kept a fresh NCO commanding each watch rotation. Plus, we'd set a ten-minute overlap so changing the guard never left sleepy leejes on the walls. With the NCOs in charge, it left me to manage the larger picture. I was pleased at the rotation the experienced corporals set. It was an easy one to figure out—"five-and-five" was standard doctrine for inclement weather conditions. Five hours on watch, and five hours to recover. Long enough to get some meaningful sack time, but not so long that those on watch were overexposed to the harsh elements.

The next several hours passed without incident. The calm lasted until 1st Section was on their second full watch shift.

"You've got to sleep too, LT," Faulkner said.

"I'll sleep later, I need to be ready for—"

"Sir... go. We need you in the fight, so rest until we've got something to shoot."

Only Faulkner's insistence that I rest prevented me from remaining awake the entire time. He was right, and my mental faculties were clearer once I'd slept. When I woke up, I received an alert from Pool, who was back on watch.

"Sensors went offline, LT. Should I send someone to check on them?"

"Negative, we're in no position to send leejes. It's probably a trap… or they're about to come. Either way, I need every blaster in the fight."

Great, now our only early warning was eliminated. We were on our own. Worse, Captain Archer still hadn't heard anything from higher up.

***

I was leaning against the parapets with Corporal Pool. Searching the horizon for any sign of the enemy activity. Even though I was on alert, I was still surprised when we heard a distinct rumble coming from somewhere down below. I didn't know what the noise was, but it didn't sound good. It felt sinister. Ominous.

"LR-01, sir… there's been a development here," I said. "I don't recognize the sounds, but the rebels are doing something down there. LR-24 out."

"I'm aware, Fetch," said Captain Archer. "Fleet is monitoring from orbit; the fuzzies have some sort of mobile armored weapons platform. It appears to be a fighting vehicle, but it's not repulsor-driven like ours. Definitely not friendly. Get your A-P launchers online. Take out those vehicles the moment they appear, or things could get dicey."

I wanted to ask if the Fleet being aware meant that we'd get some kelhorned air support. But figured that since the captain didn't mention the possibility, it was off the table.

"Roger, sir. KTF! LR-24, out."

Like all good NCOs, Corporal Pool seemed to know when something big was coming. He was by my side waiting for me as I cut comms with the commander. I don't know if I gave something away, or he spied on the officers' secure L-comm channel. I never did find out, but I would've loved that trick as a corporal, doubly so as a sergeant. I connected with him via a secure bucket-to-bucket comms link and gave him the update.

"The rebels have some sort of tank coming our way," I informed him. "I want our A-P men prepped, but otherwise maintain the five-and-five so our boys can rest. When they make the next push, I want clear heads. They're massing their firepower, and Fleet can't help."

"Yes, sir," Pool replied. "I could hear the rumbling, too. I'll make it happen."

I left the wall and headed for the chow tent. We couldn't use the mess hall, it was too far away. Instead we'd repurposed the support building closest to us, turning it into the new dining facility. Across the camp, the mess hall served the marines and runners ferried the hot food to us.

With an enemy this numerous, getting too far from our post was risky. But in those moments, I enjoyed the simple comforts of the warm building. Taking off my bucket was a rare treat, and I relished breathing fresh air. Your bucket kept you alive, but the air recyclers weren't miracle workers and eventually your personal funk could drive you bat-shit crazy.

Knowing I could breathe clean air, that my bucket was clipped to my belt and not on my head, was a glorious feeling after so long on duty. I savored it like a thirsty man worships water, while I shoveled hot food into my belly. The chow wasn't good, but I was too tired to care. And the chef inside my head? He was easy to silence when your only other choice was a ration bar. I don't remember what we ate, but I remember the hot kaff.

Some of the men of Rage Company took the opportunity to prod me for intel. "How long will we need to hold out before Fleet sends help, LT?"

"I don't know, Stern, I just don't know."

"Can we hold that long, sir?"

"We're Rage Company, of course we can."

"Ooah, sir!"

I was pouring my second cup when an explosion rocked the base. It wasn't loud, but the rocky nature of the construction made everything vibrate. I gulped down as much of the beverage as I could and slammed the mug onto the table. I slapped my bucket onto my dome as I ran toward the walls.

"Pool, report!"

My HUD was on auto-pilot, scrolling a steady stream of data across my visor. I took it in, cursing. The enemy tanks had crested the hill while I was stuffing my face. Our A-P teams had gotten off a few missiles, but the rebel gunners were quicker in amassing their forces. Too dang quick. I'd thought I had at least another hour.

With no reply from the corporal, I tried again. "Dammit, Pool, report in!"

Still nothing. I scrolled through my HUD's updates—Salvador and Pool, gone! That left Padagas and I the sole surviving members of Berserker Squad.

I cursed myself for failing to keep my word. I'd failed to bring all of them home. Rationally, I knew it wasn't my fault, but a weight slammed into my heart. I struggled to breathe as I ran for the walls. Rage Company—my brothers, my squad!

Archer bellowed over L-comm, "To arms, to arms! Man the walls—enemy at the gates."

The alert spread like wildfire. Up and down the walls of Camp Jericho, legionnaires and marines rushed into position—all tense, all looking for targets.

"Make your shots count!" I took the stairs two at a time up the parapet walls.

There were troops beyond the walls, and swift enemy tanks. Much smaller than the Republic hover tanks or even the old Savage models I'd seen. No wonder these things rushed through the forest so quickly! They were maneuvering through and around the tree line with remarkable agility as their four independent treads propelled them into combat. On top of each boxy rectangle beast, I saw a hatch.

"If anyone pops their head out of that hatch, KTF!" Dwyer said into the L-comm, his usual steadiness calming everyone's nerve.

Virgil must've thought the hatch allowed the vehicle commander to pop out and visually inspect the battlefield.

Above that exit sat the main gun. I wanted no part of it. I didn't know what these strange vehicles were, but one of the marines had already nicknamed them the crawling devils. It fit the bill, so we went with it.

"Least there's only a few of those crawling devils," I said to Rage Company, hoping to buoy their spirits.

But their numbers continued to climb. Five, ten, and finally thirty tanks. Fear and despair clenched my gut. I wanted to cry. We'd almost held them back and completed the mission. But that was over now; we didn't have the resources to fight off so many tanks. There were more of them than we had missiles. Assuming every shot was a kill, which wasn't likely.

"Back blast area clear... Fire in the hole!" shouted one A-P gunner.

We kept firing, and took out as many tanks as we had missiles for, but soon even that advantage was gone. The large bore cannons on the massed tanks began adjusting their aim. The shelling was about to start, and there was nothing we could do about it.

"Hunker behind the parapets!" I yelled.

Scanning the field, I tried looking for a strategy that would beat these beasts. I went through every sophisticated tactic I could remember from the sergeant's course, but I had nothing. My heart pounded in my throat. When my men needed me to be on my game, I came up short. I could see that a few of vehicles were on fire. Six had already been taken out by our missiles. But we didn't have an unlimited supply of the things.

"Make your shots count!" I yelled at the nearest gunner. Then, to Dwyer, "How many missiles do we have left?"

"Eleven, sir."

Even if we managed one kill per missile, we could only take out half of them with what we had left. That still left us with thirteen of these monsters to fight off. Would the walls of Camp Jericho hold? The fortified castle that the Repub had reclaimed was old. It had been built in a more primitive time, when the weapons weren't as powerful. We were about to find out how good these ancient engineers were, and it was going to get bloody.

"Be ready for more wounded leejes," I warned Doc Tran over the L-comm.

"You think?" the doc spat back.

It was clear that this second volley wasn't meant for casualties, though. They were aiming for the dome of doom and took out our portable anti-missile defense system. I didn't know if we could salvage it, but even if it could be saved, we lacked the technical expertise to do the job.

More rounds came at us, easily taking out one of the main gates into Camp Jericho. The one on my section of the wall. If we couldn't keep the enemy outside the camp, we'd die. The rebels outnumbered us, and now they outgunned us.

"Looking grim, Virgil."

"We're not dead yet," he growled.

The crawling devils continued to advance, despite the best efforts of our gunners. We took out nine more of them—half, but not enough. They threw rounds at us with wild abandon, without a care for fire discipline. The tanks adjusted their angle to lob shells into the camp itself. One of which slammed through one of the barracks, sending rock and debris everywhere.

Baboom.

Dust and dirt floated in the breeze, obscuring our vision, and still they kept firing. Our missile mules were spent.

"I want someone scouring the camp for more A-P missiles!" Captain Archer yelled over comm.

A squad of marines peeled away from the wall for the search.

"Status on Fleet, sir?" I shouted into L-comm.

"They're back. Hold position at all costs." The grave tone of Archer's voice made me wonder if he had gotten word and just didn't have the heart to share the answer—that help wasn't coming from the Navy.

"Sir, there are still fifteen of them," I told Captain Archer. "We did the best we could but couldn't get them all. Sir, they've already taken out the gates. It might be time to consider a danger close—"

"No! We won't call fire on our own position, understand me, Ocampo? We aren't there yet. I've kept our superiors updated, they're working out a strike package now. Hold what you've got, and KTF."

"How?" I asked in frustration. "How do we kill them when we're out of missiles? Our blasters won't even singe these tanks. If we had more missiles, we'd be good to go. Sir, how do we continue the fight?"

"You're an officer in the Legion! Find a way."

24

Stern was the first of my men to snap. "We gotta fall back! Call in the ALTO!"

"Hold your ground, Stern!" I shouted over the open comm, hoping the rage I let fly would cow him and stop anyone else from joining his call for retreat. "Don't give an inch, there's nowhere to pull back to."

The besieged walls rumbled beneath our feet, but we stood our ground. The rebel tanks were turning our covered firing positions into craters, thinning out my already understrength unit. Yet the leejes of Rage Company leaned over the parapets and sent bolts downrange.

The wall before me boomed and sent a spray of splintered stone and dust falling down on top of me, covering me in grit.

"How many shells do those kelhorns have?" I yelled to myself as the little bits of rock tinked down on my LARK.

We'd fire bolts at any troops in the open, knowing that it would be them who would overwhelm and kill us if they started to pour through the holes the tanks would make. That would draw more fire from the tanks, causing us to drop back down behind the wall. Initially, the MCR infantry were sparse. But once it was clear that we'd fired the last of our missiles, the fuzzies became emboldened. They flooded out of the woods and into our camp. The krankers waltzed right in through the destroyed gates.

"Sket!" I shouted, turning to find Corporal Pool. I stopped short.

He was dead. In so many pieces it would take a bio-recovery team days' worth of DNA scanning to find all of him. Now Padagas was again leading a squad of legionnaires. Our numbers were getting dangerously low.

Kaboom.

I reached for the nearest leej only to be thrown down onto the rocky walkway of the parapet I'd been standing on over the gates—it'd taken another direct hit. The structure shook as another round followed the last. I struggled to regain my feet, despite the swaying movement from the castle walls. For a moment I thought the entire wall was going to come down, ending me and the rest of the defenders in one cataclysmic avalanche of stone.

The rebel tanks hit the walkway over the crumpled gates a third time. And now I could tell this section above the gate was definitely going to topple.

"Move!" I shouted at other nearby leejes. "Off the walkway!"

Modern weapons proved to be too much for the structure—the arched walkway crashed to the ground. I scrambled, desperately trying to reach for something to hold onto, but I fell to the rocks below.

I hit the ground with a thud, my bucket smashing onto the castle rubble. My ears rang. My vision blurred. I struggled to remember where I was. I wasn't even sure who I was for a few moments, but my bucket kept feeding me data. A howling horde of additional MCR swarmed past me in even greater numbers than we'd previously seen, completely oblivious to those of us on the ground.

I'm sure we all looked dead. A frightful sight, dozens of broken and mangled bodies.

I'd landed badly and twisted my leg. It wasn't broken, but it hurt. What concerned me more was the pain in my left arm. My HUD lit up a red icon, warning me that my arm was fractured, but I could already tell. Fortune was on my side again, because I hadn't broken my suit integrity. With the fight going on all around me, I knew I'd have to deal with my injuries later. The synthprene suit underneath helped stabilize my arm, buying me time until death or Fleet ended my pain.

Momentarily safe between waves of MCR, I hopped onto the L-comm and sent a message.

"LR-01, the archway over the gates is compromised," I managed. "Rebels pouring in... my HUD estimates over five hundred of them. That can't be right, but my bucket hit the rocks pretty hard when I fell. I'll KTF, sir. Do my best."

Despite my best efforts, I still slurred my words. Moments of brilliant white pain temporarily obscured everything else.

"Roger," Archer acknowledged. "Commander's report indicates you've fractured your arm and sprained your leg. We'll get a medic to you as soon as the situation allows. Hold tight, and don't do anything stupid. We're pulling some of Red Company over to relieve your men. The 9th is finally freed up and is dropping an HK-PP behind those monsters, one of those tank-hunting mechs. Just hold on. We'll turn the tide and pull you back, Lieutenant. LR-01, out."

Holy muck buckers. That wasn't fleet support but an HK-PP mech was more than welcome!

The pain was getting worse. My limbs throbbed and white specs of light danced across my vision. I felt nauseous, even though I knew my LARK had issued meds. They weren't helping. I must've looked dead, because the rebels continued to stream past me into Camp Jericho.

"Oba," I groaned.

I couldn't wait for rescue, not while my men were still fighting for their lives. I knew that I couldn't trust the updates from my damaged bucket, so I shut them off. Until I could affect the outcome, I didn't want to know whether my boys lived or died. I needed to focus on the here and now, on what was immediately in front of my blaster.

The stream of rebels had slowed to a trickle. They were probably all in the camp. Then I was alone with the tanks in front of me. Those crawling devils continued to blast away at the walls of the Camp Jericho, not satisfied with the damage they'd already wrought.

Nothing I could do about that.

I took stock, pushing them from my mind. I evaluated the enemy ground forces. They appeared unarmored, but they carried a wide variety of weapons—blasters, flamers, rockets, slug throwers.

I could put in some work against those guys.

I ignored those armed with pistols and blasters. They were deadly, but our leejes could handle them in a stand-up fight. The rockets and flamers, those were a serious threat. And I was in position to take them out.

The flamers and rocket wielding fuzzies had to die. I targeted them, immediately excluding all other targets. All I needed were a few uninterrupted shots. I'd go down fighting, take a few of them out before they killed me. If I was lucky, their flamers and rockets would explode, killing even more of them. If not, I'd still be buying my men some time.

Oba help me, but I was ready for the pain to end. I was ready to walk among my ancestors, to tell them that I'd honored my family. I'd returned their name unstained. I lay broken at the gates of Camp Jericho, with one simple request. I prayed that every bolt flew true, that what I sacrificed mattered. I wanted my unborn baby to know that his daddy had done something important. To know my suffering had merit, that it was worth the blood debt I was about to pay.

Biting my lip against the pain, I rose up to an awkward kneeling position with my bum leg off to the side. I used my injured left arm to create a stable firing platform for my blaster and scanned for targets. I took one last calming breath and brought my face down to the scope of my blaster.

"Where are you?" I whispered.

My HUD and scope quickly synced. I was ready for action. I panned the confines of Camp Jericho for the right targets. Then I saw it, the telltale bulk of a flamer. If I could hit the fuel container, it would end badly for the enemy. It was as good of a first target as I could think of. I got to work.

"Oba guide me..." I prayed.

The first bolt went into the tanker's pack and ignited it and the wearer into a ball of flames.

"... that I might do thy bidding."

A rocket clattered to the ground next to its dead owner.

"Make me the swift and deadly instrument of your will."

Two more dead.

"Let my aim be true..." I recited by rote, entranced by the battle around me. I was dropping targets in rapid succession.

"... and my cause righteous."

More.

"Make my hand faster than those who seek to do me harm."

Please, just a few more.

"Grant me victory over my foes, that I might protect your people."

Them. Stop them.

"And Oba, if today is truly the day you call me home..."

That one.

"... then let me die..."

Him, too.

"... with my foe prostrate at my feet."

I wasn't sure that Oba would truly approve of a prayer like that. It was likely a conceit of the warrior seeking to understand his war. But it brought me solace as I prepared to meet my end. I was afraid, and I might've pissed myself, but I wanted to go out on my terms. I needed to know that my family name remained unstained by cowardice.

I fired bolt after bolt, depleting several blaster battery packs. Changing batteries was difficult with a fractured arm, but adrenaline let me ignore the pain. The enemy had finally recognized that I was there, that I was a threat, but I ignored their shots. I fired through it all, letting my HUD prompt me where to shoot as my muzzle swept Camp Jericho.

I watched rocketeers and flamers die, some of them exploding gloriously at my hand. I screamed my fury, I cried, but I kept shooting. Bolt after bloody bolt. Eventually, some of the other wounded leejes near me regained consciousness and joined my hunt. There were eight of us against the entire Bar Kokhba Revolt and their MCR allies.

That's how it felt, anyway.

Our war was focused on the few meters around us, on the compound swarming with rebels.

"Target the flamers and the rocketeers," I screamed over the L-comm. "When you can't find those, go for the teams on the crew-served platforms. KTF, and I'll see you in Paradise."

The snarling Arthava returned fire at an increasing rate, but I wasn't afraid. If anything, this helped us. It prevented the tanks mobilizing in our rear from firing on us without also inflicting friendly casualties. Bolts slapped the rubble around me. One lucky rebel shot me in the chest, but the bolt deflected off my armor. It was painful, but my armor held. It didn't help my fuzzy vision, though, so I let the computer in my helmet do its job.

I'd found my peace, and I continued reciting my prayer. I begged Oba to let each bolt save my brothers, and zeroed in on the enemy. A hand grabbed my shoulder. I swung around wildly, blaster waving, arm searing in pain, and came face-to-face with Corporal Faulkner. I almost panicked, afraid a fuzzy had gotten in that close, but it was just one of my leejes.

"Follow me, LT!"

The large Corporal Faulkner had led a fire team to pull us out. There were only three of us left, still firing, as we were dragged toward Rage Company's line.

"I can't walk."

"Stern and Kowalski!" Faulkner bellowed, motioning his men to some of the broken leejes near my side. "Grab the carry handles on the back of their LARKs. I'll grab the LT."

We didn't stop firing. We couldn't, we were lost in our own personal wars. I didn't count how many lives I ended, and I've never checked the data from my bucket. I never want to know.

"We're coming in hot," Faulkner called out as he ran.

We were among our lines, clinging to the shadow of Camp Jericho's walls as the legionnaires above us sent suppressing fire into the MCR ranks that had poured inside the base. I turned on my alerts to assess the situation. My ears suddenly hurt; I'd gotten used to the silence during my solitary battle at the gates. Now I could hear all of the chaos going on around me. Without the isolation, I had to fight to maintain my objectivity. I wasn't just a leej with a blaster, I was an officer leading whatever was left of Rage Company.

"LR-01, I'm back with an isolated pocket of Rage Company. What's the situation where you're at, sir? Your HUD beacon went offline," I asked Archer.

There was only static over the direct comms line. I switched to the open command channel and repeated the message. This time I received an answer, though it wasn't from my commander.

"Sir, First Sergeant Rodney Bonner here. Captain Archer is down. Medics are working on him, but he's out of the fight for now. He's unconscious, so it's all you now. Red Company's officers are all dead. I think I'm the senior non-com left, and I've assumed command, until properly relieved."

"Roger, Gunny. Consolidate your troops into a defensible perimeter. Get them off the walls, we can't hold them."

"Aye, sir. They're already pulling back."

"Good, focus on repelling the fuzzies, Marine. Last word from Archer was that an HK was dropped behind the tanks. When they're out of the picture, we'll coordinate a counterattack with the mech pilot and reclaim Jericho. LR-24, out."

With a clearer view of the situation on the ground, I assessed what was going on around me. The rebels were attacking from the roofs of the buildings around us. Our only surviving mortar team was making that approach costly. They had been firing almost nonstop through multiple engagements with the enemy. Thankfully we found Jericho well stocked with mortars. If only the same had been true of A-P missiles.

Still, we could hold for a while longer if those mortars kept the enemy at bay.

"Shift your fire to the dining facility—priority mission. They're attacking the med station!"

"Aye, sir," replied the marine mortarmen.

Krump.

The brassy boom reverberated off the stone buildings.

"Good hit—fire for effect!"

After giving the order, I left the mortar team to man their guns. I had a more pressing concern. My biggest fear was the unknown. We were cut off from the marines of Red Company and all my men seemed to be fighting in isolated groups, making last stands as best we could. I could see them on my HUD and speak to their leaders, but we couldn't physically link up. The area between us might as well have been a million miles apart. And every second, more KIA icons appeared where leejes once stood. Our company would be lucky to man a section if this continued.

"Dwyer, report."

"I'm alive, LT. Pinned down by the support buildings. How 'bout you? HUD says your arm is broken."

I grimaced from the reminder. "I'll be fine. Who's with you? There're so many fuzzies, my HUD can't find you in any of the groupings."

"I'm by myself. I'll link back up with the main element with all possible speed."

I continued firing while I analyzed the situation. My training hadn't prepared me for this. If I didn't adapt and overcome, we'd all die. I fired again, my bolt slicing through the thin uniform of a nearby rebel grabbing for one of the flamers from his fallen comrade. The bolt punctured the fuel tank of the flamer. Soon the Arthavan was fully engulfed in flames and running among the other rebel troops, a yelping brushfire on two legs.

"Great shot, LT!"

"Look at him run," Stern cheered.

The chaos created by the flaming fuzzy allowed the leejes to score a few more kills. Howling their dismay, the rebels pulled back behind cover.

"They're retreating," Faulkner warned.

"Shoot them as they run for cover," I ordered.

The fuzzies were smart to duck and run. If they were smarter, they would've let their tanks soften us up some more before regrouping for another attack. It's what I'd have done.

The lull in the battle gave me time to reach out to higher headquarters, but we couldn't get through. I called to the mech pilots, but again got static. I wasn't sure who or what was jamming us, but we would be in trouble if we didn't figure it out.

25

"LR-136, you've got the lead," I said over the L-comm. "Hold what you've got, I'm going up to the walls for a peek at what those tanks are doing on the other side. If I don't come back in ten, assume I'm dead. Coordinate with Sergeant Dwyer and Gunny Bonner. He's the senior marine non-com."

"I'll go, sir. We need you alive."

"I need better visuals than what you can provide me. I'm doing this."

"Roger, sir."

"Faulkner, the men are counting on you. No heroics, just hold what you've got. I'll be back with news before you know it."

The decision to brave the enemy guns was easy; executing it proved to be as nerve-racking as it was dangerous. I knew I couldn't ask one of my leejes to do it. I had to do it myself... once I got up my courage.

"You can do this, Fetch."

I could say it. Convincing myself was harder.

When I'd made it halfway up the steps, I better saw our positioning: scant few men hugging whatever cover they could find, trying to watch the backs of their brothers and knowing that there weren't enough guns in the fight to do it well.

"There are so few of us..."

Tears leaked out. I couldn't stop them. We'd started the day with ninety-eight legionnaires, and now there are barely fifty of us at best. So many of my neighbors would never leave Rhyssis Wan alive.

Thank Oba for the marines.

They hadn't been hit as hard; most of their losses had been to their overzealous officers and NCOs. If we could minimize the losses while regrouping, we might hold out through another assault. We were close to the precipice of disaster, but perhaps we could turn the tide.

"Dwyer, they're massing near you. Watch the mess hall."

"I see it."

"Mortar team, adjust fire," Bonner interrupted. "Target the troops around the dining facility. We'll break that cluster of fuzzies, LT."

"Understood," I said.

Taking one last calming breath, I stood up and raced up the stairs to the walls. Some rebels noticed my movement, and blaster bolts tracked my progress. None of them hit me, but boy, can fear make a man's feet fly.

When I got to the top of the walls, I ducked down behind the battlements and caught my breath. The bodies of my brothers littered the passageway, all leejes from Rage Company. HUD icons told me that some of them clung to life, but without medical attention, they'd be dead soon.

"Doc, I got wounded on the walls."

"We've got wounded everywhere, sir! Until you can bring them to me, they're on their own."

Win first, help later, I told myself.

It felt cruel, but it was the truth. I crawled down the line scrounging battery packs for my blaster, and anything else I could use. The pain in my bad arm was incredible, but it needed to be done. Besides, if a wounded leej looked like he could still defend himself, I wanted to have something for them. Each time I found a man alive, I put a blaster in his hand, patted his shoulder, and moved on. There were precious few still living. I only managed to get enough charge packs to outfit four leejes with basic combat loads. It would have to do.

Oba must've been watching out for me, because when I popped over the parapets I didn't get shot. In fact, I saw something so good that I would have been half-okay with getting shot, just for having the privilege of seeing a large HK-PP mech as it clanked around the battlefield.

"HK on site!" I called into the comms.

I don't know whether the men cheered or not, but I was elated. The HK pilot skillfully ran circles around the tanks, overpowering them with superior firepower.

Staring, I took it all in. I'd never seen one of these before. Cally had some, but they were boxed up somewhere collecting dust until now. Several missile pods were mounted on the mech's shoulders, and it carried chain guns in its hands. It was a machine built for one thing—destruction—and piloted inside by a single highly trained individual.

The MCR tank crews had been too slow to recognize the threat. The HK's pilot didn't hesitate, firing several missiles at the crawling devils. Two of the beasts erupted, flames bursting from their hatches. The missile penetrated the tank before exploding in a concussive blast. Checking my threat icons, there were only five of the enemy vehicles left.

"How d'you like it now!" I shouted.

The crawling devils' treads churned up the ground as they moved frantically through their turns. One tank shuddered as it took a blast and then went up from the inside out as two consecutive detonations sounded...

Boom.

BOOM.

The crawling devil exploded from the HK-PP's missile. Millions of shrapnel shards burst across the field and clattered into the damaged walls of Camp Jericho. The surviving tanks managed to turn to face the HK while it catapulted missiles at its next target. Though tall, the HK was narrow and nimble, and danced past most of the blasts in jerky movements.

"Aw, yeah! You mess with the bullitar, you get the horns!"

I was yelling nonsense, cheering the mech on like this was some sporting event. I tensed in anticipation when the enemy tanks fired again.

Ba-boom.

One missile slammed into its side, sending the HK-PP careening backward into a stand of trees. Snow cascaded and missiles launched, but with a leap, the giant mech burst into the air, mechanical arms firing and destroying two tanks in an instant.

"Get some!" I screamed, slamming my fist onto the parapet walls. My battle cry was followed closely by a scream of pain. I'd forgotten about my injured arm, but the pain brought it all back into focus.

Outside Camp Jericho, the crawling devils churned after the mech pilot, giving our compound a break.

"Faulkner, Bonner, rebel tanks are distracted with the HK-PP," I called in. "Use the time to push back against the fuzzies inside the wire. Get that mortar team cracking."

Meanwhile, the tanks worked to eliminate the newfound threat. The mech pilot was good, certainly better than the fuzzies. Whoever the pilot was had anticipated the enemy's attempts to bracket the HK-PP into a corner. It was bizarre, a choreographed ballet... except it was deadly serious, and the dancers were heavily armed.

The tanks moved in sync, all trying to corral the massive HK against the walls of Jericho where movement would be constrained. The mech pilot replied by thrusting into the air, constantly on the move. The pilot kept his movement parallel to the walls, never letting the tankers trap the mech. Another quick-powered jump brought the HK-PP behind one of the tanks.

"Get him!" I shrieked.

The pilot beat the tank with its large metal fist. The sound was deafening, even behind my bucket. The clanging rang across the mountains, and I was sure even the ghosts of Kusiba could hear the sound. The other tank crews tried to get rounds off, firing despite one of their own being between them. The decision proved to be a fatal one—for the fuzzy tank crew.

With a graceful bounce, the mech launched away, and missiles streaked toward its last location, and found the enemy's tank instead. It exploded in flames so hot, they burned blue, and smoke billowed out from its skeletal insides.

"Sucks to be a tanker!"

I was having too much fun.

The mech pilot jumped his HK-PP again, landing on another of the tanks that had formed into a semicircle around where he'd just been. Overeager tankers tried firing again, missing the pilot, but blowing the treads off the tank he'd been near. Seizing the opportunity to put the vehicle out of commission, the HK-PP used a short jump and landed on top of the tank.

Reaching down with its free hand, the mech grabbed the tank's cannon barrel. Placing his boot on the turret, the mech pilot pulled up.

Kreech.

"How's it looking, sir?"

"The HK-PP pilot is ripping them apart, Virgil! He just ripped the barrel off one—it's so mangled that it'll never fire again!"

"How many are left?"

"Just two now. Looks like Oba is tilting the scales in our favor!"

Having neutered one tank, the HK-PP pilot jet-jumped away, taunting the rebel tank crews into shooting.

"He's making them waste their missiles, Virgil!"

"Tanks still have their main cannons, LT."

"It'll make it harder for the tanks to attack the HK-PP," Bonner cut in. "Still a win—he can pick those devils off one by one."

The tankers weren't giving up. They backed up as a unit, clearly leery of another offensive.

"They're running!" I laughed with surprise. "The tanks are retreating!"

"Watch it, sir—could be a trap," Bonner cautioned.

"How many are running, LT?"

"Just the two, Virgil, but cowardice is contagious! The mech is turning the tide!"

While the dance resumed, both sides wary of the other, I reached out to Wendell over the L-comm.

"LR-86, connect me to..."

"Wendell died, sir. His position was overrun... I couldn't get to him in time."

"Roger. Thanks, Virgil."

Taking a deep breath, I connected to Padagas.

"LR-133, I need you to patch me over to the HK pilot. What's the frequency or comms channel? I can't reach it and that needs to be fixed. Can you make it happen?"

"Yes, sir. I can make it happen. Give me a few minutes and I'll get you in, LT."

"The sooner the better."

Meanwhile, one of the marines managed to get onto their portion of the walls. He'd picked up one of the MCR's rocket launchers...

Whoosh.

The marine fired off a missile toward one of the undamaged enemy tankers. He was a great shot and scored a range-perfect hit. He didn't destroy it; the tank crews were too skilled for that. The fuzzy tankers moved just in time, avoiding a fiery demise. Instead, the missile struck one of its treads and limited its mobility. I reached out to Red Company, trying to reach the SOAR marine.

"Gunny, can you patch us into the marine on the walls?" I asked. "Does he have more of those rockets? Can he start targeting the other tanks? If we limit their mobility, the mech pilot can finish ripping them to shreds."

"We only salvaged the one, sir," replied Gunny Bonner. "We're pinned in, taking heavy casualties right now. I can't spare anyone to look for more."

Not bothering with the niceties of radio protocol, I cut the comms and went back to observing the battle. Nothing really happened. The tankers seemed more intent on protecting their own and avoiding the HK-PP. The mech pilot seemed to be a patient man, not wanting to get himself dusted with the battle of behemoths so close to being a victory. During the ballet of death that followed, Padagas somehow managed to patched me into the mech pilot.

"HK-PP pilot, this is LR-24. I'm the ground forces commander, do you copy?"

"Little busy here—you know, trying not to die. Whaddya want?"

Even with the distorted signals, I could tell he was blunt. Manners didn't seem to be his strong suit. I liked his moxie, but I hadn't expected anything different from a hot-shot mech jockey.

"If the tanks run, let them," I said. "We need you to enter the camp and relieve the defenders. We're being overrun and will fall without relief."

"I'll help when I can," the pilot replied through gritted teeth.

The voice was high-pitched, boyish almost. Was the pilot a woman?

The mech leaped up in an aerial twist that landed her daintily behind the newly damaged tank. She planted her feet and kicked it. She kicked it! Bashing giant dents in the black metal side.

Clang. CLANG!

The crash rang out, overshadowing the sounds of the firefight happening inside the walls of Camp Jericho. I'd have hated to be the crew of that crawling devil; the ringing probably gave them a concussion. They didn't suffer long—she ended their migraine in a spectacular fashion. Unleashing her chain gun, she rent into the tank's armor and eviscerated the crew. She didn't stop there, but ripped the missile pods off the tank and tossed them aside.

The process wasn't without risk, and a plasma round connected with her shoulder. She'd taken other hits, shrugging them off like they were nothing. But this hit was different. This hit did visual damage. She continued fighting, despite the sparks and smoke flying from her shoulder joint.

"Behind you!"

My warning came in the nick of time. Another short burst of her jump jets put her beside the offending tank. This one had been disabled earlier in the fighting, but was still in well-enough shape to aim its main gun. This time she merely lifted it by its right treads and flipped the beast over. The tank appeared to be weaker there, and the pilot used her two massive robotic hands to rip open the tank like a can of sardines. With a quick burst from her chain guns into the exposed guts, she finished the tank. But the fight wasn't over.

"Only one left, Virgil! If she eliminates the crawling devils, we might get her to clear the fuzzies out of Jericho."

"It ain't over until they're dead, LT. Don't count them out yet."

The functioning enemy tank closest to the tree line seemed to give up.

"It's running, Virgil!"

It was using a zig-zag evasion pattern as it ran from the battle. She sent several long bursts into the fleeing tank. I don't know where she hit it, but the crawling devil started trailing smoke as it disappeared into the snowy forests. With the tank threat eliminated, the HK pilot strode through the damaged gate. I hoped that those leejes we'd left at the fallen gates were already dead, because I couldn't stand the thought of my men getting crushed under the boots of several tons of HK mech.

"Make ready!" I told my leejes. "Take advantage of the mech support."

When the mech entered the camp, it jumped on top of a support building and landed with a crunch. Rage Company desperately tried to maintain its defensive perimeter nearby. From the building's roof, the mech could no doubt see most of the camp.

Unslinging her chain guns, the HK fired at the massed rebels, knocking them down like lines of dominoes.

"Haha!" I screamed in jubilation at the fuzzies.

Legion forces had been stuck against the walls, unable to find a way to break out from the stalemate. We couldn't fight back, and the enemy used our inaction to slowly pick us off. The furry Arthava snipers whittled us down, killing leej after leej from their vantage point on the roofs of Camp Jericho's buildings.

Now the tides had turned. Rebel leaders seemed to realize the danger they'd created when they'd boxed themselves in. Rather than risk having their tactics turned against them, the screaming hyenas charged the HK with bolts blazing.

I couldn't help it, I laughed at the stupidity.

Then I realized my joy was premature.

The fuzzies were charging right at us, at my line of leejes. I watched in horror as my boys had to duck down again, trying to create the tiniest sliver of a profile they could. The rebels were trying to make a run for it. But the Arthava would have to run by us to escape...

"Watch out!" I yelled to my leejes.

The fuzzies kept coming, but they couldn't outrun the plasma bolts the mech pilot threw their way. Furry bodies piled up feet from where Rage Company was hunkered down. I yelled like a loon with the rest of my men.

The HK paused while it cycled a new drum into its plasma chain gun. The silence was unnerving. The clash of battle, the screams of dying men, and the explosive discharge of shot and shell had become my new normal. The absence of that sound scared me more than any of the previous explosions.

In the silence we heard that ominous grinding. Another tank? One that hadn't been as damaged as I thought? Turning to look across the other parapet toward the open field, I saw the smoking tank heading straight toward the damaged gate. With her back turned, the pilot was a sitting duck.

"Behind you!" I yelled into the mech's comms.

The HK turned, but it was too late to prevent the massive missile volley. The enemy tank had fired everything it had left, a last gasp. Sensing the threat, the mech pilot fired as she turned, guns blazing. I watched it like a slow-motion car crash, two mechanized fighters destroying each other in a climax of explosive energy. The pilot gave us one last victory, crushing many of the fuzzies as she tumbled to the ground.

"Noooo!"

The smoking mech lay unmoving.

I didn't even know her name, but I cried for her. She'd paid the ultimate price to save my leejes. But there wasn't time to stand around bawling. There were rebels to kill. Thanks to her, there were a lot fewer of them. The Arthava that weren't crushed to death were showered in flaming wreckage, and they weren't wearing armor. Threat icons on my HUD began blinking out. The readings on enemy activity started dropping so rapidly that the integrated targeting system in my bucket momentarily glitched.

Burning Arthava smell remarkably like burning rubber. I hadn't smelled something that disgusting since I'd been sprayed by a palm skunk during field training. I watched the carnage, entranced by the macabre death throes of the rebels. We all might've kept watching, but Gunny Bonner jumped onto the L-comm.

"You leej bubbas expecting my marines to do all the heavy lifting?"

This small battle might have been won, but the war raged on. We still had the hard task of rooting out the rebels inside Camp Jericho, and they would not surrender without a fight.

You corner an animal, and it gets vicious.

Corner an Arthava—it gets smart.

26

"Sergeant Dwyer, get this battlefield policed."

"Already on it, LT."

"Thanks. Corporal Faulkner, , move our wounded leejes to Doc and then I want every fuzzy's blaster staged by the walls."

"Might I make an alternative suggestion, sir?" asked Gunny Bonner.

"Send it."

"Sir... they've got troops to bleed. MCR is going to hit us again. It's inevitable. We need to start preparing for a last stand now, with fallback positions."

"He's right, sir," Dwyer cut in.

"Send your plans to my HUD," I replied, unsure how to proceed.

"Let's secure Jericho first, LT." Dwyer advised. "We need to be sure there are no MCR left inside the wire to shoot us in the back when the next attack comes."

"Obviously," I replied.

I had two of the most lethal KTF machines in the camp giving me ideas, I wasn't dumb enough to tell them no without a damn good reason. Even with their help, it took us longer to regroup than it should have, and we had no idea where the enemy was or where they'd strike from next time. After the HK had broken the siege on Camp Jericho, we'd been in shock. Those HKs were supposed to be the fist of Oba, unbeatable... that's how we always heard about them in the reserves. And this one had gone down to some kranker high on religion. How was that even possible?

"Padagas, divvy up the remaining charge packs."

"Yes, sir."

I set a timer on my HUD counting off the time we had for preparation. I knew I couldn't let perfection be the enemy of good enough, so I committed to launching the clearing mission when the clock struck zero, regardless of how ready we were. Every unit was preparing to kick the bloody rebels out of Jericho.

Despite our losses, Rage Company automatically reestablished a chain of command so we could continue functioning as a unit. First Sergeant Bonner did the same with Red Company.

Then the final numbers of troops now under my command showed up on my screen. It was so low, I had to double-check.

"Virgil, this doesn't need to go out over the open comms. Verify count because I'm questioning the number my HUD is showing me are left."

"It's bad... Twenty-five leejes and a hundred and twelve marines."

"Oba! We landed with two companies! We're down to two and a half squads!"

"Thank Oba for the marines, sir."

"Two hundred and six of them landed—we lost more than half of our marines!"

"Roger, of the three companies that make up our rag-tag group, we're down to twenty-six percent. You'll have a lot of letters to write, sir."

"Letters?"

"You're the commanding officer, it's your sacred duty to write their families, sir. A tradition that predates the Legion itself."

"Is it worse than Zastos yet, Virgil?"

"Not yet, sir, not yet."

The raw numbers were shocking. We were bleeding warriors at an alarming rate. The last attack had been brutal; we all would've died without the appearance of the HK. She saved the day. Did she get a medal? Nope. She must've been from a poor fringe world.

"Everyone ready to roll?" I asked Dwyer.

"No time like the present, sir!" answered Padagas.

"Charge!"

We began probing for surviving pockets of the enemy. Things were too chaotic, our forces too dispersed for anything more sophisticated than a general charge in the right direction.

We would move down the camp's main thoroughfares and find small groupings of fuzzies hiding against buildings or crouched beneath windows, trying to stay hidden now that they were outnumbered.

"Contact left!" someone would call, and then we'd light up the MCR and move on, clearing buildings as we went.

The fuzzies kept pulling back, getting closer and closer to the armory, which would have to be the survivor's last stand. The building butted up against the wall over the cliff, on the opposite end of Jericho's gates.

"We got 'em cornered!" I yelled, waving the hunter-killer force of marines and legionnaires on. "No quarter!"

It wasn't the smartest plan. We were cornering them like wild animals. When they couldn't run, they'd bite back. But we wanted them to stand and fight… so we could kill them and be done with it. We were exhausted, too angry to care about the rules of engagement insisted upon by the House of Reason. We wanted blood, and ran pell-mell at them until they boxed themselves in near the barracks.

"For Stanton!" the marines yelled.

We fought the final skirmish with the rebels over the ground where Captain Stanton died. The battle cry from the marines was quickly picked up by my leejes as we pushed the fuzzies back.

"Keep up the pressure!"

Oba must've been on our side, since the Arthava ran away from the armory and over to the corner where both walls sat above the cliff heights. The rebels had clearly failed to form any contingency plans, or they wouldn't be trapped like this. Failure of leadership, if you ask me. Maybe a command structure that didn't value their fuzzy little lives.

That didn't mean they weren't going down without a fight. Those MCR didn't want to die any more than we did. Once cut off from any further retreat, they dropped into shooting stances and tried to stand ground. They began to growl and gnash their teeth, throwing their heads back again in that same way I'd seen before they prepared to charge earlier in the day. These needed putting down.

"No quarter!" I shouted again.

And we killed them, by the dozens. I wasn't counting. It felt like Oba had dumped every fuzzy on Rhyssis Wan on our laps. I felt in an obliging mood, so I spanked 'em. One blaster bolt at a time. I'm just a generous officer.

A bolt whizzed by my bucket, and Faulkner tackled me to the ground. He saw the fuzzy who had a bead on me before I did. Rookie mistake.

A nearby leej coolly sniped the shooter, then picked off another two rebels.

"Pay attention, sir," the sniper chided. "Next time Faulkner might not be around to save you. And I might miss."

With the shooting winding down and the MCR in the camp well enough accounted for that I could take my blaster out of the fight, I attempted to reach the Brass.

"Any 9th Legion Headquarters Element, this is LR-24 of Rage Company," I said over the main L-comm channel. "In the absence of other senior officers, I've assumed control of the remnants of Rage Company, Dragon Company, and the marines of Red Company, 3/4th SOAR. How copy, over?"

"9th Actual, what do you need? We're a little busy here. Got the enemy on the run. We need to keep pursuing them until we get a decisive victory."

General Ponce, 9th Actual, was talking to me.

"Sir," I continued, "we've managed to repel the second assault on our position. We're down to a hundred thirty-seven troops, and that includes forty-three walking wounded. Sir, we need reinforcements or extraction. Jericho's defenses were compromised by enemy tanks, the HK Fleet sent was destroyed, and our charge pack supply is critical. What do you advise?"

"Advise? Hold what you've got, by any means necessary. We're pushing the enemy toward you and will link up at our earliest possible convenience. Fleet is tasked with rounding up stray elements in just as bad shape as you elsewhere on the planet, so they won't be of any more assistance. Make it happen, Lieutenant."

"By any means necessary. Roger. LR-24, out."

I kept my scream of primal rage at bay, at least until I ended the comms link. I was about to reach out to my senior non-com, Sergeant Dwyer, when he called me on the L-comm.

"By any means necessary—it's a good order," he said. "It means we can do whatever we want, as long as we win."

"You were listening, Virgil?" I couldn't believe it.

"Always," he smugly replied. "It's how I anticipate the commander's intent before he knows it himself."

Before I could answer back, Gunny Bonner called me over the general comm. "We've got some last few MCR cornered. What are your orders with the rebels?"

"Offer them an unconditional surrender. If they'll retreat without their arms, we watch them go. At a minimum, it'll cost the rebels the credits to rearm them. We can't slaughter them, we're not murderers." I said it with more authority than I felt.

"You can't murder a traitor, sir. It's an execution. And you've promised my marines a 'No Quarters' fight. Wouldn't want to disappoint on our first date, sir."

"I'm not going to preside over a war crime, Gunny."

"Looks like there are only thirty rebels left. Could be more, I'm only accounting for those not hiding in buildings. That's nothing we can't handle. Should be able to kill them in a matter of minutes. Quicker, if we let our mortar team play."

"Sergeant, I said no. We give them the chance to surrender."

I couldn't ask my men to take the risk, so I slung my blaster, and walked toward the group of clustered rebels with as much dignity as I could muster. Well, an ungainly limp, anyway... but let's not get picky. Rebel Arthava in their white and gray camouflage uniforms waited, blasters gripped tightly in their four furry fingers. That they didn't start shooting told me that they were well aware of how lost their cause was.

These MCR were using one of the nearby barracks for cover, but if we started shooting, they'd all die. I knew that. And they did, too. Turning on my external speaker, speaking in standard, I tried diplomacy.

"I come to offer you the gift of your lives. Lay down your weapons in total surrender, and you will live. I'll let you march out of here, but if we must finish this battle, you will all die. Who can speak for you?"

I never got a formal answer from the rebels. I imagine their surviving chain of command was huddled in the rear arguing over seniority, but the rank and file knew the game was up. They dropped their blasters and walked toward the destroyed gate. The rebels had their hands in the air in the universal sign of surrender, some of them sporting pretty nasty looking injuries.

Yes! It's working, they're surrendering! I thought as the trickle of deserters became a flowing mass as the Arthava headed for freedom.

And then I heard the charged whine of a single blaster bolt being fired.

An Arthava with a shiny insignia on the breast of his uniform opened fire on his own men. One minute there was silence, and then the shrieks of a renewed firefight. Men screaming, sending down a storm of bolts. Arthava screaming, as Padagas turned one of their own flamers on them. The smell of burning rubber spread, and the dizzying flow of bolts created a river of lava in the air they super-heated.

"Make 'em pay!" Dwyer hollered into the L-comm.

In hindsight, it was clear that the rebel officers were shooting their men to prevent a surrender. But the legionnaires and marines under my command had been looking for a reason to fire. And that they did to great effect.

"Cease fire," I futilely screamed into the L-comm. I slammed my injured arm down onto blasters, trying to make the bolts miss. The pain almost made me double over. I struggled to get through to them and screamed into the comms channel, "They were surrendering! Cease fire!"

The battered men continued firing, ignoring my pleas for mercy. It was a slaughter. I rushed back to where

Corporal Faulkner had been when the fighting began. He fired as wildly as the rest of them once the shooting started.

"Cease fire, Faulkner!"

Yanking on his arm, I tried to get his attention. It took a few moments, but when I snapped him out of it, the firefight was already over. There wasn't a rebel left untouched from the brutal melee. None of them got out of it alive.

"We made 'em pay, sir," Faulkner said, panting.

"Damn right,"' Padagas added. The grim resolve in his voice was heart wrenching. The boy inside was dead. All that was left was a stone-cold killer. At least he was on my side. "KTF all kelhorned night!"

"We sure did, Remo, we sure did."

When the firing stopped, fifty-nine rebels were dead, strewn across the field. Some were still smoldering from Padagas's flamer. Gunny Bonner had been a little off in his prediction of the final numbers—but he'd made what he desired a reality.

So much blood, brilliant in the afternoon sun.

I stood in shock, horrified at the events as they unfolded.

"That's how you do it, sir!" Bonner whooped.

"They were surrendering..." I started.

"Their officer thought otherwise, and we obliged. No time for niceties in war. Ooah!"

It took me a while to recover from the event, mentally anyway. The pain from my arm had me seeing stars. Pinpricks of light danced before my eyes, and the pain rolled over me in waves. I screamed in my bucket, alone. I wanted the rebels dead also, but we couldn't become them to beat them.

When I could calm down, I ordered the men to tend to the wounded.

"Was it as bad as Zastos yet, Virgil?" I asked him while we picked up a wounded leej and carried him to the med station.

"Ask me that after the final push, sir. The end of it all remains to be seen."

I didn't see how anything could have been worse than all of this. We set the wounded marine down on a table beside another man who looked too still to be alive. Doc Tran bustled about between tables, looking haggard.

I opened up comms. "All right, Gunny, I want men back on those walls. While you marines earn your rides home, Sergeant Dwyer will police up the bodies."

It was a gruesome job, but there was nobody alive I'd trust more to honor the fallen.

"Freezer filled up a long time ago, sir."

"Stack them outside, then," I said, knowing the cold would do the same. "With as much dignity as possible."

Dwyer was a veteran of many combat assaults, and he efficiently put the boys to work searching the enemy dead, looking for anything useful. Those slates and data packets were left piled near where their former owners had recently been slaughtered. Once we'd policed the gear from the rebel dead, we went through it and kept anything we could repurpose for ourselves.

"Padagas, go through their electronics. See if we can find anything useful in it."

I knew he could handle it, and he needed something to do. We were all that was left of our squad, and he was starting to show the strain of that loss. Giving him busy work, tasks that were critical to our survival, kept him out of his own head. There'd be time to cry later, if we lived that long.

After we'd dealt with the bodies that littered the camp, we set about preparing to make our last stand. "Faulkner, I need you to construct a defensive barrier near those destroyed gates. We need to defend that entry point."

"Too easy, sir, too easy!"

"Then build us a bug out shelter when you're done. Against the cliffs."

His experience in construction back home made him the best man for the job. It was a desperate hedge against our ultimate destruction. Should we be overrun, there'd be a long wait for help.

"And get me an update on the CO," I said as an afterthought.

I figured Captain Archer was still out of it, but asking made me feel better. I had been so occupied with the moment to moment fight, I'd mentally pushed our wounded troops out of head. I still feel bad about that, being such an uncaring kranker.

Guess it didn't matter because the fuzzies weren't about to give us time to process our feelings and we knew it. So we set to work reinforcing our perimeter. The work was hard and progress was slowed by our need to maintain a constant guard. I put the wounded on those watches since they didn't need to move around much for that task.

It was a small concession to their pride, but I knew that eyes searching for threats was the best we could hope for from them.

In the end my prayers were answered. The enemy left us alone for the next twenty-four hours. We had time to get as ready as we could hope for, given the circumstances. Even better—our men were able to rest. I kept the light guard schedule, counting on the rest of the men to wake up quickly should we need them.

"Full kit when you rack out, Leejes."

It made for sore muscles, but it gave us a unit-wide quick reaction force. We could all be prepared and in the fight in under a minute. I was able to keep the mess tent working around the clock, though we switched to the robotic field cook. We were eating glorified fecal paste that was dressed up to look like real food. But the grub was filling, the kaff was hot, and our bellies were full.

During the lull in the action, Faulkner and I created a contingency strategy. A last-ditch effort at making the Arthava bleed for every square inch of ground they took from us.

"Faulkner, I know your construction boys are tired. But we need to make this place as defensible as possible."

"Roger, sir. We're highly motivated to kill and not die. We understand, sir."

"Good. I want sniping platforms on roofs and hasty barricades we can fall back to. Where are we with the final bunker?"

"They're as good as we can make them without real construction gear."

It was good news. If we managed to fall back together, the rebels would have to fight for every inch. If we had to retreat, it would be to another defensive position. The traitorous scum would have to continually assault new objectives. My only regret was that we hadn't thought of it sooner, so we could've done a better job.

Faulkner looked up at the stars twinkling above us. "I hope that the 9th comes riding in to the rescue soon."

"The 9th will arrive," I said. "Only trouble is they'll be pushing the rest of that MCR element ahead of them."

27

"Have they forgotten about us, LT?" one of my wounded legionnaires asked me.

We'd just finished moving the last of our dead to the makeshift morgue and were stacking the last of the dead rebels when the white powder began coating the field in front of our position. It obscured the dead outside the walls, adding to the sense of calm we all felt.

"Not a chance," Gunny answered for me.

"Listen to the hullbuster," Dwyer drolly replied. "They're occasionally right."

I answered the legionnaire quietly, "The 9th is pushing the whole horde of them in our direction. They'll come."

After a day of inaction, I hoped that the enemy would just give up on us. That maybe, just maybe, they'd moved on to an easier target. General Ponce had said the Fleet was busy picking up other elements stranded across the planet. Maybe those had become the bigger sand-fish. And the Bar Kokhba cultists were fanatical in their hatred of the Republic, but they'd lost significantly more troops than we had. Had we hit them hard enough to buy us the time we needed for the cavalry to arrive?

Please let that be true.

The wait for something—anything—to happen began to feel almost peaceful, like the camping trips I'd taken as a kid. If you ignored the staggering losses we'd suffered and focused only on what was in front of us. It worked.

To a point.

"How do you do it, Virgil?" I asked, the fact that I'd asked variations of this question many times before not at all lost on me. "How do you stop from going insane on missions like this?"

"Accept your death. Knowing that I'm already dead brings me peace. Frees me from the survivor's guilt."

"Easier said than done, Virgil. It wasn't you in charge. It wasn't you who was responsible for so many dead leejes."

"Stop that krank! You're a Legion officer, not some kel-horned sailor. Now, man up, or we're all dead."

He was right. Hearing it hurt, but he was right.

"Guess we only have one job left," I said grimly. "When this is over, they'll bury Rage Company under the corpses of the traitors we've slain."

That sense of peace allowed me to appreciate the natural beauty of the wintery mountains. I could ignore the bloody orange tinge to the snow. I could appreciate the trees, the crisp mountain air. Even under my bucket, I could smell it. When it started snowing, it added to the tranquil ambiance.

Conversation broke out. The kind I used to relish while we were on training exercises on New Caledonia. Just the guys... talking about nothing while we worked.

"We should build a ski lodge here after we kick the fuzzies from Rhyssis Wan, LT."

"Let's just kill the traitors, there were loyal fuzzies here too."

"But the skiing would be fun!"

"We have mountains in Cally, ya know. Hell, there isn't a planet in the New Caledonia system where you couldn't ski—Pictavia, Ogham, Govan, and Talorc. Plus, all those snow bunnies. Real, human girls... why come here?"

"You ruin all the fun, man."

"It comes with deployment."

It went on like that for a while, and then the talk drifted off and someone—Faulkner—got back to business.

"Are we going to get the bodies outside the gates, sir?"

"No, Faulkner. Let the fuzzies rot where they lie. They'll serve as a natural barrier."

"It'd be funny to watch them trip over their own dead," Faulkner agreed.

"And we don't have the manpower to deal with them, anyway. Let's make this time count." I stepped over a particularly large Arthava that seemed like it would make a good base on which to stack more bodies.

As we worked, the snow hardened on the ground, turning the top layer into a thin sheet of ice that brilliantly reflected the sunlight.

Staring out at the snowy terrain, I prayed, "Please, Oba, protect my men. Keep the Arthava away, let our fight be over. Bring the reinforcements, so I can bring the rest of my men home to their families."

But all those prayers went unanswered.

Early in the morning of our third day in Jericho, we heard the thunder of boots thudding and crunching into the snow. A wind blew across the mountainous terrain, and while we couldn't yet see the troops as they hid under the tree cover, we knew they were out there.

"Do you hear that, Virgil?"

"Yes, sir. I'll start getting everyone on line. But our L-comms is a closed loop... no need to whisper, sir."

I don't know why I still acted like our bucket-to-bucket conversations could be heard by outsiders. Maybe it was paranoia, I don't know, but I couldn't help myself.

"I've got my marines coming on line, sir."

"Thank you, Gunny."

I wanted more information and the two NCOs had different tech than the LARKs I wore—Virgil with his Legion proper kit and the hullbusters with whatever sensors they had.

"Gunny, Dwyer, your armor's different from mine. Are you getting anything on your HUD?"

"My HUD overlay ain't much, sir. Damn sure ain't Legion tech. Just feeds me some quick intel and works as a target assist. But if you're wondering if those are fuzzies out there, LT, I'd say hell yeah."

"Thanks, Gunny. What about you, Virgil?"

"Negative, sir. I've got nothing you're not seeing, just the intuition from years of field experience. If those were our forces, they'd tell us they were coming. No, it's the Arthava."

There wasn't a lot to go on with our perimeter sensors down, but I trusted the intuition of my NCOs. My bucket's AI was next to useless. It couldn't identify the icons as friendly forces, but until they attacked Jericho, the AI wouldn't declare them hostile.

"Gunny, send a few marines to the rooftops. If they hit in force, we can't hold the walls. Let's prepare for the last hurrah."

Gunny Bonner never answered. The sergeant of the guard, a marine private, sent out the official alert. We rushed to our positions, making ready.

"Faulkner, it's go time. Pull your construction teams back on line."

"Yes, sir. I sent a few of them to the sniper platforms. The rest of us are en route to your location."

We were expecting a fight at any moment, but nothing happened. I expected the troops massed outside the walls to attack, but there was nothing. The unknown force stood just out of sight, hidden by the infernal trees and burnt out ruins of the tanks. Only the crunching sound of movement on the icy ground assured us that the HUD alerts weren't from some phantom army.

There was clearly a sizeable force, but they didn't attack. It was unnerving. Normally the Legion would attempt to get recon drones or leejes out there, but we didn't have that kind of manpower. We were out of options, so we waited.

And waited.

I started to think I was going mad. Was I imagining it all? If I was, so were my men. We were on alert, ready to pounce at any second. Or maybe they sensed a trap? Didn't know how vulnerable we were inside. It looked like hell had come for their buddies outside the camp, that was for sure.

"Why aren't they attacking?" I asked on the command channel.

"To mess with our heads? To hype themselves up? To pray? The fuzzies haven't exactly behaved logically, sir," Virgil reminded me.

"Let them wait, sir," Bonner added. "Only buys us time for the 9th to get reinforcements to us and—"

A whistling sound, so faint at first, stopped the Gunny's mouth from moving. I could hear it too, and I almost didn't recognize it for what it was. Then it shrieked.

"Incoming!"

Boom.

When the attack finally started, it wasn't another frontal assault. They seemed to have learned their lesson. Mortars, they were shelling us with mortars.

Boom.

The rebel forces fired another mortar salvo, and this time the telltale whistling had our full attention. They were overshooting their marks, destroying the support facilities. They hadn't even adjusted their fire from the first round.

Amateurs.

We began to return in kind, sending our own mortars into the tree line where we suspected them to be.

The ground around us rumbled and shrapnel flew through the air, rocky bullets that killed a few of my leejes and injured a dozen marines.

"Doc, we need you to get the wounded fit to fight!" I called in, my mind scrambling for what to do next.

"Doing the best I can, but I'm no miracle worker. Now leave me to my work, I'm a little busy here, Fetch."

Our boys injured by the shrapnel were tough, refusing medical aid and staying on the line. It was hard, being attacked by an enemy you couldn't see. It was even harder watching our numbers continually dwindle. What made it worse was that we couldn't do anything about it.

Boom.

The shelling continued...

Boom.

Destroying more of the ancient buildings...

Boom.

And showering us in shrapnel and debris.

Boom.

I willed myself to keep my eyes on the hills. Hoping that what we were giving back was hurting them as much as we were being harmed by their own fire. The MCR could rush out of those woods at any moment, we had to be ready. I checked the sensors in my bucket and extrapolated from that data as I watched the field in front of me.

Sket.

They were walking the shells closer and closer to our position on Jericho's castle walls.

"Be ready to abandon the walls," I ordered. "We'll take up the position just behind it. It'll let us miss the worst of the attack so we can KTF these kranking hyenas."

The shelling continued, until their mortar crews found the mark. We lost twenty marines. Trigger pullers we couldn't afford to lose. The Arthava found us, but they never fully bracketed our position on the walls. The Legion would never accept such imprecise fire, but even clumsy shots can kill.

"Be ready," Dwyer called out.

"How're your marines, Gunny?"

Huddled down behind the walls, I waited for an answer. None came.

"Gunny, report."

A missile shrieked overhead.

Boom.

"Gunny, report!"

He hadn't survived the wait for the final assault. First Sergeant Rodney Bonner died during the shelling. I was pissed. Bonner had grown on me and his competence had helped us halt the last attack. With every man we lost, our collective viability became more and more unstable.

Spirits remained grim, but resolute. It was largely because Doc paced the lines rendering aid to those with minor wounds. He was our angel, seemingly oblivious to the war going on around him. After every circuit along our perimeter, he'd return to the medical tent and check on the more severely wounded.

"Be careful, Doc."

"We can't have you getting hurt!"

"Can't kiss it and make it better if you're dead, Doc Tran!"

Leejes were taught to be protective of our docs. There wasn't much else we could do while we waited for the shelling to end. Just try to keep the medic safe. An assault would follow the mortar rounds, and we'd need our medic available when that happened.

"Damn it, Doc! We'll bring 'em to you," Dwyer hollered after him. "Get your ass back!"

I had to fight back the urge to go full Fleet on him, but Dwyer was right. "Doc, keep to the medical tent. They'll hit us any moment now," I ordered through the L-comm.

"Yes, Mom," Tran chuckled.

His laugh was contagious. It helped the rest of my dwindling command relax, just for a moment. He'd just returned to his med-tent when the mortaring assault resumed.

Maybe they had to switch out their barrels?

Shrugging, I continued watching and waiting. The first three rounds landed among the rubble and nobody was hurt. The fourth arched overhead and landed near our medical tent.

Boom.

"Doc?" I called into the comm. I had just seen his vitals wink out on my HUD. "Doc!"

There wasn't an answer. Just... silence.

Smoke and dust plumed from where the medical tent once stood. Doc had been there when the mortar landed. He was killed instantly. He died with the men he labored to save. I screamed again, fighting against the primal rage that threatened to boil up. It almost drowned me in the futility of our situation.

"Why the hell couldn't you let the locals help us? Why, Archer, why?" I screamed into my bucket.

For the thousandth time, I cursed that fatal decision. A larger force would've given us options right now, like counterassault.

"Get it together, LT. KTF, that's how we honor Doc now," Dwyer said to me, via private link.

He was right, but it galled me to sit there and take the shelling.

Something out of nowhere reminded me of my training instructor.

"Son, if you get shot, Doc can patch you up. But if Doc bites it, everyone is screwed. They earn their title and place in the unit. Protect 'em with your last breath."

Faulkner's came up next to me and his shoulders sank. "What'll we do without Doc? Who'll save the wounded?"

"We've got Sergeant Dwyer... but first we gotta hold out for a few more hours. Calm down, Corporal Faulkner. Head in the game."

But Faulkner kept shaking his head. "This is it, LT. This is it."

Grabbing him by the shoulder, I shook the big man. "We'll make 'em pay for this. KTF, with all we've got left."

"KTF, sir."

The grim resolve in his voice assured me that he'd be okay. A runner reached the tent and shot me back visual from his HUD. Doc Tran was draped over a patient, protecting whoever it was from the shelling.

"Check Doc's vitals," I ordered, hoping that somehow my HUD was wrong.

The runner rolled Tran over and checked his pulse. "Nothing, sir."

I could see now who Doc had died protecting. It was Captain Archer—the shining armor gave it away. Tran's final act had given the captain another day.

"How's Archer doing?"

Still in his armor, the captain lay still as the doctor.

"He's unconscious, sir. Probably won't survive without a real hospital."

The readout on Archer's HUD interface showed that Archer was suffering from several internal injuries. I worried about his risk for internal bleeding, but we couldn't help him with those wounds. I wasn't sure if Archer's extra time would be worth much, given the dire straits we were in.

"Faulkner," I said, "get to the tent and take the captain to the bug out shelter you made. Mark the unit HUD interface, just in case we need to retreat there. Take Padagas and move as many consumables you can. Be discreet about it, but make it happen. Take anyone else you need. We don't have much time. I'll check the rest of the bodies here, but the reports don't look good."

"What are you gonna do, sir?"

"Nothing else to do but KTF."

Faulkner stood, and sprinted to complete his task.

"LR-99, take three leejes and secure anything we can use from the med tent. And Paige, be quick about it. LR-24, out."

Boom.

The shelling continued, but they shifted their fire to the unbroken gate near the Red Company sector of our lines. It didn't last long, and soon a loud thud reverberated the camp as the large wooden door crashed to the ground. Nobody was under it when it fell—a fortuitous thing. The weight would've killed them.

"Barricade, we need a hasty barricade at that gate!" I called.

"On it, sir!"

The senior marine, a staff sergeant whose name I never had the chance to learn, led a group of men to build a hasty fortification. The rebels sniped at them as they worked, and the sergeant and seven more marines died erecting the position. And still the enemy didn't show themselves, preferring to lurk in the trees like cowards.

"Come on already!" I screamed and shook my fist.

I received a blaster bolt to my wounded shoulder for my trouble. Least I could still shoot with the other arm. Not that we had any targets to kill. Just empty trees and mortar salvos. I couldn't see the action in the marine's sector, but I monitored it over the HUD. It was disheartening. Those were men we couldn't afford to lose. With each loss we had to stretch our lines. How much longer would we last?

"9th Actual, come in, over."

Static was my only response.

"Any Caledonian Fleet forces, come in, over."

I still didn't receive a response.

We were on our own. It had been a desperate gamble to call them, but I knew that we were doomed without immediate assistance. The shelling shifted again, causing me to regain my focus. They were walking the rounds inward, a maneuver we'd all practiced. They were trying to take down as much of the walls as they could to add more entry points into the camp. The final assault was coming.

"Make ready! They're coming for us. Monitor your HUDs. If the line breaks, regroup on our last defensible position. We can't hold the intermediary lines, so don't try. If this is it, our final moment, it's been a pleasure. KTF! LR-24, out."

My voice quivered a bit, but I was too tired to care. We had all resigned ourselves to death… we were just hoping it'd be quick and painless.

"I'm sorry, Ashley," I whispered. "I'll see you on the other side."

I'd been right about the timing. Cold comfort that was. It wasn't long after we'd manned the walls again that the shelling stopped.

"Is this a trap? Are they luring us to the walls, Virgil?"

We stood side by side on the wall, scanning the silent trees for movement.

"This, LT, this is the final dance."

"Is this worse than Zastos yet?"

"Ask me when it's over."

I didn't have to order our troops to start shooting. The moment they had a target, they let loose. After hours of shelling, they were hungry for blood. There wasn't much of the battlements left, but enough remained to put a few troops up there with blasters. Height advantage and all—not that it mattered when they outnumbered you by numbers nobody would believe. I read the final reports and even I don't believe it.

"Should I move the crew-served weapons to the walls, sir?" Sergeant Navin asked me over the comms. "The heights would add to their lethality."

"No, leave them focused on the gates. That's where they're going to breach. When the fuzzies come, we make them pay."

"I don't have any det cord to blow the guns when we fall back, sir."

"When we fall back, set the charge pack to over-cycle and abandon the guns."

"I can carry—"

"No, Navin. It'll slow you down. Make it back to the bunkers to ride it out."

With so little room on the damaged walls for men, I concentrated my boys in the positions that protected the breaches in the walls.

"Make every shot count," I cautioned.

The fields in front of us were still pristine, their snowy beauty giving us a last look at the promise of hope Oba provided. The beauty didn't last. Nothing good seems to in this arm of the galaxy.

Howling their war cries, the enemy rushed our position with numbers I couldn't even begin to count. There were so many of them, moving so fast, that they blurred into an amorphous blob of fur and claws, sending up vicious if poorly aimed blaster fire at the parapets.

"Wait for it!"

The Arthavans were running and gunning, spraying blaster fire everywhere. Some of it at us on the walls, yes, but other times just scattered into the open spaces around the camp. Shooting the walls themselves. Shooting at shadows behind the tanks. Just always shooting. And maybe to an effect, because the din of fire and the brilliant flash of so many blaster bolts felt more than overwhelming. It felt like the end.

"Paige, execute contingency plan alpha. I'll stay on the lines, hold them back for as long as possible. Go, now," I ordered.

Paige was a good legionnaire; he didn't argue or make grand sentimental gestures. He pulled half the men back as I abandoned the parapets. Despite the pain in my arm, I manhandled some of the leejes off the wall. They'd lost themselves to the bloodlust, firing wildly at the wall of furry hyenas.

"Fall back—now, damn it!" I shoved one man over to the stairs.

The rebels fired their weapons, but didn't slow down. The traitors clearly wanted to get in close rather than fight it out at longer ranges. We slaughtered them, but I knew we'd be dead the moment they got within arm's reach of us.

"Pull back, by the numbers!"

I wanted to keep up the slaughter, but time was rapidly running out. Maybe it was already up. I fired anyway, sending as many bolts toward the enemy as my trigger finger could manage.

"For Santos!"

I shot the enemy, standing shoulder to shoulder with my men. We killed rebel after rebel, but they kept charging. If this was where I died, it had to matter. Someone had to know we'd died doing our duty.

"9th Legion Actual, this is LR-24. Our position is lost, but we'll fight to the last. Camp Jericho has fallen. I'm sorry, sir. KTF."

With my final update sent, I narrowed my focus to the choke point where I fought. The enemy would have to funnel in through the gates, and we stood resolutely in their path. They were getting closer. When they were a few meters from us, they slowed their pace and began firing their blasters into our ranks, actually aiming now. It wasn't quite volley fire, but the massed bolts were having a devastating effect.

"Die!" I screamed as I held my trigger down and fired.

I ignored the warning that my blaster was in danger of overheating, of going critical. I wasn't worried about that, not when the rebels were almost on me. I could hear their growls, guttural and primal. Legionnaires dropped beside me, and I silently prayed my death prayer.

"Harken to me, my ancestors. Walk with me, until I stand at the foot of the one most high. Reunite me with my people, back to the beginning. Complete my circle. Call me to you, Oba. I am ready."

Released from my fear of death, I got angry. No longer was I willing to calmly accept my demise. The Bar Kokhba Rebellion had taken me from my family, stealing irreplaceable precious moments from me. I mourned the child I would never meet, and the dreams I'd never fulfill. I'd kept the anger at bay before, but now I had nothing to prevent me from fueling the flames of my fury. I wanted blood. Dying could wait a few moments more.

My blaster finally died. I screamed, "Take that!" and hurled it at the fuzzy horde.

Dropping to one knee, I scooped up a blaster from a dead brother to resume firing. Those of us on the wall kept trading bolts with them, but it couldn't last. The enemy would be close enough to end it all any second. If we didn't pull back soon, we wouldn't be able to. We'd done as much as we could, and I knew it. I got onto the L-comm, resigned.

"Fall back by the numbers, good order! LR-24, out."

Standing, I felt my legs groan in pain. Even kneeling on the cold ground for that short time was painful. But dead men didn't worry about such things. I forced the pain away and increased my rate of fire as I hobbled back to our next position. I couldn't see them, but I hoped the marines at the other gate managed to fall back as well.

We hadn't made it to the next barricade before the Arthava finally rushed through the gates. An explosion echoed from the Red Company gate. The marines had somehow managed to improvise an explosion. I hoped the bomb killed dozens of fuzzies, but I couldn't worry about that anymore. The rebels in front of me were demanding my attention.

"Run for it!" I yelled.

We'd started pulling back with twenty men, a mix of legionnaires and marines. There were only nine of us left when we hit the first barricade. The troops Faulkner had placed on the roofs were making their presence known. Those angels of death forced the rebels down, crawling over piles of their own dead. Those brave warriors saved us, keeping the enemy off-kilter for a few more precious seconds.

I used the time they bought us to fire more bolts into the rebel ranks, stopping only to reload charge packs. It was exhausting work and my injured arm was throbbing. The pain medicines administered by Doc Tran had worn off long before. Simply holding the blaster was difficult. Despite the pain, I continued firing and hitting my mark.

"Pull back to the final position," I bellowed.

There were more troops with me now, men from the advanced group I'd sent to man the barricades. They stood with me, manning crew-served guns and spewed their hatred at the rebels with each blast. I'd waited too long. I should've pulled back sooner.

"Virgil, are you with me?"

"Little busy, LT."

"Ooah."

Some of my boys were ripped to pieces at the barricades by the enraged Arthava. That's not a metaphor—the hyenas literally ripped them apart. I could hear their screams, but we couldn't help them. We were close enough to see the blood dripping from the snouts of the kranking hyenas. Screaming my rage and regret, I fired several bolts into the maw of the roaring Arthava.

"Eat that, you kranker!" I yelled through my external speakers.

We fired as we pulled back. And we only had one line to pull back to. I wanted the rebel scum to bleed for it, KTF-style. The orderly withdrawal fell apart, and we ran toward the next barricade. It was every man for himself, though I slowed down to cover the retreat.

Blaster bolts kicked up debris all around us as the men ran.

"Come and get it!" I yelled, quickly depleting another charge pack before joining my men in retreat.

It was hopeless, but we ran anyway. It was a rout. The cultists had won the fight for Camp Jericho. Still, we weren't about to just roll over and die. Instead we fell back to the next position. It was near the final row of barracks, where we'd lost Captain Stanton.

When I made it to the final barricade, I dropped my rifle and manned an empty crew-served blaster. Wendell had been on it, and I had to shove his corpse out of the way, but he always was a practical sort. He'd understand the unceremonious treatment. Even touching the butterfly grips hurt, sending white hot pain up my arms. I didn't care, I welcomed the pain. It reminded me that I was still alive, that there were more rebels to kill.

"For Cally!"

I fired controlled bursts until the enemy got closer. Then I opened it up, holding the trigger down. I fired until the barrel overheated, and the battery began to scream in protest. When it finally couldn't take the heat of the overcharged weapon, the battery pack cycled down completely. I was shot at point-blank range by an Arthava. My side blazed with fire as I struggled to maintain consciousness.

Funny, I'd always assumed that dying would hurt more.

28

"I thought angels would be prettier," I groaned.

"You got better than an angel, you got me."

"Is this hell, then?"

Padagas laughed as he slapped my shoulder. The pain was unreal. I managed not to cry out, I think.

"Did Virgil make it?"

"Not sure who all made it, sir. Let me treat your wound first, LT."

They say Oba has a soft spot in his heart for fools, and it must be true because he watched over me. I didn't die. Corporal Faulkner and Stern pulled my battered body back to a small bunker he'd made. They'd piled the bodies of Arthava dead on top of it, hiding us in plain sight.

"Faulkner… thanks."

"Don't thank me. Just didn't want your job, is all. We've been over this."

The Arthava were a superstitious people; they treated their dead with such reverence that they never disturbed the bodies. If they'd stuck around to bury them, they would've found us, but after Camp Jericho fell, they refocused on the larger war. Or maybe with the 9th chasing them, they didn't want to stick around. Either way, their big picture thinking let them miss what was right in front of them.

Not all of us made it into the bunker; I counted only a dozen. Captain Archer was already there and he made thirteen, but he was as good as dead if we couldn't get him to a hospital. His shallow breathing worried me, but there was nothing I could do for him. Watching out the only viewing slit in the confined space, I saw rebel Arthava scrounging among our dead.

"There's one close by," I whispered.

The Arthava's furry snout was covered in blood, human blood.

He was eating Navin.

Bile choked my throat. They were eating our dead!

"Let's go—" I started, my vision blurred in anger.

Padagas grabbed my shoulder. "We'll make 'em pay, sir. But not today."

How much he had changed.

The fuzzies spent several hours hunting for war trophies while hundreds of other rebels milled about aimlessly. As day shifted into night, they moved out of view. I didn't know if they'd left the camp or were just in another part of it.

"Faulkner," I whispered through a secure connection, "were any other hideaways like this built?"

"Yes, sir, we made four. Until they leave the area, we can't check them. Maybe the leejes and marines on the roofs hid early enough? Maybe they're still alive as well?"

I didn't answer him, but I suspected we both knew the truth. They were all dead. These bunkers wouldn't have cut off our communications with each other. I wanted to ask him where the other bunkers were, but I was distracted by the sounds of blaster fire. Mortars followed the pitched sound of the blaster bolts.

"They're shelling the camp, I think?"

"Our luck will hold, sir. I'm too pretty to die."

I only shook my head. When did Faulkner become the jokester?

Boom.

Boom.

The rebel cultists were finishing the destruction they'd started. I was close to panicking, close to rushing out of the bunker to get it over with. But then our HUDs lit up in the most glorious shade of green I've ever seen.

Those weren't MCR mortars, they were ours! And they were accompanied by legionnaires, lots of them. Help had arrived.

"Faulkner, check everyone's kit. We're gonna get back in the fight."

He stared at me for a long minute, his expression hidden by the black and tan helmet. I was afraid he was going to disobey. I could almost imagine his disgust pulsing from his helmet. But he's a good leej, and he nodded. In just under a minute, we were all kitted back up for the final showdown in the ill-fated Jericho. There weren't many of us, but we couldn't let our reinforcements fight alone. We were leejes. We supported our own.

"All right, Leejes, we're going back out there to aid our brothers," I said over the company L-comm. "If you're too wounded too fight, you can guard the captain. The 9th is out there. They're our family. Nobody hits our family without paying for it."

Turning, I faced the three marines huddled for warmth in the opposite corner. In the dim lighting, they were hard to discern. Almost like you couldn't quite tell that they weren't one of us, that they weren't legionnaires too.

"This is a leej fight. You can sit it out if you want. But you're legionnaires in my book. You earned it," I said, as dispassionately as I could. It had to be their decision, I didn't want to unduly pressure them into going back into that mess.

"I'm with you, sir," one growled, "but I'll castrate you if you demote me to legionnaire again. I'm no bubba, I'm a SOAR marine!"

I didn't know his name, but I imagine that I'd have gotten that same answer from any of Stanton's brave warriors.

I smiled and took the spot by the low bunker door, if you could call those wooden planks a proper "door." When everyone was set to go, I made sure that I'd be the first one out. None of our wounded sat back down, and we stacked by the exit, prepared to meet our fate.

"One..."

Thank you, Oba.

"Two..."

We'll make this mean something.

"Three!"

I opened the door, bursting out into the frozen night air. In the moonlight, the carnage looked even more horrific. Broken and bloodied bodies lay strewn about like trash after the Pictavian harvest festival. We stopped, looking around for targets, anything to shoot, but there were only dead. Stumbling, fighting the pain from multiple injuries, I was momentarily blinded when a flare went up. Sure, my bucket compensated, but my reaction was more from the shock of the event, than the event itself.

When I could see again, I picked up the silhouette of a legionnaire. We ambled toward him, as best we could. We looked like drunk soldiers, trying to play twister after a night of self-indulgence. When we got within arm's reach of the relief force, my HUD registered it as Sergeant Major Logan Scott.

"Sergeant Major," I managed weakly, but Scott interrupted.

"Stand down, Leej. Medivacs are en route, you're relieved," he said and gave me in a bone-crushing hug.

29

After telling the barkeep my story, we sat silently staring into our drinks. The Sleeping Legion bar was somber, but it was warm. For just a moment, I could forget that icy hellhole. Even thinking about Rhyssis Wan gave me chills. I shuddered despite the temperature.

I don't know how long we sat there, for I was beyond caring. Only the next drink mattered. The silence dragged on.

"So, what happened to your captain?" Wetmore asked.

"He made it," I said, "but he's paralyzed from the waist down. Could be a long while before nanites get him walking again. Probably take a medical retirement. It's a kranking shame, he was a decent officer. Poorly trained, but the ingredients for something better were all there. I'd follow him again, should the Republic beat the war drum."

"And Faulkner? Padagas? Dwyer? The marines?"

I sat there, staring at the amber whiskey before answering.

"There aren't many leejes left." I slammed back the last of my whiskey. "All told, nineteen marines and nine leejes made it."

The barkeep poured me another drink as I'd answered his question. I slammed that one back too. It burned all the way down. My throat felt like it was on fire. Not enough to hide the pain, but it was a start. Gesturing, he poured another fresh finger of whiskey. When I'd regained my composure, I answered the rest of his question.

"One of the other bunkers hid a few marines, who were too scared to try the comms for fear of the MCR listening, but no other leejes made it to the bunkers before they were overwhelmed. Two bunkers sat empty. Nobody made it to those."

"Then how did Sergeant Dwyer make it out alive?"

"He never said, but he must've hid under the bodies of the fuzzies, too."

"Did he ever tell you about Zastos?"

"Only in passing. He said that Rhyssis Wan was a picnic compared to Zastos. Maybe he was kidding, hard to say with that old timer."

"What about Padagas?"

"He's strapped to a bed, heavily sedated. When the fighting stopped, he broke down. He'd kept his emotions in check, fought like a beast, but when it was over, he broke."

I couldn't continue. My eyes were leaking. It wasn't pretty, but the barkeep played the role of a good therapist. He waited me out.

The barkeep looked down and shook his head. "They say time heals all wounds, LT. I hope that they're right. Whatever happened to the big guy, Faulkner?"

"He stands watch outside Padagas's room. He's appointed himself an unofficial honor guard. Won't let anyone else do it. When we leave this kranking place, we'll escort Padagas home. Then it's up to the med boards to determine if he stays in. We plan on stopping by Archer's home on the way to Pictavia. His family deserves to know what kind of man they raised, a leej through and through. After we escort the captain home, we'll do the same for Padagas."

"What about you, Fetch? Can I call you that? Why do they call you that?"

I laughed at that question. The memory of my drill sergeant telling me that my first name was once the most popular choice for K9s still brought a smile to my lips. The smile was harder than it was before, with a finer edge to it, but it was still there.

"Someone thought Benjie was a dog's name, so my drill sergeant dubbed me Fetch. And as for me? I'm going home to kiss my wife, and my son. I just got the message that she had the baby. She wants to surprise me with the gender, but I already know. It's a little boy, I can feel it. After that? I don't know. How do I go back to cooking for corpulent rich idiots after what I've seen of the galaxy? There has to be more to the world than cooking. I don't know, but I've got a few bottles of whiskey to swim through before I decide."

The tinkling of the bell told us we had company, and like that the spell was broken. Turning, I started to size up the interloper. It was Sergeant Major Scott, resplendent in his Legion dress uniform.

"It's time to go, son. Your ride leaves in a few hours and your men still need you. Bring them home with their pride intact. Can you keep it together for one more mission?"

Nodding, I stood up and saluted the barkeep and stumbled out into the blinding Utopion sunlight.

ORDER OF THE CENTURION CITATION:

Name: Benjie Ocampo
Rank: Lieutenant
Organization: Legion Reserve
Company: Rage Company
Legion: 9th Legion
Corps: New Caledonian Reserve Corps
Born: February 18th
Entered Service: November 11th
Serial Number: LR-24-1043-0915-2017
Date Earned: March 25th
Place Earned: Battle of Camp Jericho, Kusiba, Bar Kokhba

CITATION:

Conspicuous gallantry and intrepidity in action at the risk of his life above and beyond the call of duty, while serving as an officer with the 9th Legion of the New Caledonian Reserve Corps during operations that occurred as a result of the Bar Kokhba Revolt. After the Reserve Corps suffered catastrophic losses during the contested landing on the planet of Kusiba, Lieutenant Ocampo led and inspired the remnants of his command to assault their main objective. He single-handedly led the attack which not only took the orbital guns offline, but also showing great initiative he turned those guns on the rebel faction, thereby saving the Republic naval fleet.

After silencing the enemy guns, Ocampo led the surviving members of Rage and Dragon Companies in the capture of Camp Jericho from enemy forces. During the subsequent assaults by combatants under the command of the Mid-Core Rebellion, he demonstrated uncommon courage, repeatedly disregarding his own well-being to complete the mission. During the first breach into Republic lines, he laid down such a sustained rate of targeted suppressive fire that his men were able to pull severely wounded legionnaires to safety.

Despite being repeatedly wounded himself, Ocampo continued to suppress enemy fire while allowing medics to attempt life-saving action on fellow legionnaires. He repeatedly refused medical care so he could secure the critically wounded, before organizing the successful counterattack that ultimately delayed large numbers of enemy forces, thereby taking pressure off the main body of the 9th Legion.

For his service to his men, the 9th Legion, the Caledonian naval assets, and the Republic, I recommend Lieutenant Ocampo for our highest award for valor, the Order of the Centurion.

Signed, by my hand,

Russo Ponce
General Russo Ponce
Commander, 9th Caledonian Legion

THE REPUBLIC ...
TO ALL WHO SHALL SEE THESE PRESENTS, GREETINGS:

THIS IS TO CERTIFY THAT

LEGION COMMANDER KELLER

HAS AWARDED

TO

FOR

CONSPICUOUS GALLANTRY AND INTREPIDITY IN ACTION AT THE RISK OF HIS LIFE ABOVE AND BEYOND THE CALL OF DUTY, WHILE SERVING AS AN OFFICER WITH THE 9TH LEGION OF THE NEW CALEDONIAN RESERVE CORPS DURING OPERATIONS THAT OCCURRED AS A RESULT OF THE BAR KOKHBA REVOLT.

DESPITE CATASTROPHIC LOSSES UPON LANDING, LT OCAMPO LED HIS COMMAND FORWARD. HE SINGLE-HANDEDLY DIRECTED HIS TROOPS IN TAKING THE ORBITAL GUNS OFFLINE, SHOWING GREAT INITIATIVE IN TURNING THOSE GUNS ON REBEL FACTION AND ON TO THE TAKING OF CAMP JERICHO.

LT OCAMPO CONTINUALLY DEMONSTRATED UNCOMMON COURAGE, REPEATEDLY DISREGARDING HIS OWN WELL-BEING TO COMPLETE THE MISSION. DESPITE BEING REPEATEDLY WOUNDED HIMSELF, LT OCAMPO CONTINUED TO SUPPRESS ENEMY FIRE WHILE ALLOWING MEDICS TO WORK ON HIS FELLOW LEGIONNAIRES. HE REPEATEDLY PUT FELLOW LEGIONNAIRES BEFORE HIMSELF. FOR HIS SERVICE TO HIS MEN, THE 9TH LEGION, THE CALEDONIAN NAVAL ASSETS, AND THE REPUBLIC.

I HEREBY AUTHORIZE LIEUTENANT OCAMPO TO RECEIVE OUR HIGHEST AWARD FOR VALOR, THE ORDER OF THE CENTURION.

Warrior's Prayer

Oba, guide me, that I might do thy bidding.
Make me the swift and deadly instrument of your will.
Let my aim be true, and my cause righteous.
Make my hand faster than those who seek to do me harm.
Grant me victory over my foes, that I might protect your people.
And, Oba, if today is truly the day you call me home,
Then let me die with my foe prostrate at my feet.

Death Prayer

Harken to me, my ancestors.
Walk with me,
until I stand at the foot of the one most high.
Reunite me with my people,
back to the beginning.
Complete my circle.
Call me to you, Oba, I am ready.

Prayer Before Charging Enemy Troops

Oba, protect my family.
Make their lives long and fruitful.
Protect my men.
Bring them home to the arms of their loved ones.
Make my feet swift, my aim deadly,
and welcome me into the embrace of my ancestors.
Walk with me, until I stand at the foot of the one most high.
Reunite me with my people, back to the beginning.
Complete my circle.

JOIN THE LEGION

You can find art, t-shirts, signed books and other merchandise on our website.

We also have a fantastic Facebook group called the Galaxy's Edge Fan Club that was created for readers and listeners of *Galaxy's Edge* to get together and share their lives, discuss the series, and have an avenue to talk directly with Jason Anspach and Nick Cole. Please check it out and say hello once you get there!

For updates about new releases, exclusive promotions, and sales, visit inthelegion.com and sign up for our VIP mailing list. Grab a spot in the nearest combat sled and get over there to receive your free copy of "Tin Man," a Galaxy's Edge short story available only to mailing list subscribers.

INTHELEGION.COM

GET A FREE, EXCLUSIVE SHORT STORY

THE GALAXY IS A DUMPSTER FIRE...

J.R. Handley is a pseudonym for a husband and wife writing team. He is a veteran infantry sergeant with the 101st Airborne Division and the 28th Infantry Division. She is the kind of crazy that interprets his insanity into cogent English. He writes the sci-fi while she proofreads it. The sergeant is a two-time combat veteran of the late unpleasantness in Mesopotamia where he was wounded, likely doing something stupid. He started writing military science fiction as part of a therapy program suggested by his doctor, and hopes to entertain you while he attempts to excise his demons through these creative endeavors. In addition to being just another dysfunctional veteran, he is a stay at home wife, avid reader and all around nerd. Luckily for him, his Queen joins him in his fandom nerdalitry.

Jason Anspach is a best selling author living in Tacoma, Washington with his wife and their own legionnaire squad of seven (not a typo) children. In addition to science fiction, Jason is the author of the hit comedy-paranormal-historical-detective series, *'til Death*. Jason loves his family as well as hiking and camping throughout the beautiful Pacific Northwest. And Star Wars. He named as many of his kids after Obi Wan as possible, and knows that Han shot first.

Nick Cole is a dragon award winning author best known for *The Old Man and the Wasteland, CTRL ALT Revolt!,* and the Wyrd Saga. After serving in the United States Army, Nick moved to Hollywood to pursue a career in acting and writing. (Mostly) retired from the stage and screen, he resides with his wife, a professional opera singer, in Los Angeles, California.

HONOR ROLL

We would like to give our most sincere thanks and recognition to those who supported the creation of *The Reservist* by subscribing as a Galaxy's Edge Insider at GalacticOutlaws.com.

Guido Abreu
Elias Aguilar
Bill Allen
Tony Alvarez
Galen Anderson
Robert Anspach
Jonathan Auerbach
Fritz Ausman
Sean Averill
Matthew Bagwell
Marvin Bailey
John Barber
Logan Barker
Russell Barker
Eric Batzdorfer
John Baudoin
Steven Beaulieu
Antonio Becerra
Mike Beeker
Randall Beem
Matt Beers
John Bell
Daniel Bendele
David Bernatski
Trevor Blasius
WJ Blood
Rodney Bonner
Thomas Seth Bouchard
Alex Bowling
Ernest Brant
Geoff Brisco
Aaron Brooks
Marion Buehring
Daniel Cadwell
Van Cammack
Zachary Cantwell
Steven Carrizales
Brian Cave
Shawn Cavitt
David Chor
Jonathan Clews
Beau Clifton
Alex Collins-Gauweiler
Garrett Comerford
James Connolly
James Conyers
Jonathan Copley
Robert Cosler
Andrew Craig
Adam Craig
Phil Culpepper
Ben Curcio
Thomas Cutler
Alister Davidson

Peter Davies
Ivy Davis
Nathan Davis
Ron Deage
Tod Delaricheliere
Ryan Denniston
Christopher DiNote
Matthew Dippel
Ellis Dobbins
Ray Duck
Cami Dutton
Virgil Dwyer
William Ely
Stephane Escrig
Hunter Ferguson
Ashley Finnigan
Steve Forrester
Skyla Forster
Timothy Foster
Bryant Fox
Mark Franceschini
David Gaither
Christopher Gallo
Richard Gallo
Kyle Gannon
Michael Gardner
Nick Gerlach
John Giorgis
Justin Godfrey
Luis Gomez
Gerald Granada
Gordon Green
Tim Green
Shawn Greene
Erik Hansen
Greg Hanson

Jason Harris
Jordan Harris
Matthew Hartmann
Adam Hartswick
Ronald Haulman
Joshua Hayes
Jason Henderson
Jason Henderson
Kyle Hetzer
Aaron Holden
Joshua Hopkins
Tyson Hopkins
Christopher Hopper
Ian House
Ken Houseal
Nathan Housley
Jeff Howard
Mike Hull
Bradley Huntoon
Carl Hutchens
Wendy Jacobson
Paul Jarman
James Jeffers
Tedman Jess
James Johnson
Randolph Johnson
Tyler Jones
John Josendale
Wyatt Justice
Ron Karroll
Cody Keaton
Noah Kelly
Caleb Kenner
Daniel Kimm
Zachary Kinsman
Rhet Klaahsen

Jesse Klein
Travis Knight
Ethan Koska
Evan Kowalski
Byl Kravetz
Brian Lambert
Clay Lambert
Grant Lambert
Jeremy Lambert
Dave Lawrence
Alexander Le
Paul Lizer
Richard Long
Oliver Longchamps
Brooke Lyons
John M
Patrick Maclary
Richard Maier
Brian Mansur
Robet Marchi
Deven Marincovich
Cory Marko
Lucas Martin
Pawel Martin
Trevor Martin
Tao Mason
Mark Maurice
Simon Mayeski
Kyle McCarley
Quinn McCusker
Alan McDonald
Caleb McDonald
Hans McIlveen
Rachel McIntosh
Joshua McMaster
Christopher Menkhaus

Jim Mern
Dylon Merrell
Robert Mertz
Pete Micale
Mike Mieszcak
Brandon Mikula
Ted Milker
Mitchell Moore
William Morris
Alex Morstadt
Nicholas Mukanos
Vinesh Narayan
Bennett Nickels
Andrew Niesent
Greg Nugent
Christina Nymeyer
Colin O'neill
Ryan O'neill
Tyler Ornelas
James Owens
David Parker
Eric Pastorek
Carl Patrick
Dupres Pina
Pete Plum
Paul Polanski
Matthew Pommerening
Jeremiah Popp
Chancey Porter
Brian Potts
Chris Pourteau
Chris Prats
Joshua Purvis
Nick Quinn
Eric Ritenour
Walt Robillard

Joshua Robinson
Daniel Robitaille
Thomas Roman
Joyce Roth
David Sanford
Jaysn Schaener
Landon Schaule
Shayne Schettler
Andrew Schmidt
Brian Schmidt
William Schweisthal
Aaron Seaman
Phillip Seek
Christopher Shaw
Charles Sheehan
Wendell Shelton
Brett Shilton
Vernetta Shipley
Glenn Shotton
Joshua Sipin
Scott Sloan
Daniel Smith
Michael Smith
Sharroll Smith
Tyler Smith
John Spears
Peter Spitzer
Dustin Sprick
Graham Stanton
Paul Starck
Maggie Stewart-Grant
John Stockley
Rob Strachan
William Strickler
Shayla Striffler
Kevin Summers
Ernest Sumner
Carol Szpara
Travis TadeWaldt
Daniel Tanner
Lawrence Tate
Tim Taylor
Mark Teets
Steven Thompson
William Joseph Thorpe
Beverly Tierney
Matthew Titus
Jameson Trauger
Scott Tucker
Eric Turnbull
Brandon Turton
Jalen Underwood
Paul Van Dop
Paden VanBuskirk
Jose Vazquez
Anthony Wagnon
Christopher Walker
David Wall
Andrew Ward
Scot Washam
John Watson
James Wells
Ben Wheeler
Scott Winters
Jason Wright
Brandt Zeeh
Nathan Zoss

Made in the USA
Columbia, SC
15 November 2023

26394567R00204